Fic
Har   Harrison, Stuart
       The Snow falcon

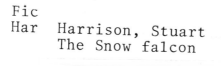

INFORMATION NETWORK

W9-CEV-188

MAY 2 0 1999   ✓

Parsippany-Troy Hills Public Library
Parsippany Branch
292 Parsippany Road
Parsippany, N.J. 07054

THE SNOW FALCON

THE SNOW FALCON

Stuart Harrison

ST. MARTIN'S PRESS ❧ *New York*

THE SNOW FALCON. Copyright © 1999 by Stuart Harrison. All rights reserved.
Printed in the United States of America. No part of this book may be used or reproduced
in any manner whatsoever without written permission except in the case of brief
quotations embodied in critical articles or reviews. For information, address St. Martin's
Press, 175 Fifth Avenue, New York, N.Y. 10010.

Design by Abby Kagan

Library of Congress Cataloging-in-Publication Data

Harrison, Stuart.
    The snow falcon / by Stuart Harrison.
        p.   cm.
    ISBN 0-312-20166-4
    1. Gyrfalcon—Fiction.   I. Title.
PR9639.3.H324S66   1999
82—dc21   98-44017
                                        CIP

First Edition: February 1999

10   9   8   7   6   5   4   3   2   1

FOR DALE,
WITH THANKS

PART ONE

1 THE FALCON SHIFTED UNEASILY, SENSING DANGER. From her perch high up in the rocky cliffs she could see a figure far below crossing open snow. He was a mile away, a solitary blemish against a vast white landscape, but the falcon's keen eyesight enabled her to clearly distinguish his features. She could see the rifle slung over his shoulder and the deep tracks he'd made leading back toward the trees.

Every now and then the man stopped and turned his face to the sky as if searching for something. He shielded his eyes against the glare of the sun and looked all around; then, after a moment, he walked on. The falcon was wary of him, though she didn't know why. She'd seen him several times over the last few days, and her instinct had warned her to keep her distance.

A week ago, storms had ravaged the area, bringing high winds and snow from the north. For days the winds had blown the falcon south from the icebound land she knew as home. For much of the time she had sheltered as gales whipped up blizzards and turned her world into a maelstrom of swirling white. In the end, hunger had driven her to the air and she'd been carried in the path of the storm until the worst had abated. Now she found herself in an unfamiliar landscape. The mountains rose in the distance, blue gray against the sky; the valleys beneath her were forest-clad, dark green. High up above the tree line there were only rocky cliffs and snow.

In some of the valleys there were rivers, and lakes of deep aqua. Food was plentiful. Two days ago she had killed a ptarmigan, stooping down from above as it flew across open ground, but now she was hungry again. Earlier, she had seen a hare feeding on a patch of grass that lay in the cover of a rock where the snow lay thin on the ground, but the man had been close by and she had let the opportunity pass.

A breeze blew across the cliff and the falcon let her wings hang open, the flow of air teasing her feathers. She was dusky cream in coloring, with chocolate markings across her breast and thighs. Her wing primaries grew darker toward their ends, where the cream became light gray. At twenty-six inches in length, with a wingspan of more than three feet, she was of a race of falcon that is the largest and swiftest on earth. She had no natural predators. Only man threatened her.

THREE QUARTERS OF a mile away, Ellis paused for breath.

"Goddamn," he said hoarsely. Phlegm rattled in his throat and he spat to the ground. He was tired from the long climb and warm beneath his parka. With each step he sank to midshin, crunching the surface of the snow. It was heavy going, and his head ached.

But for the lure of the money, he would still have been home in bed. He shifted the strap of his rifle and looked to the sky. There was nothing there but the odd drifting cloud and the glare of bright sun. The light bounced off the snow and made him squint. It felt like needles being shoved through his eyes into the back of his head. Ahead, dark rocks rose in a sheer cliff four hundred feet high. He wiped a thin sheen of sweat from his brow and rubbed his eyes, which were bloodshot from all the drinking he'd done the night before. He was regretting that now. He figured he'd spent more than sixty bucks buying rounds and drinking Wild Turkey chasers. Red Parker and Ted Hanson had asked how come he was so damn generous all of a sudden, but he hadn't told them, except to say he was about to come into some money. They'd started buying him drinks after that, probably hoping they could share in his good fortune, but he was too smart for that.

"Come on, Ellis, you got some rich old lady we don't know about, gone and left you all her money?" Red had asked.

"Well, maybe I have," he'd answered, "but I ain't saying one way or the other."

Hanson had snickered. "You damn stud."

Ellis frowned. Maybe he'd been a little hasty, talking about the money. Could be he'd exaggerated things a little, too, when he'd seen they doubted him, let them think he was going to get his hands on a fortune. Maybe there wasn't going to be any damn money at all, he thought sourly, and then he was going to look stupid. He'd been walking now for two hours, and there was no sign of the falcon. His head was hurting and his mouth felt like he'd been chewing sand. He knelt down and took off a glove, then scooped snow into his mouth with his bare hand. It tasted slightly bitter but it quenched his thirst. He took off his cap and rubbed a little snow over the stubble on his scalp. It helped to ease the pain. He blew on his hand before he put his glove back on, then beat his arms against his sides. Once he stopped walking, it became cold real fast.

It could be the falcon was long gone, or even that he'd been wrong about its being an arctic gyr. Uncertainty worsened his mood. The idea of losing out on an easy thousand bucks was bad enough; that he might be wasting his time up here when he was suffering from a king-size hangover just made it worse. He thought about just turning around in his tracks and heading back to his truck, and for about two seconds it was an appealing notion. Then he thought about the money again and decided he'd give it a while longer.

It occurred to Ellis that for all the trouble he was going to, it was still Tusker who was getting the better deal. They'd agreed on a thousand for the gyr, but now that Ellis thought about it, Tusker had rolled over with hardly a murmur, which Ellis realized probably meant he was getting stuck with the short end of the stick.

He'd seen the falcon for the first time three days ago, early in the morning, when he'd stopped to take a leak. At first he'd thought it was a peregrine; then he'd decided it was too big. This had made him curious. He knew from the shape of the wings that it wasn't a hawk or an eagle. He'd watched it ride a thermal over the trees; then it had turned and dropped, flying low, and he'd caught a glimpse of its coloring, a pale flash. He would have shot it right then, but his rifle was back in the truck and there hadn't been time to fetch it. Since then he'd never been as close.

Later he'd had to deliver an order of lumber for a guy who was building an extension on his house over toward Williams Lake. The guy had really screwed him on the price, but what the fuck, business was lousy and any kind of sale was better than no sale at all. He'd made up for it anyway by putting some second-rate crap in among the load, which the guy wasn't going to find until it was too late. Afterward he'd driven on to town and stopped in at the library to see if he could find something that looked like the bird he'd seen. As soon as he'd found the picture of a gyr falcon, he recognized it. He didn't know how it had come to be so far south, since the book said they were generally found way farther north, but when he'd read that the species was rare, especially one so light colored as this, he'd had a feeling Tusker might be interested.

Tusker had been working on a grizzly when Ellis walked in the door. It was a female, posed in an aggressive stance, up on its hind legs, menacing teeth bared, huge and frightening. In the dim light of Tusker's workshop it had looked almost alive, and Ellis had involuntarily hesitated. Tusker had glanced toward him, his sharp black eyes flashing with amusement.

"Looks pretty good, wouldn't you say?"

"I guess so," Ellis had said. He didn't like to go to Tusker's place; the sharp smell of the chemicals Tusker used in his work made him feel sick to his stomach—that, and the underlying stench of death that always clung to his clothes long after he'd left. He'd looked around, feigning a casual air, not wanting Tusker to get the better of him.

"What can I do for you?" Tusker had said, straightening up and wiping his hands on a grimy rag.

"I might have something for you."

"Business ain't so good right now."

Ellis had looked away, a quick bitter anger rising. Tusker always said business wasn't so good, just to establish ground rules so nobody would think he was going to pay much for anything a person might be hoping to sell. The showroom out front was filled with Tusker's work. Raccoons and beavers; foxes slinking through grass; salmon, even, mounted and fixed with a plaque all ready to be inscribed. Tusker did a good trade in selling trophies to fishermen who went home and bragged about the fight their fish had put up before they'd finally hauled it in. Lotsa guys like that, wanted something to show for the hours they'd spent standing in freezing water. Tusker said some of them even got so they almost believed the stories they made up in their heads. Ellis had to admit that Tusker was good at what he did, though it was hard to imagine a more unpleasant way to make a living. Surrounded by dead things all day, ripping out their guts and flesh, which all went into a stinking drum out back that attracted swarms of fat blackflies when the spring weather came. Ellis stared at a fox that stared right back at him, its eyes glinting, looking about ready to turn tail and run, so lifelike he would almost have sworn it moved.

"You ever get people looking for falcons?" Ellis had finally said. It hadn't come out as casual-sounding as he'd wanted, and he didn't miss the way Tusker hesitated, his eyes getting narrow before he answered.

"What kind of falcon we talking about?"

"An arctic gyr."

There was a pause. Tusker turned back to his work. "Where you going to get a gyr falcon, Ellis?"

Ellis had seen the look in his eye, the sudden quickening of interest he'd tried to hide, and his confidence jumped a notch or two.

"You got some people you sell to, if I remember right," Ellis had said. "Collectors and such. Think maybe one of them might be interested?"

"Maybe. Thing is, Ellis, a gyr falcon, that's a protected bird."

Ellis had snorted, amused that Tusker should even think he'd believe that such a thing would be of any concern. "Well, if you ain't interested, that's fine by me. I just thought I'd give you first pop since we've done business in the past is all." Ellis had started to make as if he were heading for the door, which both of them knew he wasn't.

"You're sure about it being a gyr falcon?"

"I wouldn't be here if I wasn't," Ellis had said.

"They don't usually come this far south," Tusker had mused. "What's it look like?"

Ellis had described it. "Almost pure white, too," he'd added. "That makes it a pretty rare bird, I'd say." Then he'd told Tusker what he wanted for it, plucking from the air what he'd thought at the time was a pretty outlandish sum.

"A couple of hundred is no good. I want a thousand."

Tusker had hesitated, but just barely. "That's a hard bargain, Ellis, but okay, I guess I could go to maybe six hundred."

Six hundred! That one bird could be worth so much had just about floored him, but Ellis had hidden his surprise. Coming on top of that and almost as quick was the thought that Tusker had never given

six hundred dollars for anything in his life without it being worth a
hell of a lot more than that. Ellis had stuck to his guns and shook
his head, hoping like hell he wasn't pushing things too far, a nervous
lump forming tightly in his throat.

"A thousand," he'd said emphatically.

Tusker had frowned, pursed his lips, then stuck out his hand. "You
got a deal."

As Ellis had left, hardly able to suppress the grin forming on his
face, he'd caught sight of a cage in a dark corner, something moving
around in there. He'd paused long enough to recognize a bear cub,
which suddenly started snuffling and crying in a high-pitched wail.
Tusker had followed his look.

"Guy brought it in a week ago, with this." He gestured with his
thumb to the female grizzly already stuffed and mounted. "He shot
the mother, then found the runt. Said he didn't know what he could
use it for, so he brought it in."

"What you going to do with it?"

"Put it right next to its momma," Tusker had said, grinning. "Female grizzly protecting her cub. It'll look good in some city guy's
house. He can tell all his friends about how he just almost got himself
killed. Make quite a story, I'd say."

Ellis had felt bad for the cub. It seemed a sorry fate, and he'd
turned away, Tusker's laughter following him through the door.
There was something wrong with a person who could find such a
thing amusing.

Now that he'd had time to think about it, it seemed to Ellis that
Tusker had accepted his terms a little too easily. Ellis had sold him
stuff before, mostly to order, and he knew Tusker wasn't stupid. That
son of a bitch was probably going to make five times what he was
paying for that falcon by the time he'd finished.

Just thinking about it got Ellis steamed up. He felt like Tusker
had taken him for a sucker and was trying to cheat him. What he
ought to do is tell him the price had gone up, that he wanted two
thousand for the gyr, maybe even more. Could be he'd underesti-
mated its value altogether. He felt like he should try some other
dealers and see what kind of price he could get elsewhere. There
were plenty of taxidermists around, though maybe not all of them
were as unscrupulous as Tusker.

He reminded himself, however, that before he could do anything, there was the small problem of finding the damn bird. He stopped again for a breath; the cold air made his lungs ache. He was above the tree line, crossing a broad open snowfield that was getting steeper all the time. He searched the sky, but it was empty.

Ellis wiped his hand across his unshaven jaw. He was beginning to think that if he didn't find the gyr again soon, the damn thing would just move on. He raised the glasses he wore around his neck and scanned the sky, then swept around to the cliffs ahead. Just as he was about to drop them, something moved, and he swept back until he saw the flick of pale wings.

THE FALCON WATCHED the figure far below, which had stopped moving. The wind coursing across the rock face ruffled her feathers, giving a slight tempting pull to her wings. She turned her attention back across the valley in the direction of the forest, dark green, covering the slopes downward. Hunger pangs gripped her, and she searched for movement. A solitary bird appeared, following the course of the valley slope, coming toward her. She could see the rapid beating motion of its wings rowing it through the air, the turn of its head as it warily surveyed the landscape, itself in search of food and alert for danger. The falcon watched, and turned her body slightly toward it. She felt the pull of the wind and the need to satisfy her hunger, but she was wary, made nervous by the continuing presence of the figure coming from the opposite direction. Something held her back, warning her, a deeply embedded instinct she could not ignore. The approaching bird was closer now; its light gray plumage and the fat-breasted flight that gave it an awkward sculling motion marked it as a pigeon. If she left her perch and rose, she would be poised above and slightly behind it, her descent from the sun giving her cover. The pigeon was unaware of her presence, but soon it would be close enough that it would see her as she left the cliff and would then have time to veer away and drop for the sanctuary of the trees. Again the falcon shifted, opposing instincts compelling her. She looked again to the far figure, uncertain, then hunger drove her forward and she took to the air, leaving her perch with rapid wingbeats until she felt rising air currents sweep her aloft.

ELLIS WATCHED THROUGH the scope on his rifle, his finger resting on the trigger, tightening the pressure. He saw the color of the falcon's plumage clearly against the dark rock as it took to the air and knew he hadn't been mistaken. He was already thinking about the money and grinning as he followed the falcon in his sight, waiting for the right moment. The falcon was farther away than he would have liked, but he was a good shot. He could have killed it then, but he wanted one clean body shot. Tusker wasn't going to pay much for a bird with its head blown off.

He watched the falcon stoop toward the pigeon, moving so fast he lost it in his sight, then found it again as it leveled out. The angle wasn't right and he hesitated, starting to squeeze the trigger.

"Come around, dammit," he muttered.

He was tempted by an image he imagined: of himself walking into the bar and taking out a roll of bills, buying drinks for everybody. Maybe he'd take Rachel somewhere to eat and this would be a whole new start for them. Things would pick up at the yard, they wouldn't fight so much, he'd quit drinking the way he'd been. All he needed was one clear shot.

ON OUTSTRETCHED WINGS, the falcon banked and turned. Positioning herself, she waited until the pigeon was closer; then, judging time and distance with effortless precision, she closed her wings and stooped. She gathered speed quickly, her wings folded back into a tight V, and from the ground she was simply a blurred shape, too fast to follow. The sound of rushing air roared in her head as she plummeted earthward; beneath her, the pigeon wavered in its course, sensing danger, but by then it was too late. The falcon came from behind, throwing her feet forward to strike with the long talon on her back toe. As she swept by, there was a split second of impact, a cloud of feathers, and the pigeon dropped limply toward the earth. The falcon turned and came around to catch it fifty feet from the ground, then carried it toward the cover of nearby trees.

RELUCTANTLY, ELLIS DROPPED the sight. The falcon was too small a target and, as he watched, was quickly lost from view.

"Damn," he said bitterly.

His chances of seeing it again that day were remote. Once it had fed, it might not take to the air for hours. He lit a cigarette, then coughed and spat into the snow. His head was pounding now and he was starting to feel dizzy. He turned around and started back on the long walk down to the road.

He'd come out again in the morning. Right now he just needed to get some sleep and maybe a beer to quench his thirst.

2 Michael Somers pulled over across the road from the church on the edge of town. It looked just the way he remembered it, small and wooden, painted white, in a cold February landscape of snow, surrounded by a cemetery and a picket fence. Behind it rose the dark green of spruce and cedar that made up much of the forest. He got out of the Nissan he was driving, and went through a gate, and followed the path leading to the porch, hunching his shoulders against the wind that came down from the high ground. In the northwestern corner of the cemetery, a solitary cottonwood tree stood where it had been for as long as he could remember. In the summer its spreading branches provided a shady spot, but now the bare limbs seemed lifeless. This part of the cemetery was being reclaimed, new graves taking over from those so old nobody remembered the people who were buried in them. It was untidy, with lopsided crosses and angels missing limbs, the ground uneven. Here and there, new plots had been created.

He found the grave his parents shared, marked by a polished black gray headstone inscribed with gold lettering. He'd come home from college for his mother's funeral when he was eighteen, the last time he'd been in Little River Bend. Maybe that was when a thread had started to pick loose in his mind, something that had been sewn there a long time before that. He was living in Toronto with a wife and child of his own when he learned, twelve years later, that his dad had been killed in an accident, and that time he hadn't returned for the funeral. As his father was lowered into the ground, he'd been attending a business meeting, pretending his life was functioning normally. Only later did it become clear how rapidly it had already begun to unravel, and how the event of his father's death accelerated the process, which ended catastrophically with events that had destroyed more lives than just his own. Standing by the grave, he felt it all pressing against the inside of his head, and he thrust his hands deep into his pockets and looked up beyond the fence across the snow, letting the whiteness fill his mind.

Two weeks earlier Heller, the psychiatrist at St. Helen's, had come out to wish Michael luck as he'd left. He'd shaken the younger man's hand. Michael had come to like Heller, and had appreciated everything the doctor had tried to do for him. It was Heller who'd put the idea of coming back to Little River Bend in his mind in the first place.

"Three years and you haven't said a damn thing about where you come from, you know that? What is it you're afraid of there?"

"Who says I'm afraid?"

"If you're not, then go back there."

He'd thought about it for a while. Then, during one of their sessions, he'd asked, "Can you arrange it with the parole people?"

Heller had said he'd already made some inquiries. "You can report to the local RCMP in Little River Bend, or else you can check in with the authorities in Williams Lake. There's a doctor in Prince George, a guy by the name of Patterson. You can talk to him if you feel the need. I'll send him your files."

"You've got it all worked out," Michael had said. "Were you so sure I'd go?"

"I think you know you have to," Heller had told him.

The day he'd left he'd said, "I'll miss watching the Blues together."

"Yeah." Heller had smiled ruefully. Hockey was about the only thing they talked about. "Call me if you need to."

"I will, thanks."

And that had been that.

Michael turned away from his parents' grave. A dull ache had begun to seep into his skull, and he knew it would migrate to his temples. Sometimes it was like a clamp had been tightened against his head, and it could grow in intensity until it took his breath away. When he reached his car, he breathed deeply, massaging his head with his knuckles until the pain subsided.

He drove into town along Main Street. Some things had changed over the years, but mostly things looked the same. Memories started flowing back; he recognized the Apple Market, then the house just off Fourth Street where old man Spencer had once lived, whose habit was to sit on the porch all day nodding and smiling as people went by, calling to everybody by name, even the little kids. He'd been the oldest person in town and had lived there his entire life. Michael wondered about that, trying to think how it would feel for Little River Bend and its surrounding environs to represent a person's entire experience. He slowed as he passed the corner and craned to get a look at the house. Spencer would be long dead, but the house still looked the same, even to a sagging window shutter that hung lopsided from the frame.

Farther along Main Street, a paint-blistered sign remained over the store his father had run until he'd died. The insides of the windows were covered with black paper, so the building resembled a dark empty hole between its neighbors. It was flanked on one side by a drugstore that had been a lunch bar when he'd last seen it: On the other side, though, Greerman's Clothing hadn't changed at all. It seemed as if the same work jeans and checked shirts were displayed in the window alongside a faded poster showing a bunch of guys posing beside big-wheel trucks. Seeing his dad's store again brought a quick tightening feeling to the base of his throat. Memories shifted and jostled, crowding into focus, and images of his parents leapt and receded. He slowed as he passed by; a sudden swell of emotion rose and brought with it a bitter taste in his mouth, and he bit down, unconsciously clamping his jaw tight. He thought of Louise and Holly, and a deep ache he'd come to live with flared and died like a struck match. He turned away and drove on, banishing his memories to the recesses of his mind.

Along the street he parked outside the office he guessed Carl Jeffrey had taken over after his father had retired. Now Carl, it seemed, was the town's only lawyer. Michael remembered him from high school, an overweight and unpopular kid who wore thick glasses. He hadn't been a natural scholar, but his old man had chivied him along mercilessly, grooming him to take over the family firm. As Michael got out of the car, a woman passing on the sidewalk glanced his way, and for a second he felt conspicuous, reading something into her quick scrutiny, but she walked on by, no flare of recognition on her features.

She looked to be in her mid-thirties and could have been, for all he knew, somebody he'd gone to school with. His pulse raced and then went back to its normal rhythm. He wondered how people were going to react to him coming back here. Sometimes during the journey he'd thought that twenty years does a lot to change people; maybe nobody would remember him; and if they did, maybe they wouldn't care about what had happened seven years ago back East. Maybe it hadn't even been reported here.

He went up the stairs and entered an outer office. A young woman smiled at him as she looked up from her word processing.

"Hi. Can I help you?"

"I'm here to see Carl Jeffrey."

"Sure, I'll get him for you. Can I give him your name?"

"Michael Somers."

Her smile faltered the way it might have if she'd reached to pet a dog that had then unexpectedly growled at her.

"I'll tell Mr. Jeffrey that you're here."

Though there was a phone on her desk she could have used, she got up and went through to an inner office, glancing quickly back at him as she closed the door behind her. When the door opened again after a minute or two, she returned to her desk, avoiding his eye as she went. Carl was just behind her, his expression split into a wide smile.

"Hey, Michael! It's been a long time. How are you?" They shook hands, then stood back a second to look each other over, Carl shaking his head. "Hell, you look just the way you did when I last saw you."

"You look good yourself, Carl."

In fact, Carl was as Michael had imagined he might have turned out. The face was the same, only fleshier than he remembered, neck and jowls merging into rolls that flowed over the collar of his shirt. The suit he wore was wrinkled at the arms and stretched tight around his middle, and there was a faint stain on his tie. Carl waved an arm and ushered him into his office.

"How about some coffee or something?"

"Coffee would be great."

Carl called back to his secretary. "Jenny, did you hear that? Fetch us some coffee, would you? How about a doughnut? There's a bakery a couple of doors down that does pretty good food. You hungry?"

"I'm okay, thanks."

Carl's expression creased into a slight frown of indecision, his eyes growing smaller in his face. He made up his mind while Jenny waited by her desk. "Just get me one of those cream-cheese bagels. Poppyseed," he called out. He turned back to Michael and patted his expansive stomach. "I have to watch what I eat."

Michael didn't comment, thinking that it seemed he was fighting a losing battle.

Carl smiled broadly again, shaking his head in disbelief as he went behind his big wooden desk. "How long has it been? Twenty years? How'd you manage to stay looking so good? Sit down, make yourself at home. Smoke?" He picked up a pack of Camel Lights from the desk and offered them across.

"No thanks. I quit."

"Yeah? I should do the same. These things'll kill you, that's for sure." Carl lit a cigarette and speculatively blew smoke across the room as he settled his bulk back into his chair.

They were the same age, thirty-seven, but Carl looked older. He had the smooth features that overweight people often have, and his size made him look prosperous in a small-town kind of way. It was the suit, partly, and the office, with its big desk and chair and its windows overlooking the street. In the city he would have looked like a rumpled, slightly seedy second-rate lawyer and his features might have adopted a harassed attitude, but here he appeared well settled—rooted and confident. In contrast, Michael knew he himself looked edgy. He saw it in his own expression when he caught himself unawares, passing his reflection in a window or a mirror. He thought he appeared guarded, his brow vaguely furrowed, as if he was worrying at some internal problem. His hair, though, was thick and fair, and sometimes he caught in the way he looked a trace of the younger man he'd once been, even the boy back beyond that, and he guessed that was why Carl seemed surprised by his appearance. Maybe he didn't fit Carl's idea of what an ex-con ought to look like.

"So tell me, when did you get here?" Carl asked.

"I just arrived."

"I've been expecting you ever since I got your last letter. I was starting to think maybe you'd changed your mind when you didn't show up. I thought maybe I had the dates wrong, but when I called that hospital—St. Helen's?—they said you got out a couple of weeks ago."

"I decided to drive here," Michael said.

"All the way from Toronto? Jesus, that's a long way. They have planes now, you know, Michael."

Michael shrugged. "I felt like driving."

It was something he didn't feel like explaining. The fact was, he'd used some of the money his father had left him to buy a Nissan Patrol and had set out across the continent, following Route 1 all the way to the Rockies and across them before eventually turning north on Route 97 toward Williams Lake. He'd stayed in cheap motels, spending only as much time in them as he needed to sleep. The rest of the time he was either driving or sitting in diners at night sipping a beer and watching people come and go. A lot of the time he ate junk food, stopping at a Dairy Queen or a McDonald's. The food in prison, and after that at St. Helen's, had featured hamburgers and the like on a regular basis, but he'd learned that it was small things that people on the inside missed the most. For him, one of those things had been the particular taste of a Big Mac, even though it was something he'd hardly ever eaten before his life had disintegrated in such spectacular fashion. He supposed it had something to do with missing what he couldn't have, and maybe it was just a way of stopping him thinking about the other, more important things he'd lost in his life. Maybe he should have mentioned it to Heller. The psychiatrist would have rubbed the side of his forehead with one finger and given that small disarming shrug. "What do you think, Michael?" He said that a lot, and sometimes Michael had wondered why he needed Heller at all if he had to figure everything out for himself.

Driving to Little River Bend had been a way of getting used to the idea of having his freedom again. It had felt good to be surrounded by empty spaces, and every now and then he'd felt the need to stop just so he could walk around. Flying to Vancouver and then catching a local plane to Williams Lake would have made the transition all too sudden, the change too abrupt for him to absorb. He'd needed time to adjust, to prepare himself and think about things, though in all honesty he'd done precious little of that. All the way, a trepidation about returning had grown in him, to the point where he'd considered just turning back. He didn't, however, say any of this to Carl.

Carl's secretary tapped lightly on the door and came in carrying takeout coffee cups and a paper-wrapped bagel that she put on the desk. Michael saw the way she leaned over from the side, making sure she didn't get too close, and when he thanked her, she still wouldn't look directly at him. Carl didn't seem to notice anything amiss and started unwrapping his sandwich.

"You want cream or sugar?" he said with his mouth full.

"No thanks." The secretary left them, and when she'd gone Michael said, "I think she's wary of me."

Carl looked to the door, his eyebrows rising. "Jenny? What makes you say that?"

"Just a feeling, I guess."

Carl waved his hand. "She's young. Don't worry about her."

Carl started sorting through stuff on his desk while he drank his coffee and chewed his bagel vigorously. "By the way, Karen said to say hi when I saw you."

"Karen?"

"My wife, you remember Karen White? We've got a couple of kids..." He passed over a photograph, then his expression fell. "Hell, me and my big mouth. I guess you probably don't want to hear my happy-family talk. I wasn't thinking."

"It's okay," Michael assured him.

A moment passed and Carl said, "You mind if I ask about your wife? I mean, have you seen her?"

"We're divorced now."

"You had a little girl, right? What was her name?"

"Holly." A picture of her sprung to Michael's mind, the way she'd been when he'd last seen her, just a baby. He didn't even know if the picture was accurate, or if it was simply a generic image of a baby. She would be almost eight years old now, he realized, and he had no idea what she looked like. He was aware that Carl was watching him, no doubt trying to decipher the thoughts in his mind. For a second, a silence enveloped them. Then, when Michael didn't volunteer any other information, Carl moved on.

"Anyway, I'd call Karen up so she could come in and see you herself, but I know she's tied up with some meeting she had to go to. Something to do with school." He waved his hand airily.

Michael looked at the photo and did recall Karen White. She'd been kind of a chubby blonde with an unnerving lazy eye that sometimes drifted inward. The picture showed Carl and Karen beaming smiles at the camera, two well-fed children in front of them.

"She'll be sorry she missed you," Carl said, his smile slipping back into place.

"I'll see her around, I expect."

"Oh, sure." Carl appeared vaguely puzzled, then the feeling was gone. "Anyway, I guess you want to get down to business," he said, becoming brisk.

He appeared happier dealing with straightforward issues that held no minefield of misunderstandings. He picked up a folder and started to read from it. "Everything's pretty much as I told you when I wrote. There's the house, of course, which is kind of in a poor way, which you'd expect after being empty for so long, but it's not too bad. I had someone go out and take a look for you. The roof needs fixing in a couple of places and it could use a coat of paint, but nothing serious. Then there's your dad's old store. As you know, his insurance covered the mortgage when he died, so that's freehold as well."

"I saw it on the way in," Michael said, thinking of the black papered-over windows. "I see Greerman's is still there."

"Yeah, I guess nothing much changes in a town like this," Carl said. He flicked over a page and looked down a column of figures. "The money your dad left has been sitting in an account at the bank since he died. The taxes have had to be paid from it over the years, so the amount's reduced a fair bit even after interest, but there's still almost twenty thousand."

Carl paused and looked as if he were about to say something, and Michael knew Carl had to be curious about why he'd never touched the money before, and why he hadn't sold the house and store instead of just leaving them empty all these years. "More like eight," Michael said, explaining that he'd bought the Nissan, and whatever had been in Carl's mind he put it aside and went back to the sheet in front of him.

"Right, okay." He made a note. "All the same, you're not exactly destitute when you add it all up. Of course, you won't get big-city prices here, but it should be enough to get you started again."

Michael nodded, though his mind had been wandering. He went over to the window and looked down to the street.

Carl watched him, then got up and stood beside him. "You've had a hard time over these last years, Michael. I think I know how it must feel. That's why I'm glad to give you some good news."

Down in the street, a snowplow had stopped at the side of the road. A truck pulled up, and a guy got out and started talking to the man who looked to be in charge of the plow. Michael watched them, then turned his attention to a woman with two young children who pulled up in a big Ford F250 and started taking bags out of the front seat. The roof of her truck was covered in a layer of snow. Winter this year had been comparatively mild. He could remember when, as a boy, it had been forty below here in February and the snow five feet thick. He tore himself away, realizing that Carl was waiting for him to say something.

"Good news?" Michael echoed.

"Things'll get better for you now, you'll see," Carl assured him. "You'll be able to put all this behind you. Hell, I know it's easy for me to say that when I haven't been through everything you have, but you have to think positively about life. In a couple of years, you won't even remember all this."

"I appreciate the sentiment," Michael said, uncertain where this was heading.

Carl put his arm around Michael's shoulder. "Well, what did you expect? We've known each other for a long time. Times like this, old friends need to stick together. Soon as I heard you were getting released, I started putting this thing together."

Michael allowed himself to be guided back toward the desk, puzzled as to how his relationship with Carl had been promoted to that of old friends. As far as he could recall, they'd had little to do with each other in the time he'd lived in Little River, and since then the only correspondence between them had related to his father's estate. Carl's overfriendliness held the smooth oil of insincerity.

"Anyway, I guess you're keen to hear the details." Carl sat down again at his desk and started looking through some papers.

"Details?"

"I think you're going to like this, Michael. I didn't say anything earlier, because I thought it would kind of be a nice surprise for you." He handed over a sheet of paper for Michael to look at. "Now, I got to tell you, the first offer this guy made was way too low. I told him that, I said you wouldn't even be interested. I got him up to what I think you'll agree is a fair deal."

Michael looked over the figures, still unsure what Carl was talking about.

"So where will you go, anyway? Back East?"

It took a minute for Michael to see the assumption Carl had made, and for a few moments they sat in silence, Carl's brow beginning to furrow with unease, or puzzlement, or both. "I'm not selling," Michael said eventually. The sheet of paper, he belatedly understood, was an offer on the house and store. This was Carl's good news.

"You're not selling?" Carl blinked. "I don't get it."

"I mean I'm staying here, Carl."

Carl took off his glasses and stared hard at the lenses while he polished them with a handkerchief he took from his pocket. His smile remained frozen on his face, but it looked forced, as if it were threatening to be swept away without his full consent. Eventually he looked up. "You mean you're planning to live here? In Little River?"

Michael heard the underlying tone. "You look like you don't think it's a good idea."

Carl started to shake his head and protest, but changed his mind. "The truth is, Michael, I should counsel you to think about this. I'm speaking as your friend here, not just your lawyer. This is a damn good offer," he added.

"It's not the money."

Carl fiddled with a pen. He got up, looking uncomfortable about the whole situation, the expression on his face changing to one of irritation. If he'd had to guess, Michael would have said that Carl was wishing Michael's dad had taken his business someplace else before he died—only there *wasn't* anywhere else in town. He wondered if maybe Carl had put some kind of deal together that was going to make the lawyer some money, and now that he understood Michael wasn't selling, he was pissed about it. Another possibility occurred to him, however, one he hadn't anticipated and hoped wasn't true.

"The truth is," Carl went on, choosing his words carefully, trying to sound reasonable, "I just assumed you wouldn't want to stay around here. I mean, it's lucky you didn't sell everything when your dad died. There's enough to start somewhere new."

Luck, Michael thought, had nothing to do with it. Back then the last thing he'd wanted was anything that had belonged to his dad. He wouldn't have cared if the house and store had just fallen apart.

Carl was warming to his new approach. "I wish sometimes I'd got out of here when I was younger the way you did. I don't know why you'd want to think about living in a place like this. What would you do, for a start? You were in advertising, weren't you? I mean, there's not much call for that kind of thing around here."

"I doubt I'd be much in demand these days," Michael said.

"Well, maybe not in Toronto. There're other places. New York. California, maybe."

The mention of the States made Michael think of Louise and Holly again. The last he'd heard, his wife had remarried and was living in Boston.

"I wasn't planning on going back to the advertising business," he said.

"What will you do, then?"

"I don't know. I'll get a job of some kind, I suppose. It doesn't matter what." The fact was, he hadn't considered the practicalities of his situation too much. What was uppermost in his mind was that he needed to be here, he needed to reconcile his life, and after that, he didn't know. He didn't know if there would even be a time after that.

Carl changed tack, adopting a cautionary tone. "You're turning down a good offer, Michael. I mean, it might not be so easy to get a job around here." There was the ring of prophecy in the way he spoke.

"Because I've been in prison?"

"It's not that. Jesus, there's other people around here had their brush with the law. But, well, you know how people are."

Michael thought about Carl's secretary and the way she'd acted around him earlier, the way Carl was acting now. He thought he was beginning to see how people were. "I grew up here, Carl," he said, not entirely sure what point he was trying to make. Maybe it was an appeal of sorts, for some kind of understanding. He started to try and explain a little of how he felt, why he'd needed to come back here, but Carl was already talking again, Michael's words barely registering.

"Little River is a small town, Michael. People aren't like they are in the city, you have to remember that. Think about how long it is since you lived in a place like this. I mean, I guess you left here in the first place because you hated it, and let's face it, you haven't exactly been back here on a regular basis now, have you? Before you got locked up, I mean."

That was true enough, but Michael's reasons for not coming back went a lot deeper than that, something he knew now he wasn't about to explain. "Do people here know about me, Carl?"

Carl seemed surprised by the question. "Do they know about you? Hell, of course they do. It was in the papers."

It had been a faint hope, Michael saw now, to think the news hadn't traveled this far. "Maybe they don't remember, or they don't care. It was a long time ago."

"In a place like this, people have long memories." Carl paused. "Listen, think about this. If you sold up, you could just go somewhere where nobody knows you. The papers here didn't get their facts exactly straight when they reported your case, Michael. Plus, you know how things get twisted when stories go around. Murder is a touchy subject."

"I didn't kill anybody," Michael pointed out.

"Doesn't mean you weren't intending to," Carl said flatly.

Michael didn't say anything for a moment, and suddenly he thought he'd been foolish not to have foreseen this. "This isn't about the town, is it, Carl? I mean, you're not just talking about how the people out there feel about me?" He gestured toward the window. His tone had become bitter with disappointment, and maybe Carl misinterpreted that as something else. Just for a second, something flashed across his face, a flicker of apprehension.

"You have to understand this thing from other people's point of view," Carl said.

Michael stood up to leave. He guessed he could see what their point of view was. "Thanks for your time, Carl."

Carl followed him to the door. "I think you're making a mistake here, Michael," he called after him.

Michael didn't reply. As he left, Carl's secretary looked up from her screen, then quickly looked away again without meeting his eye. He paused momentarily, saw her shoulders stiffen against him, her back resolutely turned his way, and for a second it seemed like a portent of things to come, the way his life would play out, and he was suddenly deeply saddened by that.

THE HOUSE WAS situated off a country road a couple of miles out of town. An unpaved track wound down between the trees, full of potholes and, at the moment, inches thick with snow. At the bottom there was a clearing surrounded by woods, and a quarter of a mile beyond that flowed the river from which the town took its name.

Michael turned off the engine and let the silence settle over him, punctuated by the pinging of hot metal. Just then the sun burst through cloud and lit the mountains, chasing a shadow down across the snow-covered slopes and the forest all the way to the clearing. The house was awash with light, and for a few moments it was as if somebody had thrown back dusty curtains in an old room. It was a two-story weatherboard place with a porch running along the front and side, and despite the paint flaking like burst blisters, it looked solid enough. He absorbed the feeling of being there again and felt a shadow of the past behind him. The sun vanished as the cloud closed over again, plunging the landscape into gray. The sky seemed low, pressing down, and the house all at once was desolate.

The memories he had of growing up here were forbidding, and he pushed them out of his mind. Inside, the air was dank and still, and the walls felt cold to the touch. He wandered through the rooms, pulling sheets from the furniture. He thought the place might have altered after his mother had died, but it remained largely the way he remembered it.

Upstairs he went into his mother's room. The bed where she'd died was still there. She'd swallowed a bottle of sleeping pills, late on a Wednesday afternoon when she knew his dad would be home, as always, around six. Their lives had revolved around long-held routines; for years, the only night he came home late was Thursday, when he stayed at the store to do the paperwork. It was just a month after Michael had gone back to college after the first break. He'd found a holiday job, which meant he'd come home only for a weekend. He remembered telling his parents the job meant he might not get home again until the summer, and he could still see the shock of disappointment in his mother's face. The way something behind her eyes collapsed was testament to the fact that she'd been counting the days until he came home. She'd never wanted him to go to college; he'd always known that, and despite himself, he'd felt guilty at leaving her. He couldn't imagine how she and his dad would get along together, and he'd guessed that was her reason for not wanting him to leave her alone. The truth was, he'd been glad to go, to be free of the claustrophobic atmosphere of this house, and once he'd left, he'd never wanted to come back again, not even for the holidays. He hadn't needed the job—his mother had said she would give him the money—but it had been an excuse to stay away.

The night she died, his dad had come home around eleven, inexplicably breaking the routine of a lifetime. When he'd found her, she was unconscious, and by the time the paramedics arrived, she was dead. There were rumors that he'd come home earlier, found her, and then gone right back out again, not returning until he was sure the pills had done their job. When Michael had asked his dad where he'd been, he'd said he'd been at the store, but he couldn't explain why he'd stayed late. The question had stayed unanswered in Michael's mind ever since.

He stood in the doorway of the silent room, thinking that everything that had happened here had figured in his own decline. He knew now that his mother had been mentally unstable. Maybe he'd inherited a fragment of that in his makeup. Heller had asked him if he felt guilty about her death, if he thought his leaving had been at the root of it. He'd smiled and shaken his head. That would have been too pat an answer.

After the funeral, he'd never seen his dad again. They had stood side by side at the graveside like the strangers they'd always been, and afterward he could find no words to express how he felt, only a bright anger that he'd kept wrapped tightly inside. He remembered only later that he hadn't shed a tear for his mother, and years later he was reminded again when he'd found himself sitting at his desk, tears coursing silently down his face after the call that informed him of his dad's death. This was a man from whom he'd always been remote, whom he hadn't laid eyes on for twelve years, a man whose funeral he would refuse to attend.

The present merged with the past, and he looked around at the quiet shrouded room and saw that this homecoming was the fruit of all his efforts. He'd sworn that he would never screw up the way his parents had, that he would make a happy home for the wife and children he'd imagined would one day be his. Now he had a daughter he didn't know, whose mother had probably told her that her dad was crazy and had once planned to harm her.

Welcome home, he said to himself with sad irony.

when the guy lived right next door to her. She didn't like her own opinion to be influenced by gossip, but it wasn't always so easy to go by her principles. The bottom line was that she had to think about Jamie. No smoke without fire: It was something her mother used to say, one of the many annoying clichés she used to comment on life, and even as it popped up in her mind, Susan grimaced.

"God, don't let me start turning into my mother," she said, feeling a pang of quick guilt as she turned away and resolving that to make up for it, she'd call her during the weekend.

When Susan went through to her son's room, Jamie was still in bed and showed no signs of moving. She shook him by the shoulder, and he turned over to look up at her sleepily, his straight brown hair hanging in a fringe almost to his eyes.

"Did you hear what I said?" He shook his head. "Bob's rolling in something outside. Did you go down and let him out?"

They could hear him barking, and Jamie's eyes went to the window. He nodded.

"Then you better get up and clean him up before you go to school." She pulled back the covers from his bed and went out of the room. "Breakfast in ten minutes," she called over her shoulder.

Downstairs in the kitchen it was warm, the heat having already been on for an hour. Susan turned on the radio while she made coffee and cracked eggs into a pan for Jamie's breakfast. The weather report said there was a front coming, and she wished she didn't have to drive to Prince George later. Through the window she could see the track that rose through the trees toward the road into town. At the moment it was only lightly covered with snow, nothing her Ford couldn't handle with ease even without chains. Sometimes in winter she had to call Hank Douglas from down the road to come up in his tractor and dig out her access road for her, though that was rare.

Jamie appeared and went to the refrigerator to help himself to milk for his Cocoa Puffs.

"Want some hot chocolate?" she asked him.

He nodded, then Bob came to the door and jumped up against the window, slobbering all over the glass. Jamie went over to let him in.

Susan shook her head. "Uh-uh. Not until he's cleaned up, okay?"

Jamie turned to her and pointed back at the dog, making an exaggerated shrug.

She shook her head. "No way, buddy. You heard me."

3 LITTLE RIVER BEND WOKE TO A STEADY SNOW-
fall that looked set to continue for at least the rest
of the morning.

Susan Baker pulled back the curtains of her bedroom
window. "Hell," she muttered under her breath. Down
in the clearing at the front of the house, a patch of frozen earth
showed brown and bare where Bob was thrashing about like he was
having a fit. She rapped hard on the windowpane and the dog stopped
what he was doing and looked around, his tongue hanging out the
side of his mouth, appearing deliriously pleased with himself and
completely stupid.

"Jamie!" Susan called. "Bob's out there rolling around in something
dead. He's not coming back in this house until somebody cleans him
up, and it isn't going to be me."

Before she turned away from the window, she looked across the
trees toward the house in the clearing about a quarter of a mile
beyond. All she could see was a wisp of smoke rising and the top of
the roof. She wondered about the man who'd moved in there just a
few days ago, and if the things she'd heard people say about him
were true, that he was supposed to have killed somebody once. The
details were sketchy, but she'd already heard two versions, and it
seemed that with each telling the story was becoming more lurid.
One version said that he'd killed his wife, the other that he'd killed
several people, including his own daughter. This last she was certain
was untrue, and even though she didn't like the apparent relish with
which some people spoke about it, she couldn't help but be concerned

porch with such haste that both Jamie and the man she knew to be Michael Somers looked toward her in surprise. She faltered, suddenly uncertain.

"I found your dog over at my place," Michael said, indicating the way he'd come. "At least I thought he was yours."

He sounded unsure of himself, and Susan guessed he'd been asking Jamie, which of course would have elicited no response. As he stood there, unmoving, she couldn't help thinking about the stories going around about him, and the fact that she and Jamie were alone. It made her acutely aware of how isolated they were out here.

"I was just asking your son here—"

"It's our dog," she said quickly, cutting him off. She hadn't meant to sound so abrupt, and he seemed taken aback and halted midstep toward them. "Bob, get over here," she said, and after a second Michael let go of the collar. She turned to Jamie and said, "We have to go. We'll be late for the bus. Go inside and get your things ready. Take Bob with you."

He did as she asked, looking at her curiously as he went past, and she put a hand on his shoulder to hurry him. When she turned back, Michael was looking on with a strange expression. He looked almost angry, she thought, which caused a flutter at her throat. She pushed a hand back through her hair.

"We have to go," she said. He nodded wordlessly, and before she could say anything else, he turned away and went back toward the trees. She felt a moment's regret for the brusque way she'd sounded and belatedly called after him.

"Thanks for bringing Bob over." He didn't respond, and as he vanished into the woods, she wasn't even sure if he'd heard her. "Damn," she said quietly. "Nice work, Susan."

SNOW WAS SETTLING on the road that led into town. A solitary pair of tire tracks in the oncoming lane was evidence that this was a country road, little used except by people whose properties were accessed by it or by logging trucks heading up into the forest. Jamie hugged his bag to his chest, looking out the window at the falling snow. His gaze was distant; he was absorbed in whatever thoughts were going through his head. Susan wondered, as she often did, what they were.

Jamie pointed back again, and frustration flashed in his expression. It was clear he was telling her there was nothing to clean up, which she had to admit was true; whatever it was he'd been rolling in outside must have been frozen enough that it hadn't got caught in his fur. All the same, she made out she didn't understand him; then she knelt down in front of him.

"Is there something you're trying to tell me?"

Immediately he frowned and went back to the table. He was getting wise to her, she thought. It was no use trying to fool him anymore. He knew when she was playing dumb when he was signing, had worked out that it was a ruse to get him to a point of frustration that he'd just talk without even thinking, and he wasn't falling for it. She glanced over at him as he picked at his eggs listlessly, his expression morose. Now who was fooling who? He knew how to get to her, how to make her give in, but she turned away and looked out the window, resolving to stay firm. Dr. Carey cautioned her that she had to be tough. "Make it too easy for him and he's got no incentive to speak," he'd reasoned. She knew this was good advice, but then, he wasn't Jamie's mother. It was she who had the lump come to her throat every time she put him on the school bus in the morning. He looked so small and alone, and it made her want to hug him, to tell him everything would be okay. Being tough wasn't such an easy thing.

Outside she saw Bob run across the snow in front of the window and head for the trees. Automatically she started to go to the door to call him back, and then she saw Jamie looking at her, his eyes making a silent plea. She sighed, acknowledging defeat.

"Okay, okay. Go and bring him inside." She shook her head as he went, then glancing at her watch, said, "Jesus, look at the time," and hurried from the room.

She was just finishing getting dressed when she glanced from her window and saw something that stopped her dead, her fingers poised at the top button of her shirt. Jamie was below, standing close to the house, and he was facing a figure who had come from the trees, his hand gripped through Bob's collar. He wore blue jeans with a fawn-colored coat, and he had thick hair that made her think of overripe corn gone from yellow to deep burnished gold. For a second she didn't know who it was, then suddenly she knew and was heading for the door. She ran down the stairs and outside, bursting onto the front

Jamie pointed back again, and frustration flashed in his expression. It was clear he was telling her there was nothing to clean up, which she had to admit was true; whatever it was he'd been rolling in outside must have been frozen enough that it hadn't got caught in his fur. All the same, she made out she didn't understand him; then she knelt down in front of him.

"Is there something you're trying to tell me?"

Immediately he frowned and went back to the table. He was getting wise to her, she thought. It was no use trying to fool him anymore. He knew when she was playing dumb when he was signing, had worked out that it was a ruse to get him to a point of frustration that he'd just talk without even thinking, and he wasn't falling for it. She glanced over at him as he picked at his eggs listlessly, his expression morose. Now who was fooling who? He knew how to get to her, how to make her give in, but she turned away and looked out the window, resolving to stay firm. Dr. Carey cautioned her that she had to be tough. "Make it too easy for him and he's got no incentive to speak," he'd reasoned. She knew this was good advice, but then, he wasn't Jamie's mother. It was she who had the lump come to her throat every time she put him on the school bus in the morning. He looked so small and alone, and it made her want to hug him, to tell him everything would be okay. Being tough wasn't such an easy thing.

Outside she saw Bob run across the snow in front of the window and head for the trees. Automatically she started to go to the door to call him back, and then she saw Jamie looking at her, his eyes making a silent plea. She sighed, acknowledging defeat.

"Okay, okay. Go and bring him inside." She shook her head as he went, then glancing at her watch, said, "Jesus, look at the time," and hurried from the room.

She was just finishing getting dressed when she glanced from her window and saw something that stopped her dead, her fingers poised at the top button of her shirt. Jamie was below, standing close to the house, and he was facing a figure who had come from the trees, his hand gripped through Bob's collar. He wore blue jeans with a fawn-colored coat, and he had thick hair that made her think of overripe corn gone from yellow to deep burnished gold. For a second she didn't know who it was, then suddenly she knew and was heading for the door. She ran down the stairs and outside, bursting onto the front porch with such haste that both Jamie and the man she knew to be Michael Somers looked toward her in surprise. She faltered, suddenly uncertain.

"I found your dog over at my place," Michael said, indicating the way he'd come. "At least I thought he was yours."

He sounded unsure of himself, and Susan guessed he'd been asking Jamie, which of course would have elicited no response. As he stood there, unmoving, she couldn't help thinking about the stories going around about him, and the fact that she and Jamie were alone. It made her acutely aware of how isolated they were out here.

"I was just asking your son here——"

"It's our dog," she said quickly, cutting him off. She hadn't meant to sound so abrupt, and he seemed taken aback and halted midstep toward them. "Bob, get over here," she said, and after a second Michael let go of the collar. She turned to Jamie and said, "We have to go. We'll be late for the bus. Go inside and get your things ready. Take Bob with you."

He did as she asked, looking at her curiously as he went past, and she put a hand on his shoulder to hurry him. When she turned back, Michael was looking on with a strange expression. He looked almost angry, she thought, which caused a flutter at her throat. She pushed a hand back through her hair.

"We have to go," she said. He nodded wordlessly, and before she could say anything else, he turned away and went back toward the trees. She felt a moment's regret for the brusque way she'd sounded and belatedly called after him.

"Thanks for bringing Bob over." He didn't respond, and as he vanished into the woods, she wasn't even sure if he'd heard her. "Damn," she said quietly. "Nice work, Susan."

SNOW WAS SETTLING on the road that led into town. A solitary pair of tire tracks in the oncoming lane was evidence that this was a country road, little used except by people whose properties were accessed by it or by logging trucks heading up into the forest. Jamie hugged his bag to his chest, looking out the window at the falling snow. His gaze was distant; he was absorbed in whatever thoughts were going through his head. Susan wondered, as she often did, what they were.

At the stop in town, the school bus was waiting, chugging soft clouds of exhaust fumes into the cold air.

"Don't forget what day it is," she said as Jamie started to get out. "I'll pick you up at twelve, okay?"

She leaned over to kiss his cheek, but he avoided her. She watched him walk over to the bus, where some other kids about his age were milling about at the doorway, jostling one another to get on. Jamie hung back from them, shuffling his feet in the slush, and waited until the way was clear before he climbed on. She imagined him walking up the aisle to find a seat by himself somewhere. All the kids would be noisily talking over one another, arguing about a hockey game or something on TV, and Jamie would sit by the window, tracing patterns on the glass with his finger.

She waited until the bus moved off before driving to her office on Main Street, across from the diner. Depending on her mood when she drove in each day, she found the town either instantly depressing or comfortingly familiar. That it was small and that she knew just about everyone who lived here struck her as a good thing on some days. On others it drove her crazy, and she dreamed of being anonymous, in the flow of a city.

Occasionally over the past year or so, she'd thought about moving away, thinking it might be good for both her and Jamie. Sometimes when she was taken with an urge to evaluate her life, she made lists on a sheet of paper: everything positive down one side, the negative down the other. It was supposed to be a technique for figuring things out logically. The idea was that if the negative side was disproportionately long, then you had a problem, but at least you could see it there in black and white, which provided a focus. She didn't know what conclusion a person was supposed to reach if the result was the other way around, but she imagined it probably never happened that way. People whose lives were so good didn't feel the need to analyze why.

Her own columns always came out evenly balanced. There was nothing startlingly bad about her life, nothing that gave her a compelling urge to change, but still she felt an undercurrent of discontent.

On this day she pulled up outside her office with its sign painted on the window that read LITTLE RIVER BEND REALTY and switched off the engine. She paused for a moment to look along Main Street. Most things she needed could be bought in town; there was a drugstore, some clothes stores, a grocery store, a hardware store. Everything was covered so long as having a wide choice wasn't a priority. If a person wanted to go out at night, there was the Valley Hotel, which was about the only place that served a decent meal, or there was a bar called Clancys that served food, but mostly just stuff that could be heated in a microwave.

Richard Wells from the bank came by and saw her sitting in her car. He paused, then came and tapped on her window. "Everything okay there, Susan?"

She came to, aware that she'd been daydreaming, and wound down the window. "Fine, Richard. I was miles away, I guess."

He smiled. He was a friendly guy in his fifties with a wife and three kids, all at college. He looked up at the sky. "Think this is going to get any worse?"

The weather was a constant topic of conversation in winter, though around Little River they missed the worst of it. They were in a protected valley at the edge of the Cariboo Mountains, the Columbia ranges beyond and the Rockies still farther east. This winter had been mild compared with others she'd seen in the time she'd lived in the town. The lack of severity was being attributed to the El Niño effect, but all the same, there had been some heavy falls already that month, and more were expected.

"The weather report said there was a front coming in," Susan said.

"Is that right?" Richard stamped his feet. "Looks like we're in for a cold one, then."

They chatted for a minute, then he checked his watch and said he had to be going. "Bye now." He raised his hand and moved on, snowflakes settling like a shawl across the shoulders of his heavy dark coat.

She watched him go, then went into her office. Things were quiet this time of year, and she wasn't expecting to be busy. She planned to make some calls to people who she knew were thinking of selling their houses, and later she'd go over and have coffee with Linda Kowalski, who as well as being her best friend owned the diner across the street with her husband, Pete.

The morning passed quickly, and at eleven-thirty she switched on the answering machine and hung a sign on the door. Outside, the snow had stopped falling, but it felt colder, the breeze cutting to the bone. She scraped snow from her windshield and drove to Bakerstown, where she picked Jamie up from school. He was waiting for her inside the entrance hall, and when she pulled up, he came out and climbed sullenly into the passenger seat. Before heading toward the highway, she turned around and went back toward Little River. On the edge of town she stopped outside the church and reached into the backseat for the flowers she'd bought earlier.

"Jamie, are you coming?"

As usual whenever she brought him here, she might as well have been talking to herself. He continued looking out the window as if he hadn't heard her.

For a brief second she was angry, but it passed. The frustration got to her sometimes, but getting upset was pointless. She had been down that road before. She had been down every road. With a resigned sigh, she climbed out and walked back through the snow.

The headstone was a simple granite marker, with his name and the dates of his birth and death carved into it. Underneath it read BELOVED HUSBAND AND FATHER. She often thought the words were inadequate, but at the time she hadn't known what else to put. He'd been thirty-six years old when he'd been killed in a hunting accident, of the sort that happened regularly, if not in epidemic numbers, throughout the country. Just a moment's carelessness, and the man she had loved for eleven years was dead. There had been a stage afterward when she'd felt bitter that he could have let it happen and left her all alone to deal with the aftermath. It hadn't lasted, but sometimes she still felt a trace of it when she came to his grave. She looked back across the cemetery toward her car, where Jamie was still determinedly looking the other way.

She remembered the morning she'd waved from the window as they'd left. Jamie had been alone to witness his father's blood leaking away into the ground, his life ebbing with it into the forest floor. It wasn't clear exactly what had happened, and as Jamie hadn't spoken a word since, it had remained mostly a matter of conjecture. It seemed, though, that David had simply tripped, and somehow or other the gun had gone off, blowing a hole in his chest. When Jamie had been brought home, he'd been soaked in his father's blood, as if he'd taken a bath in it. The sheer volume of it had shocked her deeply; the sight of her eight-year-old boy, red from head to foot, still came back to her sometimes at night and numbed her with horror.

She turned away, her eyes stinging. She wiped them and took a breath, blinking up at the sky. She missed David with a deep physical ache that gripped her inside. At night, sometimes, she still hugged a pillow to help her sleep, forming in her mind a picture of his face to carry her though her dreams.

Overhead the cloud was clearing, revealing brief glimpses of blue sky. The ground around the church was covered with a few inches of white snow; the forest beyond rose up the mountain, a green canopy of spruce that in summer would be broken up with patches of dazzling green willow. Right now it appeared dark, above a gloomy interior. The country looked big and empty, as empty as the bare glacial slopes above the tree line high in the mountains. She wanted to put David behind her now and she knew she ought to, but with Jamie it was difficult. Perhaps, she thought again, a new start somewhere else, maybe in Vancouver or even in the East, might be the best thing for both of them.

As she turned and started back toward her Ford, a vehicle came along the road from the direction of town, and as it got closer, she saw it was Coop. He pulled over, the engine of his RCMP Chevy cruiser idling with a throaty rumble. She always thought it incongruous that the Mounties kept the rider-on-horseback motif on their motorized vehicles. The big truck with its fancy yellow, red, and blue flashing on the sides was about as far removed from a horse as it was possible to get. Coop had the window down. The police lights on top of the roof bore a cap of frozen snow.

"Going to Prince George today?" He looked over at Jamie and raised a hand, but got no response.

Susan frowned. She hated the way Jamie simply blanked out anything he didn't want to know about; but then, that was his whole problem.

"Don't worry about him," she said. "You know how he is."

Coop flashed her a smile. "He'll come around. Listen, how about when you get back I take you both out for supper at the hotel? What do you say? I bet Jamie'd like that."

She doubted that somehow. Not for the first time it struck her that Coop seemed immune to the way Jamie treated him. It bordered on outright hostility at times, but Coop didn't seem to mind. A lot of people would have given up long ago, she thought. She tried to remember at what point her relationship with Coop had altered, when

exactly he had become more than simply David's friend looking out
for his widow and young son. She couldn't get a fix on it, and wasn't
even sure what exactly their relationship was. It had been on her
mind lately, seeping into her consciousness that some kind of understanding seemed to have developed around them without her really
being aware of its happening. She wondered if it was possible for a
thing to happen like that. Or had she been aware all along and just
lacked the energy or the will to acknowledge it? For now she put it
out of her mind. She begged off his invitation, claiming she would
be tired, which was true enough.

"Okay," he said easily. "How about just you and I have dinner
sometime, maybe on Saturday? The break would do you good."

"I don't know, Coop. . . ." She was unsure of what to say, or even
why she was backing off. It just seemed like things had drifted beyond her control, and she needed some space to think.

"Come on. Saturday at eight, okay?"

She relented. Maybe he was right, maybe the change would do
her good, and she could think of no good reason to turn him down.
She knew he'd be hurt, and she didn't want that. She didn't know
what she would have done without him in those early days, so she
smiled and said that eight would be fine.

"Okay, see you then." He raised a hand to Jamie as he left, and
called out for Susan to drive carefully on the way home. "It'll freeze
up later," he warned.

She waved and watched him go, then got back into her Ford, where
Jamie sat with his shoulders hunched, a sullen expression marking
his features. "You didn't have to do that," she told him, but he just
looked out the window as if he hadn't heard.

DANIEL CAREY WAS a child psychologist Jamie had been referred to
by Dr. Peterson in Little River.

The therapy had been going on for more than a year now, though
it was closer to eighteen months since the accident. That morning,
when she'd last seen David alive, Jamie had looked back at her and
waved, yelling that they'd bring home a deer. It was the last time
she'd heard his voice. She had nightmares occasionally in which he
spoke to her again, but though she could see his lips move, the sound
he made was unintelligible. She would wake distressed and try to

recall exactly how his voice had sounded, and each time it seemed
her recollection was less clear.

It was shock, everybody had told her initially, it would wear off,
and she'd tried to believe it. For the first few weeks she'd been a
mess herself, dazed from loss and prescription tranquilizers, but one
morning as they sat at the kitchen table, the two of them like zom-
bies, she'd gone right upstairs and flushed the rest of her medication
down the toilet. After that she'd put her own feelings aside. There
would be time for grieving later, she'd told herself, and since then
Jamie had been her first concern.

Slowly he'd come out of himself, a little at a time, and she'd been
careful not to push him. She let him decide when to go back to school,
and one day he'd just brought his books down to the breakfast table
without ceremony. He hadn't looked at her but just carried on eating
as if nothing had changed. She hadn't let him see the tears in her
eyes when she drove him to the bus. After that he seemed to be
coming back to her a little more each day. He started to smile again,
and life resumed an almost normal rhythm, except that Jamie still
wouldn't speak. There were other things, too: He didn't hang out
with kids he knew from school, and he never acknowledged the pictures of David she'd placed around the house; nor would he refer to
his dad in any way. That was when she'd agreed to take him to see
a psychologist, though she was unsure now about what good it had
done.

Dan Carey perched on the edge of his desk, reviewing Jamie's file.

"So tell me how he's been," he said.

"The same. He's out there now, staring into space as if nothing
exists. It worries me," she added.

During the drive, Jamie's behavior had followed a familiar pattern.
She could almost feel him retreating from her as if he were slowly
drawing a cloak around himself, burrowing down deep. After Coop
had gone, he'd flicked radio stations a few times, changing them
without apparent reason, rhythmically kicking his heels against the
seat bottom. But then, like some clockwork figure slowing down, his
jerky and unnatural movements had stilled. She'd glance over at him,
watching the lines on his brow smooth out, as if he were falling into
a trance, and then he'd sit there motionless, staring out the windshield
in an unseeing manner. The first few times this had happened, it
had scared her, but Dr. Carey had said not to worry, that it was just

Jamie's way of coping with the visits, that it would pass. Only it hadn't. Every time she brought him here it was the same routine.

She knew what to expect when they got home. Often he was difficult, angry with her, and sometimes he broke things. The last time it had been a Florentine vase he knew she treasured. Another time, he'd spilled hot coffee over her.

"He doesn't want to come here, and he blames me," she said to Dr. Carey.

"So how do you feel about that?"

She gave him a wan smile. How did he think she felt? Hurt, unsure that she was doing the right thing making Jamie attend these sessions. Sometimes his anger even scared her a little.

"It's not that I'm afraid for myself," she explained. "It's just the situation. I'm afraid he'll start to hate me."

Carey nodded with understanding. "But this only ever lasts for a few days?"

"Until the next time."

"And you want to know what I think you should do?" He put down the file and sat in the chair beside her. "You know why he's doing this, don't you?"

"Because he doesn't want to come here," she said.

"Yes, but that's only part of it," Carey told her. "It's the underlying reason you need to think about. It's really about the fact that he doesn't want to confront what happened—the same reason he's refusing to speak, a form of denial. My guess is that Jamie has blocked out the day of the accident. He wants to pretend it never happened."

She'd heard this before and it made partial sense, but what she couldn't understand was why Jamie seemed to have erased any notion that he'd ever had a father. Why was he oblivious to David's pictures?

"It's as if David never existed," she said.

"We won't know that until he starts to talk again," Carey said. "Maybe it's the only way he can blot out that day. Maybe he's angry with his father."

"Angry? Why?"

"Because his dad left him, or maybe it has something to do with the accident, something we don't know about? It's impossible to say. How is he with other people?"

"Most of the time he's okay. I mean, inasmuch as he is with anyone."

Carey paused a moment. "How about with your friends? Is there anyone who comes to the house, for instance?"

She saw what he was getting at and thought of Coop. "There's a guy who was a friend of David's, he's the local cop. He comes around now and then. Jamie doesn't like it. He does his best to ignore him."

"How do you think Jamie sees this guy?"

"I don't know. He's just a friend."

"But Jamie's attitude has changed toward him since his dad died, right?"

"I guess," Susan said. She thought back, trying to recall when it had started happening. It hadn't been right away, but maybe a month or so after the accident, that Coop had started showing up unexpectedly at the house, just making sure they were okay. Sometimes he'd stay for supper.

"Jamie's probably afraid this guy is going to take his dad's place. It's a conflict he can't deal with, so he does his best to put him off."

"But it's not like that," Susan said quickly.

"Maybe that's not how Jamie sees it. It's *his* perception we're talking about here."

There was a short silence, then Carey got up and walked around his desk. "Look, the way I see it, you have two options at the moment," he told her. "Jamie hasn't made any outward progress since you started bringing him here, am I right?"

"In some ways he gets worse, like the way he is now." She pictured him in the waiting room, his gaze vacant. She'd had a nightmare once in which he just stayed like that forever, locked in his own reality.

"Okay, here's what I think," Carey said. "You can keep coming here and hope that one of these days Jamie'll start to trust me, or else you can give it a break for a while and take the pressure off him."

"And if I take the second option, what do you think will happen?"

"Maybe nothing. But the same could be said for the first. To be honest, I don't think a break is going to hurt right now. Jamie's stubborn and he's a bright kid. All he ever does is stare at the wall when he's here. He knows what's going on, and he's just decided he doesn't want to play ball. He could do that forever."

It was the last thing Susan wanted to hear. It was her greatest fear that Jamie would never speak again, that he'd gradually withdraw from the real world and sink ever further into himself. She voiced her concerns to Dr. Carey.

"I don't think it's going to come to that," he said. "I think he'll find a way to deal with this in his own way. Take him home and tell him he doesn't have to come here anymore, and let's see what happens. Try to treat him as normally as possible, and don't make allowances for him. You're still not letting him sign?"

"I try not to." At one time she'd thought she ought to consider having him taught sign language, but Dr. Carey had advised her not to. It would just make it too easy for him, he'd said, and she'd gone along with that.

"Good," Carey said. "Let's give it three months, and call me if you need to. And another thing: Don't let him stop you from seeing anybody. That's not going to help him in the long run."

She was surprised and started to say again that it wasn't like that with Coop, but she stopped herself, uncertain. Instead, she smiled and shook his hand as he led her to the door. Outside, Jamie sat in a chair, staring blankly into space, not even blinking when Carey crouched down and said good-bye. Then, as Susan bent down to him, she saw a flicker of puzzled response in his expression.

"Dr. Carey says you don't have to come here anymore."

She held out her hand and hesitantly he took it, watching her as if this were some kind of trick.

"Come on, let's go home," she said.

4 CATCHING SIGHT OF A REFLECTION IN THE plate-glass showroom window, Michael had to look twice to recognize himself. The last time he'd worn a suit on a regular basis had been seven years ago, when he'd worked in an office on the fifteenth floor of a glass and steel tower in downtown Toronto. Back then he'd been the agency's most successful account manager, and in return for his skills, the company had provided him with a BMW and paid him a ridiculously high salary. He was literally the blue-eyed boy: clean-cut, six feet and lean, wearing thousand-dollar suits, and outwardly confident that it would all last forever. He didn't look much different now, despite the intervening years and all that had happened. A little older—mostly around the eyes, where the lines were etched deep—the hair darker and a little longer; seeing himself was like encountering a ghost.

The suit was an old one, but it was still conspicuous in a place like Little River. If people here wore suits at all, they bought them at a department store in Williams Lake for $125 on sale.

A guy came over, smiling curiously, wearing a sport coat and pants that sagged at the knee. "Morning," he called cheerfully. "Something I can help you with today?" He sounded doubtful, maybe thinking that Michael didn't look like their regular truck-buying clientele.

"I'm looking for George Wilson," Michael said, adding, "I'm here about the job."

The salesman's smile stayed curious as he gestured through the doorway. "Just ask the girl behind the desk over there, she'll find him for you. He's around here somewhere." He looked Michael up and down while trying not to show it, taking in the suit, the silk tie, and the loafers.

"Thanks," Michael said.

"Anytime."

The job of promotions manager had been in the paper next to the twice-weekly full-page ad Wilson's ran to sell their cars. Michael had read about the job and looked over the ad with the eye of somebody who'd spent a lot of time in the advertising business, and he'd thought he had something to offer. A phone call had secured him an appointment. The girl behind the reception desk looked up as he approached.

"Hi, there. May I help you?"

"My name's Somers. I have an appointment with Mr. Wilson."

She ran her finger down her diary, where Michael could see three or four other names. Her expression gave no sign that his name meant anything to her, other than that he was there about a job. "I'll tell him you're here."

He took a seat while she spoke into the phone. "He'll be down in a couple of minutes," she told him. "Can I get you anything? Coffee, maybe?"

"I'm fine, thanks."

"Okay." She seemed reluctant to go back to whatever she'd been doing and fiddled with her pen for a moment. "It's not so cold out today," she ventured.

"No," he agreed.

She was maybe twenty-five, he thought, and he was flattered by her attention, but it also made him nervous. He picked up a magazine from the table and started to flick through it, thinking about what he'd tell her if she asked him where he was from. He could feel her watching him now and again as she looked up from her work, and once he met her eye and they exchanged smiles. He started to think the suit had been a mistake, that he should have made himself less conspicuous—which he thought was ironic, given the job he was applying for.

After ten minutes or so a door opened, and a tall, upright-looking man with a shock of white hair stopped by the desk and then came over to Michael, extending his hand. His grip was firm, belying the

age his leathery, deeply lined skin gave away. He smiled and introduced himself as George Wilson, his quick, intelligent eyes meeting
Michael's and holding the look for a half second.

"Come on through," he said, pointing the way.

Stairs led up to the offices on the first floor where the administra-
tion was handled by half a dozen women and one man who had a
desk in a small corner office. Some of them cast curious glances their
way. Wilson's office overlooked the front of the lot and contained a
huge desk, some visitor's chairs, and a liquor cabinet. The smell of
cigar smoke permeated the room, ingrained deeply into the carpet
and the furniture. Wilson closed the door.

"You're not from around here?" he began.

"No," Michael said, thinking that now wasn't the time to elaborate.
"Toronto."

"I didn't think you bought that suit around here."

Michael didn't reply, feeling that nothing was required. He had the
feeling that Wilson was shrewd, sizing him up. The old man gestured
that they should stand by the window, and together they looked out on
the vehicles arranged in lines on the lot below. This had about it a little
of the feeling of a king surveying his domain, and Michael guessed that
Wilson spent a fair bit of time standing right at this spot. At that moment, the salesman who'd approached Michael earlier appeared outside
and went over to a young guy who'd wandered in off the street. The
salesman just appeared at his side, scuttling like a crab, and from where
he and Wilson were standing, Michael could see the smile that automatically arrived on his face. Michael saw the salesman glance up, and
for a brief instance their eyes met, then the salesman was casually
touching the customer's elbow, starting to guide the guy further onto
the lot, gesturing toward a line of Ford trucks.

Wilson nodded toward the lot. "That fellow there has worked for
me for five years now. He's a good man. He wanted to apply for this
job you've come about, but I told him he wasn't right for it. The
truth is, I'm looking for somebody with some fresh ideas, and that
puts most people around here out of the running." The old man
turned, and for a second their eyes met. "I believe in cutting through
the b.s.," Wilson said briskly. "I rely on my instincts when it comes
to business; the same applies to people. So, you're from Toronto, eh?"

"It's where I've lived most of my adult life."

"What kind of work did you do there?"

"I was in advertising." He held up his résumé. "It's all in here."

He'd put it together using the computer in the library at St. Helen's. After a lot of thought, he'd decided to end his career record at a point six years earlier without giving any explanation as to what he'd been doing since then. It was something he'd thought was best handled face to face, when at least he could explain.

Wilson made a dismissive gesture. "We can get to the paperwork later. I like to hear what a man has to say about himself first. The way somebody talks tells me a whole lot more than some fancy résumé ever will. So, what brings you to a place like Little River?"

It was a question Michael had expected, but for the moment he sidestepped it. He wanted a chance to explain what he thought he could offer before he got into that. "A lot of things, I guess. But you could say I needed a change of scenery."

"It'd be that, all right," Wilson said. "And what makes you want to apply for a job like the one I'm offering? I mean, don't get me wrong, it's an important position for us. We never had a promotions manager here before, but somehow I doubt this is the kind of thing you're used to."

"Advertising is what I know about, Mr. Wilson, and everything that goes along with it. I understand that Little River is a different environment from the one I'm used to, but I knew that when I decided to come here."

Wilson nodded as if he understood. "I guess I can relate to that. Any man who decides the city doesn't have everything this life has to offer has got my vote." He looked out the window toward the mountains. "I've lived here all my life, and I'm seventy-four years old now. I've done a bit of traveling in my time, and I never found a place that offered anything better than what I've got here. Of course, I'm fortunate. My dad started this business, so I've always had something to work on, something I knew would be mine one day, which it was when he retired. I've done all right here, and I'm thankful for it." He paused a moment, then added, "You married, Mike? Can I call you Mike?"

"Sure. I was married, I'm not now."

Wilson frowned and looked thoughtful. "That's a shame. I've been married for nearly forty years now myself. All of them to the same woman, too," he added, and laughed briefly. "It's a great thing, marriage. A family is important, don't you think? Gives a man stability, something to work for. My only regret is that neither of my kids were interested in coming into the business. They've both done well by themselves, though. One of them's a lawyer, the other's a doctor. I'm proud of them. You got kids of your own, Mike?"

"Just one," he said. "A girl."

Wilson considered this for a moment. Michael had the idea that being divorced was a mark against him, but Wilson must have decided it was something he could overlook, and he waved a hand as if dismissing the subject.

"Let me tell you about the job, Mike," he said.

They sat down, and Michael listened as Wilson outlined what the position involved. It was about what he'd expected. The business had done well enough over the years, but as Wilson had recognized, things were changing. Competition from out of town meant that some people, especially the younger ones, were tempted by deals and all kinds of offers. A lot of fancy stuff on the side, as Wilson put it. The company's reputation, which was what they'd always traded on, was getting forgotten about when it was measured up against the glitz and glitter of their competitors.

"This business has been around a long time, Mike. My dad started it after the war, and he had a philosophy that's always worked well for us: Treat people right, they'll do the same by you. That's it in a nutshell. See, we look after our customers, and that's why they come back. Of course, it means the automobiles we sell cost a few dollars more because we back every one up with a guarantee, but people come back because they know they can trust us. We're good people, I guess." He grinned at himself. "Guess that sounds old-fashioned these days."

"I don't think the values you're talking about ever go out of fashion," Michael offered. "It's the way you communicate them that has to change."

Wilson cocked an eyebrow. "Values. That is what I'm talking about, I guess. It's a word you don't hear too often these days. I think you may have hit the nail on the head, Mike. Values is what we're all about here. We stand for the way things used to be, when it wasn't all a fast buck and make it anyway you can." He shook his head sorrowfully. "Nowadays, seems like that's all young folks care about."

"I guess it seems that way sometimes," Michael ventured.

"Even a town like this isn't immune to it." Wilson gestured with a sweep of his arm toward the window. "We've always provided a service here, a fair deal for a fair price, and we've always taken care of our customers. If you have a problem with a vehicle you bought from us, we'll take care of you. Not like some of these places. Once they have your money, they don't ever want to hear from you again. If you got a problem, it's your problem, not theirs. People forget that when they sign up on some deal that gets them a fistful of Texaco vouchers and a free case of beer. That won't do them any good when the damn head blows a mile or two down the road."

Wilson shook his head ruefully. "I guess there's no point in just complaining about it, that won't do any good. We have to move with the times, I can see that. We have to let people know about what we stand for. Tell them about our values." He paused. "You've had a chance to take the place in a little. What would you do if the job was yours, Mike?"

Michael gave the impression of giving the question some contemplation before replying, though in reality he could see what the issues were. "My opinion is that what you've got here is essentially an image problem," he said eventually.

He watched for Wilson's reaction to see just how open to new ideas the old man was. It was okay to pay lip service to the recognition a business needed to change, but sometimes when it came down to it, the people in charge balked at the practicalities. Wilson, however, indicated with an almost imperceptible nod that he was still listening.

"The thing is, reputation can work for you, as it always has here, but just as easily it can work against you if it isn't presented in the right way. What you have to do is make your reputation for a fair deal the very foundation of your marketing, which in a way you already do." He recalled the ad that Wilson's ran, which showed a photograph of the old man himself alongside a banner of the company name and a slogan that said, "You Can Trust Me."

"What that communicates, especially to younger people who're getting bombarded by sophisticated messages all the time from magazines and TV, from radio and billboards, is that Wilson's is old-fashioned," Michael explained. "Also, they probably don't believe it, and they probably don't identify with your image." He paused, unsure how this would go down, especially the last part.

"So, what would you do about it?" Wilson asked after a moment.

"Don't use your picture, for one thing. You need an image that appeals to young and old. And that would be just the start. I'd recommend a total overhaul of your marketing from the top to the bottom. But I'd make it a gradual change. Nothing too dramatic all at once. That would just run the risk of alienating all your loyal customers."

Wilson got up and went to the window again, where he stood with his back to Michael for a short while. When he turned around, his expression was serious.

"So, you'd take me out of the advertising, huh?"

"That would be my recommendation."

"And that would be just the start?" He looked back out the window and appeared to be trying to envisage how things might change. "I guess I'd have to hand over the reins a little bit, wouldn't I?"

"It would be a consultative process, I imagine," Michael said. "Like I say, a little at a time."

Wilson nodded slowly. "I like your ideas, Mike," he said. "I guess you must have learned something in the city. I'm not so old and pigheaded that I don't know I don't have all the answers myself anymore. I guess we could use somebody like you around here."

"Ideas are no good without someone to listen to them," Michael said. "I admire you for being willing to accept change. Not everybody can do that."

"Well, nothing stays the same, I guess," Wilson allowed. "Even in a place like this. We're a friendly bunch here, Mike, at least I like to think we are. We all get along together and we don't stand on ceremony too much. You could even afford to dress a little more casual if you wanted to," he added jokingly. "I think you'd like it here. I have to tell you, though, the kind of money I can offer probably wouldn't match the expense account you'd have in a some big-city firm."

Michael got to his feet. "I understand that. There's something I think you ought to know about first, though." He handed over his résumé, and while Wilson flicked through it, Michael revealed he'd been in prison.

Wilson stopped turning the pages and looked up sharply. "Prison?"

"For three years. Then I was at a unit called St. Helen's," Michael said. "I was released a couple of weeks ago. That's why I came to Little River. I was brought up here."

Wilson's friendly expression dissolved and hardened; his brow furrowed while he looked down at the résumé, rereading the title page.

"Somers? Michael Somers?" The name meant something, but it took him a moment or two to place it. "Your dad was John Somers who ran the hardware store?"

"That's right," Michael said. "You probably heard about what happened. I had a kind of a breakdown, but I had therapy while I served my sentence. I'm fine now."

Wilson shook his head, barely listening. "This changes everything." He closed the résumé abruptly and handed it back. "You should have told me about this right at the start."

Michael could see the change in him, the tight line of the older man's jaw, the hard, unrelenting light in his eyes. A wave of disappointment swept over him, and he wondered why he'd ever thought that it would be any different, that people would overlook his past. All the same, he found himself arguing his case.

"And if I had told you, would you have listened to what I had to say? Would you have even agreed to see me?"

"I think you ought to leave," Wilson said.

Michael uttered a short and bleak derisory laugh. "What happened to the way you liked my ideas? How about those values you were talking about earlier?"

Wilson's expression remained closed. "I'm sorry. It just isn't possible." He started toward the door.

"Wait a minute," Michael said. "You're telling me you can't give me a job because I've been in prison, is that it? I mean, I just want to get this clear, so that I know. Even though I served my sentence, even though I've paid my dues to society."

"It's not just where you've been," Wilson said. "It's what you did. People around here know you, they read the papers. I couldn't have somebody like you working here. Even if I thought it wouldn't affect business, I couldn't have you here. It just wouldn't sit right with me."

"What about all that stuff about treating people right? 'We're good people,' didn't you say? Shouldn't people get another chance?"

"I think you ought to leave," Wilson repeated, moving toward the phone. "I don't want to have to call the police."

Michael felt suddenly deflated; his anger faded to a dull buzz. He should have known better. Wilson held open the door for him, saying nothing. Michael met the old man's eye and saw only distance and hostility there.

"Take my advice," Wilson said as Michael left. "Go somewhere else. Where people don't know you."

There was no sympathy in his tone, no desire to offer wisdom for the sake of helping. He was just saying that the town didn't want him around, and that if Michael had any sense, he would just move on. Michael didn't reply. On his way past reception downstairs, he noted that the girl who'd smiled at him earlier was speaking on the phone. She looked up and met his eye, then looked quickly away. When he reached his car, he got behind the wheel and screwed his eyes against the pain throbbing in his temples, taking deep breaths, massaging his head with his knuckles until the pain faded to a dull ache.

IN THE AFTERNOON, Michael left the house and walked down to the river, needing time to think and clear his mind. He crossed the river by an old footbridge that creaked and swayed above the dark water. The air was filled with the muted roar of water where the banks narrowed between two black rocks that glistened wetly in the weak sunlight. Beyond them the river dropped and surged in white rapids for a hundred feet or so before it widened again to continue its course. On the far bank he climbed through the woods, which down here were mostly hemlock scattered through with aspen and poplar. When he came out beyond the trees, where the snow was thick on the ground and the air was still and quiet, he found a place among the rocks where he could sit for a while.

When Holly was born, he'd thought life was full of promise and had painted mental pictures of how his family would be. The one thing he wanted for her was that she should be happy, that her life would be free of the tensions he'd grown up with himself. He envisioned only an existence where nothing intruded to upset the balance.

He'd married Louise when he was twenty-six; she was three years younger. He was already doing well, and they'd bought an apartment that they moved into the week after their honeymoon in Tobago. He'd written his dad a letter a month later to give him the news, and he sometimes wondered now what pain that must have caused him to receive it after the event. Louise herself came from a happy family, with two brothers and parents who welcomed Michael as one of their own. He'd never talked about his own family except to say that he was an only child, that his mother had died when he was eighteen and he didn't get on with his dad. He'd never tried to explain why, or revealed that his mother had taken an overdose. Louise had tried to persuade him to invite his dad to the wedding, a conversation that had developed into a serious argument.

"You don't understand about him, okay! Just forget it," he'd said, aware that his voice was rising uncontrollably but unable to stop it.

After that, she'd let it drop. A couple of weeks after he'd written, a wedding present had arrived from his dad, and a card. He'd put the present, unopened, in the spare room, but Louise had found it, and one day when he came home from work, a hand-blown glass vase was standing on the table.

"Call him. Just do that, please," Louise had said. "What harm can it do?"

He'd refused, and she'd let it go. But it was there between them, a taboo subject he wouldn't discuss, and it festered.

The first years of their marriage had been happy. Louise had honey-blond hair and serious gray eyes, but when she smiled, they melted. He'd loved her then as completely as any man could. Her body was slim and firm and she knew how to dress so that she turned men's heads in the street. He'd been proud of her. He'd thought he was lucky to have her, and looking back now, he could see that that was the first sign something was slightly wrong. It was as if he'd already felt that nobody should expect things to go so well, that it couldn't last. He had a beautiful wife, a career going places, and at the back of his mind there was a shadow lurking, a gloomy tendency to wonder when it would all go wrong.

His dad called once or twice from Little River, and they'd had stilted conversations. After a while the calls had stopped coming, but there'd been letters instead. Every time he'd read one, he'd felt the need to be alone for a while, and sometimes he'd read them over and over again. Perhaps he was searching between the lines for a message that wasn't there. His dad wrote about the town and small things that were happening. He never mentioned Michael's mother or asked him to come back and visit. Louise had periodically tried to persuade him that he should try to work out whatever had gone wrong between them, or at least talk about it, but he could never bring himself to do that. If he and Louise ever argued, it was over this one thing, this part of his life he excluded her from.

When Holly was born, Louise had given up her job. About that time, Michael had been headhunted to a new agency where he was paid more money. It should have been a perfect time, but the shadow in his mind had grown longer and darkened his thoughts. From a vague feeling that he was undeserving of his existence, he became convinced that disaster was just around the corner, that all of his good fortune had been devised to lull him into a false sense of security. He looked for the warning signs. The birth of his daughter had made him wonder how it was possible to have so much love for a person. He'd look at her, so helpless and vulnerable, and the emotions he'd felt constricted his throat. He kept thinking that he was responsible for her life, that everything she experienced when she was young would shape her and stay with her for all of her days, and he'd promised he would make her life perfect the way his own had never been. He would lie awake at night, and when Louise would question him, he'd tell her that he was afraid for Holly, afraid that it would all come apart. She'd tried to comfort him, but he could see in her eyes that she was worried.

"But why should anything go wrong?" she'd said. "Everything's fine."

"It's just the way I feel."

He'd started calling home at odd hours, checking that everything was okay, sometimes turning up unexpectedly at the apartment. At first Louise had been touched by his concern, then one day it had got to her. Maybe Holly had given her a bad time because she was teething, and maybe the strain was just beginning to show. She'd flown at him when he'd come in the door early in the afternoon.

"Michael, what are you doing here? Why are you doing this? You keep sneaking around as if you expect to find something!"

"I just want to make sure you're okay."

"We're fine. Michael, we're fine." She'd spoken slowly, trying to maintain control. "You have to stop doing this. You're smothering me," she'd said in a softening voice.

He had stopped—for a few days, anyway—but then started again, and it got to the point where she persuaded him that his insecurities

stemmed from his own upbringing and that he ought to see a ther-
apist or else get in touch with his dad.

"I could maybe understand if you'd at least tell me something
about your parents. What is it that made you this way?"

By then, though, it was way too late. The mention of the subject
was like opening a sore every time they spoke, and they argued. At
the time, he'd been surprised by her insight, but when he thought
about it later, he saw how obvious it must have been. As time went
on, she talked more about his seeing somebody. His moods had started
to affect her, too, she claimed. There were days when they hardly
spoke, and he began to suspect her of having an affair.

When Holly was about a year old, Michael got a call one day from
the RCMP in Little River. His dad's car had been traveling on the
wrong side of the road when he came around a bend outside of town,
and he'd hit a logging truck head on. The impact had flattened his
Dodge, killing him instantly. The cop that called Michael said that his
father wouldn't have known anything about it. Maybe a moment's
awareness and then oblivion. Michael was numbed by the news, and
then the knowledge filtered through that they would never be recon-
ciled, that all the things he'd kept locked up now had nowhere to go.

Louise had all but begged him to go to the funeral. She'd said
they would all go, that he could show her and Holly where he'd
grown up. The break would do them good. He'd refused, and refused
even to discuss it. He didn't tell her about the way he'd cried silently,
grieving for a father he'd never really known, about how he remembered that he hadn't even cried at his mother's funeral. He kept it
all locked inside, and though he wasn't aware of it at the time, his
reason began to slip away.

Things got worse after that. His work started sliding, and people
at the agency were starting to ask questions. He'd overhear Louise
on the phone, and when he'd try to discern what she was saying,
she'd hang up, avoiding him if he questioned her about who she'd
been talking to. He spent hours at night in Holly's room, just sitting
quietly in the dark watching her sleep. He remembered thinking it
was all falling away from him, that he was letting Holly down, unable to live up to the responsibility he felt for her happiness. Louise
came in one night and found him holding Holly, pleading with her
not to grow up hating him as she cried in distress.

It went on for months. Near the end, he knew Louise was planning to leave him and was convinced she had found somebody else. He bought a gun, unsure of what he was going to do with it, and he kept it for weeks in his desk at work. When he followed her one day, she met a man he didn't recognize, and he watched them have coffee in a café, talking earnestly across the table with their heads close together. Before they left, the man took her hand and a look Michael recognized passed between them. It was the way Louise had once looked at him. At the door he watched them kiss and part regretfully. He followed the man and found out his name and where he lived.

A week later, Louise told him she wanted a divorce. She explained at length how the last year had made her life a misery. Even then there was something in her tone he hadn't picked up on until later. She'd pleaded again with him to see somebody, and maybe if he'd agreed, they might still have had a chance. Instead, he'd got up from the table in silence and left the apartment. He'd driven to the office, let himself in, and taken the gun from his desk. Then he'd driven to the address of the man Louise had been seeing, and when he opened the door, Michael had shot him twice.

There had never been a time since then that he could recall anything of what he'd been feeling. And yet every action from the moment he'd risen from the table was etched in his mind and he could recall it with ease; not a second had dulled in his memory. It was like a film in which he was an actor. He didn't even view the figure he watched go through his paces as being himself in any real sense.

He'd driven home and told Louise what he'd done, and he remembered most clearly of all her frightened look and the way she pleaded with him while she held Holly close. Holly had cried, not understanding what was happening. It came to him eventually that Louise had thought he intended to shoot them both and turn the gun on himself; this was something he'd thought about often since, unsure exactly what had been in his mind. The police arrived, and he held them at bay while he tried to work out what was happening and what he was going to do. The enormity of it all had hit like a crushing blow that he felt he would never recover from.

The last time he saw his wife and child, they were being led away while he was handcuffed. Louise had looked back for one brief moment, and in that instant he touched bottom, knowing he would never see her again.

Coming back to the present, Michael rose stiffly, aware he'd been lost in thought for hours. He'd been sitting hunched against the cold while it seeped into his bones from the rock. He stretched and thought back to the meeting with Wilson. Maybe the old man had been right not to hire him. Maybe people had a right to be wary of somebody who'd done the things he had. Heller had asked him once, not long before he left St. Helen's, if he thought he was cured.

"I thought you were the doctor," Michael had said.

"You don't exhibit any psychotic signs, but then you haven't for a long time. I want to know what you think, up here." Heller had tapped his head with his finger.

In truth, Michael didn't know. He recalled the dog that had strayed over to his house a few days earlier, poking its nose through the kitchen door, and the expression of the woman in the house through the woods when he'd taken it back. She'd been afraid of him, which had both angered and saddened him. Maybe she was right to feel that way. Who was to say that what happened once might not happen again?

He looked to the sky, which was just starting to change its hue as the afternoon became late, and he felt insignificant beneath it, as if he might be the only person in the world, and the air was empty and still around him, like an emptiness of his own inside. As if to prove him wrong, a movement across the snow caught his attention.

Down the slope from where Michael stood, a man with a rifle over his shoulder walked into view, and as Michael watched, he wondered what the man was hunting.

5 ELLIS DIDN'T NECESSARILY BELIEVE IN SUCH things, but he'd almost swear that falcon knew what he was about and was making a fool of him. It wasn't just the money anymore that drove him out here every day, though that was still a big part of it. Now there were other things at play, like he had something to prove to one or two goddamn people, and maybe to himself as well.

What he should have done, he saw clearly now, was he should have kept his big mouth shut. Since that night in Clancys when he'd been shooting off about how he was going to make himself some easy money, people had been laughing among themselves when they saw him coming. Only the night before, Ted Hanson and Red Parker had been shooting pool when Ellis walked through the door and ordered himself a beer.

Red had straightened up from taking his shot and called out, "Hey, Ellis, I see you ain't gone and bought yourself a new truck yet with all that money you was coming into."

Hanson had snorted into his beer, wiping his mouth with the back of his hand. "What happened, Ellis?" he'd said, adding his own piece to the general amusement. "You go and lose your winning ticket?"

Fuck, he'd had to just grin and take it, laughing along with them as if he didn't mind being the butt of their crummy jokes. He didn't know where Hanson had got the thing about the lottery; he couldn't remember having said anything to give them that idea. What he'd said was that he was coming into some money, if he remembered rightly, but he was sure that was all. He hadn't even said how much he was talking about. Maybe he had dropped some hints about it being more than those dumb assholes would ever see at one time, and he might concede he'd allowed things to become exaggerated, maybe even encouraged it by being so secretive, but he was absolutely positive he'd said nothing about winning any lottery.

The thing was, a week had gone past and he was no closer to getting that falcon now than he had been when he'd started. Every time he showed up in Clancys, he was going to hear the same old jokes until either he proved them wrong or they just forgot about it. It was all getting out of hand, like a big old snowball gathering size as it rolled along out of his control. He hadn't been able to resist telling them what he was going to do with the money when he got it. It had seemed harmless enough at the time. Jesus, times hadn't been easy these last few years, and it had felt good to be on the right side of a little luck for a change. The trouble was, he'd sounded like he was rubbing their noses in it, and now they were just paying him back. They didn't even believe him anymore.

What was funny was that he'd called some other dealers and found out that he'd been right about Tusker planning on cheating him, so he'd called Tusker back and told him the price for the gyr flacon was now two thousand, which seemed about right. Tusker had played it like he thought it was too much and had offered him fifteen hundred and made a big fucking deal of it, like he was cutting off his right arm or something. In the end, though, he'd agreed that he could probably stretch to the two thousand. This had made Ellis feel pretty good, since the most he'd been offered elsewhere was eighteen hundred. So he was on the right side of the money.

"When do I get this bird?" Tusker had said, his voice irritable.

"Soon," Ellis had replied. "A couple of days."

"I already contacted somebody I know, and he's waiting," Tusker said.

So what did Tusker think, that he could just go out and whistle the damn thing to come and get itself shot?

"I don't know how long I can guarantee that price," Tusker had added. "And it had better be in good condition. I can't use anything that's been all blown to hell."

Ellis had hung up, his good mood banished in a second. Nobody ever wanted to give a guy a break.

He stopped for a moment, aware that he'd been so engrossed in his mood that he'd forgotten what he was looking for. He'd seen the falcon a half dozen times over the past few days—which was good, because it meant it was staying in the area—but never close enough for a decent shot. He took a cigarette from a pack in his pocket and flipped his Zippo, cupping his hands around the flame. Sucking smoke into his lungs made him cough, but he hardly noticed.

Some crows were making a fuss around the tops of some trees, flapping around and squawking, and he raised his glasses to get a better look. The falcon flew among them, casually ignoring the half-hearted feints the crows were making. It was something that always puzzled Ellis about crows. They were like a gang of street kids, full of bullshit and bravado when the big man sauntered past, maybe making up in numbers what they lacked individually. He'd seen them do the same thing with hawks and even eagles. The falcon could have killed any one of them at any time. It was bigger and faster, like a luxury car compared to some old wreck that had seen better days, but the falcon just ignored their taunts, disdaining them with a kind of haughty disregard. Ellis had to admit to feeling a kind of grudging admiration.

He watched the falcon rise and guessed it had been somewhere on the other side of the woods. As it always did, it flew away from him, too far away to risk a shot. He had the feeling it knew he was there. He watched it grow smaller, rising toward a rock face in the distance, and he followed it with his glasses until he saw it land; then he marked the spot.

A hundred yards to his left, the woods ran off the same way, and Ellis thought if he could make a path through the trees, he might get close enough undetected to finally have a clear shot. The odds were about even at best. He might get there and find the damn thing had flown, but it was going to be his last chance that day, he was sure of that. The light was beginning to fade already. He dropped his cigarette and started down toward the trees.

MICHAEL WATCHED ELLIS from the rocks high up on the right, and followed the way he'd been looking with his glasses. He saw the mob of crows and another bird that had flown leisurely from their midst, leaving them calling insults in its wake. He didn't know what kind of bird it was, and without glasses all he could tell was that it was large and pale in color. He thought it must be some kind of bird of prey, maybe a falcon. He knew it wasn't a hawk, which were quite common in the mountains. He'd seen several that day, soaring high up on thermals of rising air, riding effortlessly on their broad rounded wings. Their calls echoed among the valleys, a kind of high-pitched plaintive mewing.

He watched Ellis vanish into the trees. The falcon had flown into the distance, lost against a distant rock face, and the crows settled so that the landscape was empty again. He was cold and he thought he should be heading back to the house before it got dark, but instead he turned and headed the way the falcon had flown. It seemed the right thing to do, or else he had guessed what was happening and was curious. But whatever his motive, he didn't question it.

THE FALCON STOOD perched on a narrow ledge high in the rocks. She had chosen a spot where she was sheltered from the prevailing winds and where she had roosted for the night several times before. She wasn't hungry, having killed a squirrel earlier in the day, and she was fully recovered from the battering she had taken in the storms that had swept her south. During the days she had flown this territory, she had seen peregrines, which she recognized as being cousins, and hawks circling high in the air, but no other falcons of her own race. An instinct was beginning to call her north again, like something whispered on the wind. She turned her eye to the peaks rising blue gray as far as the eye could see and shifted restlessly. She was in her first year, having fledged from the nest the previous summer. Later in the year she would need to find a mate, and it was partly this need that was calling her.

She looked back across the snow. The figure she'd seen from the edge of the woods had gone, though his tracks were clearly visible leading down to the tree line. She knew it was the same figure she'd seen almost daily, and she felt a familiar unease. She always saw him first, and sometimes he never knew she was there, watching him from a far vantage point. On this occasion there was something different in the situation. Another figure was coming her way across the snow, keeping high on the slope and making no attempt at concealment. She watched him approaching steadily. Her uneasiness increased, but the reason for it was unclear. She felt it had something to do with the figure who'd vanished into the woods. The one she could see she remained wary of and wouldn't allow to get too close, but she didn't sense danger. The signals were confusing, and as the light faded, she was reluctant to leave her roost without good cause.

She flicked open her wings, feeling the breeze give her lift, but she settled again uncertainly and watched.

ELLIS WAS TEMPTED to make his way to the edge of the woods so that he could use his glasses to see if the falcon was still there or if he was wasting his time. It was dark in the trees, the light fading fast, and he was beginning to regret his decision to try for a shot today. Whichever way he looked at it, by the time he walked back to his truck, the sun was going to have gone down, and he was already cold and tired. He resisted the temptation to take a look, sure that if he did, the falcon would be there but that it would see him and he'd lose it again. He labored on, thinking that another twenty minutes would do it.

He started to think about what he was going to do when he finally got the money. First thing, he thought, was that he was going to go into Clancys and put a hundred bucks on the bar and tell everyone the beers were on him. It wasn't that he wanted to make a big deal of it, or make anyone feel stupid for making fun of him, but he wanted to see their faces. Especially Red and Hanson. He just wanted that one minute when he could show them a wad of notes so thick it would make their eyes bulge; then, just to show there were no hard feelings, he'd give them a hundred each. Or maybe fifty. He'd tell them how he'd got it then, just so they wouldn't think he'd really won the lottery or something, and so they wouldn't come around asking him for a loan to buy a new truck or something stupid like that, which he wouldn't put past them.

He was also going to buy Rachel something, maybe a new dress or whatever women liked. And he was going to take her somewhere for dinner, maybe the Red Rooster out on the highway, which despite the name was actually a pretty classy place. She deserved it. She'd had to put up with a lot over the last few years, and he guessed if he was going to be honest about it, he hadn't made things any easier.

It bewildered him sometimes the way things turned out in life. He remembered Rachel at school, a good-looking girl he'd hardly ever spoken to back then. He'd known she was out of his league. Not only was she pretty, she was smart, too. Not that he was dumb, it was just that around his house there hadn't been a lot of emphasis on school and learning. His old man had made all the kids, his brother and sister and him, feel like losers right from the word go. He'd made damn sure of that, molding them in his own drunken image. Ellis remembered hearing his father slapping his mother around when he came home with a skinful. At least that was something Ellis had never done.

The army had straightened him out. Enlisting was probably the best thing he'd done in his life, apart from marrying Rachel, which even now he sometimes couldn't believe he'd had the good fortune to do. The army had made him see things clearly, see the way he was going to turn out, which was just like his old man if he didn't do something about it. It had given him self-respect—enough to ask Rachel for a date when he'd got back. Jesus, but he still remembered how knocked out he'd been when she accepted. She'd said later that she didn't even recognize him as the same Pete Ellis she'd known at school. She was the best thing that ever happened to him. He wondered where the fuck it all went wrong, but he knew the answer. It always came down to money and getting an even break, and the way the business had gone downhill the last few years, he guessed he really was a goddamn loser like his old man, after all.

Ellis stopped and peered through the trees. He guessed this was about it, though he was going to be lucky if the light was good enough now to give him much of a chance. He reached for the rifle slung over his shoulder and started back toward the open ground. When he was close, he moved from tree to tree until he could get a view of the rock face about two hundred yards away. He found the fissure he'd sighted earlier where the falcon had landed and moved his glasses over the rock. At first there was nothing, and then a movement made him stop. There it was, standing there as clear as day. The sun was going down but he had a few minutes. He raised the rifle and found the falcon through the sight. Not so smart after all, he thought. Just for a second he felt something like regret, but he pushed it from his mind. He started thinking about walking into Clancys with all the money he was going to get. He shifted his position and leaned against the tree to steady his aim.

IF ELLIS HAD looked, he would have seen Michael across the slope. Michael had stopped and was looking up at the rock face, thinking the falcon was up there somewhere. He still didn't know what he was going to do. High up, he caught a movement and saw a pale shape. He looked toward the woods, and down there at the edge of the trees he saw Ellis kneel on the ground and raise a rifle.

There was no time to think, just the knowledge he didn't want this to happen. He raised his arms and shouted, and almost at the same time a shot shattered the quiet air, echoing through the valley.

THE FALCON WATCHED the figure below. When it stopped, she shifted position. Her unease had grown, but she was confused. She scanned the terrain spread out below her, sensing danger but unsure where it would come from. Conflicting impulses to remain where she was, high up in the safety of the rocks, or to take to the air made her flex her wings. She was reluctant to leave this ledge where she could spend the night. The figure below made a sudden movement, and even as his voice carried on the air, she flew into the gray light, banking and rising on silent wings, another sound, like the sharp crack of a bough breaking in the woods, shattering the stillness.

"SHIT," ELLIS MUTTERED. He raised the rifle again for another shot, but it was too late. The falcon fled beyond his line of sight.

He dropped the barrel to see what the hell had happened, and somebody was up there, across the slope. Whoever it was looked straight at him, then turned and started walking away. For a second, just an instant, it flashed in Ellis's mind that he could pick him off as easy as swatting a mosquito. Then the impulse passed, and he loosened the tight grip he had on his rifle and rose to his feet.

He shook his head in disbelief. He was jinxed, he had to be.

6 FROM HER BEDROOM WINDOW, SUSAN SAW A beam of white light flash through the trees, then swing around as Coop's car came down the access road. She heard the dry crunch of tires on the snow as he came to a stop outside the house. Fixing an earring, she stood back to examine her reflection in the full-length mirror. She was wearing jeans and a loose woolen jersey that came to mid-thigh; her hair, shining coppery hues, fell over her shoulders.

"Will I pass?" she murmured to herself.

As she always did these days when getting ready to go out, she'd dressed down. She hesitated, wondering if for once she should wear something different, but it was just Coop taking her into town.

She turned out the light and went down the stairs, reaching the door before he knocked. He stood in the porch light, filling the space with his size. He was tall and broad-shouldered, his hair close-cropped, his skin weathered.

"What have you got there?" she asked, indicating the package he carried in one hand.

He held it up. "It's something for Jamie. It's just a fishing reel. I thought the one he has is getting kind of old."

"Coop, you didn't need to do that." She stood aside to let him in.

"It's no big deal," he said.

"Let me have your coat. You can take that in to Jamie while I fetch you a beer; he's watching TV with Wendy."

She went through to the kitchen and popped the cap on a beer; she usually kept some in the house for when Coop stopped by. She lingered for a minute. The kitchen was her favorite room, the heart of the house. Half the room was occupied by the huge pine table where she and Jamie ate their meals and where sometimes at night she sat to work or read. The room had large windows that looked out toward the mountains and let the natural light flood its open spaces, bouncing off the stainless-steel refrigerator and the row of copper pans that hung above the range.

Through the glass doors that led into the TV room she watched Coop show Jamie the reel. Unaware that she was watching, Jamie remained impassive. He and Coop stood apart from each other, striking an unnatural tableau. Jamie should have been crowding close, eagerly, wanting to hold it and work the ratchet the way boys do. Instead, when Coop held it out to him, he hesitated before accepting it, then without even looking sat on the floor and turned back toward the TV, the reel beside him. If Coop noticed his lack of enthusiasm, he gave no sign of it.

She took his beer through, carrying her own glass of wine. "Hey, that looks great," she said, trying to make up for Jamie's poor grace with her own enthusiasm. "What do you think, Jamie? I bet you can't wait to try it out."

She knew she sounded forced. Coop took his beer and pretended not to notice.

"It's no big deal," he said easily.

"Did you thank Coop, Jamie?"

Jamie looked at her, then to Coop, and kind of nodded, which was a gesture he could make convey as much or as little as he chose. That this was a token response was obvious. She felt a flash of anger with him and sympathy for Coop, who was trying not to let on that his feelings were hurt. He watched a commercial on the TV with patently false fascination.

Hank and Sarah Douglas's oldest girl, Wendy, sat on a chair with her legs curled up underneath her. "Where are you guys going tonight?" she asked in the awkward silence.

Susan seized the opportunity gratefully. "Just the hotel, aren't we, Coop?"

He nodded his agreement. "How's your dad, Wendy?"

"He's okay."

"Everything okay at school?"

Wendy pulled a face. "I guess."

Susan was eager to get away. "Come on, Coop, let's finish our drinks in the kitchen and leave these two to the TV," she said.

She could never relax in the company of both Coop and her son. The tension was too much for her. She bent to kiss Jamie's cheek and he barely acknowledged her.

In the kitchen she apologized, even though she knew Coop understood how things were with Jamie. "You know he doesn't mean it."

"Don't worry about it."

"I think I'm too soft with him. I ought to send him to his room for what he just did," she said.

"He just misses his dad," Coop said simply.

She looked through the door at her son. "Yes, I know."

In the quiet moment that followed, their eyes collided.

"You look great, Susan," Coop said.

She smiled and reached out to touch his arm. "That's sweet," she told him. Then, turning quickly away and putting her glass in the sink, she saw Coop's frown reflected in the window.

THE BAR OF the Valley Hotel was busy even for a Saturday night. George Jones scanned the restaurant reservation list with a creased brow.

"Looks like you might have to wait for a little while," he said apologetically.

"We don't mind waiting," Coop said.

"Maybe fifteen minutes?"

"That's fine."

They left George going over his table plan and walked to the bar. Coop nodded to people as they went. Everybody in town knew Coop. He'd been a cop there since he'd joined up straight out of college, and after Dan Redgrave had retired, a few years back, he'd been promoted to sergeant in charge of the station house in town. As far as his career went, that was the end of the line unless he chose to leave Little River, but Susan couldn't ever see him doing that. Sometimes she envied him for a certain air he had about him. She'd puzzled over it for a while, trying to find the right term to describe it. It wasn't contentment, exactly, but it had to do with the fact that he was comfortable with his place in the world, and a feeling that the respect people paid him was no more than his due. At times it annoyed her, too, that he could be so self-possessed when she herself didn't know what she wanted.

"You know we're going to be taking somebody's table, don't you?" she said when their drinks arrived. Coop looked at her as if he didn't understand. "Come on. You know George is going to bump somebody back to make room for us."

Coop smiled at her. "He'll work it out, Susan."

She could see he hadn't given it any thought, nor would he. It was George's problem. It didn't occur to him that somebody who'd booked might have to wait longer for their meal because of them. It was just a tiny little thing, and she didn't know why it should concern her. He was as honest as anybody could be without being a saint, and in every important way imaginable he upheld the law just as it was written down. So what if he bent the rules a little? He didn't do it for himself, though undoubtedly he did benefit in small ways. The Valley Hotel, for example, sometimes stayed open beyond the hours permitted by George's license, a fact that Coop overlooked and which coincidentally meant he never had to wait long for a table even when the hotel restaurant was busy.

Then there was Tommy Lee, who she knew occasionally dropped off half a deer at Coop's door and who she also knew sometimes carried loads over the limit in his truck when he was hauling around the back roads. She doubted he ever got a ticket. Once she'd asked Coop about it, and though he'd looked a little puzzled by the question, he'd explained his reason. He'd said that Tommy struggled to keep his truck on the road, what with all the competition from the big out-of-town companies, and sometimes he had to cut a few corners. What good was it going to do if Coop just made things harder for Tommy than they already were? She'd seen his point, but all the same, she wondered if Coop ever questioned whether he was setting himself up as judge and jury, as if Little River were his own little state and he the benevolent dictator. She'd never asked him because she knew it was an exaggeration, but she thought if she had asked, he would have been astounded.

While they were waiting, Craig Saunders, who ran the Texaco station on the east side of town, came over with his wife, Julie. Craig and Coop were friends from way back in their school days, and when Susan had first moved to Little River with David, the Saunderses were among the first people she'd gotten to know. The three guys

had sometimes gone fishing together, and Julie would come over with
her three kids and they would spend the afternoon getting food ready
for a barbecue. It had all felt a little strange to Susan, the whole
notion of the little women taking care of the domestic stuff while
the men went off together and had a good time. It hadn't really been
like that with her and David, though; he'd never been the kind of
guy to expect her to fill that role. With Craig and Julie, however,
she thought it wasn't far off the mark.

"How's Jamie?" Julie asked her when the men's talk had turned
to hockey.

"He's fine."

"I saw you guys the other day when he got off the bus. I waved,
but I guess you didn't see me. You know, he looks more and more
like his dad when David was younger." She put a hand on Susan's
arm. "It's such a shame. It must be hard for you, coping the way you
do."

"It's not so hard, Julie. We get along just fine," Susan replied. She
hated the way some people patronized her, as if living alone was such
a remarkable feat. Even more, she hated the tone certain people took
when they were speaking about Jamie, they way they oozed pity.

"How's he doing at school?" Julie said.

"He's doing good. His grades are fine."

"I guess you must be worried about what'll happen when he goes
to high school," Julie said as if she hadn't heard.

"Worried?"

"Well, I can imagine what it must be like for you. God knows, I
worry about my three enough, and there's nothing..." Julie's voice
trailed off and for a second she looked stricken; then she smiled
brightly and added, "I guess there're tutors maybe."

Susan clenched her glass; the smile she was wearing froze. Silently
she counted to five and told herself not to react. What had Julie been
about to say? That there was nothing wrong with her kids. Unlike
Jamie.

"Jamie doesn't speak, but it hasn't affected his mental abilities,"
Susan said.

Julie reddened. "Oh, no! I didn't mean that." Her hand went automatically to Susan's arm again and rested there for a second before
she let it drop away. "Don't take any notice of me. I always say the
wrong thing. I just meant that it must be harder for Jamie to keep

up. I mean, it *has* to be if he can't ask questions and the like, doesn't it?" She fell silent and looked at her drink. "I didn't mean anything," she said again.

They were both relieved when the topic of conversation between Coop and Craig moved away from hockey. Craig started talking about his business, complaining about how it was getting harder these days to make a decent living, the way he was apt to if given a chance. Susan listened to him detailing how tough things were; he was a perpetually dissatisfied man, and she felt a moment of sympathy for Julie, who had adopted a bored but dutiful expression. She knew that Julie hadn't really meant any harm, and she wished she hadn't been quite so short with her. Craig droned on and Coop glanced toward her. There was an amused tightening around the corners of his eyes because he knew what she was thinking, and she hid her smile and looked down at her drink.

"I heard that Somers guy moved into his parents' old place," Craig said after he'd exhausted the topic of his business. "That's the old place along the road from your house, Susan," he added. "I guess you must be worried having a guy like that living next door."

"Why should I be worried?" she said, taking a tone that set her opposite his way of thinking just for the hell of it. She swallowed a twinge of guilt, recalling the way she'd acted toward Michael Somers the other day.

Julie said, "Don't tell me you haven't heard about him, Susan?" She looked at Coop and reprimanded him. "I thought you would have at least warned her, Coop."

"I've heard people talking," Susan said, annoyed at the implication that she needed Coop to look out for her in some way. "I just don't listen to that kind of thing."

She'd snapped more than she'd meant to, and she saw from Julie's expression that the other woman was offended.

"I was only thinking of you," Julie said in a hurt tone.

There was a moment of awkwardness, then Susan relented. "I'm sorry. I just meant that I don't like listening to stories about people third-hand. You know how things get exaggerated."

"But there isn't anything exaggerated about this," Julie said, quick to justify herself. "Craig knows him, and Coop, too. They went to school with him."

"Yeah," Craig agreed. "He was always a little strange, that guy."

"He went crazy," Julie said. "He tried to kill his wife and baby girl and he shot some guy who was trying to get them away or something. I remember when it happened. It was over in the east somewhere—Toronto, I think. Michael Somers moved away after he went to college. His mother killed herself, at least that's the story, but she always was strange. I guess that's where he gets it from."

There was a note to Julie's tone that Susan found distasteful. She hated the way people took pleasure in regurgitating other people's misfortune, as if their own lives were lacking something and they needed to feel someone else was worse off in some way. She glanced at her watch, wishing George would come and tell them their table was ready.

"The way I heard it," Coop said, "it wasn't exactly like that. He did shoot some guy and hold his wife and daughter hostage, though."

"And you know what?" Julie said, her voice rising with self-righteous indignation. "It was only six years ago, and already he's out of prison. Can you believe that? And he's living here. I mean, it shouldn't be allowed. People like that, they ought to lock them up forever, I think."

"He spent the last few years in a psychiatric unit," Coop corrected. "I guess they decided he was okay."

"Come on, Coop," Craig said. "You know what these freaking doctors are like. They let all kinds of people back on the streets just so they can go and kill somebody else. I mean, the guy shot somebody, for chrissakes! How do we know he isn't gonna do it again someday?"

Coop shrugged. "He's served his term. We can't lock people up for something they might do."

"It doesn't mean we have to have the guy living in our own backyard."

Coop held up his hands. "Hey, I don't like it any more than you do."

Susan shook her head. "I can't believe I'm hearing this. I'm not condoning whatever it is he did, but if he had some kind of breakdown or something, we can't hold that against him for the rest of his life." The others looked at her in silence, and she knew what they were thinking: that she was sympathetic because of Jamie, because he had been seeing a psychiatrist. But that had nothing to do with it.

"I met him," she said. "He came over the other day, and he seemed like just a regular kind of guy." She wasn't even sure why she'd said it, distorting the truth like that, making out that she was so different from the rest of them, and she felt another twinge of guilt.

"You didn't say anything," Coop said.

"There was nothing to say. He just came over to say hello." She felt a surge of irritation that Coop should assume she had to report to him everything that happened. He didn't answer, just looked over her head.

"Excuse me." Susan put her glass down on the bar and made her way back to the rest rooms, wishing she hadn't said anything. She should have just kept quiet. Inside, she looked at herself in the mirror. Her eyes were blazing angrily. She rummaged in her bag and started vigorously brushing her hair. Behind her, the door pushed open. Linda Kowalski came in and grinned when she saw her.

"Having a good time?"

Susan made a face. "Don't ask. I didn't know you were here."

"We were going to come over, but I saw Julie and Craig join you. I didn't want to interrupt."

"Thanks a lot," Susan said. She stopped brushing her hair while Linda lit a cigarette. "That woman just gets to me sometimes."

"Are you eating with them?"

"God, I hope not."

Linda raised her eyebrows. "So it's just you and the good policeman again."

"What's that supposed to mean?" Susan said.

"Whoa. It was just an observation."

"I'm sorry. I guess I'm on edge. There seems to be this idea that people have that Coop and I are more than just friends."

Linda met Susan's eye in the mirror, a skeptical slant to her look. "This is new."

"Meaning?"

"The 'just friends' part. You think Coop sees it that way?"

Susan sighed. "I don't know what to think. I don't know how this happened without me noticing it. I didn't mean to encourage Coop to get the wrong idea. Do you think I did?"

"By dating him? Having him over to supper?" Linda shook her head, smiling. "Of course not."

"I wasn't dating him," Susan pointed out. "He just offered to take me out a few times, that's all." She could see Linda remained unconvinced. "That's not true, even I know that. It just seems like this thing has crept up on me. I'm not interested in any man in that way."

"You could do worse."

"I know. I like Coop. I mean, he's been good to us, to Jamie and me. I just don't feel ready."

"You know that as far as this town is concerned, you two are as good as married, don't you?"

"What?"

"What did you think?" Linda took her friend's hand. "Why else do you think the guys around here aren't swarming over you like bees around honey? It's because of Coop." She paused, letting what she'd said sink in. "Are you sure it's such a bad thing, Susan? Are you planning to stay by yourself forever?"

"I'm not by myself. I have Jamie. Anyway, it's not something I even think about. I'm not in a hurry to find myself a man."

"Don't wait too long, that's all I can say. And what *about* Jamie, since you mention him? I mean, don't you want more kids? Don't wait until he's too old to be bothered with his own brothers and sisters."

Susan squeezed back on Linda's hand. She knew how much Linda and Pete had wanted children, and that they'd never been able to despite all the treatments they'd undergone. It was such an unfair world sometimes, Susan thought.

She really hadn't meant to encourage Coop, but if she was really truthful, she must have known what would happen. Maybe her holding back had nothing to do with him at all, maybe it was just that she was caught up in the past. She still missed David. She thought about him a lot, finding herself at odd times disbelieving that he was gone. She still expected him to walk through the door at the end of the day. Then, of course, there was Jamie. How could she think about anything else, really, while Jamie occupied so much of her thoughts?

"Can I just say one thing?" Linda said. "Coop's a good man, and there aren't too many of them in this town. Sometimes we don't appreciate the things we have until it's too late. Don't write him off yet."

"I'm not writing him off. I promise," Susan said. "I guess I should get back."

"Say hi to Coop for me," Linda said, and together they went back out to the bar.

AFTER DINNER THEY drove back to Susan's house. She'd had a few glasses of wine and was feeling mellow, content to listen to the low sound of music on the radio and watch the headlights flash through the trees along the road. It didn't strike her until they pulled up outside her house that Coop had been unusually quiet on the way home. She'd been absorbed herself, thinking about her conversation with Linda. There had to be a time when she moved forward with her life, she thought. Perhaps it wasn't a good thing to dwell on the past and cling to her memories of a dead husband. She looked at Coop in a fresh light, asking herself how she felt about him.

"How about a cup of coffee?" she asked when he turned off the engine.

Normally when he dropped her off, he didn't come in, and she expected nothing different, but tonight he was looking at her in a different way. It made her suddenly aware of the quiet, of how the porch light cast his features into shadow.

"I'll just come in for a minute," he said.

She covered her surprise and, inside, reminded him they had to be quiet because Jamie was upstairs and Wendy was staying over. She wondered why she'd felt the need to mention something he couldn't have forgotten.

She made coffee and they stood together in the kitchen, side by side, leaning against the bench in the soft light from the lamp in a corner. It occurred to her that she didn't really know a lot about Coop. Sure, she knew the basics—where he lived, how old he was, that he liked fishing and was content with his life—but there had to be more to him, personal things they'd never discussed. Looking back, she realized that he'd listened to her talk often enough, especially after David had died. He'd always been there for her, a sensitive ear when she'd needed one, but to her slight shame, she'd never delved into his life, his inner life. He wasn't the kind of man who talked much about himself, about what he thought.

"Coop?" she said, and he turned to her, his face half in shadow. "Can I ask you something? How come you never married?"

He considered her question thoughtfully, then gave the smallest of shrugs. "I guess I never met the right woman before."

It was a stock answer, but there was an implication in the way he added "before." Before what? Was she supposed to read something into this? she wondered. A silence that was fraught with meaning extended between them, and Susan felt her heart hammering in her chest. She felt the vibrations in the air and knew that something subtle had altered between them. I could stop it now, she thought.

He finished his coffee and put his cup down. She held her own cup to her lips, looking ahead. Neither of them spoke. When I put it down, she thought, that's when something will happen, unless I say something. She felt panicked, but at the same time there was a current of excitement about the situation. Coop was going to kiss her, and she was unsure exactly how she felt about that. Her eye caught David's picture on the bulletin board. A part of her questioned how she could have allowed things to come to this, while another argued she must have always known it would. It had been a long time since she'd been held, since she'd felt that she wasn't all alone. Her conversation with Linda came back to her. Maybe Linda was right, maybe she didn't appreciate what she had right here beside her.

She placed her cup on the bench. He put his hand on her shoulder almost tentatively, then turned her toward him. Her heart was thumping wildly and her breath fluttered in her throat. His lips touched her own, slightly parted, firm to her own softness. She closed her eyes, and in the darkness she could feel his body and the pressure of his mouth. She responded to his movements. His big hands held her lightly, gently, almost reverentially at her shoulders, her own against his arms. A spark of warmth ignited in her belly and glimmered.

They kissed for half a minute. It was a little awkward and strange, but nice, too. She waited for the glimmer to become a glow, but it failed to happen, and she thought it was just the situation. They were both nervous, which was strange for people of their ages, and then she thought that maybe it wasn't strange after all. He'd been David's friend and he must feel his presence in that way, as she did in other ways. All at once she wanted to be alone; she needed time to think.

Perhaps he sensed that she was hesitant. He let her go, for which she was grateful.

"I should leave," he said quietly.

"Coop . . ." she said. "I don't know if I'm ready . . . I mean, I need time." She shook her head, uncertain of what exactly it was she was attempting to say. She let him move away, feeling the cool space of air between them, and smiled uncertainly. She didn't trust herself to speak again.

"I'm not going anywhere," Coop said.

"Coop, I can't promise . . . I mean . . ." Her voice faltered. She felt like a fool, stumbling over her words like a tongue-tied teenager.

"It's okay," he said, and started for the door.

She walked him out, and on the porch he brushed her lips, their mouths barely touching, and she watched him until the lights of his car vanished in the trees and the sound of the engine faded.

When he'd gone, she washed up their cups and turned out the lights. Before she went upstairs, she checked that everything in the TV room was off. The reel that Coop had bought for Jamie lay where he'd left it on the floor.

In her bed she closed her eyes, but sleep was slow in coming. She kept thinking about Coop's kiss, the feeling of being close to another human being after so long, but it was David's image that filled her mind, and though she screwed her eyes tight and bit her lip, she couldn't stop the tears from coming.

7 IN THE EVENING, MICHAEL SAT ON THE PORCH while twilight faded. Since moving in, he'd discovered he liked the light best around dawn and just before night fell. In the mornings he rose early and went out to walk. He'd watch the sky lighten over the mountains, their dark shapes changing from black to ink blue before the first sunlight hit the snow. At the other end of the day, as the sun went down, the clearing was awash with a soft pinkish light.

The woods around the clearing had fallen silent, not a breath of wind to disturb the air. The chatter of birds preparing to roost for the night had vanished, and the sound of nocturnal prowlers rustling in the undergrowth beneath the trees hadn't yet started. The color of the snow had altered from its customary crisp white and seemed to possess a hazy radiance. Occasionally at this time of the day everything was suffused with tones of purple and pink, and it was eerie enough to believe that somebody somewhere had begun the end of the world.

Michael felt he might be the only person still living, marooned somehow to inhabit this small, mysterious clearing. He smiled at the track of his own thoughts. He was startled by a cry from beyond the clearing and searched for its source. It had sounded close, and brought goose bumps to his flesh.

He heard it again. *Kek kek kek kek.* High-pitched, echoing. A shape passed above the trees, dipping down toward the far edge of the clearing, and another came close behind. The first shape darted into the cover of trees, and its pursuer twisted and banked so that for a second he saw its back and outstretched wings. The impression was fleeting, gone in the blink of an eye, but vivid, and then silence returned and the clearing was empty. It was almost as if he'd seen a ghost. The image he retained was of a large bird, pale in color, almost white. The experience left him feeling he'd witnessed something strange, and for no reason that he could put his finger on, he was certain it was the falcon he'd prevented the hunter from shooting. He waited, half expecting something more to happen, but time passed and twilight faded to dark.

He used only a few rooms in the house. He discovered, as he wandered around when the mood took him, that memories he'd buried for so long he'd forgotten even their presence began rising to the surface. Perhaps because so many times he'd told himself and others who'd asked, like Louise, that he'd left Little River because he'd hated the town, he'd come to think of it as the truth. He knew now that it wasn't so. He would have left anyway, he was sure of that; as plenty of other people shed their small-town roots to search for something else in the wide world to satisfy their needs, so he would have done the same. But he doubted he would have hated the town. He would have thought about it fondly, maybe, in a hazy kind of idealistic way, redolent of images of youth. That he'd buried it so far in his subconscious that he never thought about it in any terms was because the town, his growing up, was all so tightly interwoven with his hate for this house that he could never separate them.

He sat in an empty room where once they had sat, the three of them, his mother, himself, and his dad, to eat their evening meals. He could remember that when he was young he would hear the sound of his dad's Dodge pulling up outside the house, and his mother would fuss anxiously. They would be in the kitchen, where he would be sitting at the table doing schoolwork while she prepared dinner.

"Go outside and meet your dad, Michael," she would say. She'd walk over to him, wiping her hands, looking nervous. She always got changed into some kind of nice dress about an hour before his dad would arrive, and put makeup on and fixed her hair. She'd quickly hug him to her, pressing his face into her breasts as he stood up.

"We have to be nice to him," she'd say as they parted, holding his eye. "You know we have to be nice to him, don't you?"

So he'd go outside and his dad would see him coming and give a sort of tired-looking smile. Michael always tried to do what his mother told him, to be nice to his dad, so he always went out to meet him; but he hung back. When his dad wasn't around, his mother always told Michael that his father had a temper, that he could be very mean to her.

"But I can put up with it, Michael. I can for you. That's why we always have to be nice to him. That's why I always get dressed nicely for him when he comes home, though he doesn't notice. Just don't say anything to upset him."

At dinner maybe his dad would tell them a thing or two about his day at the store, but his mother would just smile and lean over to Michael, maybe ruffle his hair. She would speak only through him.

"Ask your father if he wants more beans, Michael. Tell him if the meat's tough, it's because it was ready at six." This last, said with bitter reproach, was if his dad was even a few minutes late.

In the quiet empty room, he tried to remember his dad ever raising his voice, ever raising his hand in anger. He couldn't. When he thought of his parents, his mother was all softness and flowing dresses and his dad was just remote, a figure on the edges.

THERE REMAINED THE pressing need to earn an income. Michael calculated that the money he had left would last him for a while, but he was aware that sooner or later it would run out. Despite the experience at Wilson's car lot and what that might signify about the attitudes he was likely to encounter, he circled several ads in the help-wanted column of the local paper. He decided to lower his sights and chose only the kinds of jobs where he might expect employers wouldn't be so concerned about who he was.

The next morning he presented himself at a tire shop on Seventh Street dressed in boots and jeans and asked to see the manager. A short fat guy wearing greasy overalls came through a door, holding a thick cheese sandwich in one fist, his mouth full of food. When he spoke, he sprayed pieces of chewed bread from between his lips.

"What can I do for you?"

Michael gestured with the rolled-up paper he was carrying. "You ran an ad for someone to fit tires."

The guy looked him up and down. A badge on his overalls labeled him as the manager. "You done any work like this before?"

"A little."

The fact was, he'd done some machine work while he was in prison, so he was used to working with his hands. He didn't think it would be so hard to learn how to fit tires. The shop was small, with racks of tires lined around the walls, a couple of mechanic pits in the floor and some trolley jacks lying around. Behind the smeared glass pane of the office cubicle, a middle-aged woman worked on some paperwork that had an oily thumbprint at one corner. Another small and ancient desk behind her had a girlie calendar pinned on the wall above it.

"You live around here?" the manager said. He took another bite out of his sandwich and looked at Michael suspiciously, as if he didn't look like the type of guy who normally came around looking for work in his shop.

"A couple of miles out of town," Michael told him.

The guy grunted and sauntered over to the window, where he asked the woman for an employment form. "We start at seven here and go through until four. You get a break around noon unless it's busy. The work comes first, that's my rule."

He gave a belligerent look, challenging Michael to find fault with his terms. "Pay's eight bucks an hour to start. What's your name?"

"Somers. Michael Somers."

The manager started writing on the form, then he stopped and looked up. "How do you spell that?"

Michael spelled it out. The manager stopped again. The night before, he'd been in Clancys having a couple of beers and he'd heard some talk about a guy who used to live in town. It was all before his time, he'd only lived in Little River for three years, but they were talking about how this guy had shot his wife and kid and now he'd come back here to live. He looked at the name he'd written. Somers. That was the name he'd heard. He'd thought there was something about this guy that didn't fit.

"I just remembered," he said. "The job's gone."

"Wait a minute . . ."

As the manager started to turn away, already crumpling the form into a ball, he felt Michael grip his arm. For a moment they were both frozen there. Michael was taller and his grip was strong, and when the manager looked into his eyes, he thought they were a funny kind of blue, real dark. He was wondering if he could reach the wrench that was just behind him on the bench, then Michael let him go.

Michael struggled to control his anger. "A second ago you were telling me the rate for the job."

The manager relaxed, seeing that nothing was going to happen now. "Yeah, well, I guess I changed my mind."

Michael saw the woman behind the window watching everything that was going on and he imagined how she'd tell her friends about what she'd seen, and how she'd embellish it just a little to make things interesting. He considered trying to persuade the guy to give him a break, but when he searched the other man's expression for something that would indicate he might find some empathy there, he could see he would be wasting his time. The manager stared at him with small black eyes that poured out what felt like hate. This was a mind closed to reason; a small mean spirit resided behind those eyes, one whose opinions and narrow reactions were set immovably in stone. Prisons were full of people like that, and Michael had learned long ago that he would search in vain for a compassionate human being behind the facade. He started to turn away without another word.

The manager called out to him. "And if you need tires, fella, don't come around here. We don't carry your type."

Michael walked out onto the street. For a second he had to stop and take a few deep breaths before he could walk on. He could hear the manager's voice still ringing through his head, the malice and derision that rippled within it. He felt the curious looks people threw him as they moved around him, and when he met the eye of a woman walking a dog, he saw the flicker of recognition in her expression before she hastily turned away. She went on by and glanced back, stopping at the side of the road, then crossed, looking back again as she neared the other side. He felt a dull kind of acceptance that was crossed with anger. She avoided him the way somebody might avoid a drunk weaving along the sidewalk, with distaste and slight apprehension, as if at any moment he might act in some violent and unpredictable manner.

He tried a few more places, but it was the same story with differing reactions wherever he went. After the tire shop he expected it and didn't stop to argue. Once or twice he thought he saw a glimmer

of something approaching regret or maybe embarrassment in the
way a person's look slid away from his own and hands became suddenly busy shifting around pieces of paper, but he was probably
imagining it.

At noon he went into the diner, feeling the eyes of the other
customers following him as he slid into a booth by the window. The
waitress who approached to serve him smiled unexpectedly.

"What can I get you?"

"Just coffee, thanks."

"Nothing to eat? The food's pretty good here, if I do say so myself."

He looked up at her, thinking she hadn't recognized him, waiting
for her attitude to abruptly change. She had red hair, which he
guessed was dyed, and was in her middle to late thirties. The hands
that held her pad and pencil were reddened from the heat and constant cleaning, and the lines around her eyes showed her age. Her
expression, however, remained friendly.

"What would you recommend?" he asked. Beyond her, a guy at
the counter looked over his shoulder and then away again, saying
something to his buddy, who looked over briefly.

"How hungry are you?" the waitress responded. "The broiled bacon
and tomato bagel is good, or we have a homemade vegetable soup
with fresh foccacia bread on the side." Her smile became a grin, and
she nodded back toward the counter, beyond which a man in a white
apron worked at the grill. "My husband is kind of a gourmet. He
makes the bread himself. I think he's trying to educate his fellow
citizens, though between you and me, I think he's wasting his time."

"The soup sounds fine," Michael said. He felt a sudden surge of
warmth toward this woman. Just in the simple fact of not being
treated like some kind of pariah, he was reminded of how life had
once been, what it felt like to walk in the flow of society. He watched
the waitress walk away, and felt other eyes returning to their plates,
the quiet hum of conversation resuming, though more subdued than
when he'd come through the door.

The waitress brought over the soup and bread and placed it in
front of him with what he felt was slightly more care than a customer
might ordinarily have expected. A napkin was neatly folded on the
side of the plate.

"Enjoy," she said, and he thanked her.

Though he hadn't felt hungry when he'd entered the diner, and though he still couldn't muster any real enthusiasm to eat, the food was undeniably good. After he'd finished, he sat drinking his coffee and wondering if coming back to Little River had really been such a good idea. He had a house and a store that had both stood empty for years and needed work if he was to stay, and yet he felt no attachment to either of them. The prospect of staying also presented practical problems, aside from the fact that he'd be resigning himself to estrangement from the people of the town. He wondered what the point was. He had a dwindling money supply and little chance of finding work. He pondered the alternatives: Perhaps he should go down to Vancouver, or maybe, as Carl Jeffrey had suggested, to the States. In a city he would at least have anonymity. But then he reasoned that he'd escaped from this town and his past once before, or thought he had, and it hadn't done him any good. He knew he'd stay—for the time being, at least.

Across the street, a woman emerged from the real-estate office and walked toward the diner. He watched her absently, and then, as she moved, he noticed her in more particular detail. He saw it was his neighbor, the woman from the house next door to his own. As she approached, he studied her. He guessed her to be in her early thirties; she was slim, with high cheekbones, and as she walked, her hair, shot through with deep reds and mahogany, caught the sunlight as it bounced around her shoulders. She came though the door, and as she took a seat at the counter, she smiled to the man at the grill and said something he couldn't hear. Maybe it was her smile that struck him then, perhaps because it lit her features in a way that was in marked contrast to the way she'd looked when he'd taken her dog back and she'd come onto the porch. Then he'd felt only coldness from her, but now he glimpsed that there was another side to her, what he guessed was her everyday nature. She stood out from the few other women in the room—and would stand out in any crowd in this town, he thought. He saw the flash of white teeth in a generous mouth and all at once he was thinking about Louise. It was an old memory, from a long time ago when she had put her hands softly to his face and rested her head against his chest, his arms encircling her, feeling the warmth and smoothness of her skin. He felt as if a hole had opened up in him that he stared into, seeing only emptiness and everything he'd lost. Without knowing how it happened, he felt his coffee cup shatter in his hand.

The waitress came over with a cloth. "Don't worry about it," she told him when he apologized. "We got plenty more of those old things." She peered at him. "Are you okay?"

"I'm fine." He stood up, aware that people were looking over, muttered his apology again, then dropped some notes on the table to cover his bill and quickly left.

"SO WHAT DO you make of him?" Susan asked as Linda put the broken pieces of Michael's cup in the trash. She watched him through the window as he crossed the road until he was out of sight, aware that when he'd broken the cup, the noise of voices in the diner had hushed but was now rising again in volume. The atmosphere had changed suddenly as he'd left, a release of slight tension.

"He seems like a guy with things on his mind."

Susan raised her brows. "Wouldn't you be if you were him?" She gestured around her. She could hear Rudy Pearce talking to John Helsinger from the auto-repair shop on Sixth and Barker.

"I read just the other day about some crazy son of a bitch who went into a Pizza Hut with a shotgun and started blasting everything all to hell," Pearce was saying. "Couple of people got themselves shot up before the cops came and took this guy away."

"Uh-huh." Helsinger stuffed half a cheeseburger into his mouth. Mayo dribbled down his chin, and he wiped it away with the back of his hand.

"Well, what's to say this fella won't get it in his head to go and do something like that? You see the way he looked just then?"

"There ain't a Pizza Hut in Little River, for one thing." Helsinger laughed at his own joke, but Pearce just scowled.

"Listen to them," Susan said.

"Well, can you really blame them?" Linda said. "I mean, these things do happen, Susan."

"You mean you agree with them?"

"I'm not saying that. I'm just saying you have to understand how some people might feel."

"To them anyone different is crazy."

Linda looked at Susan skeptically and put her hand on her friend's arm. "You're thinking about Jamie, aren't you? This is different, Susan."

Susan shook her head. "I don't know. Maybe I am thinking about Jamie. I hear the way people sound sometimes when they talk about him, as if because he doesn't talk he's subnormal or something. I worry about him. It's not just that, though. It just seems unfair the way Michael Somers is getting treated, that's all." She shrugged. "Let's change the subject."

"Okay. So how's the good policeman?" Linda grinned.

Susan groaned. "Please, maybe I'll just have my coffee to go."

AFTER LUNCH SUSAN went back to the office and spent an hour catching up on the notes she kept of people who mentioned to her that they were thinking about selling or buying. People often sounded her out in some vague manner if she met them on the street or in the store, and long ago she'd gotten herself into the discipline of following up on these random connections. Now and then something came to fruition that otherwise might never have happened. Somebody finally got motivated enough to put months or even years of indecision behind them and put their house on the market.

As she considered people she should call, she came across the name Carol Johnson. On impulse, she picked up the phone right away. Carol's husband, Jeff, had lost his job a few months back, and when Susan had talked to her one day, Carol had said they were thinking about moving to Kamloops, where Jeff had a brother who ran a printing shop. Susan recalled that a couple of days ago she'd overheard somebody saying that Jeff had gone down there to try it out for a while.

Carol answered on the fourth ring.

"I wondered how things were going with Jeff down there in Kamloops?" Susan said.

"He likes the job," Carol told her, "and he's getting on well with his brother. He was worried about that."

"So, does that mean you're going, too?"

"I don't know. Jeff wants us to, but I'm not so sure. Everybody we know lives around here, and there's family and all."

Susan understood her reluctance. Carol had two children under four years old, and as long as she was in Little River, she could rely on help from her mother and sister. In Kamloops, she'd be all alone. It was a tough choice, but she guessed that in the end it would come down to money, and Kamloops was where Jeff had work. Susan wanted to get the Johnson house as a listing if they were moving, because it was a nice place, a two-story log-cabin-style house that Jeff had largely built himself, and she was sure she could sell it quickly. She always had to be on top of the situation with a place like that, because a good property west of town might end up getting listed with a realtor in Williams Lake if she let it slip by her. A lot of people still had the idea that they might get a better price if they listed with one of the bigger firms, though this was absolutely untrue.

"Listen, why don't you let me come over and give you a valuation of your house?" Susan suggested. "It might help to make the decision easier."

Carol was reluctant at first, and Susan guessed she felt that taking that step might make her move irrevocable, but while she hated to pressure her, Susan knew that if she didn't, then somebody else might. Sometimes people needed a little shove in the right direction anyway, she reasoned. They made an appointment for that afternoon, and Susan left pretty much straightaway. As she went out the door she wondered about asking Linda to meet Jamie at the bus, but checking her watch, she thought she ought to get back in time.

As it turned out, the valuation took longer than Susan had expected. Carol had had second thoughts by the time Susan arrived, and it took half an hour to talk her round.

"Look, at least this way you've got the information you need," Susan said. "It doesn't commit you to a thing."

She called Linda and told her she was running late. "If I'm not back, can you meet Jamie?" Linda said she would, and Susan thanked her and hung up the phone.

"So, where shall we start?" she said to Carol.

IT WAS CLOSE to four-thirty by the time Susan got back, and as she pulled up outside the office, Linda came over from the diner. The second Susan saw her friend's face, she felt the cold grip of intuition.

"What is it? Where's Jamie?"

"I'm sure he's okay," Linda said, though her expression was pinched with worry. "I called Coop right away when Jamie wasn't there when I went to get him, and he's looking for him now. He can't have gone far away."

"You mean he wasn't on the bus? Oh my God, I can't believe I wasn't here. Did you call the school? I mean, have they seen him?"

"No, he was on the bus. The driver said he definitely remembered him, said he got off in town. I was a few minutes late, and by the time I got there, he'd gone." Linda shook her head in self-recrimination, tears stinging her eyes. "I'm sorry, Susan. This is all my fault."

Susan saw that her friend was on the verge of breaking down, and she managed to get hold of herself. That Jamie had definitely been on the bus went a long way to calming her fears. If he'd gotten off in town, then he couldn't be far away. The sudden overwhelming clutch of fear that had gripped her abated a little.

"It's okay, Linda. It's not your fault. I should've been here myself. I'm sure he's okay, he's just wandered off somewhere." She heard her own voice as if from a distance, calming Linda's unjustified guilt. She started sorting through the places where Jamie might have gone. Maybe a friend's house—only he didn't really have any friends anymore—or maybe the store. She glanced down the street, half expecting to see him sauntering toward her, unaware of the panic he was causing. It was irrational, she thought. What harm could come to him anyway? She was simply being overprotective, the way she had been ever since the day of the accident. That nightmare image of Jamie soaked in blood forced itself into her mind, and her heartbeat quickened again. At that moment, Coop came around the corner in his cruiser and pulled up. For a moment, Susan's hopes soared as she peered into the cab beyond him; then she saw he was alone.

"No sign of him here yet?" Coop said. "I'll take a ride through town. He's most likely just lost track of the time."

"I'm coming with you," she said, moving toward the door.

The radio in his cab crackled, and Coop picked up the microphone and spoke into it. Susan couldn't make out what was being said through the static, but Coop glanced at her quickly and the look he wore scared the life out of her.

"What is it?"

"That was Ben Miller. A trucker said he saw a kid sounded like Jamie getting into a utility out on Deep Ridge Road, heading out of town."

"Out of town?" A million ideas went through her mind. She felt numb for a split second, and then all kinds of questions beat against her skull. "What kind of utility? I mean, is he sure it was Jamie?" She felt her voice start to break despite herself and covered her mouth with her hand, fighting back tears. Then it struck her what Coop had said. "Deep Ridge Road? That's the way home."

COOP FOLLOWED HER as she drove, keeping close enough that every time she looked in the rearview mirror she could make out the shape of his face behind the wheel. His presence there was both comforting and not. She was glad that it was him, but she kept seeing the lights on his cruiser, which somehow deepened her worry.

It was a fifteen-minute drive, but it seemed on this occasion to take forever. She tried to concentrate on the road; she knew she was driving faster than was safe, and there were patches of ice here and there where she felt her Ford slide a little. It would do Jamie no good, she told herself, if she ended up in a ditch. She kept asking herself why he hadn't waited at the bus stop. He knew she always met him, and that if she couldn't make it, Linda would. She imagined finding him and later asking him why he hadn't just gone to the diner or her office when nobody was there at the stop. He'd be unaware of the worry he'd caused, shrugging his shoulders. She knew she should be mad at him for scaring the life out of her, but she also knew she wouldn't yell at him; instead, she'd hold him tight and tell him he mustn't ever do that again. But even as she was imagining this scene, a part of her mind was thinking she might never see him again. She tried to tell herself that things like that didn't happen in towns like Little River, and that was part of the reason she'd agreed to come here in the first place, partly why she hadn't left after David had died—that, and inertia. She kept thinking about what Coop had told her, that some trucker had reported seeing a kid get into a utility. It could have been anyone. It didn't mean it was Jamie, though when Coop had called back, Miller had confirmed that the driver had said the kid he'd seen was wearing a red-and-blue coat. Just like Jamie's. But it could be coincidence. She bit her lip, her thoughts tripping over themselves in their headlong rush through her mind.

She was five minutes from home before the thought that had sat hunched like a shadow in the dark corners of her mind took shape and she thought of Michael Somers. She rationalized that there was absolutely no reason to think he had any involvement in this. A flush of heat rose to her face, borne of guilt at thinking about him at all, but his name stayed in her mind. He drove a utility, she'd seen him in it once or twice—a Nissan, she thought. He also had reason to be on Deep Ridge Road, though why Jamie might have been there she had no idea. He could have walked there, it wasn't that far from the center of town, but why would he? The more she thought about it, the more her unease grew. It was just too much of a coincidence that somebody had seen a boy answering Jamie's description. Who else could it have been but him? And who else around there would have picked him up without letting her know? Her heart raced, and she put her foot on the gas, clenching the wheel tightly.

When she turned down the track to her house, the back end of the Ford slid sideways in the grit and snow, and then the tires gripped as the vehicle plunged down through the trees. As she stamped on the brakes and threw the truck into neutral as it slid to a halt, she saw the dark-colored utility stopped outside the house, and then she was out the door, running. For a moment she didn't see anybody, then Michael Somers opened the door of his Nissan and got out from behind the wheel. She stopped dead, her heart still thumping. Behind her, Coop's truck was coming down the track, at a slower pace than she had driven.

Susan's eyes fled from Michael's face, searching for Jamie, half expecting him to get out of the Nissan, but when he didn't, she looked around in confusion. Just then Bob barked and approached from the back of the house, Jamie just behind him. He stopped when he saw her.

"I came across him on the road," Michael said. "I think he was walking here, so I persuaded him I could give him a ride. I thought I better wait until somebody got home."

Relief flooded every cell in Susan's body, and she felt suddenly weak, as if she were going to collapse, and in her relief she lashed out.

"Are you crazy? Didn't you think I'd be worried about him? He's just a child, didn't it occur to you to call?" She ran to Jamie and fell on her knees, crushing him to her, tears flowing across her face. "Thank God," she said, pressing his head to her face, smelling his hair.

Michael looked on, bewildered at first, until he understood what she'd thought, and as he turned away to get back in the Nissan, he felt Coop grab his arm.

"Hold on a second. What's going on here?"

Michael looked at him. "Like I said. I gave the boy a ride. He was a long way from home."

"Where'd you pick him up?" Coop said.

"Outside of town."

"You didn't think someone might be worried about him when you found nobody home?" Coop nodded in Susan's direction, and Michael followed his look. She was getting to her feet, wiping her tear-ruined face.

"I decided to wait awhile," Michael said. "It seemed like a good idea at the time." He felt Coop's grip on his arm loosen just a fraction, though the cop's eyes remained fixed. Coop's face was weather-beaten, his eyes pale. "Am I under arrest here or what?" Michael asked.

For a moment Coop said nothing, but Michael could feel his thoughts like waves of hostility.

"Coop."

They looked around at the appeal in Susan's voice, and saw her watching them uncertainly. Then Coop let go of Michael's arm.

Susan started to speak. "I'm sorry about what I said before. . . . I mean, I was . . . I didn't know what to think."

Michael didn't say anything, just got in the Nissan and backed around. He looked in the mirror as he drove up the track: They were watching him go. His mouth compressed in a thin line.

8 THE FALCON HAD SPENT THE NIGHT HIGH ON A rock face, hugging close into the back of the ledge where she stood. She had slept with her feathers ruffled so that warm air was trapped against her body. With one leg raised, the foot clenched and tucked into her breast, she resembled some sleepy children's toy, puffed up and rounded like a portly owl.

As the sky lightened, the first faint streaks of yellow and amber suffusing into the inky blue darkness at the horizon, she opened her eyes and stood square on both feet. Her plumage settled sleek against her body; her eyes, bright and intent, surveyed the landscape below. The transformation was instant. She became again the efficient predator, her lines sculpted and streamlined, her shape honed to perfection.

Far below her, the terrain rose and fell in sharp rocky valleys high above the tree line. The glacial slopes shimmered with the first touch of sun, the frozen snow throwing back light from ice crystals. The falcon roused herself, shaking her plumage from head to tail, then stretched each leg and wing in turn, awakening and warming her muscles. She clenched her talons against the rock beneath her feet, and bent to nip at shreds of matter that clung to their polished points. Watching, feeling the slight changes occurring in the air as it was fractionally warmed by the rising sun, she observed the world as it came awake. Stars faded until their light became a glimmer, then vanished one by one, and the pale orb of the moon faded out against the winter-blue sky. A streak of high cirrus smudged the horizon above the mountains to the west, but otherwise the day dawned cloudless. A breeze came up out of nowhere, its cold caress rippling across the falcon's feathers and sliding away like the kiss of a fine rain mist. Feeling its call, she stood on the edge of her ledge and extended both wings, feeling the lift from the movement of air as she harnessed it with her flight feathers. Her feet gripped tightly as she savored the sensations she experienced each waking morning. Breast thrust forward, the deep curve telling of the powerful muscles beneath feather and skin, she cocked her head sideways and peered with intent curiosity skyward and back again across the mountain cliffs. Her eye missed nothing. Her blue-gray beak, curved to a fine point, possessed a soft polished hue. In the far distance, a speck rose into the sky and circled slowly, an eagle she watched for a moment with interest. Then with a flick of her wings she was airborne, rising quickly on the currents that came up from the valley floor below.

Her wingbeats were fast and powerful, carrying her farther out toward open space where she found a thermal and hung on out-stretched wings, allowing herself to be borne aloft, effortlessly bank-ing and coming around as she quickly rose. The sun was above the horizon now, the air warming quickly, and below her the mountains peaked and glistened white in the fresh light. She soared higher, swiveling her head and ranging her eyes across the land below. Feel-ing her thermal peter out, she banked sharply and rode down on a roller-coaster ride toward the valley slightly to the southwest where the spruce and cedar pushed high and dark. Rising air from the valley floor bore her aloft again, and she repeated this procedure several times, ranging back and forth, catching thermals to bear her up and then banking and sliding down, air rushing across her body, the pat-terns of thermals invisibly mirroring the terrain below. All the while she took in and registered the movements of animals and birds in the forest; she watched a squirrel sit up high on an exposed limb and nibble at a nut held in its paws, saw it freeze suddenly, its nervous eyes looking left and right as it sensed danger, then it quickly dashed for cover. She saw it all, but she was not hungry yet and had not positioned herself to hunt. She merely soared, the sun glancing off her pale back as she swooped and turned, and occasionally her call echoed across the valley, a sharp *kek kek kek*.

———

ELLIS HAD PARKED his truck down off Falls Pass Road on a logging track when it was still dark and made his way up through the trees with his rifle over his shoulder and a thermos of hot coffee laced with whiskey in his pocket. His plan was to find a place to conceal himself in the general area that he thought was the falcon's territory and just to wait and hope it would show. He'd come to believe this was a battle of wits, and it was him pitted against the falcon and a whole bunch of other forces ranged against him. He knew he was being fanciful, but it was like that damn bird represented the way his whole life had been. Every time he got close to making a little headway, it all came down around his ears and was snatched away from him. Ellis felt that if there was a God, He didn't have time for people like himself. Instead Ellis was just a plaything for minor devils to taunt for their amusement. How else was he to explain what had happened the other day when that guy had appeared out of nowhere? He still didn't know who the hell it could have been.

It had become crucial to Ellis that for once in his life he should come out on top. He had an idea this was a test and that if he could pass it, then things might generally improve in his life. He'd begun to consider that the bird wasn't just a regular falcon, that maybe it was something else, something supernatural. All of this he kept to himself. If anybody had heard him talking that way, they'd have put him in a straitjacket for sure. He hadn't told Rachel what he was doing, though she was curious about where he was spending his time. A couple of days ago she'd gone to the yard and he hadn't been there. That evening they'd had a fight, her yelling that if he didn't work, how were they going to get by just on what she made working afternoons at the grocery store in town? That had really got to him. He hated the fact that without the money she brought in they would really be in trouble, and she knew it. What did she expect him to do, for chrissakes? There was no work. Sometimes he thought she'd leave him. He saw it in her eyes that she wished she could have her time over again and then she never would have married him. That made him afraid of losing her, and he felt powerless to stop it. At times he came close to hitting her. Jesus, he hoped he never did anything like that; it was just he hardly knew what was happening to him sometimes.

He'd found his spot, hunkered down in some rocks, and he'd sat there waiting. It was damn cold and he was freezing his ass off even with the coffee. He'd been thinking about how he could have stayed in bed with Rachel curled up warm beside him. Maybe they could have made up in the best way there was, her soft breasts against his chest as he lay over her, though it had been a hell of a long time since they'd done anything like that. It made him uncomfortable just thinking about it, and he had to shift position and think about something else. If things worked out, he promised himself they'd have a real night out. It would be a new start for them. She'd see how hard he'd tried to do this thing right, just for her. Mostly for her, anyway. Things would get better.

In the meantime he found a spot in among some rocks where he was well hidden but where he would have a good view of the surrounding terrain when it got light. He started to unroll his groundsheet and took his rifle from his shoulder; then he poured some coffee and sat down to watch the dawn arrive.

MICHAEL, TOO, HAD risen early and had crossed the river and climbed to a high rocky promontory, where he sat to look back the way he'd come. He was sweating from the climb, and his chest ached from the cold air. It had taken him an hour and a half, and now he was hungry and was wondering how long it would take him to get back. The return journey would be quicker, downhill all the way to the river he could see far below snaking its course westward, where it would eventually pour into the Pacific.

As the sky lightened, his house was visible from where he sat, and not far away through the woods he saw his neighbor's house with smoke rising from the chimney. When he'd been young, an old couple had lived there. He remembered them vaguely, assumed that they were long dead by now. A vehicle was parked outside the house, and as he watched, a figure emerged, though it was too far away for him to distinguish even if it was a man or a woman. Whoever it was went back into the house for a moment, pausing on the porch and looking toward the mountains. For a second he had the idea that the woman, which is who he decided he was watching, had felt his distant gaze and was searching for him. He imagined that for a brief moment their looks met, then she turned and went back inside. He knew that in reality he would be invisible to anyone down below unless they had glasses and were specifically looking for him, and he put his idle fantasy down to some unexpressed desire.

The day before, when he'd stopped to pick up the boy as he walked along the road, it had been their second encounter within an hour. Earlier he'd been walking toward his car, having parked at the bottom end of town, when he'd seen the boy sitting across the road on a fence by the bus stop, swinging his legs. Two other kids of around the same age had been passing by, one on a bike, the other on skates, being towed behind. He'd watched as they stopped and looked for a while at the boy, who acted as if they weren't there.

"Hey, stupid," the bigger of the two kids had said. "How come you're still here? It's time to go home, stupid, don't you know that?"

Michael had paused, then started to move on, thinking they were just kids and it was none of his business anyway. He heard the kid wearing skates tell the other one they should go.

"He's just dumb, Jerry. You're wasting your time talking to a dumb kid."

Michael had heard their laughter, high-pitched, cruel and mocking. He turned around and saw that the boy hadn't reacted, was just staring at his feet.

"Hey, why don't you say something, huh? Come on, just say one little thing. Say 'I'm a dummy,'" the big kid had said. "What's the matter? Haven't you got a tongue, dummy?"

The smaller kid had suddenly stepped forward and grabbed the silent boy's bag and tried to yank it out of his hand. "Give me that thing!" he'd yelled.

There had been a quick tussle. The bigger kid had joined in as the two of them tried to steal the bag, but the boy wouldn't let go. All of a sudden the boy had been yanked from his perch on the fence and went sprawling facedown, landing hard on the frozen ground. Michael had shouted out, just as a woman had come out of the house behind. He'd helped the boy to his feet, and then before he could do anything more, the boy had just run off. He'd watched him go, then figuring there was nothing more he could do, he'd headed back to his car, still watched by the woman at her door.

When he'd seen the boy again walking on the side of the road just out of town, he'd been surprised that he was out there and as a natural gesture had stopped to offer a ride.

"It's okay, you can get in," he'd said when the boy didn't move. "It's a long walk," he'd added after a moment. He'd begun to wonder about the boy. Was there something wrong with him? His silence didn't seem quite right; it went beyond mere shyness, which had been his first assumption. The other kids had been calling him "dumb," "dummy." Michael studied the boy, and some old familiar chord was struck by the expression in his eyes. He flashed back to himself at that age, and saw himself as an observer might have, sitting on a rock staring at the mountains, tossing pebbles down the slope to the river, quiet and habitually alone.

"Come on, get in," he'd said again, and this time the boy had come over and reluctantly climbed in and stared out the window. On the drive back he hadn't uttered a word, just kept himself squashed up against the door, his face averted. Then, once they'd arrived, the boy had slipped out without a glance and vanished around the back of the house. He'd followed after a minute, and seen him playing with his dog. Then, walking around the house, Michael had concluded that nobody was home. He'd begun to wonder then why the boy had apparently been intent on walking all the way from town, and wondered, too, if his parents knew where he was, a thought that had caused Michael a slight unease.

He'd been on the point of going over to his house to call somebody when the boy's mother and the cop had arrived, the woman with fear etched deep into her face. Fear of him.

He had slept poorly throughout the night thinking about it. Every time his eyes fluttered closed and he sank into a light slumber, it was as if he'd given leave for images from the past to crowd his mind, jostling for space. Uppermost he kept seeing that day seven years earlier when he'd returned to the apartment. He'd been waving the gun around, wildly, indiscriminately, while he poured out his pain and anger. Louise, frightened and wide-eyed, had stared at him from where she had been huddled against the wall with Holly, who'd been crying inconsolably. He could recall her voice.

"Michael, you're frightening me. Why don't you put the gun down? Please don't hurt us, don't hurt Holly."

He closed his eyes, pushing the memory back, shutting out the scene below. The wind swirled around the rocks where he was sitting, the cold seeping into his bones. He could feel his blood grow sluggish, his thoughts slow down as his body temperature dropped. It was getting harder to feel his fingers, or even his hands if he didn't move them, and he knew he was experiencing the first signs of hypothermia. The sweat on his body had dried and cooled, and now he was starting to shiver. He knew that if he didn't move, lethargy would invade his senses and soon after he'd feel a kind of euphoria. He opened his eyes, and as he did, he heard a high-pitched call and turned his gaze skyward. He saw the falcon circling above him on outstretched wings, with the sun behind her so that he could make out her shape only when he managed to lift his arm and shield his eyes. He was certain it was the same bird he'd seen twice before, and as he watched, he caught a flash of her coloring as she came out of the glare of the sun. She appeared to be almost white across her back, which puzzled him. When he was young, he could remember seeing peregrines in these mountains, but they were smaller than this bird and blue gray in color.

The falcon came around, positioning herself as if intent on something below, and he took his eye away and searched across the slope. As he did, a brown shape rose several hundred yards away and flew toward the trees with a whir of wings; at the same time, the falcon stooped earthward. In that instant a shot rang out, startlingly loud, its source close by, and the falcon began to corkscrew out of control. She dropped like a stone, wings flapping uselessly, and vanished behind some trees while her quarry fled safely in the opposite direction.

MICHAEL CAME UPON on a hollow where rocks had collected at the bottom of a snow-covered slope. At first he couldn't see anything; then a movement in the shadow of a boulder the size of a doghouse caught his eye. The falcon stood on the ground, camouflaged against the white snow and the mottled browns and grays of rocks, her dark bright eyes fixed on him. Cautiously he went closer, surprised to find her alive. As he drew nearer, he saw clearly that one wing hung limp at the shoulder and trailed against the snow, spots of blood staining red against white. When he was ten feet away, he crouched on one knee and considered what he should do.

The falcon never took her eyes from him, watching every movement warily but without fear. Her coloring, as he'd thought earlier, was pale across the back and wings, though it was a dusky cream rather than white, and toward the tips of the primaries and secondaries it darkened to a slate gray. Her breast and thighs were flecked with markings of chocolate, and the talons of each toe were of the same glistening black as her eyes. Up close, she was bigger than he'd thought, perhaps a few inches over two feet from head to tail.

It was clear that the falcon was incapable of flight, but less clear was what he could do. The idea of getting within range of what looked like razor-sharp talons and beak made him nervous, and her manner as she held his gaze steadily was unbowed. On the other hand, the alternative of simply leaving her to her fate was inconceivable, and so he took off his coat and shuffled forward on his knees. Sensing his intention, the falcon backed against the rock behind her and flicked open her one good wing, which startled him. He moved close and she lunged for his hand as he cast his coat like a net. It covered her so that he was able to gather her up and hold her contained within, like some precious and dangerous prize. Then he turned and made his way back down toward the river.

ELLIS HAD HEARD the falcon before he saw it, craning his head all around, and then there it was, flying high, turning with wings outstretched. He'd raised the rifle slowly and took aim with his finger on the trigger. This time he knew he'd won. He'd outsmarted it, and this was the end of the road. The falcon presented a clean shot, and in a way he was almost sorry, but there were always winners and losers. He could have given up before then, but he hadn't, he'd kept going, he'd shown he was a man of determination. Tusker, start counting out that money, he'd thought, and squeezed the trigger.

It was unclear at first if he'd hit it. As he fired, the falcon started to dive, and he thought again that all the forces of the world were lined up against him; then he lowered the rifle and saw the falcon spiraling down in the wind. He'd grinned, taken out a cigarette and lit it with his Zippo, and calmly began to pack up the thermos and groundsheet he'd brought with him.

Ellis had marked the area where the falcon had fallen and reached it quickly. He came on the hollow from above, and the first thing he saw were tracks in the snow going both ways. Beneath him there was an area of scuffed snow, spotted with blood. It took him several full seconds to absorb what must have happened.

He stumbled down into the hollow, and by the time he reached

the bottom, his mood had turned grim. He wondered if it could be
Red or maybe Hanson, or maybe they were in it together. It was
possible that somehow they'd known all along what he was doing,
and he thought back to that first night when he'd gotten drunk and
shot his mouth off. He wasn't entirely clear about what he might
have said. Possibly he'd let something slip and they'd been tailing
him ever since, all the jokes and stuff in Clancys at his expense just
a double bluff. He got madder just thinking about it. It made perfect
sense. He'd never trusted either of those sons of bitches in the first
place. As he went at a trot into the woods, he was vaguely concerned
that something wasn't right with his theory. It had to do with the
guy he'd seen the other day who he knew hadn't been either Red or
Hanson. But then he lost the tracks where there was no snow, and
he stopped thinking about that. It occurred to him that those bastards
must have parked somewhere close to where he'd left his own truck
and that's where he ought be heading. He changed direction, running
along as fast as he could go, cursing under his breath.

9 Tom Waters was examining Katie Mullins's dog, which she had just led in on a leash from the waiting room. Katie was twelve years old, and the dog was a crossbreed. There was a little Labrador in there and perhaps some collie and German shepherd. All in all the dog didn't particularly resemble any of its various gene lines, so it was hard to tell, but it was a nice enough looking animal, rough-haired and friendly with a patch of dark fur around one eye that gave it a kind of roguish look. Right then, however, the dog was looking pretty sorry for itself.

"What's his name, Katie?" Tom said as he felt the animal's abdomen.

"It's Roy." She looked worried. "He's going to be okay, isn't he?"

"Well, let's see here," Tom murmured. "What was it he ate, do you know?"

Katie held up a hand and started counting on her fingers as she reeled off a list. "There was a tin of shortbread that my aunt sent over from Toronto, and a packet of raisins, I think, but it was hard to tell just how many of those he ate because they were just scattered everywhere. Then there was a bar of dark chocolate that Mom uses for baking and some dried fruit and some cans of beer. That's all, I think."

Tom looked up. "Some beer, did you say?"

Katie nodded. "He likes beer. He crunches up the cans with his teeth until he makes a hole in them, then he licks up all the beer that leaks out. Dad gets pretty upset about it sometimes," she added thoughtfully.

"Well, I guess that's understandable," Tom said, suppressing a grin. "And some dried fruit, you said?"

"It was apricots and dates, I think."

Very little about animals surprised Tom anymore. He'd been the vet in Little River for thirty years, running a mixed practice, and there was almost nothing he hadn't seen. About two thirds of his time was spent looking after domestic pets like Katie's dog, the rest taking care of horses and farm animals. Around here, though, the term "domestic pets" could cover just about anything, from the usual hamsters, cats, and dogs to beavers and owls and even the occasional orphaned bear cub. A plain old mongrel that had drunk a little too much beer on top of some dried fruit was no big deal.

He gently squeezed the sides of the dog's stomach, and in response it looked back at him with a trusting but sorry expression.

"How did he get to eat all that stuff, Katie?"

"He got in the cupboard when we were out," she said in a scolding tone. The dog turned mournful eyes on her. "You're sure he's going to be okay, aren't you?"

He walked her to the door and signaled for Rose, his nurse, to take her back to the waiting room. "He'll be fine, I think. You just go on and sit in there a bit while I fix him up. He's just a little bloated, that's all, and it's making him uncomfortable."

He gave Katie's mother a smile, to which the exasperated woman shook her head.

"It's one thing after another with that dog," she complained.

"Well, he's a character, I guess," Tom agreed.

The process of pumping out Roy's stomach was unpleasant and pitiful for man and beast. The dried fruit had been reconstituted in the dog's gut by the beer, swelling up and bloating the animal. With Rose helping, Tom filled a bucket from the pipe he'd fed down Roy's throat. He let nature take over the job of expelling what hadn't been digested. While they did their best to control the mess, the dog farted and shat its way around the surgery floor.

"Jesus," Tom muttered, hit by a particularly foul odor.

After forty minutes, Roy was back to his old self and was led out to the waiting room, where Katie threw her arms around his neck.

"Just keep him away from beer and fruit," Tom cautioned.

"I will," she promised, and knelt down and began lecturing Roy about eating things he wasn't supposed to.

While Rose sorted out payment with Katie's mother, Tom finished cleaning up. He opened all the windows to let the smell dissipate a little and sprayed the room with pine air freshener.

"Anybody else coming in that you know of?" he asked when he went back out front.

"No one's called," Rose replied.

"Okay. Well, I have to go up and see Dave Thomas's mare some-time today, so I may as well do that now."

Even as he spoke, a car pulled up outside. He rolled his eyes. "Spoke too soon, I guess."

THE INJURED FALCON was helpless, her good wing and both feet secured with a piece of elastic that Tom had slipped around her body. With practiced hands he stretched out the injured wing and felt along the bones. The falcon watched with bright eyes, trying to twist her head and bite him.

He felt a slight movement in the bone around the wound. "This is one lucky bird," he murmured. "The bullet just grazed the bone and passed through the flesh. I can feel a grating here in one of the ulnas. I'll need to do an X ray, but I think it's just fractured. Did you see who it was that shot at her?"

Michael shook his head. "Not exactly. You said 'her'?"

"I'd say she's a female, by the size of her. They're usually bigger than the males by about a third."

"You know what she is, then?" Michael asked.

Tom gestured to a bookcase in the corner. "Well, she's some kind of falcon, I know that much, but she's not any type we get around here. There's a volume over there on birds of prey. Get it out, could you?"

Michael found the book and leafed through the pages until about a third of the way through he stopped at a picture of a falcon perched on a rock high above a winter landscape. He compared it with the bird on the table. The coloring matched. He started to read out loud from the text.

"It says here she's a gyr falcon, pronounced *jer*. Native to the arctic regions, normally. 'The largest falcon on earth, ranging in color from pure white to almost black.... Preys on lemmings, large birds, et cetera.... Sometimes known as the snow falcon.... Females weigh up to three and a half pounds, with a wingspan of more than three feet.'" He left the book open on the desk. "So how did an arctic species come to be here, do you think?"

"She might have drifted south. Maybe an immature bird caught up in winter storms. It happens sometimes."

Michael watched while the vet continued probing the wing. If the falcon was in pain, she gave no indication of it. She suffered the intrusive examination with dignity, despite the ungainly way she'd been trussed. The sharp eyes and the way her head sloped toward her powerful-looking beak gave her a noble, almost defiant appearance. He recalled her flight above the woods, scything through crisp mountain air, in complete mastery of her element. From childhood he'd always admired birds of prey; it had to do with the fact that they were predators, but it was also because they possessed an innate grace. In a way, he envied them their existence, attuned to each breath of air, each rising thermal and current that they could exploit with such ease to carry them across great swaths of land spread out below.

"Why would anybody want to shoot a bird like that?" he said softly, speaking to himself.

Tom looked up and really noticed Michael for the first time. He didn't recognize him but was struck by his eyes, which were a deep shade of blue, hinting at things kept hidden deep inside. Tom had long ago formed the opinion that anybody who had empathy with animals had something still pure in his soul that too many people had lost touch with. He peeled off his gloves.

"Money's usually the reason. That, or just plain stupidity."

"Money?" Michael said.

"When something is rare, you can be sure it has a value to somebody."

"Even dead?"

"The taxidermy trade caters to a certain kind of person, I guess. I never saw the appeal of having some poor animal stuffed and mounted in my house the way some people do. Takes all kinds." Tom shook his head, studying the falcon. She was beautiful, there just wasn't any other word for it. Why somebody would want to see a bird like this shoved in a glass case instead of flying free where she belonged was beyond him. There were times when he was ashamed to be a part of the human race.

"What'll happen to her?" Michael said, absorbed with similar thoughts.

"We'll get her fixed up, and when the wing's healed, we'll try and give her another chance." There was a fatalistic note in the vet's tone that sounded off-key. His brow was furrowed in lines of doubt.

"You don't sound convinced," Michael said. "Don't you think the injury will heal?"

"It's hard to say," Tom admitted. "A bird like that, the way she hunts, she can't afford to have a wing damaged. You ever see the way they hunt?" He demonstrated with his hand. "They fold back their wings and just go straight down, like this. Remarkable sight, and they get up to more than a hundred miles an hour, I read somewhere. That kind of speed puts a hell of a lot of pressure on the wing. It's like an athlete—a sprinter, say. The wrong kind of injury can spell the end of a career, even after it's healed. It might look okay to you and me, but that doesn't mean the person is ever going to compete again."

Tom saw that Michael wasn't following what he was getting at, and he gestured toward the falcon. "The problem here is that in a few weeks her wing might look as good as new, but there'll be no real way of knowing. I'll have to keep her in a cage and make sure that wing is held in place so she can't move the joint. By the time I release her, she'll be out of condition, but she'll still need to catch her food. She may not be up to it."

Michael absorbed what the vet was saying, reflecting that it was unfair that having survived the hunter's bullet, the falcon might still succumb in the end, suffering a slow death by starvation. It seemed like maybe he hadn't done her any favors after all.

"Don't worry about her," Tom said as if reading Michael's mind. "You did what you thought was right. If it wasn't for you, she'd be dead by now."

"What would you have done if *you'd* found her?"

Tom considered the question for a moment before replying. "I've been taking care of animals all my life, but you can't do this kind of work in country like this without having some respect for nature and her ways. It's hard for us to understand sometimes, isn't it? We like to root for the underdog, I guess. Show us some animal that's helpless and injured and we want to take care of it, but the fact is that it's the strongest and smartest of a species that survive. Your falcon here was just unlucky. Maybe out of the nest she came from, she wasn't the one nature decided was going to make it."

"Except it wasn't nature that shot her," Michael pointed out. "Are you saying she ought to be euthanized?"

"No, I'm not saying that. Now that she's here, I don't see it can hurt to give her another chance. There's a guy over near Williams Lake I might call if I can find his number. He came in here once a couple of years ago with an injured hawk that he'd trained; he might be able to help."

"Help in what way?"

Tom explained an idea that had occurred to him. "The best thing would be to immobilize the wing to allow time for the fracture to heal, and then train her to fly free. She could build her strength up, and we'd see if there was any problem before she was let loose. At least that way she wouldn't starve to death. Maybe this guy would take her on."

Michael thought back to the bird he'd glimpsed in the slightly eerie twilight of the clearing outside his house, certain it was this falcon. He was equally sure she was the same bird he'd prevented the hunter from shooting several days earlier. It seemed they were fated for each other, he mused, only half serious, and yet as the falcon met his gaze, her bright eyes shining with a fierce intensity, he wondered if maybe that wasn't so far from the truth. He couldn't explain why, but he'd felt some kind of empathy with her as he'd watched her soaring high and free in the mountains.

"What if *I* was to train her?" he said.

Tom looked at him curiously. "Are you serious?"

"Why not? What exactly is involved?"

"Well, frankly, I don't know." Tom paused. "It's something you ought to think about pretty carefully. There's a lot to consider."

"Like what?"

"Like the time it'll take, for one thing," Tom said. "She's going to need to stay here for a few days while I do something about that injury; then the wing's going to have to be immobilized for a couple of weeks. You'll need a place to keep her, fresh food."

"I've got the time," Michael said. "The rest I can organize."

"If you're going to train her, you'll need to learn how."

"You mentioned this guy you were thinking of calling. Maybe he could help."

"If I can find his number," Tom said. He went over to his desk and started looking through his papers. After turning out the contents of three drawers, upending them on the desktop and sorting among the debris, he found what he was looking for. He came back with a piece of paper on which he'd written a name and number. "His name's Frank Dobson. Maybe you should speak to him before you commit yourself. Leave the falcon with me for a few days, and let me know what you decide."

"No need for that. I can tell you now that I'll be back for her." Michael was as certain of that as he was of anything. The idea had occurred without forethought, but now he was sure this was something he wanted to do.

Tom nodded, seeing that he meant it. "I believe you will. Do you live far from Little River?"

"Just out of town. My name's Michael Somers."

Tom didn't react, though he recognized the name sure enough. He'd known Michael's dad before he died, and he knew that Michael had been to prison and for what, though what he read in the papers he always regarded with a degree of skepticism. He'd heard something about Michael's coming back to town, and the things people were saying. He saw the way Michael was watching him, a little uncertain, maybe a little defiantly, as if he expected the mention of his name to provoke a particular response.

Tom held out his hand. "Welcome home."

Michael hesitated, then took it. "Thanks," he said, and for the first time since he'd been back, he started to feel as if maybe he really was coming home after all.

THE SOUND OF a vehicle slowing and then pulling off the road drifted down to the clearing, and then a few moments later a police Chevy appeared through the trees and pulled up behind Michael's Nissan. Coop got out, took his sunglasses off, and then put them in his pocket. He looked over the clearing and the house, and when his gaze settled on Michael, he inclined his head in a brief, barely perceptible nod.

"How's it going?" He walked over and introduced himself, extending his hand, one foot on the bottom step of the porch. "We didn't meet properly yesterday."

Michael felt the strength in his grip, the hard callused palms, and met his unflinching gaze. "The name's familiar," he said.

Coop nodded. "We went to the same school. I was a year ahead of you, so I guess we didn't have much reason to know each other well."

Michael remembered him then, but only vaguely. "This just a social call?" he asked.

Coop considered his answer. "Not entirely, I guess."

Michael waited for him to go on, finding Coop's honest answer amusing in a way. "Coffee?" he offered eventually. "I was about to have a cup myself."

He went into the house and poured two cups from the pot and took them both outside. "You said this wasn't a social call," he resumed.

Coop nodded. "I thought you might want to tell me about what happened yesterday."

Though he knew he ought to have expected the question, Michael still tightened his jaw. "Nothing happened. I gave the boy a ride home, that's all."

"That's right, you said. You picked him up on the road out of town."

"That's right."

"You know how he got there?"

"Why don't you ask him?" Michael said.

Coop just nodded. "His mother was half out of her mind with worry."

"I saw him walking on the road. Next time I'll be sure to just drive by. I thought I was doing him a favor."

"Well," Coop said, "no harm done, but it might be a good idea if you remembered the way things can sometimes appear to people. Might be sensible to stay on your side of the woods." Coop looked back toward Susan's house.

"Are you trying to tell me something?"

"Just offering advice, that's all," Coop said. "You can't afford any misunderstandings with you being on parole."

Michael wondered if he was being given some kind of warning, which is what it felt like, but as if Coop could see what he was thinking, his expression creased into a smile of sorts.

"I've always liked it here," Coop said, looking toward the mountains.

"Yeah, I like it too," Michael agreed.

Coop looked back at the house, unhurriedly drinking his coffee, then passed over his empty cup. "I should be going. Thanks for the coffee."

"Anytime," Michael said with faint irony. He watched Coop stride back toward his cruiser. There had been something in his tone, something vaguely proprietary in the way he not very subtly told Michael to stay away from the house across the woods. He wondered if the woman there had asked Coop to come over. Or was there something else to it? Did Coop have his own reasons for warning him off? Michael watched Coop back around and drive up the track, the sound of the motor slowly receding down the road.

"What the hell was that all about?" he asked himself.

10 THE GYR FALCON STOOD ON A PERCH MADE from a length of timber run across the width of the woodshed behind the house. Her injured wing was bound with a fitted leather brail to prevent the joint from moving. The X ray had showed a fracture in the ulna, as Tom Waters had suspected, but the good news was that the radius was intact, so an operation hadn't been necessary. The brail around the carpus joint was secured at the humerus, which immobilized the joints on either side of the fracture. Tom's advice had been to leave it in place for about two weeks, and then he'd take another look.

Right now, Michael was concerned about a more pressing problem. Several days had passed since he'd found the falcon, and in that short time her condition had deteriorated. Even in the gloomy light it was plain to see that she was thinner, and the ragged appearance of her feathers, some of them bent and some broken from her confinement in a wire cage at the veterinary office, only made her look worse. The piece of beef he'd left on her perch remained untouched. During her stay at the vet's she had also refused food, and when Michael had collected her, Tom had warned him that sometimes when a wild animal was brought in, it refused to eat and failed to respond no matter what he did. It was just the way things were, as if sometimes an animal simply chose to die rather than be imprisoned. The falcon was shivering in the cold, her ability to keep warm depleted through lack of energy. When Michael had looked in on her early that morning, he'd been alarmed to see that the gleam in her eye had lost its luster, and he was certain that if she didn't eat, she would not survive another night.

"What can I do?" he asked Tom when he called the veterinary office.

"Not much, I'm afraid." Tom's voice sounded heavy with regret. "It's her choice, in the end."

Michael refused to accept that he was helpless. He was standing on the upper landing in the house, looking out of the window across the woods while he talked. A magpie flitted between the branches of a poplar, settled on the snow, and began strutting about. Two rabbits on the edge of the trees nibbled at roots, occasionally looking about nervously, ears twitching, alert for danger.

"There must be something I can try," he said into the phone.

The line was silent while Tom considered what he could suggest. "What are you giving her?" he said at last.

"Fresh beef."

"You could try something a little more tempting. Maybe something fresh she's used to," Tom suggested. "I don't know if it will help, but it might."

Michael's eye went back to the rabbits he could still see at the edge of the clearing. "Thanks." He hung up.

"HEY," SUSAN SAID. "Want a cookie?" She offered Jamie a plate of Oreos and he took one and bit half of it off and munched while he looked out the window. She took one herself and sat down at the table. Bob was lying on the floor at Jamie's feet.

"We could take Bob for a walk," Susan suggested. She felt like getting some air. It was Saturday and she hadn't gone into the office that day but had stayed around home doing odd jobs; earlier, she'd gone to the market. Jamie had stayed close to the house, alternating between being outside with Bob and playing computer games in his room. Trying to be casual, Susan had said that she needed to see Fran Davies on the way back from the store, and she asked Jamie if he'd wanted to stay awhile and hang out with Fran's son, Peter. Jamie had stayed outside when they arrived, but ten minutes later Peter had come into the kitchen, where Fran and Susan were having coffee, and announced he was going skating with some other kids in the neighborhood.

"Take Jamie with you," Fran had said.

Peter had glanced at Susan. "I already asked him, but he doesn't answer."

Through the window they could see Jamie outside, idly drawing shapes in the snow with his finger. Fran had given Susan a helpless shrug.

"It's okay," Susan had assured her. "Have a good time," she told Peter. "Maybe Jamie will go next time."

It had been Fran who'd told Susan about the kids who'd been bothering Jamie at the bus stop. "Jenny Harris went out to break it up, but some guy was already there. She said the kids ran off, but she knows who it was. It was that little rat Craven and the Jones kid. You should call around and see their parents, Susan."

But Susan had shook her head. "I don't know if that's such a good idea. It might just make things worse."

Now, as Susan nibbled on her Oreo, she wondered how long this bullying had been going on. The school had never said anything about it, and Jamie just looked away when she tried to ask him. Fran had heard from Jenny Harris what the other kids had been calling Jamie. Kids were cruel. Though Jamie's teachers all said he was bright, how was this going to affect him if it went on? How long before getting called "dummy" and "stupid" stuck, and what would that do to a small boy's self-esteem? She felt so powerless, so unable to intervene, to get past this wall of silence that Jamie had built around himself and refused to let anybody breach.

She'd guessed it had been Michael Somers who'd stopped the kids at the bus stop from hassling Jamie, and through a laborious question-and-answer process Jamie had eventually confirmed it on the ride home. It made the blood rush to Susan's face to think about the way she'd thanked her neighbor for his trouble. When it came down to it, she was no better than the rest of the people in this town, and she was ashamed of herself. She was thinking about what she could do to make it up to him, and decided that all she could do was apologize. She was thinking that she ought to go right then, before it got dark.

THE PORCH STEPS creaked as she climbed them. She knocked at the door. It swung open on its hinges, but nobody came. Susan looked at

Jamie and then peered inside the gloomy hallway. The air smelled faintly musty from the place having being shut up so long. A staircase straight ahead led up to a landing and turned the corner, vanishing out of view.

"Hello? Anybody home?" There was no answer. She went along the porch and peered in the windows, feeling nosy but also curious now that she was here. The house had been empty for as long as she'd lived across the way, and she'd never given it much thought, but now as she saw the old furniture inside, the heavy dark wood, she wondered about Michael Somers having grown up here, about what his parents had been like. With no sign of anybody being home, she turned to tell Jamie they'd come back again in the morning. Jamie, however, had gone. She looked around, wondering for a second if he'd wandered into the house, thinking, great, now she would have to go in and fetch him and then Michael Somers was going to come back from wherever he's been and find them inside his house and how was she going to explain that? Her eye fell to tracks in the snow, obviously adult-size, leading around the house, and beside them were Jamie's. She called out as she followed them around.

"Hey, where are you?"

Jamie was standing at the doorway to a shed around back, and when she reached him and looked inside, the first thing she saw was Michael crouched in the gloom; next she saw the dim, pale shape of the falcon. Michael heard them and turned to see who it was. Their eyes met for a second and Susan saw the deep worry lines around his eyes, then she pulled Jamie back out of the way. A moment later, Michael stepped outside and closed the door behind him.

"We didn't mean to intrude," Susan said. "I knocked at the door around the front, but nobody answered."

He nodded. "That's okay." His eye fell to Jamie, then came back to her.

"Is that a hawk you've got in there?"

"She's a gyr falcon. I found her up there." He gestured back to the mountains. "She's injured."

Susan saw again the deep worry lines around his eyes. "Is she going to be okay?"

"I don't know. She's not eating." He paused as if wondering whether to go on. "She needs fresh meat, rabbit or something like that."

"There're plenty of those in the woods."

"I don't have a gun. I'm not allowed to own a weapon."

He met her eye as he spoke, then looked away, and for some reason she felt as if he were accusing her of something. She didn't know how to respond; his expression had become hard and sort of distant. Involuntarily, her hand fell to Jamie's shoulder, reminding her of why she was here. The situation was awkward now, as if Michael too was recalling their last meeting.

"I came over to apologize," Susan said. She faltered when he didn't say anything, just looked at her. "About the other day, I mean. I heard what happened. I'm grateful for what you did, I guess I was just worried, I didn't know what to think ..." Her voice trailed away. She thought she should just shut up before she dug herself in any deeper. "I just wanted to thank you."

Silence hung over them for a moment, then she made a move to leave. He hadn't accepted her apology or acknowledged it, and she couldn't blame him. In a way, he looked as if he hadn't really heard her, as if his thoughts were elsewhere. "I hope your falcon is okay," she said. They were at the corner of the house when he said something she couldn't quite hear; she turned around.

"Thanks for coming over," he repeated, then turned and went back inside the shed without another word.

When she and Jamie got back to the house, he went to turn on the TV and she stood thinking in the kitchen for a while, then she went out to the hall and to the door that led down into the basement. Flicking on the switch, she made her way down the steps, keeping her hand on the wall to guide her. The bulb cast a dim yellow light that barely reached the back corners of the room, and in the corner where the locked cupboard stood against the wall it was gloomy and cold. Susan hesitated, feeling her heart beat and a tightness around her chest. She hadn't been down here for almost a year and a half, and reaching out to grope on the top of the cupboard among the cobwebs and dust, she could feel a tremor in her hand. She felt the cold metal of the key and clasped it, then put it in the lock and took a breath before she turned it. It moved smoothly, with a sharp click, then the door swung open a little and she reached to pull it wide, letting the faint light illuminate the inside.

David's rifle was inside, buckled into its case, with two boxes of ammunition on the shelf. She'd put the gun there the day of his funeral, when her mind was still numb, and had never looked at it since. Once or twice she'd thought about giving it away, but the idea of coming down here had been too much, and instead she'd simply left it. Now, as she reached out for it, she couldn't help but feel a shudder as she felt its weight, knowing that this gun had killed the man she loved. Briefly she was seized with an impulse to slam the door and go back upstairs, just leave it there, but taking another deep breath, she took it out and put it under her arm, then placed one of the boxes of ammunition in her pocket. She went back up the stairs and turned off the light.

When she reached Michael's house, the front door was slightly open, the way she'd left it, so she went straight around back. The door to the shed was closed, so she tapped on it and waited. Michael seemed surprised to see her when he opened it, and even more so when she held out the gun.

"Take it," she said, and perhaps he detected some quality in her voice that made him realize this was an effort for her, if not why, and he reached out and took the gun. She gave him the ammunition too. "It's been locked away for a while, but I think it should be okay. You might want to clean it first."

She didn't wait for him to thank her, just turned around and went back to her house as quickly as she could. Later, sitting at the kitchen table hunched over a coffee cup, her mind full of memories, she flinched when she heard the distant crack of a rifle shot.

MICHAEL WATCHED SUSAN as she vanished around the house, walking quickly, her hands thrust deep into her pockets, shoulders set, not hearing him thank her. He looked down at the rifle in his hands, a perplexed expression marking his features, then back again to the now empty space between the woodshed and the side of the house.

He took the rifle into the woods across the clearing. After a short walk he came to the banks of the river, where smooth gray rocks lined the shore. He practiced until he'd got the feel of the rifle and could hit a small fist-size target from fifty yards. With the gun loaded, he walked along the riverbank until he came to the bridge, where he crossed the gray-green water flowing beneath him.

After twenty minutes on the far bank he found a rabbit nibbling at a patch of green in the woods. As a boy he'd owned a slug gun briefly, and with it he'd once shot a squirrel that had been feeding on the high branch of a tree. He'd taken careful aim at the little animal as it sat up on its hind feet eating a nut, then fired. It had dropped like a stone. For about ten seconds he'd experienced a rush, and then he'd crouched down and looked carefully at the small, still warm body with a patch of blood on the breast. The eyes had retained a glimmer of brightness, though already they'd seemed glassy. He wished then that he hadn't killed it, because there had been no purpose to killing it. After that he'd only ever shot at targets he made from rocks or marked on the trunks of trees. Now he justified shooting the rabbit by reasoning that though he wasn't killing it for himself, he *was* taking it for food, and that in the wild the falcon would have killed prey anyway.

He took aim and fired, and when the animal dropped where it stood, he experienced a mixture of triumph and remorse. When he approached, it lay perfectly still, its eyes open and staring, a bloody stain in the fur behind its neck. He picked it up and carried it back to the woodshed, where he gutted and dismembered the carcass and cut pieces of still warm meat for the falcon.

She watched him from the far end of her perch when he showed her the meat, which he dangled in front of her to be sure she could see what it was. She showed no interest, so he left it beside her, and for a while he crouched by the door, hugging himself in the cold, watching her, willing her to eat. After half an hour she hadn't moved. The more his eyes became accustomed to the dim light, the more clearly he could see her shivering. He found himself talking to her, quietly and soothingly. He spoke of her need to eat, to regain her strength so that her wing could heal. He hardly knew what he was saying, but the quiet flow of his words seemed to soothe them both.

"I saved you," he told her. "You can trust me."

Though he knew she didn't understand what he was saying, he felt that the spirit of his intent might pass to her in the sound of his voice. He made a pact with her that if she would eat and regain her strength, he would return her to the freedom of the skies, and as he spoke, she watched with what seemed a slightly altered posture, her dark eyes intent on him.

Eventually he fell silent. An hour later, he left her, not sure if she would survive the night. He decided to go back and check before he went to bed. If she still hadn't eaten, he would take her into the warmth of the house in the hope that would at least give him another day.

Inside, he made a quick meal and sat by the fire and tried to read. His thoughts turned to his neighbor. He couldn't work her out. He pictured the deep ocean green of her eyes and held her image in his mind until it dissolved slowly, re-formed, became Louise. She was smiling, and then her features twisted and her eyes grew wide with fear as he saw her hugging Holly against the wall. He wondered what his daughter looked like now, how tall she was, the color of her hair. Mostly he wondered if she was happy. The only thing he'd ever wanted was her happiness, but he'd discovered that was something it was beyond his power to give.

After a while, he rubbed his eyes. A tiny throb had begun at his temples, which slowly eased when he massaged it. The hands on his watch marked the passage of time. An unwelcome image periodically flashed in his mind of discovering the falcon dead beneath her perch, and he thought he would lose something of himself if that happened, though he was unsure why he should feel that way. When he'd glimpsed her in the clearing at twilight, there had been a tremor in the air, a vibration that he'd tuned to for an instant, which had linked them together. He thought that somehow this was meant to be.

At eleven he took a flashlight and went outside to the woodshed. It was bitterly cold and pitch-black, with no moon to light the way. With trepidation in his heart, he opened the door a fraction. The falcon stood on her perch, feathers ruffled so that she seemed even bigger than normal, one foot raised and clenched to her breast. She blinked at him sleepily over a bulging crop stuffed with rabbit, and when he shone the flashlight at her perch, he saw a few scraps of fur and nothing more remaining of what he'd left her.

OUTSIDE, THE MOON appeared through misty cloud, and for an instant the snow reflected back its pale gray light and the clearing was empty. Fresh snow that had fallen during the evening made a smooth unblemished world: untouched, unspoiled. Michael stood on the porch in the darkness drinking a shot of whiskey. He drained his glass, raising it in a silent toast; then, as the breeze rattled the undergrowth among the hemlocks and poplars in the woods, he went inside and closed the door.

PART TWO

11 FEBRUARY HAD GIVEN WAY TO MARCH, AND two weeks had passed since Michael had first brought the falcon home from the vet. During that time he'd confined her to the woodshed while she gained weight and recovered from the shock and stress of her injury. After that first evening, when she'd eaten part of the rabbit he'd shot for her, she'd never looked back. Michael's time had been occupied with keeping her supplied with fresh food, shooting rabbits and dissecting them. When he wasn't roaming the woods with a rifle, he was often in the woodshed, sitting quietly by the door at first to allow her to get used to his presence, then standing and moving around a little as she began to accept him.

When Michael had called the number Tom Waters had given him, he'd spoken to Frank Dobson and explained the situation. Frank had told him he was about to go away for ten days, but that when he got back, Michael was welcome to come over and Frank would give him what help he could.

"In the meantime, what you need to do is keep her somewhere dry and sheltered, and feed her plenty of fresh food," Frank had advised. "Spend some time with her so she gets used to having you around, but don't pet her like a dog or crowd her. Just give her time."

He'd asked Michael for his address, and two days later a package had arrived containing two books and a handwritten note. One of the books was a slim tattered-looking paperback novel called *The Goshawk*, by somebody called T. H. White, and the other was a newish-looking hardback written by an American that explained how to keep and train a falcon. Frank's note said that he thought Michael might find the novel interesting; the other book, he wrote, was a practical guide he might like to flick through. His advice was to read the novel first. Also in the package was a pair of leather thongs, a swivel, and a two-foot length of nylon cord with a thick knot tied at one end. A postscript at the bottom of the note told Michael that he would understand their purpose after he'd read the books.

Michael followed Frank's advice and read the novel first. The author, he discovered, an Englishman, had been a schoolteacher in the years before the Second World War. He'd given up his profession and retreated to a country cottage, where he'd virtually shunned the world and all that was happening in it to train a goshawk he'd had sent from Scandinavia. The novel was first published in 1951 and described an England that Michael was certain no longer existed. It was a place where rural life followed the rhythms of nature, where fields were bordered by hedgerows and woods, where what little traffic passed on the narrow country lanes was as often as not a bicycle. Agriculture had not yet become a highly mechanized affair where fertilizers and chemical sprays ensured that the land is worked year-round, one crop planted the moment another is harvested, where hedgerows are torn out to transform the landscape into barren prairies for the overproduction of unwanted subsidized crops, where wildlife becomes extinct because its habitat has vanished—except for small pockets where reserves have been set up or tradition prevails in the face of great odds.

The story told of the struggle between man and bird, and the bond that the man felt with his captive, but the novel also gave a background on the sport of falconry. The training of birds of prey for hunting, Michael learned, went back more than three thousand years. There are pictures in Egypt that show men carrying birds on their fists. As a sport, falconry flourished throughout the ages and across the world, but it declined in the twentieth century. A paper marker, which Michael assumed Frank had inserted between the pages for his benefit, had just a single large exclamation mark on it, and when Michael read the passage, he understood why.

During the Middle Ages, the marked place explained, English society decreed that a person's rank determined the kind of hawk or falcon that he might keep. At the bottom of the list, a lowly knave might keep a kestrel, whereas a yeoman might keep a goshawk, and so on up to the king, who might own a peregrine falcon. At the very pinnacle, however, only an emperor could own a gyr falcon. They were highly prized for being the largest and swiftest of all falcons. Michael read an obscure fact: that the Isle of Man, in the Irish Sea off the northern coast of England, was once leased from the crown, the annual rent being two gyr falcons. It caused him a wry smile when he read it. He wondered what the people of those days would think of him, not long released from prison, sitting in his woodshed with a flashlight to read by while a gyr falcon stood on her perch ten feet away in the gloom and watched him.

In *The Goshawk*, things ended badly. The author had never trained a hawk before, and he failed to understand some of the crucial elements of the art, which ultimately resulted in his hawk flying off with leather thongs, called jesses, and a leash still attached to her legs. (The leather thongs that Frank had sent were jesses for the gyr falcon.) The likely outcome, though the author never saw his hawk again, was that the leash tangled in a tree somewhere and the hawk then hung upside down, helplessly, until it died. It was a grim fate and one that plagued the author with remorse and guilt.

In the second part of T. H. White's novel, the author successfully trained another hawk, which he called Cully, and Michael decided to name the gyr after her because he'd enjoyed reading the book and because it was the first account of falconry that he'd seen. Strictly speaking, he wasn't planning on becoming a falconer himself, but because his motive in training Cully lay in his desire to release her back to the wild, he needed to learn the skills of the sport. So Cully had to be fitted with jesses. They were about eight inches long and joined to one side of a swivel at their remote ends; the knotted cord was a leash that passed through the other side of the swivel, the swivel then preventing leash and jesses from becoming twisted.

Fitting the jesses had been a nerve-racking experience. He'd had to approach Cully carefully, getting closer each day and spending time simply sitting in her proximity while she watched him suspiciously. She would skitter to the far end of her perch, the brail that immobilized her injured wing preventing her from flying to the top of the woodpile stacked at the extreme end of the shed. He would talk softly to her, being sure to make no sudden movements that would startle her, and eventually she would tolerate him stroking her toes. It seemed a huge step backward to abuse her trust when it had been so patiently won, but there was no alternative: After twelve days of getting her used to him, he smoothly drew around her a piece of sheet he'd cut, effectively pinioning her good wing and dangerous feet. He'd practiced the maneuver repeatedly, using a vase in the house as a substitute falcon, and it all went off smoothly, though he did get bitten painfully when he neglected to be wary of Cully's powerful beak. He'd quickly withdrawn his hand, surprised at the sharp pain and the fast-welling globule of dark blood that grew until it became a trickle running back across his wrist. After that he'd been more careful, and he'd worked quickly to attach the jesses to her ankles, then had released her and gone back to the shed's farthest wall to see what she would do.

To his surprise, she didn't seem to hold the procedure against him, and when he came back after leaving her to recover in solitude for an hour, she was no more wary of him than she had been before.

Several days later, he drove past Williams Lake and, taking a country road, followed the directions Frank had given him to his house. Frank lived half a mile off the road and several miles from the nearest village. Michael turned down a track and followed it across a flat plain toward a clump of trees, beyond which he glimpsed the roof of Frank's neat two-story frame house. A stream ran past the property, flowing down from the hills that rose a mile away. Snow had fallen almost daily over the last week, and strong winds had gusted from the east, bringing freezing conditions. Without the forests that grew around Little River, the land here seemed empty, a vast white undulating scene marked occasionally by dark rocky promontories in the hills or clumps of winter trees.

As Michael pulled up in front of the house, a man came out and raised a hand in greeting. He was wearing jeans and boots and a heavy checked shirt beneath his parka. When they shook hands, his grip felt callused and tough.

"Frank Dobson? I'm Michael Somers."

"Call me Frank. 'Mike' okay with you?"

"Fine," Michael said, and as Frank's gaze traveled to the back of the Nissan, Michael realized that this was the first person he'd met recently who hadn't reacted to his name. To this man, he thought, he was just somebody who shared an interest.

"So this is your gyr, huh?" Frank went around the car, peering in through the windows.

"Cully," Michael said.

Frank looked at him a moment, then grinned and nodded. "I guess you liked the book, then? I was in England once, and I met a guy there who kept falcons and he gave me that book. He said he'd read it when he was at school—as part of the curriculum, I guess—and ever since then he'd been a falconer himself."

Michael had worked out that Frank's motive in lending him the novel went further than simply its value as a story. He thought it was about impressing upon him the privileged task he was undertaking in training a gyr falcon. And he imagined that Frank hoped he'd absorbed the cautionary aspect of the tale.

Cully sat on the perch Michael had rigged up in the back of the Nissan, tethered by her leash, which gave her freedom to walk back and forth. During the journey she'd used her one good wing to balance herself awkwardly, and now that they'd stopped, she looked much more at ease.

"How was it getting her in there?" Frank asked.

"Easier than I'd thought," Michael said truthfully. He'd read how a falcon will plunge headlong from the falconer's fist, her wings thrashing furiously until she became used to being carried that way. The thrashing was called bating. "I simply wore a glove and pressed against the back of her legs. She looked uncomfortable about it, but she stepped backward and stood there okay while I carried her out to the car."

"What about the leash? Did you wrap it around your fingers?"

"Just like the book says," Michael said.

Frank nodded approvingly. "With her wing bound up like that, she's not going anywhere, but as soon as that brail is taken off, you're going to find she's not quite so placid. You have to make sure you've got a tight hold on that leash at all times; otherwise she's going take off when you're not expecting it, dangling those jesses and leash behind her."

"Like in *The Goshawk*," Michael said to show he'd got the point.

"That's right," Frank said. "I guess I'm not being too subtle, am I?"

"I can understand that. I don't want to make any mistakes. I want to see her back safely where she belongs."

"She's beautiful," Frank mused. "I've never seen a wild one before. I've seen one or two kept by falconers, but they were captive bred birds."

"Fit for an emperor?" Michael said.

Frank grinned approvingly. "Yeah, something like that, I guess."

Michael had the feeling he'd just passed his first test with flying colors.

FRANK LED THE way around the back of the house. "Leave your falcon there," he said. "Let me introduce you to Florence."

Michael thought that Frank must mean his wife, but when they came around the back, he saw a wooden outbuilding with a long open front, and no sign of anybody else. The building had a kind of awning running its length from the roof to about three feet from the ground. At the moment, the awning was propped open with poles at either end and one in the middle, but it was hinged at the top so that it could be lowered to cover the front.

Inside, a long wooden beam ran the length of the building. Standing on this, watching their approach, was some kind of hawk.

"This is Florence," Frank said. "Just wait here a second and I'll bring her out." He went through a door and soon reemerged with the hawk on his fist, which was now protected by a leather gauntlet. The hawk had the look of an eagle, only smaller; it was perhaps slightly under two feet in length, a few inches short of Cully's size. Next to her its plumage was almost dowdy, a deep russet, and instead of Cully's almost black intelligent eyes it had bright orange pupils beneath heavily pronounced brows that gave it a perpetual glare, like a bad-tempered despot.

"Florence here's a Harris hawk," Frank told him. "She's a whole lot different to your gyr."

Michael started quoting the differences he could remember reading about between hawks and falcons. "She has the hawk's characteristic orange eyes, which sometimes are yellow, and she has broad rounded wings and a long tail that are designed for soaring and for low-level hunting—maneuvering among trees, for instance."

Frank gave an approving nod. "Falcons generally hunt by striking in the air, stooping down from above. That's why they have long pointed wings and shorter tails. There are other differences, too—like the notching in the beak, for instance. But essentially it's their hunting methods and the way they've adapted to them that separate them."

Frank started to unthread the leash attached to Florence's swivel and jesses. The jesses were different from the kind Michael had fitted to Cully. They had a knot at one end that passed through a brass eyelet that joined leather anklets on her legs, and once removed, only the anklets remained, no more obtrusive or a hindrance than marker rings.

"These jesses are what most people use these days," Frank explained. "If she decided to take off somewhere, there's nothing that's going to snarl up and hang her from a tree or something. Before you go we'll swap the ones I sent you for this type. I didn't send these right away, because you need a tool to fix the brass eyelets in place, and it's easier for you and your bird if there's two people doing the job."

He took a small piece of raw meat from a bag he had in his pocket and offered it to Florence; she seized it eagerly and swallowed it. Then Frank raised his fist, and the hawk opened her wings and launched herself into the air. She flew fifty yards across the ground, staying low, her wing tips brushing the snow, then swooped up into a tree.

She was an impressive sight up so close, slightly awe-inspiring.

"She'll wait there for a minute until I call her down," Frank said. "Or until she gets bored and decides to go off and look for some food."

He took another piece of meat and held it in his gloved fist. Raising his hand, he called Florence's name, and she came down out of the tree, her great wings flicking several times before she settled into a glide. Just at the right moment she fanned her tail and threw back her wings, her taloned feet reaching forward to grab the fist, and she landed with an audible smack against the leather. Her wings hung open for a second while she regained her balance, then she settled and seized the piece of meat.

"I wanted to show you this because it's one of the most important lessons you need to learn about training any bird of prey," Frank said. "You see, Florence and I have, I guess, what you might call a partnership going. The way it works is that she tolerates me so long as I feed her and show her plenty of respect, and that's why she stays. If she hadn't been hungry just then, I could have stood here all day calling her and she would likely as not have just ignored me. So rule number one is: Never fly a bird that isn't hungry unless you want to lose her."

Michael had absorbed this lesson from *The Goshawk*. T. H. White had lost his bird partly because he'd flown it when it wasn't hungry. However, it was one thing to read about it in a book, something else to see a practical demonstration.

"One thing I don't understand, though," Michael said. "She could catch her own food if she wanted to, right? So why doesn't she just take off?"

"She could," Frank agreed. "The thing is, these birds are basically lazy but they're not stupid. She knows she has it good with me. So long as she stays here, she doesn't have to hunt every day, which for a hawk takes a lot of effort and uses up a lot of energy. She knows I'll feed her, and she's got a dry warm place to live. She'll hunt rabbits with me, and she'll let me take them from her after she's eaten the brains, but she lets me do that only because she knows that's the deal. Plus, it's her decision. Every time I fly her, there's nothing stopping her just leaving if that's what she wants to do."

"How long have you had her?" Michael asked.

"About four years. I've had falcons as well as hawks, but falcons are more trouble to keep."

"In what way?"

"Because of the way they hunt, they have to be trained and flown differently. Florence here just comes to my fist, and when we're hunting, I either carry her until we see something she can catch, or else if there're trees around, I'll let her just follow me around from branch to branch until I scare something out. Falcons often take birds on the wing, flying high and fast, and you have to train them to fly to a lure instead of the fist."

Michael had read about these different methods. It sounded as if training Cully would be difficult, and he wasn't sure he could do it. "Let me ask you something," he said. "I've never done this before. Can I train a wild gyr falcon?"

"Sure. If you know how, it's not hard. Like I said, they're intelligent birds. All you need is patience, and I guess you've got to respect them—love them, even."

It sounded incongruous in a way to hear this big man, a workingman who looked as if he'd spent his entire life outdoors, who was hardened and pragmatic about the natural world, talking about love for a hawk. But it was also clear in the tender way he looked at Florence, and from the way he handled her, that love her he did.

"You can't force her to do what you want," Frank went on. "She'll die before she'll submit to mistreatment. How's her wing coming along?"

"Tom Waters thinks she has a fractured ulna."

Frank frowned. "That can be bad. Sometimes they don't heal properly, the bone gets infected. You can give them antibiotics, but they don't always work."

"How will I know that?" Michael asked.

"You'll be able to tell when she's flying free after a lure. That puts a lot of stress on the wing, which is natural. An injury that won't heal is always going to show up then. That's why it's best to train any injured wild bird before releasing her. It's the only way you can see for sure if she can survive."

"What happens if the injury doesn't heal?"

"That's a tough call, but with a wing fracture where the bone's infected, there's only one thing you can do, and that's amputate. If it was me, though, I can't see how that's doing a bird any favors. Better to just do the right thing."

"You mean, put her down."

Frank nodded. "It's hard, but it's right. That's my belief, anyway." He replaced Florence's jesses and returned her to her perch. "Now let's get your falcon fitted with some new jesses."

MICHAEL SPENT THE rest of the afternoon with Frank, leaving as it was beginning to get dark. By then he had a much better understanding of what he'd let himself in for. Frank answered his questions and gave him some of the things he was going to need to train Cully, and showed him how to make others. He'd also said that anytime Michael needed help, all he had to do was call. The last thing he'd done was to wish Michael luck, and to tell him that if somehow it went wrong and he changed his mind, then he could bring the gyr over and Frank would take over.

Michael was sure he wasn't going to do that. He was gripped with excitement. Watching Frank's Harris hawk fly had made it possible to visualize the moment when he'd be able to do the same with Cully, when she'd come to his fist and then, later, to a lure. It stirred feelings in him that were hard to define, but had partly to do with the sense that he was embarking on something worthwhile, something that

would not only return Cully to freedom but would also return something he himself had lost: a sense of purpose.

He stopped in Williams Lake on the way home to buy a set of
balancing scales at the local junk shop. When he got home, he removed the measuring pan and replaced it with a perch that he made
from a piece of wood, so he was able to weigh Cully. Over the following few days he kept a record of her weight, noting it down every
morning along with the amount of food she ate every day. He also
began the first stage of her training, noting how responsive she was.
In a few days he'd established that when her weight was within a
few ounces of three and a half pounds, she was hungry and co-
operative, or "keen set," to use the falconry term. But if he allowed
her to eat too much and her weight increased beyond that, she was
sluggish and slow to respond.

She learned to eat while standing on his fist, balancing square-
footed and tearing at a rabbit leg held firmly beneath her talons. At
first she picked tentatively, but her trust in him grew noticeably each
day. When he wasn't feeding her, he was carrying her on his fist,
which he now protected with a leather gauntlet that extended along
his forearm. It was made from doeskin and was soft and comfortable
to wear; the sections covering the wrist, the meat of the thumb, and
the first two fingers—where Cully stood—were reinforced with extra
stitched layers.

He loved walking with her. He spent long hours in the woods
along the riverbank carrying her around so that she got used to him,
his mind empty of everything except a kind of bemused wonder at
finding himself with a powerful and beautiful falcon standing on his
fist. She carried herself stiffly erect, arching herself away from him,
shifting uncertainly on her feet, constantly throwing out her good
wing for balance. Her eyes never wavered from his, though he
avoided returning her stare, as he'd read that in the wild this is a
signal that presages attack. He talked soothingly; when he ran out of
things to say that meant anything, he'd recite lines of poetry or
snatches of song lyrics, anything to put her at ease. She heard the
words to the Cowboy Junkies' track "Bea's Song" over and over while
he listened to the melody in his head. It was a mournful tale of a
woman reflecting on her life and the things that she had let go, and
its theme of regret touched a chord in him.

During this time he drank in the details of her form, from the bright yellow skin—called cere—around her beak and nostrils, which was the same color as her legs and feet, to the gunmetal blue gray of her razor-sharp beak. Her beak was designed for tearing strips of meat from prey, and for breaking bones. He learned from his reading that in the wild she would kill with her feet, primarily with her long back toes, which were used like bayonets at impact, piercing her victim and often breaking the neck. Though her coloring was overall a dusky cream, with dark flecks across her powerful breast, he noticed now that these flecks broadened underneath to bars across her feathered thighs and the underside of her tail. Her head was primarily of a softer brown gray color that was a mixture of the chocolate and cream that predominated elsewhere, and it was to this color that her long wing primaries and secondaries faded.

As she became used to him, she relaxed her posture a little and spent less of her time on the fist watching him, more time taking note of her surroundings. She missed nothing and took an avid interest in everything. She would watch a beetle crawling across the bark of a tree with the same keen interest with which she observed squirrels dashing across the uppermost limbs of gray winter trees. In the forest, where the smell of pine resin sharpened the air and the snow lay unevenly in drifts where it had penetrated the close-needled canopy overhead, she watched small birds flitting in the half-light.

He avoided crossing the river and heading up to the high ground where he'd found her. He still wondered about the identity of the hunter who'd shot her, reasoning that whoever it was might be determined enough to try more than once. It occurred to him that the hunter must have worked out that somebody had found the falcon, and might even know it was Michael.

Sometimes Cully's feet gripped the glove and she tensed, her good wing flicking open as if she planned to take to the air. In those moments, whatever illusions Michael had been building about the nature of the bond between them quickly evaporated. He couldn't think of her as a pet. Without the brail on her injured wing, she would have launched herself from his fist, and without the leash and jesses to restrain her, she would have left him. This reminded him that she was wild, and what his purpose with her was. She would bite at her restraints and glare at him, as if she blamed him for holding her captive, but then, five minutes later, it would be as if she understood their pact, and she'd be quite settled again.

When she was completely relaxed, she would bob her head up and down, an endearing gesture that transformed her from a sleek predator to something much less threatening. Then she would rouse her plumage and shake herself vigorously from head to tail and sometimes stay that way, puffed out like a ball, one leg raised with the foot clenched to her breast, at rest. At those times she became utterly benign and seemed incapable of delivering swift death, as indeed she had been designed for by nature. He discovered that she liked to play with windblown leaves or small twigs. He made a perch for her that he'd leave outside the house just off the porch in the clearing, and she would jump down from it and step daintily around in the snow to the limit of her leash, then hop back to it awkwardly, propelled by her one good wing, grasping some stick she'd discovered, which she'd dance around with as if amusing herself. He guessed there was more to it, that her games practiced her skills at grabbing with her feet, and that some future victim would suffer the consequences.

The first part of her training was to encourage her to step from her perch to his fist for food, which after a hesitant start she would readily do. In a couple of days she was jumping the length of her leash, and that was as far as Michael could go with it until her brail was removed. The rest of the time, if he wasn't walking with her, he was getting her used to a hood that Frank had given him, which he said he'd made especially after Michael had first called. The hood was constructed of three pieces of leather formed into a shape that roughly approximated the shape of Cully's head, with the sides that covered her eyes being slightly bulbous. Its purpose was to keep her in the dark (from where the term "hoodwinked" originated, he discovered from his reading) so that she would stay calm and not be startled by strange sights if he was, for example, taking her somewhere in the car. It was a beautifully constructed thing, the side panels made of red leather, the middle section light tan, and the long leather drawstrings used to tighten it a contrasting black. On top, an ornate spray of feathers transformed it from something merely practical to a small work of art.

He'd discovered that the hood, like many other things used in falconry, was cleverly designed for one-handed use, as a falconer often has to accomplish certain tasks while carrying a falcon on his left fist. There was, for instance, a special falconer's knot used to attach a leash to a perch that could be tied and released with one hand; Mi-

chael practiced this endlessly, to perfection. Similarly, the design of
the jesses meant that they could be taken on and off the swivel one-
handed. For Michael, there was a certain pleasure in becoming ac-
complished at these things: It was all part of training a falcon and
meant he was moving closer to the time when Cully would fly free
again.

A week after his visit to Frank, Michael called Tom Waters and
told him he thought the brail was ready to come off. Tom promised
to come over the next evening.

"That wing is going to be stiff," Tom warned after he'd examined
her. "We'll take the brail off, but just go easy on her for a while. I'll
come back in a few days and see how she's doing. Don't let her get
excited and overdo it."

"What about the fracture?" Michael asked.

"I can feel a callus, so that's good, but we won't know for sure
until we see how she is with that wing."

They were in the woodshed. It was dark, and Cully was sleepy and
hardly seemed to notice that she was no longer restrained. Michael
decided to leave her inside for a few days while she got used to the
idea.

The next morning, when he brought her food, she was standing
on her perch, flexing both wings, flapping them while she gripped
tightly with her feet. He hung back at the door, startled at how large
she was with her full wingspan exposed, feeling the air she disturbed
flow across his face. He was worried that she would aggravate her
injury, but after a moment she settled again, panting from exertion.

Relieved that she appeared to be able to use her wing, he fed her
and retreated. He would give her a few days, and then her training
would begin in earnest.

12 FOR THREE WEEKS MICHAEL HAD AVOIDED going into town, even to the point of driving all the way to Williams Lake for his groceries, but with Cully temporarily confined, he had time on his hands again, and his thoughts turned to the need to make some kind of living. He knew the money he had in the bank wasn't going to last forever.

One day, while he was contemplating his options, which seemed few, he was startled by the phone; this was the first time anybody had called since he'd been in the house. He picked it up, wondering who it could be.

"Just thought I'd see how everything is going." Carl Jeffrey's voice came through the line, like a friend just keeping in touch.

"Everything's fine," Michael said cautiously, wondering what the lawyer wanted. "What can I do for you, Carl?"

"Well, I've been thinking. It seems like we got off on the wrong foot. Why don't we bury the hatchet and get together sometime soon?"

Michael hesitated, unconvinced by this apparent change of heart. "Is this an invitation to come over for dinner, Carl?"

"That's a great idea. Tell you what, I'll talk to Karen, and we'll let you know when." There was a pause. "But if you're coming into town sometime soon, why don't you stop by for a cup of coffee?"

"You called to ask me to have a cup of coffee?"

"Well, why not? Like I said, I think we just got off on the wrong foot. I want to make sure things are okay with you, that's all. I mean, they are, aren't they?"

"About as well as I could expect, I guess," Michael said, wondering if Carl was planning on getting to the point.

Carl hesitated before continuing. "Look, this is probably none of my business, but what about financially? I mean, are you getting by okay in that department?"

"You're right," Michael said. "It isn't any of your business."

Carl chuckled as if this were a joke between friends. Then his tone became conciliatory. "I guess you've a right to be mad with me," he said. "Look, I was just trying to give you good advice when we talked. You can see that, can't you?"

"Is there something I can do for you, Carl?" Michael said. "Because if there isn't, I've got things to do."

Carl's tone altered, as if he was losing patience. "Okay, Michael, if that's how you want it. I need to talk to you about the store."

"I'm listening."

"This isn't something I want to discuss over the phone. I thought you might want to drop into the office next time you're in town."

"I don't get into town very often. I think it works better for everyone that way, don't you?" Michael could hear Carl on the other end of the line, absorbing his remark.

"I heard you didn't have much luck finding a job."

"It seems I'm not qualified for any of the vacancies around here," Michael said, not attempting to disguise his sarcasm.

"I tried to warn you."

"You did," Michael agreed. "So, what is it about the store you wanted to talk to me about?"

"I could still get you a good price for it. I think you should reconsider your position."

Michael started to say he wasn't interested, but then he asked himself why he was hanging on to the place. It was just sitting there empty, costing him money in taxes, and he hadn't even been near it since he'd arrived.

Sensing his hesitation, Carl became friendly, cajoling. "Look, why don't you just come in and talk about it. What harm could it do?"

Michael thought about the money. "Okay," he said reluctantly, "but not in your office. Meet me at the store." The words stuck in his throat.

"Why there? My office would be more comfortable."

"I just feel like taking a look, if I'm going to think about selling. Call it nostalgia." Seconds passed in silence.

"About two-thirty?" Carl said at last.

"See you then." Michael hung up and went outside to the porch. Selling the store made good sense, he told himself. It would give him breathing space. It would also, he realized, loosen his attachment to Little River, which he guessed was at least part of Carl's motive.

HE WENT OVER to where Cully stood on the perch he'd rigged for her in front of the house, and held out his fist with a piece of meat held between finger and thumb. She turned toward him as he approached, and when she saw the meat, she flicked open her wings and hopped three feet to the glove. After she'd eaten, he produced the hood. When she saw it, she snaked her head left and right to avoid it. He'd discovered this was not unusual: Sometimes she accepted it, other times she acted as if she'd never seen it before. Finally he managed to slip it over her head and tighten the draw thongs at the back; then he untied her leash and took her to the car, where he set her on her perch in the back. Her movements now were accompanied by the distinctive, oddly flat note of the bell that was attached to one of her legs. It was small, about the size of a marble, and made of an alloy that produced a tone he could clearly hear from the far side of the clearing. It was something else Frank had given him, and its purpose was to help locate a lost bird—if the unthinkable should happen.

Michael drove into town and parked outside the store his father had run for forty-five years. There were few people about on the street, and nobody saw him take Cully inside. The only light came from the open door. The store was cold, the air slightly damp. It felt like walking into a tomb. He tried the light switches before realizing the power wasn't connected; then he put Cully on top of a wooden fixture that would serve as a perch and ripped down the black paper covering the windows. Daylight filtered through the streaked glass, and he stood amid the dust he'd raised, assailed for a moment by a feeling of sadness at the neglect he saw.

Once he'd worked here after school and on Saturdays, when in the afternoons he had the place to himself: Inexplicably, his father would go to Williams Lake to visit suppliers when he could simply have phoned with his order. Michael hadn't questioned it much back then. It was all part of the mysterious routine of his dad's life: like the way he'd spend every Thursday evening doing the books at the store and wouldn't come home until late, smelling of booze, or the way when he was at home he'd stay much of the time shut up in his study, building intricately detailed models of sailing schooners, inspired by plates from the leather-bound books on the shelves of his bookcase. He always had a bottle of bourbon on the table beside him, and he sipped from a never empty glass. The books were still in the house, though oddly, Michael thought, not the models. He wondered what had happened to them.

The store had wooden fixtures that once ran in aisles parallel to the door, and the counter ran along the back wall. Patches of damp showed in the walls near the ceiling, and some of the floorboards were obviously rotten. Here and there, splintered holes showed where the fixtures had been carelessly moved. They lay in a haphazard arrangement, like pieces of a puzzle waiting for somebody to put them back together again. It seemed that long ago somebody had moved through the place without care or respect; Michael supposed that this was when the stock had been taken out by the suppliers, who'd bought it back at bargain prices.

A knock at the window startled him, and he went to the door to let Carl Jeffrey in. His coat buttoned to the neck, Carl stood flapping his arms around.

"Jesus, it's freezing in here. Does that work?" Carl pointed to an old heater.

"No power," Michael said.

"We could've done this at my office," Carl grumbled, looking around.

Michael thought that if he was going to sell the place, he ought to do it somewhere he could feel the ghost of his father's presence. He associated the house largely with his mother, but the store had been his dad's.

"Funny being in here again," Carl commented. "Your old man spent a lot of time in this place. Something's missing, though. I remember coming in here when I was a kid. There was a smell I remember. Sort of sharp."

"Linseed oil," Michael said, recalling it with sudden vividness. "He used to buy it in drums and bottle it himself. He kept it out back, but the smell was ingrained."

For a few moments they were both thinking about the past.

"You spent a lot of time in here, didn't you?" Carl said. "Didn't you work here after school?"

"Yes, I did,"

"Did you get on with him? Your dad, I mean?"

There was a genuine curiosity in Carl's tone. Michael supposed people wondered why he hadn't come back for his dad's funeral, why he'd never sold the house or the store, why he'd never returned after his mother's death. In view of the fact that he'd come back now, he guessed a lot of things didn't seem to add up.

"Not really," Michael admitted, unsure why he was telling this to Carl. Partly, he was just talking to himself. "I never wanted to work in here. I hated every minute of it."

"Yeah? It's funny, I used to help out my old man around the office after school. He always wanted me to be a lawyer, like him. He was always giving me books to read, law books."

There was some note of resignation in Carl's tone. Michael wondered suddenly what secret hopes and ambitions lay buried in Carl that would now never see the light of day. It surprised him for some reason that Carl had ever harbored ideas about becoming anything but the town lawyer, just the way his dad had wanted.

"I guess your old man wanted you to take over the store back then too?" Carl said.

"No, he never mentioned anything like that." When Michael thought about it, he only ever remembered his dad encouraging him to get an education. He didn't think he'd ever wanted him to follow in his footsteps.

Carl was hunched in his coat, hands thrust into his pockets. "I thought about going to art college once," he said, and uttered a quick self-deprecatory laugh. He looked thoughtful. "I probably would have ended up designing labels for canned food or something, though. Things probably worked out for the best." He looked up as if he expected Michael to be uninterested, but the fact was, Michael found himself surprised. It seemed as if there was more to Carl than what he'd become.

"Were you any good?"

Carl looked as if he thought he was being mocked; deciding he wasn't, he shrugged. "I used to be, I think. Who knows? I guess there would have been plenty of kids at college who'd have been a lot better."

"Maybe not." Michael wondered about Carl's dad, what he'd said to give his son such a low opinion of his talent. "It's never too late," he offered, though he knew that for most people at this point in life, it was.

"Yeah," Carl said. "You know, when we were kids, I used to think we had some things in common."

"What sort of things?"

"I guess that sounds funny, huh?" Carl said with a trace of bitterness. "You didn't hang out much with the other kids."

Michael could see where this was going. Carl had been ostracized a little, the way fat kids often are, especially fat smug kids whose father was the town lawyer who nobody much liked. Carl apparently thought that made them similar, but Michael knew it didn't. *His* habit of keeping to himself was his own choice.

Carl's eye flicked to the window as somebody went by, an old man who looked curiously in the long-covered windows. Whatever mood had formed seemed to vanish, as if Carl had abruptly remembered where he was. "So, listen, let's talk about this place."

"Let's have a look upstairs first," Michael said, all of a sudden wanting to delay the moment.

Cully shifted position, and her bell made its curious flat note. Carl saw her sitting in the gloom and stepped back.

"Jesus, what the hell is that?"

Michael suppressed a smile. Quickly glimpsed, the bird's pale form was startling, more so given the strange silhouette of the hood. "She's a falcon."

Carl peered at her but made no move to get any closer. "What do you do with her?"

"I don't do anything with her," Michael said, annoyed for some reason. Carl was jumpy, a soft man wearing glasses and a badly fitting suit whom Michael didn't really like. Whatever empathy Michael might feel for the wounds Carl nursed inside himself, the man had chosen his path. Michael turned away and went to the door that led to the back stairs. Carl followed him, and they poked around the empty rooms on the floors above. Once, the rooms had been used for storage. Some contained empty boxes and faded newspapers now, but that was all. The evidence of the passing years was everywhere. It was in the badly fitting doors that sagged on their hinges, in the wallpaper faded and peeling in one of the rooms, in the floor rotted and dangerous in another.

Carl tagged along, not saying much, and when they got downstairs again, he blew his nose to expel the dust that had got into his sinuses.

"This place is falling apart," he asserted.

In truth, Michael thought, it wasn't as bad as that, but he let it go. All it needed was a little money and time spent on it. The walls were sound, and so was the roof. He waited for Carl to go on, giving him no encouragement.

"Are you still planning on staying in town?" Carl asked when he'd finished blowing his nose.

"I told you before, I don't have anywhere else to go."

"But if you had money . . ."

Michael looked around at the store. "Who is it wants to buy this place, anyway?"

"His name's Ron Taylor. He's the same guy that made you an offer before." Carl put down a folder he'd been carrying around and flicked through some papers. "He's offering you seventy-eight thousand," Carl said.

"For the store?"

"That's right."

It was about the same as the figure previously offered, with the house taken out of the equation. At some point since he'd walked through the door, however, Michael had decided he wasn't going to sell. Even while he was standing there, he could see his father's ghost working behind the counter. He was the way Michael always thought of him, in his middle fifties, gray-haired and thin, quietly unpacking a delivery of hand tools that had just arrived, checking each item against the packing slip with a pencil he usually kept behind his ear.

He'd never got on with his dad. Though they'd worked in this store together for an hour every day, they'd barely exchanged a word beyond his father's usual questions and Michael's terse answers. How was his day? (Fine.) What did he do? (Nothing.) His breath always had the lingering sourness of the couple of beers he had every lunchtime. His nose and cheeks were shot through with little red veins like spiderwebs; his eyes had an odd light. Michael never had to work very hard; in fact, he hadn't really had to work at all if he didn't want to. His dad gave him things to do and thanked him if he did them well, but if he didn't, he was never reprimanded. Once he'd tried to say he didn't want to work there anymore after school. It had been his mother's idea in the first place, another way of trying to "keep the peace," as she'd put it, though by then he'd started to understand that his mother had always used such persuasions as a way of meeting her own deluded ends. By the time he was in his teens, he was a little embarrassed and repelled by her. He could never forget the time she'd driven into town and pulled up outside the doctor's office with blood streaming from wounds in her wrists. She'd been disheveled and wild-eyed, her makeup streaked from crying so much. He'd been young then, maybe eight years old, sitting in the passenger seat of the car. His mother told the doctor she'd cut herself in an accident, but Michael knew that wasn't true, that she'd done it herself in a rage when his dad had called to say he'd be home late. The cuts, it had turned out, were superficial, but they'd waited until his dad arrived to take them home, talking quietly in the corner first with the doctor. Michael thought it was around then that his mother first started spending a lot of time in her nightgown, often not getting out of her bed until noon. She was always having headaches, taking this pill or that for some imagined condition.

His dad had been disappointed that Michael didn't want to work in the store. "I'd really like it if you did," he'd said quietly, but that was all. No other pressure. No insisting or shouting. He'd never shouted. And for some reason, Michael had given in.

"So what do you think?" Carl said, bringing Michael back to the present.

Michael shook his head. "I don't think so."

Carl didn't say anything, just drummed his fingers on the old countertop. He looked away and pushed his glasses up on his nose, then pursed his lips.

"I've got another offer," he said.

"What?"

"Two hundred and seventy-five thousand. For the house as well," he added.

The last figure, offered the day he'd arrived back in town, had been two twenty-eight, and it was about right. "How come the big jump?" Michael asked.

"You won't get a better price than that," Carl said, ignoring the question. "It's more than both places are worth. You don't have to take our word for that. Get it checked out."

Michael frowned. " 'Our'?"

"What?"

"You said 'our.' 'You don't have to take *our* word.' " Michael was puzzled, and Carl looked uncomfortable. "Who is Ron Taylor, anyway?"

"A developer. Listen, what's important here is . . . See, that kind of money is . . . Well, it's a good offer, Michael. I wouldn't tell you it was if I didn't think so."

"And it's this Taylor guy who wants the store?"

"Yes. He plans to redevelop it."

"And he wants the house, too?"

"Not really, but he's prepared to take it to get the store. Listen, you should think about this. That kind of money, you could go somewhere. Wherever you want. Europe, maybe."

"Europe?"

"I just mean, you'd have options. You're still a young man, Mike. You could get a job in advertising again somewhere."

Something didn't feel right. Michael felt that Carl was holding something back, but he wasn't sure what. "Our." Why had he said "our"? Was he a partner with this Taylor guy? It didn't matter, anyway. "I don't want to sell." He looked about the empty store again, and an idea came to him. Maybe it had been forming in his mind for a while.

"I might reopen this place," he said.

Carl blinked in astonishment. "Reopen it?" He looked around as if he expected to see workmen and tools already, as if Michael were pulling some kind of conjuring trick. "There's a hardware store in town already," he said.

"I wouldn't have to sell hardware."

Carl bit his lip and fiddled with his papers. He cleared his throat. "I, uh, I've been authorized . . . I mean, we could maybe go to two eighty-five. Two ninety." He shuffled, a little nervous sidestep.

Michael said, "You said 'we' that time. Is this you and Ron Taylor, Carl?"

"Not exactly."

The way Carl looked at him, just across his shoulder, the light catching his glasses so they flashed clear, made the moment a telling one. It still took Michael a second to get it, but then he did.

"This offer. It doesn't have anything to do with Taylor, does it?"

Carl hesitated. "No, he hasn't changed his original figures. He thinks the offer fair." His voice started weak but gathered strength as the pretense fell away.

"And it was," Michael said.

"You ought to think very carefully about this," Carl said. He was a different man now. He drew himself up, and his voice lowered. "Two ninety is a lot more than you'll ever get anywhere else. You'd be a fool not to take it."

Michael nodded slowly. "Just so I know, who is it that's making me this generous offer, Carl? I mean, I think I ought to know who wants me to leave town so much they're willing to pay over the odds. There's you, of course; I know that. Who else?"

"There's no reason for you to take it like that," Carl said. "Look at it from our point of view. We've got kids. This is a respectable town. We don't have that kind of trouble around here."

Michael echoed his words. " 'That kind of trouble.' You mean people like me? Killers. Crazy people?" He shook his head, slowly, too stunned for anger. "You know what happened, Carl. I didn't kill anybody."

"You shot a man. The cops thought you were going to shoot your own wife and daughter."

"I never once threatened them, for chrissakes." Michael didn't know why he was arguing. What did it matter? He was wasting his breath with someone like Carl Jeffrey. "Who else is a part of this deal?"

"Just some people I know. Some businesspeople."

"Like George Wilson? Good citizens of the community. He was going to give me a job, did he tell you that? I was going to be his promotions manager. He said he liked my ideas, until he knew who I was."

Michael waved a hand. He'd started to feel anger rising in his throat, bubbling up like bile he needed to spit out, but it faded. "Get the fuck out of my sight," he said wearily.

"Listen . . ." Carl took a step forward.

"This is my property." There was a warning in Michael's tone. "Get out."

His words fell hard and flat, and Carl faltered. He gathered up his papers and made to leave, skirting around Cully as he did so. At the door he turned, looking as if he was going to try one more time, but on seeing Michael's expression, he changed his mind.

"I'll tell you this for free. If you open this store again, you're crazy." He went out, slamming the door shut behind him.

RACHEL ELLIS FEIGNED sleep, waiting for her husband's deep breathing to turn to snoring. It was dark in their room, but her side of the bed was closest to the window; outside, through a gap in the curtain, she could see stars. Pete stirred, muttering something unintelligible, and his heavy hand slid from her belly to flop loose. The stubble of his chin scratched against the back of her neck.

She got out of bed and put on her robe. The kids were asleep, and the house was quiet. It was a habit of hers these days to go down to the kitchen and sit in the dark when she didn't feel like sleeping. She poured herself a glass of milk and tried not to think about the pile of bills on the shelf waiting to be paid.

Earlier that night she and Pete had argued, which these days wasn't unusual at all. It was the same old thing: no money coming in except what she made herself, him drinking, the business going to hell. Lately things had become worse. As usual, it had fallen to her to smooth it over with the bank. That afternoon, Richard Wells had looked at her across his desk when she'd gone in to talk to him, all dressed up with her hair done and wearing a skirt that showed off her legs, and she'd read sympathy in his smile. She'd clenched her hands in anger, digging her nails into her palms. She'd felt humiliated, angry at herself for thinking a little makeup and eyelash fluttering would change anything, but mostly furious with Pete for making her act like a small-town whore, or at least feel that way.

"Things have been a little quiet for Pete lately," she'd said, a flush of heat rising in her cheeks.

Richard had looked at their account record, and after a moment he'd laid down the file. "I understand how things can get, and we're not talking about a lot of money here," he'd said.

She'd known it would be okay then. When he'd shown her to the door, he'd asked about her family and said to give his regards to her dad. As she'd left, he'd given her a kind of sad smile that had cut to her heart. She guessed he felt sorry for her: for being married to Pete, for having to put on a dress and try to talk her way around a few hundred lousy dollars. All the while, Pete was drinking nights, running up credit where he could get it or stealing from her purse. People told her they'd seen him in Clancys or one of the places out of town.

She lit a cigarette, the match flaring orange in the dark, and caught sight of her reflection in the window, all shadows and light across her forehead. She was thirty-three years old. Her kids were both in their teens and becoming independent, much quicker than she had at their age. She lived in a house that needed painting inside and out, and she drove a car that regularly broke down on her. Maybe it was time she cut her losses and admitted she was fighting a losing battle. If she left Pete, the kids would go with her. They could stay with her parents for a while—over in Williams Lake, where they'd moved seven years ago—until she found herself a decent job. She could start again.

Her parents would be happy, she knew that. There would be the stuff about how they'd always told her she was making a mistake marrying Pete, but she was used to that by now and it wouldn't be for long. Seems like they'd been right anyway, though that was something she'd started to admit to herself only recently.

"He comes from bad stock," her dad used to warn her. "I know how that sounds, but it's true, Rachel. Just look at the boy's father."

Well, there was no denying that, all right, and nobody ever had, least of all Pete. His dad was a drunk and a bum who'd abused both his wife and his kids for most of his worthless life.

"Pete's not like him," she used to say, believing every word. "He knows what his dad is, and he doesn't ever want to turn out like that."

Her dad had worn a pained expression. "I hate to say it, but Pete Ellis is exactly like his old man. He's just trying hard to fight it right now."

She'd thought her father was being unfair, and she railed about how was anybody ever to make something of themselves if they never got a decent chance? She was right, of course, and her father's attitude was undoubtedly wrong. But maybe his observation wasn't.

What she remembered about Pete from high school wasn't very much because he was four years older than her, but in a town the size of Little River you get to know everybody in some way. In Pete's case, his reputation mostly preceded him. His was a loudmouth, and pretty good at throwing his weight around, always getting in fights. Had anybody said when she was sixteen that she'd end up marrying someone like that, she'd have laughed. She didn't meet him again until he came back, and then she hardly recognized him.

What had struck her chiefly about him then was his good manners, which seemed like a funny kind of old-fashioned thing to say, but it was true. The last time she'd seen him, he was this scruffy obnoxious guy she would have crossed the street to avoid; then suddenly there he was again, a whole different person. When he asked her out, he was so polite and serious that curiosity, more than anything else, motivated her to accept: She wanted to know how somebody could change so much, and if it was just an act. It hadn't been, though. He'd opened doors for her, even pulled out her chair when he took her to a restaurant, and he'd never tried to lay a hand on her.

Soon enough, his appeal had become something more serious to her than curiosity. He was kind of shy around her, and admitted it was because he hadn't been out with many girls like her. She hadn't asked much about what kind of girls he *had* been out with, guessing she knew the answer to that question. He talked a lot about the future he planned. He had this ambition to get on in the world, and as she got to know him, she found it was fueled a lot by the fact that he hated his father and was determined to prove to everyone that he would never be like him. That would take some doing, as most people had already decided otherwise.

They got married for the oldest and stupidest reason there was: She got pregnant. But if she was honest with herself, she'd have to admit that it probably would have happened anyway. It would have been nice if she could think that afterward everything had worked out well, that Pete had proved to the world he was his own person and no reflection of his parentage. Even if they'd always had to struggle for money, that would have been okay, but life, Rachel thought, is never as simple as all that.

She found out early on that Pete had a weakness that meant there was always going to be a gap between his ambitions for himself and what he was capable of. He'd done poorly at school because he hadn't studied or been expected to, and when he started the lumber business, that lack of education showed up. He was no good at arithmetic, and he couldn't read or write that well either. Things like contracts totally floored him, and any kind of complicated "legal speak," as he put it, went way over his head. None of that had to have mattered, because he could have overcome those things if he'd wanted to work at it, and she was always there to help out with the books and so forth, but Pete's real weakness was his conviction that he was as good as anybody just the way he was. He didn't want to go back to school. He didn't want to do things the hard way. He preferred to get by with bluster and determination. He used to tell her proudly that he'd work every hour of every day that came if he had to. The trouble was, hard work was only part of what was required; smart work was needed just as much. Pete was always looking for the shortcut, but he found that it rarely led him where he wanted to be.

It had been his dad's weakness, too: a generational cycle of bad parenting and poor education producing failure and bitterness. Pete had thought he could rise above it by sheer force of will, but he'd been wrong. He'd thought he could make his business work without properly understanding contracts and proposals and business plans and loan repayments and all the rest of it, and he'd been wrong about that, too. Maybe he'd sensed early on that if he married someone like her, she would somehow make up for the things he lacked, and in a way he'd been right. For years she'd been the foundation on which the family was built, this being an unspoken knowledge in their lives. Early on, the lumberyard had done okay, but she'd virtually been running it. As the kids were growing up, though, she'd had to devote more time to them, and Pete had taken on more of the quoting and office work at the yard. Business had declined—just a temporary thing, Pete had said. He'd claimed he didn't need her help anymore, but still, she'd gone out to work because he just didn't make enough money. By then she'd had even less time to check over the books, even if his pride had allowed her to.

She had seen what was happening, of course, but she'd stood back and let him try to work his way through it. Now they were in a desperate situation, she knew that. The business was all but finished, crippled with debt, no assets to speak of, and any customer goodwill had long since been used up with Pete trying to cut corners. The order book, as she'd seen the other day, was empty. The only option was for her to take charge again, the way things had once been, only this time she would have to devote herself full-time to the task. The question was, did she want to?

It kept her awake at night, thinking about it. Did she want to spend the next ten years of her life carrying the burden of keeping the family together? Whatever happened, it looked as if they would lose the house. Pete would have to accept that she would make all the decisions, would talk to customers, would try to win back lost business. He would just be a hired hand, in effect doing the manual work. That would be hard on him, adding to his sense of failure. She would have to buoy him up, sometimes be hard on him, remind him of what his dad had been like when he'd given up on himself. Did she want that? Did she want to be responsible for him?

She didn't know the answer. So she sat at the kitchen table at night, drinking milk and smoking cigarettes, and wondered what to do with her life.

IN THE MORNING, she was tired. She hadn't gone back to bed until three A.M., and even then she hadn't slept for more than a couple of hours. Her job at the grocery store had become full-time, for which she was grateful because of the money, but it depressed her to spend her days stacking shelves and working on the register—this only added to her sense that she was wasting her life. She'd graduated from high school and could have gone to college if she hadn't got married, and though she didn't kid herself that she was any kind of genius, she knew she was smart enough to do more than count change and pack orders.

When she took a break at lunchtime, she had to get out for a little while, just to clear her head. Maybe this would help her to think. She was heading along the sidewalk, going nowhere in particular, turning her problems over in her mind as if by thinking long and hard enough some solution might make itself known to her. She was hardly aware of people moving around her, now and again brushing her as she almost walked into them. Then somebody was right in front of her, and she looked up just as she collided into Michael Somers as he came out of a doorway with a stack of splintered wood cradled in his arms. He stumbled, and the wood scattered all over the sidewalk.

"I'm sorry," she said, bending down to help him pick it all up. "I wasn't looking where I was going."

"Forget it." He barely glanced at her.

She helped him carry it over to his car, where he shoved it into the back, and when they were finished, he turned around and looked surprised to find her still there. He was a couple of years older than her—maybe four or five, she thought, about the same age as Pete. Right there, however, was where any similarity ended. He hadn't run to fat the way Pete had, and though his look was kind of chilly, it wasn't desperate and mean the way Pete had begun to appear to her these days. She could see he had no idea who she was—which, she guessed, shouldn't surprise her. She would have been little more than a kid when he'd last seen her, and now she was wearing her hair tied back to save her taking any trouble with it, and she had on old Levi's that were about worn through in places and a thick sweater that had once belonged to Pete. She touched her hand to her forehead, brushing back a strand of hair that had come loose. The wood was all picked up.

"Thanks," he said before going to fetch a thermos from the front of his Nissan.

"Are you always this talkative with people?" she said when he came back. "You don't remember me, do you?"

He looked at her blankly.

"I'm Rachel Laine." She shrugged. "Actually, it's Ellis now, my married name."

He looked uncertain. Then it came to him, and he smiled. "Rachel? Sure, I remember you." He looked her over, which made her feel self-conscious. "I guess I'm getting antisocial. I'm not used to people around here stopping to pass the time of day."

She'd heard he was back in town, of course, and just that morning somebody had mentioned something about the old store his dad had run, but with her own problems crowding her thoughts, she hadn't paid a lot of attention. "They'll get over it," she said. "Something else will come along and you'll be yesterday's news."

"Maybe you're right."

An awkward silence fell between them. Rachel was about to smile and go on her way, but she realized she had nowhere in particular to go; she was just killing time. She gestured instead to the store. "You look like you're busy in there. What are you doing?"

"Fixing the place up. I might reopen it."

"Good for you," she said.

He looked surprised, then held up his thermos. "Want to take a look around? I can offer you coffee."

"Sure," Rachel said. "Why not?"

Inside, the store was a wreck. The counter was half ripped to pieces, and the floor had gaping holes in it. Michael poured her coffee into a paper cup.

"Sorry, I don't have sugar or milk."

"Black's fine." She looked around a little sadly. "I remember this place when your dad ran it," she commented. "I remember when you worked here, too." He looked surprised at that. "My dad was a builder. He ran an account with your dad, and he used to send me in to pick up things."

"I think I remember you," Michael told her.

"I doubt it. I was just a kid then."

"No, I do," he insisted. "I mean, I admit I didn't recognize you at first, but now I do. You look the same."

She laughed. "Either you're flattering me or you're lying, but thanks anyway." She remembered back to when she'd been at school. "It all seems a long time ago now, doesn't it? Sometimes I can hardly believe I'm the same person. Things don't always work out the way you plan them."

"No, they don't," he agreed in a quiet voice.

She'd been thinking about herself, but now she silently told herself she had a big mouth. What was she thinking of? She imagined the last thing he needed reminding about was the way life gets screwed up. She changed the subject, bringing up the name of a girl she thought he might remember. He took the cue and said he did.

"She's a model now," she went on. "She works in New York—can you believe that? Her folks still live in the same old house, though, and her brother lives in Bakerstown." She chatted on for a while, keeping to innocuous reminiscences about people they both knew from school, filling him in on the occasional funny story, which made them both laugh. She finished her coffee and stayed until it was time for her to get back to work.

"I should go," she said, checking her watch. "It was good seeing you, though." She meant it, too. She couldn't remember the last time she'd laughed. Maybe it had done him some good, too, she thought.

He seemed a little less withdrawn than he had a half hour earlier. He looked different than when she'd bumped into him on the street. She tried to think in what way exactly. It was his eyes, she decided in the end. He looked a little less sad.

"Good luck," she told him at the door. "Don't let the bastards get you down."

"Thanks. I'll remember that."

They smiled at each other, and she turned away.

13 MICHAEL CLOSED THE WOODSHED DOOR BE-
hind him and took down the gauntlet hanging
from a nail in the wall. It was early. Overnight the temperature had fallen and the wind had risen.
He'd lain awake in bed listening to the creaking of the
house and found it comforting. When a strong-enough gust blew, it
rattled the panes in the windows. He liked the feeling of having the
house to himself. After St. Helen's, it was a luxury not to hear the
moans and deluded mutterings of men in their sleep. Sometimes he
liked to get up and wander around at night, just for the feeling of
solitude and space. The only room he avoided was his mother's, not
because he feared her presence—he knew she wasn't there—but just
because he wanted the memories to come slowly, at a pace he could
make sense of. He thought going into her room would pull him too
far forward, to the time she'd died.

It had snowed during the night, and the wind had caused the snow
to drift onto the porch. The clearing was newly covered with an eight-
inch layer of fresh snow that concealed the tracks he'd made over
the last few days and subtly altered the contours and dips of the
ground. Trees that had been bare now held a ridge of white along
their branches, and the evergreens and undergrowth were dusted with
frost.

Up high, across the river and above the woods, the mountains
appeared forbidding without blue sky and winter sun. Heavy gray
cloud looked ominous and immovable, and the wind had died. Some

crows called from just beyond the clearing, but their cries were muffled, the landscape soaking up the sound.

Cully stood on her perch, watching him, plumage ruffled against
the cold, one leg raised in the attitude of rest. She appeared content
to remain where she was.

He held out his fist to her from a distance of twelve feet, his glove
garnished with a strip of gray fur and red meat. "Come on, Cully,"
he said softly.

She tilted her head at the sound of his voice, her look childlike.
She appeared to be contemplating whether or not she felt like playing
this game. Hunger got the better of her and she lowered her clenched
foot and roused her feathers, shaking herself from head to tail like a
dog drying itself. With her plumage then lying sleek, she clenched
her feet and leaned toward him.

"Come, Cully," he coaxed.

Her wings flicked open, and in a second she was there, looking at
him, the glove, the meat. Then she bent to eat.

"Good morning," he said quietly, and while she fed, he attached
jesses, swivel, and leash, then took her outside.

In the morning air, she bobbed her head with keen pleasure, taking
in the changes in the landscape that had occurred overnight. Her
perch in the clearing was half buried in the snow, and instead of
putting her there, he let her stand on the porch railing and tied her
leash. He'd been feeding her four or five times a day, just small
amounts each time, and persuading her to come to his fist for her
meal, extending the distance each time. She would come thirty yards
on a line without any hesitation.

Fetching the scales from the house, he weighed her; she was exactly three and a half pounds. He'd learned that at that weight she
watched his movements avidly, waiting for food. This was called
"being keenly set." He looked at his watch and started to tie a fifty-
yard nylon line to her swivel. The remote end was attached to a
wooden handle that, with the drag of the line, was too heavy for her
to carry off. He checked his watch again, then set about tying meat
to the lure he'd made from a weighted pad of leather and a pair of
duck's wings. The lure was joined to an eight-foot length of cord that
ended in a heavy wooden handle.

The sound of a vehicle turning off the road above reached him, and he heard its careful descent down the track. Tom Waters's Cherokee nosed into the clearing past the trees, where Tom killed the engine and raised a hand in greeting as he got out.

"Sorry I'm late. The roads are bad."

"It's okay," Michael said.

Tom stopped before he reached the porch, observing Cully on the rail, who in turn observed him. His expression was contemplative, thoughtful.

"I give up," he said at last. "What is it? I mean, I know she looks great, better than ever, but what is it?"

Pleased that he'd noticed, Michael pointed out that the improvement was in Cully's feathers. When she'd been confined in a cage for a few days, the wire mesh had bent half her tail out of shape and shredded the primaries on her good wing. When he'd taken a closer look, he'd found some of the shafts actually broken. Later in the year she would molt and replace damaged plumage, but until then her flying ability would have been impaired if he hadn't done something about it.

He showed Tom how he'd repaired the broken shafts by cutting them off and fixing them together again using glue and small wooden needles he'd shaped with a knife. "It's called 'imping,'" he explained. The bent and frayed feathers had been straightened just by dipping them in hot water. He'd had to bind Cully again in a sheet to accomplish the task, but she had quickly recovered her dignity.

Tom eyed Michael speculatively. "You're really getting into this, aren't you?"

Michael shrugged. "I enjoy it."

"Well, I better do my part then," Tom said. "Let's take a look at that wing."

On the phone the day before, Michael had explained to Tom that Cully's stiffness seemed to have eased a little in the last few days, but he was still concerned that the injury was bothering her.

"I can't feel anything obvious," Tom said.

"Watch this." Michael walked back into the clearing, unraveling the line tied to Cully's swivel as he went. His feet sank through fresh snow, halfway up his shin with each step. He went a good twenty yards more than she'd flown before, so that Tom would have a chance to observe her properly.

When he'd gone as far as the line allowed, he kept his body turned away from her—so that she wouldn't come too soon—and took the lure out of the bag at his side. He knew she was watching him, waiting for him to call her. The air was cold and quiet, and as he shifted position, he broke the crust on new snow, the sound like crumpled cellophane. His breath came in frozen clouds; the fingers on his unprotected hand were already numb from the cold. As always, he experienced a slight thrill of anticipation, a degree of nervous expectation. There was always the question of whether she would come when he called her, and on other occasions, when she had, he was always mildly surprised. He felt privileged. Today there was the added element of having a spectator. Michael's excitement was partly the feeling of showing off some treasured thing, like a child with a secret, but it was also the pleasure of sharing an experience that never failed to move him. If he wanted for anything, it was for this shar-ing—a very human trait, he'd thought. Something is added to the appreciation and wonder of beauty in this way.

Holding the lure in his gloved fist, he turned. Cully was fifty yards away, perched where he'd left her on the rail, standing square-footed, leaning toward him, her dark eyes fixed on his fist. Tom stood at the bottom of the porch looking on, muffled in his thick coat with his hands in his pockets. Michael raised his arm and called the falcon's name. Almost instantly her wings flicked open and she glided from the porch rail; then, with rapid beats, she was skimming across the snow toward him. He loved this moment, when he had a few seconds to admire her flight. He loved the feeling he got when she responded to his call, and though he knew she was coming for food, and that without this incentive she would probably have ignored him, he still had the sense of them working together. They were still bound in a common purpose, Cully choosing to cooperate from free will. She seemed much bigger in the air, and from this angle, with him looking down at her, her coloring appeared darker because of the way the gray tips of her wings and tail contrasted with the sharp white of the snow beneath her. She was fast, her wing strokes rapid, the whole shape of her flowing to an aerodynamic point across her head to the sharp beak. Her legs and feet were held up, tucked back beneath her tail, her eyes unerringly fixed on her target. As she left her perch, the bell attached to her leg made a small, clean sound as the tiny clapper dropped, then there was only the soft rush of air across her feathers. He hardly breathed, mesmerized by the sight of her.

There was an imperfection in her flight, however, and it was this that he wanted Tom Waters to see. Her injured wing appeared to flutter at the beginning and end of each stroke, and though she flew the distance to his fist in just a few seconds, the flaw was clearly visible. It made her passage slightly out of kilter, and the effect was to create a slight wobble. Ten feet away from him, Cully swept back her wings and rose, and as her tail fanned to act as a brake, she reached with her feet to grab for his fist. She stumbled, just slightly, flapping and scrabbling in an ungainly manner before she gained a hold. The impact knocked his arm back. She fixed her eye on his, then instinctively looked all around, mantling her wings protectively about her prize, checking for danger before bending to eat.

Michael allowed her to feed, then walked back toward the house with her perched on his fist.

"She's really something," Tom said.

"She is, isn't she," Michael said with pride. He stroked her breast with one finger. "Did you see what I meant about her wing?"

"It didn't seem too bad; it could still be residual stiffness. Don't forget that she's still out of condition."

Cully cleaned her beak, wiping it against the glove, then daintily picked scraps from between her toes. "You don't think it's serious, then?"

"I just don't think we need to worry too much about it yet," Tom said. "Give it a few more days, we'll see how she is. This kind of exercise is going to be good for her, it'll help get that muscle back in shape. How often do you fly her?"

"Five or six times a day, for small amounts."

"She seems to have got the hang of it."

"She's smart," Michael said.

"So what happens next?"

Michael held up the lure. "She has to learn to chase this for her food. It'll be a little harder for her than simply coming to the fist. She's going to have to really work for her reward. It's meant to simulate hunting."

"So the line has to come off for that, right?"

Michael nodded. The book Frank had lent him said that a falcon ought to be flying free to the fist within ten days, and chasing the lure within a few more. After that it was just a question of exercise and practice before a bird would be ready to hunt. The skills of the trainer and the disposition of the falcon made prediction difficult, but that point could be reached in anywhere from three to six weeks. Frank had told him to count on the high side of that estimate and not to rush anything.

Tom examined Cully's wing, quickly feeling along the damaged bone. "It still feels fine. Keep exercising her, but don't push it too hard. I'll come back in a week." Something in the woods caught his eye, and he looked beyond Michael to the edge of the clearing. "I see you have an audience," he observed.

Puzzled, Michael followed his look. In among the trees, half concealed though not hiding, was Jamie Baker. The boy was watching them wordlessly, his pale face peering out from the hood of his coat.

"It's the boy from next door," Michael said.

Tom raised a hand in greeting. "Hello, Jamie." He got no response. "How long has he been coming over here?"

"This is the first time, as far as I know."

They waited to see if Jamie would come closer. When he didn't, Michael called out to him that it was okay if he wanted to. "He's a strange kid," he commented when Jamie didn't move. "He never says a word."

Tom raised an eyebrow. "You've met him, then. How about his mother?"

"A couple of times," Michael said neutrally.

"The reason Jamie doesn't speak is that he can't. Or maybe he won't. His dad, Susan's husband, was a guy called Dave Baker. A year and a half ago he was killed in a hunting accident. He would have been around your age. Do you remember him?"

Michael didn't.

"Jamie hasn't spoken a word since it happened. Some kind of shock reaction, I hear. He's kind of a loner, too."

As they watched, Jamie turned around and melted back into the trees as if he knew they were discussing him, though he was too far away to have heard. Tom looked at his watch. "I guess he's got school today. And I better be going myself. Remember, keep up with the exercise, but don't push her too hard."

Michael walked Tom to his car. "I didn't ask how everything's going," Tom said. "Settling in okay?"

"As well as could be hoped."

Tom nodded. "Don't judge us all because of a few."

Michael watched him go and raised a hand. Then silence settled over the clearing again, except for the faint tone of Cully's bell as she shifted her feet.

FROM HIGH UP on the mountain across the river, Ellis watched the figures far below through his glasses. They were like tiny stick people moving about in a scene of white snow and tiny model trees surrounding the clearing, the house with a trail of painted smoke coming from the chimney. Except they were real; everything was real. The dark green Jeep that backed around and vanished into the trees emerged at the top of the track and turned toward town. He'd recognized Tom Waters; now he watched as outside the house the Somers guy went back to where he'd been standing before and the falcon flew to him from the porch rail the way he'd watched it do earlier. It was a long way off, but Ellis could see the way the line the bird had fixed to something around its legs smoothed a trail across the surface of the snow.

"Shit," he said under his breath and lowered his glasses. Without them he couldn't make out Somers except as a dark smudge and he couldn't see the falcon at all, but he'd seen enough anyway. He lit a cigarette and coughed, then turned and spat into the snow. His truck was a couple of miles away, where he'd left it at the start of Falls Pass Road. To get there he'd had to drive past the track that led down to Somers's house, and he'd been tempted to go on down and see what Somers had to say. On the other hand, there were a lot of stories going around about Somers. People said he'd shot a guy for screwing around with his wife, and then he'd tried to shoot her and their kid, too, only the cops had shot him instead. It sounded like a lot of bullshit, since Somers was supposed to have just got out of prison and this had happened only five or six years ago. If it was all true, wouldn't Somers have been inside for longer than that?

Whatever the case, Ellis had decided that first he'd find out if what he'd heard about the falcon was true. There was no point to him just charging down there and starting something that might get out of control. So he'd driven on a few miles, then left his truck, circled around the woods, and climbed up to the place where he was now sitting. The climb had been hard going and his chest was still wheezing from the effort, but at least he knew now that Somers really did have a falcon he was training. And Ellis knew it wasn't just any falcon. The question now, he thought, was what did he plan to do about it?

He was still turning it over in his mind when he got back to the lumberyard he ran on Creek Road. When he drove though the gate, he found the battered Honda that Rachel drove parked outside the old rail car he used as an office. This came as a surprise, since he couldn't remember the last time she'd been to the yard. He was transported back to a time when their children had been young and Rachel would come down most days to bring him lunch. The kids would play outside, chasing each other around the log piles, while inside Rachel did the accounts and they planned a bright future together.

She was sitting at his old desk when he went inside, huddled up inside her coat and looking at the invoices he'd written that month. Ellis paused. She looked up at him, her eyes dark and somber. She looked tired, he thought, the pallor of her face emphasizing faint smudges beneath her eyes. Despite that, her skin was still smooth and, for a woman in her thirties, unlined. Even now he was struck by how beautiful she looked, and still after all their years together he experienced a faint echo of surprise that they were married.

"Hey," he said. He went over to the potbelly in the corner and threw another log inside, raking up the embers to get some flames going.

"Where were you?"

"I had to see somebody about lumber they might want to order," he lied. He knew that wasn't what she meant, and he didn't even know why he'd said it, except that he hoped it might divert her.

"I was talking about last night. You didn't come home," she added needlessly, as if to make sure he wouldn't try to avoid the subject.

"I was here," he said, sitting down heavily. He saw the disbelieving way she was looking at him and threw out his hands. "Where the hell else would I be?"

"You tell me." She waited for him to explain, and in the silence he took off his boots and massaged his toes. He avoided looking at her. Rachel had this way of just dragging something out when she wanted to, and she knew him well enough to know how to make him squirm. He couldn't stand the pressure of her silence. Sometimes he wished she was the kind of woman who would just yell and throw things and then maybe that would clear the air, but instead she had the knack of making him feel as if he were weighed down with a burden of guilt. That was a lot worse.

"Listen, I just got drunk, if you want to know," he said, snapping at her because he wished she would say something. He reached out with a foot and kicked over the trash basket; an empty bottle of Wild Turkey rolled across the floor.

They'd had a fight the day before, and in the middle of it he'd gone outside and slammed the door behind him. It had been brewing for weeks, and the knowledge it was coming had made him ill-tempered. A letter had arrived from the bank saying they'd missed a mortgage payment on the house, on top of being two hundred bucks overdrawn against their limit. He knew she'd already been in there just a couple of days before to smooth things over, and now there was this. She'd waited until the kids had left the house and then she'd showed it to him and hadn't said a damn word, but her face had been grim.

"Dammit!" he'd shouted, gripping the edge of the table. Overcome with rage, he had lifted it up and slammed it hard against the floor. It had scared the hell out of her, and she'd jumped away from him.

The look on her face had made him feel worse. He didn't even know why exactly, except it was the same look of apprehension his mother had worn most of her life, especially when his old man was drunk or just in a mean mood—which was most of the time. Ellis had started throwing stuff around and shouting that she ought to stop nagging the hell out of him, and Rachel had shrunk away into the corner. This was a first. She was the strongest woman he'd ever known. She had kept the family together over the last few years and he knew it, but seeing her like that had confused him. In a way it felt good, like a surge of something from his balls right up through his head, but at the same time he'd known it wasn't a good thing, this feeling. Maybe that was why he hadn't gone home.

The bottle rolled into a corner, where it made a flat clunking sound against the wall.

Then there was silence, dragging on. Rachel said nothing, just watched him. He got up and went to put another log on the fire, which had caught now and was emitting a feeble heat.

"You been here long?" he said.

She shook her head, then brushed a strand of hair from her forehead. She still looked great after two kids. She was thirty-three, but when she was dressed up, she could pass for a lot younger. He tried to recall the last time he'd seen her in a dress instead of Levi's. When had they last gone out together somewhere, just the two of them? He couldn't think when. It had been a long time ago.

"So what about the order?"

He looked at her, uncomprehending. "What order?"

"You said you went to see somebody."

"Oh yeah. He said maybe next month."

He waited for her to ask him who it was. He knew he'd have to lie, and he started to try and come up with a name. For some reason Michael Somers's name sprung to mind, and he thought, wouldn't it be funny if he said that's who he'd been to see? It had a kind of roundness to it when he considered it. If it wasn't for Somers, he wouldn't be having this fucking conversation. He knew it was Somers who'd stopped him from shooting that falcon the day he'd skirted through the woods, scaring it away from the damn rock where he could have picked it off nice and clean. He didn't understand how it came to be that Somers had been on the mountain again a few days later, when he had finally shot it, but somehow it'd been him all right. Now Somers had his falcon. It was like stealing, as if Somers had taken two thousand bucks right out of his hand.

Rachel didn't ask who he'd been to see, which surprised him until he saw she already knew he was lying, that there was no order.

She flicked through the slips of paper on the desk. "Things are pretty slow," she said.

A dull fire burned in him. He didn't know what it was. She wasn't nagging him the way he knew some women would. She was just stating a fact, inviting him to talk. In one part of his mind he understood that, but in another it was too much to bear.

"Things are gonna pick up," he told her. "This is just a bad patch. There's a lot coming in soon. I've been seeing a lot of people."

He listened to himself, and it was like hearing somebody else talk, running off a lot of stuff they both knew was bullshit.

"Oh God, Pete," Rachel said.

Her voice sounded so weary and mournful and it stopped him. It was a sound he wasn't used to hearing. She was watching him out of those big gray eyes of hers and she wasn't even angry anymore, just sad. She looked so goddam beautiful. It made him think of how things had once been, but that was all a long time ago.

"What are we going to do?" she said.

14 A WEEK HAD PASSED SINCE TOM WATERS HAD come by to take a look at Cully's wing. It was mid-March, and winter continued without letup. Snow fell most days, and the temperature at night dropped to a frigid ten below. Cully was flying to Michael's fist four times a day, fifty yards without hesitation, but the line was still attached. One evening, Michael called Frank for advice.

"I feel like she's ready to fly free, without the line," he explained.

"From what you've told me, that sounds about right," Frank agreed. "As a matter of fact, I'd say she's been ready for about a week. So what's the problem?"

The problem, Michael thought, was that he was afraid to take the step. Over and over he'd read the section in the book Frank had lent him that covered this part. "If training has proceeded as described, your falcon is now ready to fly free. On the chosen day, don't vary the routine: Be sure to check carefully that she is sharp set, and then take off that line." That was it, nothing more. Michael thought it must have been a long time since the author had free-flown a falcon of his own for the first time, since he made no mention of the sinking feeling Michael felt every time he contemplated the move.

"I guess I still feel a little like that myself sometimes," Frank admitted after Michael had explained the problem. "By the time you get around to that point, you've spent a lot of time worrying about your bird, making sure she gets just the right kind of food and the right amount, making sure she's got somewhere dry and safe to sleep.

You watch her and worry she might have caught some kind of bird flu every time she sneezes, you mend her feathers for her if they get busted or twisted, you treat her like your whole world revolves around her—and then one day you have to take her line off and you know she could just take off and not come back. There'd be nothing you could do, and it would all have been for nothing."

"That sounds like a fair summary," Michael agreed.

"How's her weight?" Frank asked.

"Bang on three and a half pounds. An ounce over that and she's not quite so keen, sometimes she gets distracted. More than a few ounces and she's barely interested. I could stand and call her all day, and I think she'd just stand on the porch rail preening herself and watching clouds float past."

Frank chuckled. "I know the feeling. Do you weigh her at the same time each day?"

"First thing. I note it down, then I weigh out the day's food and note that. Everything by the book."

"Sounds to me like you know she's ready. You just have to take the plunge."

"I know. But I worry she'll just take off. It's not just that I don't want to lose her, though that is a big part of it, it's also that I doubt she could survive. With her wing the way it is, I'm certain she wouldn't last out there on her own."

There was a short silence before Frank answered. "Thing you have to remember is, between bird and man the relationship is a little one-sided," he said. "I understand how you feel about her. We get emotionally involved, we can't but help it, it's just the way we are. But a falcon isn't like a dog, they aren't going to love us back. Maybe that's partly why we like them so much. They'll respect us if we respect them and they'll stay with us because it's easier to do that than hunt their own food, but sometimes you fly them and they decide not to come back and that's it. There really is nothing you can do about it. My guess is that Cully won't take off. She knows she's injured, and she knows getting food from you is easier than hunting her own. These birds aren't stupid, you can believe that. I think you just have to trust that."

"You're right, I know," Michael said. "It's just about food, I understand that. For her, anyway."

"You'd like it to be more than that, I know, and maybe it is. I've always liked to think that there's more to it than that with the birds I've trained over the years. Until one of 'em decides to sit in a tree all day and ignore everything I can think of to try and get her down. The thing is, that's what's so special. The fact that she's a wild bird, and she'll only come back if she *chooses* to. Sure, if she's not hungry, she'll get distracted and you can lose her that way, but that isn't the real reason. Food just keeps her focused. In the end, it's her choice. Sooner or later, you just have to let her make it, and then every day you fly her, she gets to choose again. It's just the way it is."

There was nothing else to say after that. Michael knew that Frank was right, and that he just had to make the decision. By the morning, he'd found his resolve. He put Cully on the scales as normal and weighed her, noting that she was at exactly her flying weight; then he took her up on his fist and exchanged her leash for the creance, which he'd read was the term for the line he flew her on. While she roused her feathers and picked at the rail between her toes, he weighed out half her normal ration. He'd decided that this was the last day he'd use the line, and he wanted her especially hungry for the following day, something he was sure she wouldn't appreciate.

"Sorry, Cully, just a little insurance," he murmured.

Taking up his glove, he glanced toward the trees at the edge of the clearing and then checked his watch. He was a little earlier than usual, which explained why there was no sign of Jamie. Ever since that first time the boy had appeared, he'd been back again morning and afternoon, watching Cully's training from the cover of the woods. At first, Michael hadn't been sure he liked the idea, afraid that the boy might do something to scare Cully or else start to make a nuisance of himself, but neither had turned out to be the case. In fact, he never came out from the trees, made a sound, or moved a muscle. Michael had begun to be curious about him, had even spoken once or twice, trying to get Jamie to step out into the open, but the boy had stubbornly held back, leaving as silently as he arrived. In a way, Michael had to admit, he quite liked the idea of having somebody share the experience of seeing Cully fly, even if it was a ten-year-old boy who never spoke a word.

Leaving Cully on the porch rail, he went inside the house and poured a half cup of coffee. While he drank it, his eye fell to Frank's copy of *The Goshawk*. On impulse, he took it outside and wedged it into a low crook of the tree where Jamie normally stood. He had no idea if the boy liked to read, and he was sure the book was a little old for him, but if he didn't want to take it, he didn't have to. Going back to Cully, he fed her a tiny shred of meat, just to get her attention. She grabbed it eagerly, her plumage flattening, her demeanor altering instantly. She was all business now, her eye never leaving him, her talons gripping the rail tightly as she leaned forward. Michael started back into the clearing; when he turned, Jamie was there.

"I left something for you I thought you might like to have a look at," he said casually. "It's by your shoulder in the tree."

While Michael took the lure from his bag and unraveled the line, he watched Jamie from the corner of his eye. Though the boy glanced at the book, he made no move to take it. "Somebody lent it to me," Michael said. "It's about a man in England who trained a hawk. You can borrow it if you like. It's up to you." He finished preparing the line, then added, for Jamie's benefit: "If you were planning on coming over after school today, I won't be flying Cully again until the morning, okay?" He got no response, and shrugged.

It was still early and the sky was cloudless, a pale winter blue. Cully shifted restlessly on the rail while she waited. She fanned her wings, holding them half open to catch the sun on her back. When he raised his fist, she flicked her wings, and in an instant she was coming toward him, the line trailing across the frozen snow behind her. She swooped up and grabbed the glove with a quick ungainly flap, stumbled, and began to feed. Michael turned to Jamie, but the boy had gone, and with him the book.

Michael spent his days working at the store. He'd drawn up a list of the materials he was going to need to fix the place up and worked out a budget he thought he could just about stick to. The power had been restored, and he re-covered the windows with newspaper so that he could work without having passersby stare in at him. Cully stood on a perch he'd rigged up in one of the back rooms so that she didn't have to breathe the dust he stirred up as he worked.

During the first week, he pulled the old fixtures apart using a heavy claw hammer and dragged the pieces out back, where there was a small service yard. Then he attacked the old counter, ripping off the front to expose the dusty plywood shelves underneath where once there had been containers of screws and bolts, brass hinges, and all kinds of assorted inventory that wouldn't fit on the displays. He'd brought in an old heater from the house; it did an inadequate job of raising the temperature, but with all the physical work he was doing, he was sweating after an hour. It was good to be busy. With the store and Cully to occupy himself, he had little time to dwell on the thoughts and memories beneath the surface of his conscious mind, though sometimes he wondered what he thought he might sell in the store once he had it finished. He worked hard, and at the house in the evenings he'd cook himself a simple meal and read for a while. He was in bed early, too tired to think.

One night he woke suddenly, an image of Holly and Louise still fresh in his mind. He had no pictures of his daughter beyond one he had of her as a baby, and in a pool of yellow light from the lamp by his bed he took it from his wallet and studied her features, trying to imagine what she looked like now. He remembered her hand clutching his, how tiny it had been, but perfectly formed, every detail there in miniature. In the last months, before things had all gone so terribly wrong, she had been crawling and just starting to haul herself up against the furniture. When he'd come home at night, her face would beam and she'd try to say "Daddy." Until then he'd never really noticed a child's smile, the way it was like a powerful light shining from inside, the way it was an expression of the purest delight, unblemished by subterfuge or tiredness from a day at the office or bad news on the TV. It was just a smile. He kept busy to prevent himself remembering, though Holly and Louise lingered like dim regretful ghosts at the edge of his vision. He'd trained himself over the years not to wish for the impossible; otherwise, he was sure he would have fallen into the deep abyss of madness he'd once felt beckon so tantalizingly. He wondered if his daughter remembered him, wondering what Louise had told her when she was old enough to understand. When she'd spoken to him on the phone after the trial and told him she was leaving, he'd agreed it would be best for Holly not to see him or hear from him for a while, and later he'd written to say he couldn't see any future in changing that. He'd received no answer, which he'd always been unsure how to interpret. The only letter he'd had after that had told him Louise was getting married again.

Padding downstairs in the dark, he went to the phone and called international information.

"Boston," he said when the operator asked which city. "Peterson, Dr. Paul. I don't know the address."

He waited for a moment while the woman keyed in his request. His heart was thumping, and he didn't know if this was because he was nervous the number would be found, or because he was nervous it wouldn't.

"Hold for your number, caller."

He wrote it down, and after he'd hung up, he thought that all he had to do was call and somewhere in a house across the miles the phone would be picked up and it might be his daughter. He had no idea what he would say. After a while he folded the piece of paper he'd written on and went upstairs.

He paused on the landing by the door to his mother's room, then opened it and stepped inside. As if he'd been holding his breath, he exhaled, and a memory filtered back into his mind.

How old had he been when he first understood the currents of uncertainty and recrimination that swirled around him in this house? He thought he must have been about seven years old. What was distinct was waking in the night feeling thirsty and going down the stairs in his pajamas. The light was on in the passage on the way to the kitchen, and the door to the living room was slightly ajar as he passed. He stopped to listen to voices irritably batting back and forth. He could remember his dad's deep mellow tones, surprising for a man who wasn't physically large. He was thin all his life; no matter what he ate, he just burned it up. His mother was thin, too, and she moved about the house in flowing dresses looking pale. Now, thinking of her, he likened her to a fainting southern belle, pining and making herself ill. It wasn't her looks—she had sharp angular features and deep hooded eyes, lacking the appropriate softness—but she had that false frailty.

That night he'd stopped by the door and heard his mother say, "He's a child and he's our responsibility. We have to do what's right for Michael."

She spoke in a clipped tone, snipping off the ends of words like dead flowers, but underneath it there was a quiver of desperation. It was hearing his name that had struck him most.

"Who says this is right? That's what I want to know." His dad's voice, not raised but with a kind of weary patience. It was also blurry at the edges, like words on blotting paper, a sign he'd been in his den drinking.

"I don't know how you could even think it," his mother had said, her voice rising with a slight hysterical edge. "He's your son."

There was a real import to the way she had said this last piece, which he didn't understand except to realize that somehow his dad was planning something that affected him. That was the implication.

"You think this is doing him any good?" his dad had said.

"You'd have him grow up without a father?"

"Did I say that?"

"And what about me? How would I manage? You know I'm not strong. Did you ever think of that, or do you only care about yourself?"

It was a strange argument, a lot of questions thrown like daggers back and forth, nobody ever answering. He understood that the conversation was about him, and it seemed that his mother was trying to protect him.

"This is getting us nowhere," his dad had said impatiently.

Footsteps had approached the door, and Michael had scooted to the kitchen, where he'd waited until it was quiet, then crept back toward his bedroom. On his way past the living room door he'd heard his mother crying, and farther on, a bar of light spilled out from beneath the closed door of the den. He'd gone to bed troubled by it all.

Sometime after that—whether it was days or weeks he didn't know—his mother had told him quietly, whispering it like a secret and making him swear not to say anything, that she'd stopped his father from leaving them.

"He doesn't want us anymore," she'd said.

Even then he'd known his parents didn't get on, but it still came as a blow that his dad should want to leave. He remembered feeling something like shock, and after that there was a seed of doubt in him that undermined everything. His mother turned out to be a diligent gardener, and every day she watered what she'd planted. She complained of his dad's drinking and how he didn't really love either of them, and most of all she never let Michael forget that she'd stopped his dad when he had wanted to abandon them.

"We have to be nice to him or he'll leave us," she used to say. "Especially you, Michael. You have to be nice to him or he'll go away forever."

As he grew up, it became like a conspiracy between him and his mother. They stuck together, united against his father, and to please her, he did as she asked. By the time he realized that she was sick, something that was a gradual unfolding rather than any kind of sudden illumination, his feelings toward both his parents were a mess of contradictions. Some things, he thought, don't easily go away.

Memories whispered in his mind and faded until there was just the quiet empty room. Michael closed the door behind him and went back to his bed.

IN THE MORNING, Jamie was waiting in the trees when Michael brought Cully out. He weighed her, and noted her down at three and a half pounds on the button. When he offered a tiny shred of meat, she lunged forward to seize it with such haste that she had to use her wings to keep balance. He took Cully on his fist and walked over toward the woods, and as he got closer, Jamie took a step back. Michael stopped.

"It's okay." He stroked Cully's breast, at which she arched her neck indignantly, while Jamie looked on warily. "She doesn't like me doing this," Michael explained. "See, she's annoyed. It's because she's hungry and she wants me to get on with it."

He was thinking that this could be the last time she stood on his fist like this, that in a few minutes she might rise over the trees and fly from sight while he watched helplessly. He knew she wasn't strong enough to catch her own food, and the idea that she might starve to death rather than remain here terrified him. He recalled, however, what Frank had told him: that it had to be her choice, that until this point Cully had essentially been his captive. The time for delay was past, and in preparation he took a deep breath and exhaled slowly to quiet his fiercely beating heart.

To Jamie he said, "I'm going to fly her without the line today. Don't do anything to startle her. Just stay where you are."

There was a flicker of understanding and apprehension in Jamie's expression, as if he knew what was at risk here. Michael wondered how much of *The Goshawk* Jamie had read. T. H. White had described very well the risk of flying a bird free and how the prospect of losing his own hawk had felt. Michael started back toward the house, removing Cully's leash and swivel, then unthreading her jesses as he went. She examined her legs and feet and bit testingly at her

leather anklets when he lowered his fist to the rail to let her step
on. She faced the house, then turned around and roused her feathers.
Her eyes, glistening black and eager, were fixed on him; then she
looked curiously at her legs as if she understood that now she was
free. Her bell issued its clear tone across the snow, a tiny but distinct
note that carried in the still air. If she flicked open her wings and
soared away now, he knew he would spend the next days and perhaps
weeks scouring the mountains, listening for the tone of that bell,
hoping to find her alive and coax her back.

He began to walk away, his throat tight from fear of losing her.
His feet crunched in the snow, sank and lifted, crunched again. His
breathing seemed loud in his ears, clouds issuing before him. From
his spot in the trees Jamie looked on, shoulders hunched and rigid,
sharing the tension. Michael met the boy's eye briefly and tried to
smile encouragingly, though he doubted it came across that way.
Jamie's look flicked back toward Cully as her bell sounded again. For
a moment Michael was afraid she'd left the rail, but he thought that
if she had, he would have read it in Jamie's expression. He was
grateful then for the boy's presence. He didn't want to look back and
make her come too soon, before he was ready. He felt for the lure,
keeping it hidden from her in front of his body.

At fifty yards he turned, the lure in his fist, and raised his arm.

"Cully," he called. His voice sounded strangely hoarse. His throat
was dry, and he called again.

Ordinarily she would have left the railing as his fist rose, but now
she hesitated. She felt something different, sensing currents of tension. She looked skyward at a crow that flapped like an ungainly
black doll above the trees, and its call seemed to mock her. She felt
an impulse to rise, and knew suddenly that she could do so unre-
strained. Then she flicked open her wings, and in a quick movement
she was in the air.

In the half second before she responded, Michael knew that if she
left now it would affect him more deeply than he'd admitted. He
was bound up with her in ways he didn't understand except that it
was beyond its mere outward appearance. She had given his days a
purpose when otherwise he might by now have abandoned this house
and the town and all the bitter memories they held for him. A part
of him felt with her the tug of the wide sky, the inexorable pull of
the mountains beyond the river, the high wide-open spaces where

the snow lay undisturbed by human tracks. In the same instant he held his breath and willed her to come. She left the rail, her eye fixed on his fist as she swooped low and skimmed above the ground, and he knew with a massive rush of relief that she had made her choice. She rose and reached for his fist, landing with force, knocking his arm backward. He felt the tightening of her talons through the glove; then she settled, her wings held slightly open, quivering, her gaze fixed on his face, a captive no longer.

Relief flooded over him, and a feeling that made him want to shout out at the top of his voice. Cully bent to eat, and when he looked across to Jamie, they grinned at each other.

15 BUSINESS WAS SLOW, BUT WITH SPRING NOT too far around the corner, Susan was preparing for the busy period. She was working on her advertising for a monthly real-estate magazine that covered an area around Williams Lake that took in Little River Bend. Susan always took a page, though the magazine was a full-color glossy affair and was costly enough that she'd worked out that at best she broke even in terms of the revenue it created for her business. But she had other reasons for maintaining her presence: Keeping a high profile discouraged Realty World and the other networks from opening a branch in town. She knew that some of them had considered it over the years and probably concluded there wasn't enough business to support two firms, but if they ever thought she was getting lax in her marketing and they could see an opening, she was sure things could change. This was "strategic marketing," a term she liked because it made her feel that she was using the skills she'd learned years ago and wasn't just puttering around in some small-town backwater.

When she and David had moved to Little River, the business had been her lifeline. Without it she wasn't sure she could have made the transition from the ebb and flow of the city. Since he'd died, it was the business that had kept her sane, given her focus instead of allowing her mind to drift inward.

She scanned into her computer the last of the house shots she was using this month and typed up the accompanying text. She was using a desktop publishing program that allowed her to prepare her page, complete with images, description, and her company banner, then send the complete file electronically via modem to the magazine publisher, who then organized the final compilation for the printer. Though she wasn't a techno geek, she liked the control technology had given her over certain aspects of her business. She liked that she could mess around on screen with the presentation of her ads, trying out different ideas without having to explain to somebody else what she wanted and then hope they understood. When she finished preparing her page, she was pleased with the result. What she tried to achieve was a look that set her apart from the other advertisers, something that caught the eye. She thought it must work, because other agencies weren't above imitating her ideas. It was annoying, but it was also flattering.

Once she'd dialed into the publisher's system and sent off her work, she checked the time and closed up the office. The bus was just pulling in as she reached the stop, and in a moment Jamie stepped down from the bus and looked around for her. She waved out the window and watched him as he came toward her. These last few days, there was something different about him, she decided. It struck her now as he sauntered toward her with his bag thrown over his shoulder. It wasn't anything dramatic—just a spring in his step, maybe, a different light in his eye. She had a pretty good idea it had everything to do with Michael Somers's falcon. She knew Jamie had been going over there, though exactly what he was doing she wasn't sure.

"Hi," she said as he got in, throwing his bag on the floor. "Good day?" He shrugged and smiled. "How about hot dogs for dinner?" She knew he never turned down that kind of suggestion, and just for a treat she decided that maybe she would join him. The hell with watching her diet for one day.

At home, Jamie got out and ran inside. A few minutes later, she heard him running down the stairs. She caught up with him at the door.

"Hey, slow down there a second." She grabbed his shoulder. "Listen, you're not getting in the way of anything over there, are you?" He shook his head. "You're sure? Well, what goes on over there, anyway?"

Jamie looked at the door and then back at her impatiently, and she knew he wanted to get going. It occurred to her that she could just play dumb, keep him there while she asked him questions. Maybe he'd get frustrated and forget himself. She decided she would be wasting her time; he would know what she was doing. "Okay, okay," she said, standing back so he could get out. Bob came through from the kitchen, wagging his tail expectantly.

"Can't you take Bob with you?" she called out, but he paused and shook his head. "But you'll take him out later, right?" She held Bob's collar while Jamie ran off through the trees, and stood watching even after he'd gone from her sight, wondering again what he was doing over there.

Closing the door, Susan went upstairs to change. Out her bedroom window she could see the roof of the house across the other side of the trees. A tiny nagging worry about Jamie being over there tugged at a corner of her mind. She was sure there was nothing for her to be concerned about, but all the same, maybe she ought to just go over and at least make sure that Michael didn't mind Jamie being there. She hesitated, reluctant in case she might give the impression that she was checking up—which she definitely wasn't. On the other hand, what harm could it do? It was a natural enough concern for any parent. So why did she feel uncertain?

She went into Jamie's room and started picking up clothes he'd thrown on the floor. Under a T-shirt on his bed was a paperback book with a drawing of some kind of hawk on the cover; she picked it up and flicked through it. She guessed where it must have come from, and reading through a page here and there she was surprised that Jamie would read it. The style of writing was restrained and almost poetic in places, in a slightly dated, mannered fashion. Not the kind of thing somebody who plays Doom Raider might want to spend time over, especially at the age of ten. She also found a sketch pad filled with pencil drawings of what was obviously a falcon in flight. Intrigued, Susan flipped through the pages; then, reaching a decision, she went downstairs and pulled on her boots and coat.

She made her way carefully through the woods, trying not to make a sound, her steps largely muffled by the snow. She spotted Jamie from fifty yards back, standing just inside the trees with his back to her. Making her way around him, she found a place beside a pair of cottonwoods at the far end of the clearing where she could watch what was going on without being seen herself. Jamie hadn't moved; she could see the blue and red flash of his jacket; his face was turned away, watching what was happening at the other end of the clearing.

Michael was on the porch, wearing jeans and a dark coat. He changed position, and she saw the flick of wings as his falcon stepped onto his fist from what appeared to be an old-fashioned set of scales. For a moment he stood there, the open doorway of the house behind him, stroking the falcon's breast. Then, looking across the clearing, he raised his hand in a quick gesture of greeting. Susan pressed herself against the trunk of the cottonwood, afraid that she would be seen, imagining how he might interpret her sneaking around the woods to spy on him. Just as she'd moved, she thought she saw Jamie acknowledge Michael's greeting, maybe with a half-returned wave of his own, but when she looked again, he remained in the same spot.

The sound of her own breathing seemed loud, emphasizing the quiet. Her nose was so cold it had become numb, and her legs and feet were slowly turning to ice, but she resisted the temptation to move. After a short time she forgot about her discomfort. There was something oddly touching about the scene she was witnessing. It had to do with the distance Jamie kept. Despite his obvious fascination, his eyes glued to what was going on, he moved no closer. Michael went about his own routine, involving Jamie just by his greeting but accepting his reserve. There was a calmness to the unfolding scene, a kind of natural rhythm presided over by the beautiful pale falcon.

Michael lowered his fist, and with another flick of her wings the falcon stepped onto the porch rail. Leaving her there, Michael began walking toward Susan across the open snow, though his attention was focused on what he was doing with the bag at his side, taking something from it. When he was abreast of Jamie, he paused and said something to him, though Susan couldn't hear what it was. Then he walked on, his feet crunching through the surface of the snow, his breath clouding before him. Back on the porch rail the falcon waited, watching Michael intently.

Susan shivered as a breeze touched the back of her neck. Overhead, the sky was leaden, the cloud base low, shrouding the tops of the mountains. The old house stood back across the clearing, snow on the roof, the porch steps sagging a little, no longer appearing abandoned but still a little forlorn. In the clearing, Michael stopped. He was close enough that she could make out his features clearly. If he looked directly at her, he'd see her, but she couldn't make herself move out of sight behind the tree trunk. She wanted to see everything that happened, intrigued not just by the sight of this man training a wild falcon but by some other quality in this quiet, unhurried ritual. What fascinated her, she decided, was the relationship that existed among bird, man, and boy, something she felt but couldn't articulate. Michael appeared different when she looked at him, his expression smooth, unlined, his eyes unguarded, and even from this distance she could see that Jamie, too, was somehow changed.

This is all there is for them right now, she saw. Nothing else existed for them. That's what it was.

Michael raised his arm and called to Cully. The falcon left the rail and flew across the snow, wing tips almost brushing the snow, barely making a sound, moving fast. Then, when she was several yards away, she swooped up dramatically with her tail spread wide and her feet reaching out for the glove.

Susan smiled to herself, then backed away through the trees and turned toward her house.

LINDA KOWALSKI CLIPPED an order above the grill where her husband could see it. "This guy's in a hurry, Pete," she said.

Pete glanced up and flipped hamburgers on the grill. The diner was quiet, but it would start to fill up in fifteen minutes or so as the lunch trade filtered in. Linda poured two cups of coffee and sat down, lighting a cigarette as she did.

"May as well take a break while I can," she said to Susan. "You and Coop haven't forgotten about tonight, have you?"

Susan came to, distracted, then smiled. "Dinner at eight. We'll be there. Do you want me to bring anything?"

"It's all under control. Maybe some wine."

"Wine it is," Susan said.

She could have had coffee in her office, but when things were quiet, she liked to sit and talk, keeping half an eye on her office from her stool at the counter. It was one of the things she enjoyed about her life. Sometimes she tried to picture herself back in Vancouver, wearing a business suit, working long hours, perhaps becoming ruthless from necessity. It had been David's idea to leave the city, and he'd brought her up here for a weekend to persuade her to give it a try. She could picture it now, his eager, grinning expression as he'd asked her what she thought, and how she'd had to admit it was a pretty spot.

"Okay," she'd said, "but on one condition. We give it six months. If it doesn't work out, we're out of here. And I get to start my own business. Deal?"

"Deal," he'd said, then winked at Jamie in the backseat.

That had been five years ago. She'd been twenty-eight then, Jamie almost five. David had brought her to his hometown in spring, when the snow was gone from all but the high ground and the meadows along the river were lit with sparks of yellow and red from the wildflowers that grew there. She'd felt an enormous trepidation about living in a small town again. Little River reminded her of the place she'd grown up. All her life she'd dreamed of traveling, living in exotic cities, forging some kind of career. The career part had been a vague ambition, more about achieving independence for herself instead of becoming like her mother, who'd never worked after she married Susan's father. He'd been a slave to the company he'd worked for most of his adult life, only to be made redundant in his middle fifties. After that, both her parents had seemed consigned to a kind of helpless bewildered existence, their lives without direction, neither of them with a clue as to what they ought to do about it.

She'd done the traveling, or at least some of it, mostly in Europe in her late teens; then she'd come back to a job in Vancouver with a real-estate company, meaning to get qualified and then travel again. Sometimes plans go awry, as they had for her when she'd met David. He'd relentlessly pursued her until she just didn't have any resistance left. Getting married at twenty-two had never been part of her plan, even less that she would have a child a year later, but both had happened anyway. The pregnancy had been a mistake, but she'd never contemplated an abortion. When Jamie was born, they were suddenly a family, which had both pleased and mystified her.

She'd continued working while David had started out in an architectural firm, and they'd agreed they wouldn't have another child until their careers were settled. She lived a frenetic existence, trying to juggle work and Jamie so that both got the attention they needed. She'd been determined to hang on to her career, but now she remembered being exhausted much of the time. She'd sometimes envied mothers who did more than feed and bathe and take life at a constant run, mothers who had time with their kids. She would drop Jamie at his child-care group and experience pangs of guilt and longing, wondering what it would be like to have the time to sit in a park on a summer's day and watch him play. David had said they could manage without the money she made, but it wasn't just about money.

When she'd begun to sense that David wasn't happy in his job, she'd waited for what she knew was coming with a mixture of relief and fear. It had been tempting at times to surrender herself to his desires, to remove the burden of decision from herself. He'd always been uncomfortable in the city, trying to fit in when he still lived with a different internal rhythm. His had more to do with the sky and the trees in the changing seasons than the morning snarl of traffic and late-afternoon meetings, a life where the ambitious vied for recognition and didn't get home until late.

When David had finally told her he wanted to move, she asked herself if she was really happy. There had always been an undercurrent of doubt. She'd wondered if she was missing out on something, and in arguments she'd blamed David for changing her whole life. She'd told him she'd never wanted to get married and that he should have just left her alone, and then she'd felt guilty when she saw that he wondered if she really meant it.

She was cool but unsurprised about his desire to leave the city, and when he'd brought her to Little River, his tales of growing up there had depressed her initially, because they reminded her of her own upbringing. But she'd hidden that and allowed herself to be swayed by his picture of Jamie growing up by the river in the house they'd found.

"You must have *some* good memories about where you were born?" he'd said.

She'd had to concede that was true. She'd recalled herself and her friends roaming woods and hills as kids, and admitted that video parlors and shopping malls might not be such a good substitute.

"Imagine it," David had enthused.

He would have his business, designing barns and houses. ("Barns?" she'd said.) She would start a real-estate firm of her own, but she'd arrange things so she'd spend more time with Jamie and they would all take regular trips to the city. She'd found herself wondering if this wasn't what she'd wanted after all, and if her moments of unhappy doubt were simply a reluctance to admit it.

So they had moved, and almost to her surprise it had worked out. David had been happier, and he'd wanted her to be happy, too. Astutely, he'd known there wasn't anything he could do about the deficiencies of living in the country, so instead he'd concentrated on making sure she felt loved. He brought her flowers; they went for walks and he held her hand, told her she was beautiful. It worked, and even though she knew what was going on, she also knew he meant it, and they laughed about it and he never stopped doing those things. Then, three and a half years later, David had died. A year and a half after that, she was still there.

Her marriage hadn't been idyllic, but she'd loved him, never really knowing how much until she saw Coop's face that day as he climbed out of his car, not meeting her eye, and knew in advance what he was going to tell her. Sometimes, though, it seemed a long time ago.

"So, how's your neighbor?"

Linda's question penetrated her thoughts, and Susan looked up from the coffee she'd been stirring idly, creating swirls of motion in her cup. She followed Linda's look, and through the window she could see the store with the papered-over windows and Michael Somers's dark blue Nissan outside.

"He's got everybody talking about what he's doing over there," Linda said.

"Did you know him when he lived here before?" Susan asked.

"Not really. I remember him, but that's not the same, is it? He was quiet, I think. I remember his parents better—especially his dad, because he still ran the store until he died about ten or twelve years ago. He was a nice guy. His mother was a little strange, I think."

"In what way?"

"She didn't come into town much. She was always sick or something," Linda said.

After following Jamie a couple of days earlier, Susan had decided to find out for herself the truth about Michael. She'd had to drive all the way to Prince George, where in the library she'd sat viewing microfilm of the Toronto papers from nearly seven years ago, and now she knew the facts of what had happened. The things people said about what he'd done were misinformed at best, malicious at worst. All the same, he *had* shot somebody, apparently meaning to kill him. His defense had claimed temporary insanity, though the jury had rejected the argument.

"Jamie's been going over there to watch him train his falcon," Susan said. "Every morning, and again when he gets back from school."

Linda looked surprised. "Jamie is?"

Susan looked back across the street and pursed her lips in thought. "Do you think I ought to be concerned about that?"

"What do you think?"

"I see Jamie's face when he comes back, how excited he looks." She paused. "No, I don't think I should be concerned."

"Then don't be. You don't have to feel bad about that. What does Coop think?"

"Coop?"

"He does know, doesn't he?"

He didn't know. Susan was struck by the fact that Linda automatically assumed she would have expressed her feelings to him, sought his opinion, and then she wondered why she hadn't. He was a friend and he was a cop; who better to talk to?

She felt Linda watching her. "I have to go," she said, finishing her coffee and sliding off her stool. "See you tonight."

As she left, Linda's thoughtful gaze followed her out the door.

Across the street, she hesitated, then turned and walked to the door of the old Somers hardware store. From inside, she could hear the sound of hammering. She knocked when the hammering paused, and a moment later Michael opened the door and stood blinking in the light. Beyond him she could see wooden debris littering the floor, the light angling inside capturing dust in the air. He regarded her with a faint questioning look.

"Hi, I was just passing," she said. "I thought I'd stop by." It sounded lame, but she couldn't think what else to say. "Can I come in?"

He stood aside and let her through the door, swept an arm to indicate the disarray. "It's kind of a mess."

They faced each other a little awkwardly. There was nowhere for them to sit, not even a counter to position themselves beside; the remains of it lay broken on the floor, parts of the top laid against the wall.

"How's it going?" she asked.

He ran a hand through his hair. He looked tired, she thought, studying his face as he looked around. He appeared a little bemused by all the wreckage, the lines at the corners of his eyes crinkling.

"Okay, I think. I'm afraid I can't offer you anything." He made a small gesture with his hand. "I'm sort of not set up for visitors yet."

"That's okay. Actually, I wanted to thank you. I know Jamie's been coming over to your place this last week or so."

"Thank me?"

"For tolerating him. He's not in the way, I hope."

"He just watches me train Cully." Michael hesitated, then added with a faint note of wariness: "He just stands in the woods."

She thought she detected uncertainty, as if he wasn't sure of her motive. "He's not very good with people," she said quickly.

He nodded. "Well, he's no trouble. To be honest, I like having him there."

Susan sensed he had been on the verge of saying more. "You do?"

"He likes watching Cully as much as I do." He shrugged. "I catch something in his face that makes me think he feels the way I do."

His voice trailed off, and it struck her then what his life must be like, working in this store by day, seeing nobody, sitting in that house alone at night. It made her wonder why he'd come back to a town where nobody wanted him. What kind of man was he? she wondered.

"When's the grand opening?" she said, aware suddenly that he was watching her.

"I'm not sure how grand it will be. A few weeks, maybe."

"What are you going to sell?"

"I don't know yet."

It was a strange thing to say. To be doing all this work without any real plan—she didn't know how to respond. She wanted to ask him if he knew that it would be tough for him to attract business in Little River, but there was no way for her to say that to somebody she barely knew. Apart from anything else, it would imply that he hadn't thought this through. It wasn't her place to offer unasked-for advice. Unable to think of any comment, she made a show of check-ing the time, as if she had a pressing appointment.

"I have to go," she said, and he opened the door for her. She hesitated. "Thanks again. For letting Jamie watch you."

"Like I said, it's no trouble."

They said good-bye, and as she walked back toward her office, she heard the faint sound of hammering again.

16

IT WAS LATE IN THE AFTERNOON. COOP AND Miller were sitting in a patrol car five miles out of town, just off the main county road that joined the highway to Williams Lake.

"Hey, this guy's in a hell of a hurry," Miller said, his eye on the radar monitor.

Coop glanced over at the display. "He's picked us up," he said, looking in the mirror.

A truck had come around the bend a half mile behind them. The driver's detector had warned him there was a radar trap ahead. As soon as the alarm had sounded, he'd hit his brakes, trying to slow down, but it was too late.

Miller started to get out, pulling on his cap, and Coop watched him go. He had a youthful swagger to his walk; the 9-millimeter on his hip and the uniform were still novelties. He was from a place called Banner, which was about a hundred miles south, but he'd applied to transfer to Little River when he saw the vacancy. He was twenty-two and college-educated, fresh out of training, and he still had a hell of a lot to learn about being a small-town cop.

He wouldn't stay. Coop knew that. Miller was eager and ambitious. He'd be around until he thought he knew what this kind of police work was all about, then he'd be looking to move on, maybe to Kamloops or Vancouver. He probably had a strategy all written out neatly, maybe done on his computer. Coop wouldn't have been surprised if Miller had his whole career mapped out form start to finish.

He was probably planning to be commissioner or something. Miller was that type.

Coop watched as Miller stepped out into the road and flagged down the oncoming truck, which Coop could already see belonged to Tommy Lee. He could picture Tommy in the cab, a thin cigarette stuck between his lips, already cursing when he saw Miller up ahead. Coop allowed himself a smile and decided he wouldn't get out just yet. Maybe it was time Tommy met the rigid arm of Miller's law; it might encourage him to take things a little easier than he had been lately.

Coop wondered if he'd ever been as enthusiastic about writing people tickets as Miller was. He didn't think so. He'd never been the ambitious type, and couldn't exactly say what had appealed to him in the first place about becoming a cop. Apart from his training and a short spell up in Prince George, he'd worked for all of his eighteen-year career in the town he'd grown up in, only making sergeant after Dan Redgrave had retired a few years back. He fully expected that to be the last promotion he would ever receive, because he planned to remain in Little River until he retired.

He liked the job. He knew he was respected and thought himself generally fair. He was paid well enough and liked the freedom he had away from the hierarchy that existed in bigger towns, and the crime around Little River was of a fairly undemanding nature. He'd never had to threaten anyone with his gun, and he never expected to. Most people took one look at him and thought twice about getting into a fight, and those that knew him were aware that he could throw a pretty good punch if the occasion demanded. It rarely came to that, however. The worst he'd ever had to do was crack a few skulls in a barroom fight in Clancys now and again, then throw the perpetrators in jail for the night to sleep it off.

Outside, Coop could see there was a lively discussion going on between Tommy and Miller, and he thought it was about time he went over and sorted things out.

"Listen here," Tommy was saying animatedly, his cigarette bouncing up and down in his mouth. "If I kept to the damn speed limits all the time, I'd never get through enough work to keep myself going. It ain't easy running a trucking business around here, son, let me tell you that."

"That's not the point," Miller said, his jaw jutting out. "The laws are made for a reason, and you have to obey them just the same as everyone else. Now let me see your paperwork."

"Jesus." Tommy looked away and spat in disgust. "Don't you have some real criminals to catch, son?"

Coop smiled to himself. Miller was getting agitated at the way Tommy was treating the whole thing as a personal affront. His manner toward Miller's youth was starting to become patronizing, which was only going to make matters worse. Tommy saw Coop approaching then and looked relieved.

"Hey, Coop. I didn't know you was there."

"Hey, Tommy. Everything okay here, Miller?"

"This guy hasn't given me his paperwork, Sergeant Cooper," Miller complained. He glowered at Tommy Lee. "I already told him we got his speed on the radar and I'm going to have to write him a ticket."

"Jesus Christ, Coop, you know how it is," Tommy said. "I have to get this load down to Jordan's, and then I have to get back over to fetch another for Paul Davidson at the mill. How the hell am I ever going to get that done if every time I come around a corner I got to worry about other people trying to give a man grief when he's just trying to earn a living?"

"Well, Miller here's right, you know, Tommy," Coop said. "You had a fair head of steam on back there."

"Now wait a minute . . ." Tommy was indignant.

"Hold on," Coop said. "All I'm saying is, it would be good if you just kept it down a little. That'd be fair, don't you think?"

Miller's expression creased in puzzlement and a faint suspicious consternation. There was a second or two while everybody absorbed what Coop was saying.

"So I can go then?" Tommy said hopefully.

"I guess we can overlook it this time," Coop said. He stared at Tommy, then at Miller, who compressed his mouth into a tight line.

Tommy Lee climbed back into his cab, and they watched him drive away, gunning the gears as he started to build speed for the climb he had ahead, the big Kenworth spewing fumes out the back.

"Why'd you do that?" Miller demanded.

Coop sighed. Miller's self-righteous and aggrieved expression gave him a cramp in his stomach. The truth was, he'd enjoyed it just a little, showing him up the way he had.

"I did it because the man's trying to make a living and he only just gets by. He's got a wife and three kids, and if he gets behind on the payments on that truck, the bank's gonna call in the loan, and then he won't be able to make any kind of living. Then the bank'll foreclose on his house. I can't see how that would help anybody, can you?"

"He should've thought about that before he decided to break the limit. I mean, what about the law here?"

"Around here," Coop said, "I decide what the law'll be." He turned away and started back toward the cruiser.

HE GOT HOME around six-thirty and took a shower. Afterward he dressed in clean Levi's and a freshly ironed shirt and combed back his hair, then went into the kitchen and took a beer out of the refrigerator and sat down at the old kitchen table to polish his boots. He lit a cigarette and listened to a country show on the radio while he worked, singing along to the odd verse here and there when he knew the words.

Coop was confident that he could claim never to have been envious of another man in his life. With one exception. When that had happened, he'd been puzzled as much as anything, then later he'd accepted the situation, expecting the feeling would sooner or later go away. It never had, though, and when he thought about it, as he did sometimes while he smoked a cigarette on his front porch with a cold beer in his hand, it troubled him that he'd discovered things about himself of which he'd previously been unaware.

Coop took a pull of his beer. Dave Baker had always wanted to be an architect, and he'd been smart enough to achieve his aim. Coop had expected him to do well, just like Ron Taylor, who'd always had a flair for business and was now a big-shot developer, and Carl Jeffrey, who had always been bound to become a lawyer like his dad and do okay. The thing was, Coop hadn't minded that he'd always known success wasn't part of his own story. He'd wanted to become a cop, and he had, and a good one at that. He'd never envied other men their money or an easy way with women, which is what Dave had always had in spades. That was just the way it was, and everybody was different. He'd seen people over the years like Billy Deveraux, who yearned for something he wasn't ever going to have. Billy had

had ideas about selling cars in Prince George, but his business had gone belly up and cleaned him out of everything he owned. Coop could have saved him the trouble, could have told him from the start he just didn't have what it takes. Billy ought to have been content with an ordinary life. Ambition and failure can go hand in hand and destroy a person.

It had shaken Coop when Dave had come back to Little River, bringing Susan with him. Even now he couldn't say for sure what it was about her that had taken such a hold of him, but for the first time in his life he'd envied another man. She had something about her, cool intelligent eyes that lit up when she laughed, hair that made him want to feel its texture beneath his hands, a slim body he dreamed about at night. Back then, if he was with another woman, it was Susan's belly he imagined his hand lying on, her parted thighs he caressed while she lay with her head turned back and the soft graceful curve of her throat exposed.

He would be over at their house sometimes in the summer for a barbecue and watch her in a light dress with the sun showing her body when it was behind her. He'd think about her and Dave in bed, wondering what it felt like to have her feet against his chest, her sex open like an offering below him. All the time, he'd known it would never happen. She always smiled at him, never seeing what his eyes told her. Dave would affectionately smooth her rump when he thought nobody was looking and she'd grin at him. Coop would look away and hope nobody could read what was on his mind.

He'd believed it would pass, but it never had. He'd never liked Dave any less, but he'd found reasons not to visit the house so much. There was a bitter taste in his mouth sometimes when he got drunk and introspective. Then came the day he'd formed a search party to look for Dave after Susan had called, her voice tense with worry. Even then, at that exact moment, he believed he'd started to hope Dave was dead, though he hadn't admitted it to himself for a long time. When they found Dave, Coop's first thought at seeing all that gore on Jamie was that nobody could have survived losing that much blood, and following right on that he'd experienced a kind of grim satisfaction. Later, after he'd broken the news to Susan, he'd held her while she cried, and all he could think of was how warm and soft she felt. His fingers had brushed against the skin of her neck, just at the nape, so lightly she wouldn't have noticed. He'd felt her thigh against his own.

That night, he'd got drunker than he'd ever been. People thought it was because his best friend had died. He tried not to think about it anymore, but sometimes it came back to him.

His thoughts turned to Michael Somers, trying to recall him when they'd been at school, but school was about all they had in common. Coop had played sports, as had the people he'd been friendly with, including Dave Baker, and though Somers was a year younger, Coop might have known him if he'd been on the baseball team or something. But Somers hadn't ever had much to do with sports. From what Coop remembered, he'd kept to himself a lot of the time. Everybody had thought he was a little strange, though the probable truth was he'd just been a loner. The strangeness people liked to label him with came from his mother, who everybody knew wasn't playing with a full deck. It was no secret the way she spent most of her time in that house, rarely venturing into town, going around in her nightgown all day and treating herself for all kinds of illnesses she thought she had. Even Ralph Webber, who'd been the doctor then, could be heard in Clancys some nights shaking his head over a beer and remarking that the woman drove him to distraction. It was no wonder that Somers's dad had taken refuge in the bottom of a glass, which over the years had made him kind of a drunk. Basically, as people said, they were pretty fucked up as a family.

It was why the whole town was buzzing with talk about Somers now that he was back. They said that his mother had been crazy and that finally she'd killed herself, though there were others who wondered about that, remarking that it was strange how John Somers had happened to be out late on a Wednesday night, which was unusual for him. With that kind of history, Somers was on a no-win ticket. His mom had been crazy; his dad, according to rumor, had as good as killed her. No wonder, people said, he'd turned out the way he did. Some even asked Coop why he couldn't make him leave town, as if Little River were the Wild West or something.

When he'd done cleaning his boots, Coop drove to Susan's house. When he arrived, she was on the porch, wearing jeans and a shirt, with her hair swept back. Behind her, Wendy Douglas was standing in the doorway, and as he arrived, the two stopped talking, though they continued to wear odd expressions.

"What's up?" he said, getting out of his car.

"It's nothing," Susan said. "We were just looking for Jamie. He must be around somewhere."

There was some intonation in her voice that he couldn't identify. It was dark, late for Jamie to be outside. "You don't know where he is?" he asked.

"He can't have gone far."

Coop felt he was missing something. Susan and Wendy exchanged glances. "I'll go look for him," he suggested. He hesitated, unsure which direction to go, then fetched a flashlight from his truck.

"He might have gone that way," Susan said, indicating the woods.

"Toward the Somers place?"

"He's been going over there," Susan said, almost but not quite casually.

"What for?"

"He goes after school to watch Michael's falcon. He came back earlier, but then he just went again."

Coop felt as if he'd lost his footing. There were eddies and streams in the air, rhythms he couldn't make sense of. "Michael's falcon." The way she said his name sounded like they were friends, which he didn't know about. And this thing about Jamie going over there threw him. He just nodded, wondering what else he didn't know about.

"I'll go find him," he said, turning away, aware of the way Susan watched him, not saying anything, biting her lip.

Coop thought that some people have an antenna for danger, for when something comes along that might threaten the status quo. He had that feeling now. Just a sense that a subtle change had altered the balance of things.

He didn't know if he'd planned the way everything had happened with Susan, right from the day Dave had been buried, or if it had just happened. He liked to think the latter, but his conscience told him differently. It had happened gradually. First he'd just made sure that she and Jamie had everything they needed, helping out where he could; as time went by, he'd started staying for supper now and then. They'd sit up talking at night after Jamie had gone to bed, Susan doing most of the talking while he just listened. She talked a lot about Dave, and he thought that was why she'd been able to speak to him, because he'd been Dave's friend. He even wondered if in some way she thought she was actually talking to Dave, through him.

She missed Dave, and because of the way Jamie had taken it, she felt more alone and uncertain than she might have otherwise. She'd confided that she hadn't always been sure she wanted to be married to Dave, which had surprised Coop. It was a chink in their relationship Coop hadn't known was there. They'd fought like any other couple, but she'd also had doubts that went deeper, though it had all been in the past.

Occasionally she'd cried on his shoulder.

"I'm sorry, I didn't mean to do this," she'd say.

"It's okay," he'd tell her. "You don't have to apologize."

There were times he'd wanted to tell her how he felt, tell her he loved her. He could feel she needed somebody right then, and he'd thought that if he made a move, she might have responded the way he wanted, though it would have been from need and not a clear head and it wouldn't have lasted.

Instead, he'd held back and been her friend. He'd done his best with Jamie, too, though no good had come of that yet. As time had gone by and Susan had come out of herself, little by little, he knew that she'd come to understand what he felt for her. He hoped she respected the fact that he'd never pressured her with his feelings, that he'd never tried to rush her. He understood her confusion. It was partly because of Jamie, he felt. His silence was like a reminder of David, and Coop had thought for a long time that when Jamie finally accepted him, Susan would, too.

As he went through the woods toward the Somers place, there was a lot going on in his mind.

MICHAEL WAS ON the porch, wrapped up in a jacket, drinking whiskey while he watched the night sky.

The clearing was almost ethereal when there was a bright moon, he sometimes thought when he was out there in the freezing air. The snow was silver gray; the moonlight cast deep shadows where the trees fringed the clearing's edge. It felt as if this corner of the world had slipped a little out of sync, that subtle changes had taken place. The physical had melted away and he could feel himself surrounded by spirits, the ghosts of trees and animals. He wondered if he was tuning in to ancient forces that were all around. He'd once heard a theory that organized religion had missed the point, and that God and nature were one and the same. The idea had appealed to him. He thought that through Cully he was connected to the natural world.

From the porch, the sky seemed curved, like a massive dark outer sphere that encased the world. He saw the white flash of a shooting star, a chunk of ice and rock, and he wondered where it had come from before it burned up in the earth's atmosphere. How long had it spun and traveled through space?

An owl flitted across the clearing, a swift dark shape in pursuit of some victim, its wings moving with absolute silence. Owls, he knew, had given up the protective coating of oil on their feathers to achieve silent flight. Caught in a downpour, they would become sodden, unable to fly. A price for everything. Michael drank his whiskey and thought of Susan Baker coming to the store, and his brow furrowed in thought. He pictured her face, her eyes like the sea.

At the bottom of the porch steps, a figure emerged from the darkness soundlessly and was there. It startled him so that he almost dropped his glass. One second there was nothing, then a pale face materialized. He thought he was either drunk or seeing the ghost of a boy, maybe himself. It was Jamie. Michael's heart was thumping like a hammer.

"Where did you come from?" He wondered how Jamie could have crept up so close without making a sound. Michael decided he must have been lost in thought.

Jamie held something out, and placed it on the porch. Michael saw that it was the book he'd left him in the tree.

"Did you read it?"

He wasn't expecting an answer, but Jamie nodded, and in the second it took Michael to absorb this response, he realized this was the closest Jamie had ever come to the house.

"Did you like it?"

Again there was a nod. Then Jamie was peering into the dark recesses of the porch.

"Looking for Cully? She's in the woodshed, asleep by this time.

She doesn't like to stay up late." He grinned, and in the moment that followed he was sure the ghost of a smile passed across Jamie's expression.

The sound of somebody approaching through the trees, crashing against the undergrowth, reached them, and it occurred to Michael that Jamie's mother must be wondering where he was. Then a voice called out, and he recognized Coop. Michael saw him enter the clearing and take in the scene.

"Jamie? Your mom's worried about you, son." Coop looked toward Michael. "It's late for him to be out here." He stepped into the pool of light spilling from the porch.

Michael noted the way Coop was dressed, as if he had recently showered and changed. He wondered if maybe Susan and Coop were involved in some way. Coop's tone had sounded accusatory. Michael gestured to the book and picked it up. "He was just bringing something back that I loaned him."

There was a long silence that seemed to stretch for minutes. Coop's hand had dropped to Jamie's shoulder, but there was something awkward in the way they stood. The space between them seemed too large, and Jamie looked at the ground.

"We'd better go, son," Coop said.

As he started to leave, Jamie cast a quick glance back toward the porch.

"Come over in the morning," Michael said.

Coop looked a moment longer, then wordlessly turned away.

"YOU'RE A LUCKY woman," Susan said. "A man who can cook at all is a rare enough find; one who can cook like this, that's really something. You better take care of him, Linda, or one day some woman in this town is going to steal him away."

"That's what I keep telling her," Pete agreed.

"You wish." Linda got up and started to clear plates from the table, bending to kiss her husband on the cheek as she passed. "You're not so bad, I guess."

He put his arm around her waist and drew her close, grinning up at her and planting a kiss right on her mouth. "You're not so bad yourself."

Susan watched them with an affectionate smile. They'd been married seventeen years, not only living in the same house but for many of those years working together as well. The way they were around each other, the way their lives were so entwined, it was hard to imagine one without the other. They still exchanged glances across the diner when they were working, grinning at some joke they shared, touching each other frequently, a brush of a hand against the waist or an arm, a brief, almost unconscious squeeze—more intimate gestures than any passionate kiss, in their way, though Susan was sure there was plenty of that kind of passion in their relationship, too. She envied them their total comfort with each other. Would she and David have been this way if he'd lived? she wondered. Maybe not in the same way. Having Jamie had turned their attention outward from each other; probably they would have tried for another child. Linda and Pete had only each other; perhaps if they'd been able to have kids, they would be different. It was all a question of focus, she thought. She knew how much they regretted being childless, but watching them, she wondered if they fully realized that what they had together was a rare thing in itself. Would they have given a part of it up if they had the choice?

"Let me help you," Susan said to Linda, collecting Coop's plate. He gave her a brief smile, and as she went around him, she squeezed his shoulder. He looked up at her with an expression of pleasant surprise.

As she put plates into the dishwasher while Linda prepared dessert, Susan imagined a domestic scene full of kids and a husband, noisy suppers and then quiet nights in front of a fire when the children were all in bed. This contrasted with the way she and Jamie sat down to eat, the only voice her own, a wrench inside every time she looked at him.

"Penny for them?"

Susan broke from her reverie. "My mother used to say that."

"All mothers say it." Linda took some fresh glasses from the cupboard and poured chardonnay from a new bottle. "How is everything?"

Susan sipped her wine, thinking that she ought to take it easy, she was already feeling light-headed. In the dining room, she could see through the glass doors, Coop and Pete were laughing at some joke. It was the happiest Coop had appeared all night.

"Everything's fine," she answered. Linda made no comment, but her disbelief was evident. Susan explained what had happened earlier, when Coop had arrived at the house. "Apparently, Jamie went over to return a book, but he didn't tell me he was going."

Linda nodded. "So Coop went over to get him?"

"I think he was put out that Jamie was over there. You know how Jamie is with him."

"He's been kind of quiet tonight. I thought maybe you two had an argument."

Susan shook her head. "Poor Coop."

"Why 'Poor Coop'? Jamie would be that way with any man he thought you were getting involved with, you know that, Susan." Linda paused. "Or did you mean something else? I mean, everything is okay between you two, isn't it?"

"Yes, of course. I mean, we haven't had a fight or anything."

"But?"

Susan sighed. "Oh, I don't know. Coop is a sweet guy, and I appreciate everything he's done for Jamie and me. I just don't know if I can ever feel anything more than that." She watched him as she spoke, the way he lounged back in his chair, relaxed and at ease, his long legs comfortably stretched under the table, the strong line of his jaw. He hadn't said anything about what had happened at Michael's house, but she'd seen in his eyes as he watched Jamie go into the house that he was hurt. It had pulled at something inside her. It was all so confusing sometimes.

"I never told you this before," Linda said, "but when I was young, I dated Coop. I used to think one day I might marry him." She laughed at Susan's expression of shock. "Oh, it was a long time ago, before I ever met Pete. We were just kids, really."

"You dated Coop?" Susan couldn't believe it.

"Like I said, it was a long time ago." She looked down, fiddling with her glass. "You know, when Pete and I were trying to get pregnant and nothing was happening, I used to wonder sometimes how it would have been if I had ended up with Coop. Don't look so shocked. I never would have exchanged Pete for anyone; it was just that I was thinking all kinds of things at that time. It wouldn't have made a difference, anyway—turned out the problem was with me. I'm just saying I used to think about it. I think Coop would've made a terrific husband. Oh, I know he's sort of quiet, and he's happy being who he is right here in this town, but he's got a good heart, Susan."

Susan nodded slowly. "I know that," she said.

IT WAS LATE when they left, past one, and the night was freezing. Susan sat back in the corner of her seat on the drive home, leaning against the headrest. A country station was playing on the radio, and she hummed along to a tune she recognized.

"Thought you didn't like this stuff," Coop said.

"I'm making an exception tonight." She smiled over at him. The wine, and brandy on top of that with coffee, had affected her. It was more than she'd drunk in a long time, and she felt good-humored, her mind drifting in a pleasant fuzz.

"This was nice, Coop," she said. "Good food, good friends. I had a good time."

"Yeah, me too."

His expression remained serious, concentrating on the road. Susan wondered if he was still bothered about what had happened earlier. She reached out and brushed his arm.

"If you're worrying about Jamie, then don't," she said. "It's not you. It's just that he's interested in Michael's falcon."

Coop's mouth tightened fractionally. "Yeah, I know."

She didn't think he sounded convinced. Maybe it would be better to just let it drop. The sound of tires on the road lulled her, the heat made her yawn.

"Are you okay about Jamie being over there?" Coop asked after a moment.

She dragged herself up from a dreamy, half-sleepy state. "What do you mean?"

"Somers did try to kill somebody once, you know that. The guy he shot was lucky to survive. He threatened his own wife and baby, too."

"He was never charged with that," Susan said. "The prosecution accepted that he never actually made any threat. Even the judge said he needed treatment; it was part of his sentence. It's obvious he had some kind of breakdown."

"The jury still thought he knew what he was doing." Coop looked over. "How'd you know all that, anyway?"

"I went to the library. I mean, with Jamie going over there, I wanted to see for myself what really happened, instead of listening to all the talk there's been."

Coop frowned, but he didn't say anything.

They rode in silence until he turned off the road and pulled up outside her house. Susan wished again she hadn't brought the subject up in the first place. For a second they sat uncomfortably, then impulsively she leaned over and kissed him on the cheek. She started to pull away, but then he turned toward her and held her arm and they stared into each other's faces. She felt herself being drawn closer and didn't resist, then he was kissing her mouth, his arm going around her shoulders.

At first she didn't feel anything, just the sensation of his mouth against her own, then some kind of pleasant warm syrupy feeling was starting to happen somewhere in her middle, and she didn't want to let go of it just yet. Coop's male scent was in her senses, firing off little chemical receptors in her brain like little flashes of fireworks. She could feel the strength in his arms, the hardness of his body. Her hand inadvertently brushed the front of his pants and she felt his erection.

She opened her eyes, feeling cool air against her face, then pulled away.

"Coop . . . It's late. I should go in."

There was confusion in his expression, mingled with hurt and even a flash of anger she could see in the way the muscles at the corner of his mouth twitched, but he didn't try to stop her. She felt like an idiot. Worse, she felt like a tease. But she garbled some excuse, said good night, and climbed out.

Inside, as she leaned against the door, she heard the sound of the engine fading, and quiet descended over the house. She took several long slow breaths, closed her eyes, then went to the kitchen and poured herself a glass of water. Her head was swimming.

She went upstairs, and on the way to her room she stopped to look in on Jamie. He was asleep, lying on his stomach, his arms thrown out, his face turned toward her. She pulled the covers up and bent to kiss him, watching him for a moment while he slept. He breathed softly, with his mouth open a little, his long lashes lying against his cheek. His sketch pad lay on the chest beside his bed, and when she tilted it to catch the light from the landing, she could see he'd drawn more pictures of Cully. Turning over the pages, she saw sketches of herself standing on a porch rail, or flying toward a figure she supposed was Michael. She put the pad down, and stayed for a minute or two longer. On the outside, he seemed peaceful, untroubled. She remembered the sound of his laughter when he was just a baby, how he giggled when she tickled him, the first time he spoke her name. It seemed such a faraway echo, such a long time ago. She felt a swelling sensation that rose into her throat, and her eyes inexplicably began to smart. Turning away, she left his room, quietly closing the door behind her.

In her own room, she crawled into bed and turned out the light, but sleep wouldn't come. She was in a kind of drowsy half-conscious state, cocooned in warmth and darkness. Alcohol was still swirling in her brain. She recalled Coop's shoulders beneath her hands when they'd kissed. She felt bad about what had happened earlier, and in a moment of fantasy she imagined that she hadn't broken away and gone inside. She thought of him lying with her in the dark, her hands running across his back. She caressed herself beneath the T-shirt she was wearing, cupping her breasts and squeezing her thighs together. The sensations in her body came unexpectedly. The warmth that spread up from her loins took her by surprise. With one hand she described circular motions across her belly, sliding down.

With her eyes closed, arousing herself, she imagined half-formed images dissolving and rearranging themselves in her mind. She thought of Coop as she'd seen him on the drive home, thoughtful, his face in shadow, and of kissing him. His image dissolved, and memories of making love with David suffused her mind. Tears escaped her eyes to run across her cheekbones to the pillow, leaving tracks of moisture that she could feel against her skin.

She banished David from her mind, imagining being made love to by an anonymous male body. She couldn't see his face, nor did she feel compelled to, but the movements and pressure of her hands made her think of flesh molding against her own and she immersed herself in sensation.

Afterward her breathing became deep and regular; her fantasy dissolved, and when she finally fell asleep, she dreamed of things she wouldn't remember in the light of day. Only a vague unsettling discontent would linger. She curled into a tight ball, hugging her knees to her chest.

17 MICHAEL ROSE BEFORE IT WAS LIGHT AND fetched Cully from the woodshed. By the time the sun was up, he had her weighed, hooded, and on her perch in the back of the Nissan and was finishing a breakfast of coffee and a roll. For days now she'd been flying free to his fist across the clearing during their morning and afternoon sessions, and never once had she wavered, never once had she shown an inclination to rise up and fly beyond the trees, though still, each time he called her, a nervous lump stuck in his throat. Now, however, it was time to advance her training another step, and for that he needed to take her into the mountains.

He drove up the track to the road and turned toward town, but before he'd traveled far, he turned off again and drove down through the trees to Susan's house. As he stepped onto the porch to knock, he heard the dog barking inside, and then after a few minutes the door opened. Susan peered at him from sleep-filled eyes, running a hand back through her hair. When she saw it was him, she drew her robe more tightly around her.

"I'm sorry, I didn't mean to wake you," he said.

"It's okay. What time is it?"

"Early." Behind her in the passage he saw Jamie appear, his coat on, ready to go out, and he guessed the boy had been about to head for his usual spot beside the big cottonwood on the edge of the clearing where he watched Cully's training.

"I'm taking Cully to a place in the mountains, toward Falls Pass," he told Susan. "I thought Jamie might want to come along, if it's okay with you."

She looked past him to the Nissan, where Cully was visible through the window, hooded and standing quietly on her perch. "I don't know," she said, coming awake. She half turned, expecting that Jamie would already have disappeared, but he was still there, standing back a little. "I mean, I guess it's okay with me—it's Saturday, so there's no school—but Jamie's kind of funny around people." She knelt down beside Jamie. "Do you want to go with Mr. Somers?"

"Michael."

She glanced back over her shoulder. "Michael."

To her surprise, Jamie nodded. He stepped past her and went down the porch step and climbed into the passenger seat.

"He'll be okay. I'll bring him back in a few hours."

Susan was still too surprised to manage much more than a vague nod. "Okay, thanks."

She watched them go, waving tentatively, then went inside to worry.

HE TOOK THE road toward Falls Pass, above the valley, concentrating on the icy surface while they rose through the forest. In places they cut through narrow valleys where the trees rose steeply on either side, forming dark canyons where in the winter the sun never penetrated.

Jamie sat in the corner, pressed up against the door as if he were trying to keep as much distance between them as he could. Most of the time, his attention was fixed on Cully. Michael found the silence disconcerting and racked his brains for something to say. He asked Jamie a couple of questions about school, but it was hard to think of things that required only a nod or a shake of the head in response, and sensing Jamie's reluctance he gave up after a while.

A memory came back to him of driving somewhere with his dad when he would have been around Jamie's age. They were going to Williams Lake to pick up some stuff for the store, and he remembered the journey as being something like this, completed in virtual silence. He could picture his dad wearing a red checked jacket and a cap with the name of some tool supplier across the front. He had gray hair even then, almost silvery white, and the line of his jaw seemed to be dissolving into his neck in folds of skin. Whenever Michael thought of his dad, it was an image like this, as if he'd always been old.

Michael had been born when his parents were already in their early forties. They'd married in their thirties, but the family they'd planned had never happened, and a difficult birth meant his mother hadn't been able to have more children. From things he'd heard, it was this that had changed her.

On the day he'd gone with his dad, they'd taken a detour to a pond that was frozen in winter. Michael remembered it had been his dad's idea; he must have planned it ahead of time, because Michael's skates were in the back of the truck. There were lots of people on the pond: kids around his own age, whole families out together. His dad didn't skate because of an arthritic hip, and as Michael had gone around the ice, his dad had stood at the edge watching him and calling out as he went by. By the time Michael had finally come off the pond, the light was fading and there were only a few people left. His dad was still standing in the same spot, patiently waiting.

Michael remembered getting in the car feeling warm after all the exercise; his dad had been frozen, his arms stiff from standing so long in the cold. Michael remembered he'd had a good time on the ice, but he'd stayed longer than he'd really wanted to. He was glad that his dad was cold, full of this anger that he couldn't express. It was just there, a deep mixture of instinctive emotion, most of it in turmoil. He'd been silent all the way home, and gradually his dad had given up trying to get him to talk, resignation and disappointment falling over him.

By the time they'd arrived back, it was dark, and Michael's mother, having seen the lights of the truck, had opened the door to them, her expression deeply etched with worry, her eyes going from one to the other of them. Her voice was strange, kind of shaky, rising in volume.

"Where have you been?" she'd demanded, kneeling down, crushing Michael to her. He recalled the strong smell of the liniment she used to rub into her chest, the feathery feel of a dryish wisp of hair against his skin.

"We just went skating," he'd said, pulling away from her.

Her eyes had a high bright light in them, which she flashed at his dad. "Why didn't you tell me? I didn't know where you were, I was all alone. What if I'd had an attack and fallen down?" Then she'd sniffed the air like a dog and stood up. "You've been drinking!" Michael remembered thinking it wasn't true, his dad hadn't taken a drink all day, but he hadn't said anything.

It was one of the few times he could recall that he and his dad had done anything together. He saw now that on other occasions, when his dad had tried to get him to play ball in the yard or go fishing, he'd frozen him out. Thinking about it saddened him. His mother had done a good job of turning him against his dad. Her reaction after they'd been out skating, he saw now, was borne of fear; she'd been afraid all her efforts would be undone. He guessed that after that, his dad had given up.

AT THE TOP of Falls Pass Road they crested a rise, emerging from the treeline high above a valley. The road went on a little farther, then dropped down the other side of the rise toward a high pass in the mountains. Where they had emerged, the road dissected a broad snowfield, which rose in a gentle slope toward high rocky cliffs a mile away. Beyond, the mountains ranged in ever-rising white and blue-gray peaks. Michael pulled over.

"This is it," he said.

He'd remembered this place when Frank had told him he'd need somewhere open, away from trees, to fly Cully to the lure. If they crossed the slope, they'd be surrounded by pristine snow, the treeline behind them, the cliffs ahead, a ridge to the north, beyond which lay an ocean of winter-blue sky.

He fetched Cully from the back of the Nissan and they crossed a rock-strewn patch of ground close to the road. Beyond it their feet sank a little, but the snow was frozen and crisp and the going wasn't too hard. Ahead of them, sunlight hit the cliffs, bouncing back dazzling reflections from ice sheets that must have formed from water seepage high up somewhere. In places, great areas were thrown deep into shadow by the contours of the rock face, and these were like massive dark holes.

The air stung their cheeks, and each breath was like inhaling icy needles. Their steps made a sound like splintering glass. Half a mile from the road they stopped, and Michael took off Cully's hood. She stood erect on his fist, looking all around at this unfamiliar vista through gleaming eyes, her breast pushed out, reared to her full height. She flicked out her wings, testing the faint breeze. The clean smell of high air and bare rock, the unfiltered sunlight and the closeness of the sky, awakened her instincts.

In his free hand, Michael was carrying a spiked block perch, made from a wooden log, which he thrust into the snow. His plan had been to leave Cully on it while he prepared the lure, but now he had a better idea. For the moment he set her down; then he took his glove off and held it out to Jamie.

"How'd you like to help out?" he said. "I need you to hold Cully on your fist."

Jamie's eyes grew wide, and he took a wary step backward.

"Listen," Michael said. "You've been watching her for long enough. Don't you want to get a little closer?" His motive was twofold. He thought it would be nice for Jamie to get more involved, but he also thought this might help to break down his reserve a little bit. A kid shouldn't be so locked up in himself, he thought.

He crouched down to Jamie's level. "Come on, she won't hurt you," he said. "Look, she's not even worried. She knows who you are."

They stayed like that for a few seconds. Then at last, hesitantly, Jamie nodded and reached out. He looked nervously at Cully. Michael helped him pull the glove on, then brought his hand down behind the perch. "All you have to do is just press against the back of her legs and she'll step back onto your fist, okay? Just hold your arm steady, then thread the jesses and leash through your fingers like this." He guided Jamie's movements as he spoke. "Good. Now stand up."

When they were standing, Jamie's expression slowly changed. The nervousness went as he saw that Cully wasn't going to suddenly attack him. Michael smiled to himself, watching the light grow in the boy's eyes. "Just let her get used to you, that's it." Cully shifted her feet, looked at the glove and then at Jamie, nipped at her jesses, then roused her feathers, shaking her tail and settling contentedly. She turned her attention back to the landscape. "See, she's fine."

After a minute or two, Michael showed Jamie how he could stroke her breast feathers, which Jamie did tentatively, drawing back quickly when she arched her neck to watch his finger. Michael had read in one of his books that if a falcon nipped at a finger, the correct thing to do was to hold still and wait until she released it. He'd been on the receiving end of Cully's nips now and then when she didn't want to be stroked, and he thought maybe it was a good idea to take things slowly.

"Okay, we're going to fly her now," he said. "What I want you to do is just stay like this, okay? Just let Cully stand there while I walk back over there; then I'll call her. Think you can you do that?" Jamie met his eye directly. A second went by, then he gave a slight nod. "Okay. Good boy."

Michael removed Cully's leash and jesses. "Just stay right there." He knew it wouldn't take long for Jamie to feel the strain of the weight he was carrying, and he walked quickly away, taking the lure out of his bag as he went. Cully's bell sounded as she shifted restlessly. The strange flat note it made carried clearly in the air, and he imagined someone could hear it from the cliffs half a mile distant.

The next step in her training was to induce her to chase the lure instead of just coming to it held in his fist. He'd read the description in Frank's book of how this was meant to happen, and on the phone Frank had run him through it. He'd practiced spinning the lure like a lasso at his side in front of the house, imagining Cully flying around in a high wide circle around him the way Frank had assured him she would, then coming in as he called her. The aim was to swing the lure in an arc in front of his body, timing it so that Cully was just behind, then whisking it away at the last moment so that she flew on and came around again.

"A falcon will do this a dozen or more times until she tires, then you let her catch it," Frank had said. He'd promised it would quickly build her strength.

Michael felt as nervous as he had the first time about flying her free. At least then the only thing different from what she'd been doing without fail was that she wasn't encumbered by the creance. Otherwise, she'd simply had to fly to his fist. This time he was going to do something totally unexpected and she was supposed to understand what was being asked of her. To him it seemed like a big ask, but he'd prepared himself for the moment.

At fifty yards he took a breath, turned, and called her. Her wings opened immediately. Jamie ducked as feathers brushed his face, then his arm dipped and she was away. When she was three quarters of the way toward him, Michael followed Frank's instructions and tossed the lure onto the ground. For a second Cully faltered, and Michael was gripped by a quick flash of panic as he imagined her soaring past, rising and rising while he called futilely after her. But her eyesight was ten times clearer than a man's, and the meat on the lure was what she'd been watching. It was like a beacon, and as she approached, she threw back her wings and landed as if she'd been doing this forever. She mantled her prize protectively, then after checking around, she began tearing at the meat. A falcon prefers to carry her prey to a safe spot nearby if she can—a ledge on a rock face, perhaps—but if forced to eat on the ground, where she is vulnerable, she eats quickly.

Elated at their success, Michael returned to Jamie. "Let's give her a minute, then we'll do it again. Okay?" Jamie wore a slightly puzzled frown, not understanding the reason for this change in Cully's training. "You'll see," Michael told him. He was nervous as hell about what he planned to do next, and couldn't bring himself to describe it in case it all went horribly wrong. If it worked out the way it was supposed to, however, they were really going to see Cully fly. The mixture of nervousness and excitement left him feeling tense and wired.

The second time he called her from Jamie's fist, Michael threw the lure down as he had before; but now he was supposed to pull it away just before she reached it. Frank had said she'd be confused and would fly past, rising as she went, and then he was supposed to call her and swing the lure.

"Don't panic," he'd said. "She'll come around for another pass at it."

At that point he was supposed to throw it to the ground and let her take it. That was the theory.

She came quickly as before, swooping from Jamie's fist to a glide and then flying a foot or so above the snow. He waited until the very last moment before he pulled the lure away, and even as he yanked on the cord, he knew he'd waited too long. She was already poised to land, feet reaching out, tail fanned to act as a brake, and to his consternation she didn't fly past but instead came down in the snow, looking startled and annoyed. The lure, snatched virtually from her grasp, landed ten feet away, and before Michael could react, she started to run after it. She had a waddling gait, odd-looking with her wings folded, like somebody without arms, half hopping and half walking. For a second he didn't know what to do, then impulsively he jerked the lure away from her again. She stopped, bewildered now, and again she ran after it. He was dismayed; this wasn't the soaring flight he'd imagined.

He finally had the presence of mind to let her catch it, at which she seemed pleased with herself. Jamie was watching with a look of astonishment, as if wondering if this was really the way to train a falcon. Up until now everything had gone well, and Cully had looked every inch the graceful predator she was. Suddenly Michael felt he'd reduced her to farce, making her hop about in the snow like a flightless chicken.

He let her eat, then pulled his sleeve over his hand and took her back to try again. A part of him knew that he should leave it for another day, but another part wouldn't let him finish on this note. He was determined to put his mistake right. He put her back on Jamie's fist, and after offering her a scrap of meat to check that she was still hungry, he walked away again and called her.

This time he got the timing right, and pulled the lure when she was still several feet away. She flew past, rising rapidly as she headed away from them. Michael was stunned by the sight. He was suddenly certain she wouldn't respond to his call, that she would simply keep going, getting smaller and smaller until she became just a speck in the blue. It struck him that he was seeing the last of her, and it felt like something grabbing and twisting at his insides.

Her bow-shaped wings beat rapidly and evenly, the sun catching her pale color at the apex of her upward stroke, just before she started the downward movement. Michael glanced at Jamie, who was watching anxiously, waiting for him to do something. Abruptly he came to, and remembering what he was supposed to do, he found his voice.

"Cully!"

His voice carried across the snow and echoed faintly off the cliffs, but she continued to rise. He called again, swinging the lure at his side. He thought she was too far away to hear him and cursed himself for waiting too long. She was beyond the ridge now, high above the valley that lay out of their sight beyond. One last time he called her, summoning all he could to shout her name. And at last she turned.

He kept calling her all the way back while his heart beat a rapid tattoo. He was convinced she'd sheer off, change her mind at the last moment, but she didn't. As she drew near, he threw the lure up and it fell to the ground trailing the line behind it. Cully threw back her wings and seized it. She mantled her wings protectively; then, flicking the points back across her tail, she bent to eat.

After that he called it a day.

All the way back, Jamie sat turned around in his seat, his eyes still gleaming with excitement, fastened on Cully. Michael's own feelings of elation were tempered by a disturbing memory of her flight. On her turn there had been an unmistakable waver in her stroke, as if she'd been buffeted by a massive gust of wind. Then, as she'd flown back toward them, she'd appeared unbalanced, as if she were favoring her good wing and compensating for the shift in her aerodynamics.

He glanced in the rearview mirror and saw that even as she stood on her perch, the injured wing was occasionally drooping and she'd have to flick it back into place. As he drove, his frown deepened into worried lines.

TOM WATERS LOOKED up from writing a note for his nurse, Rose, who at the moment was off work with a heavy cold. He'd spoken to her earlier, and she'd said she would try to make it in the next morning. Tom had told her not to worry about it; things were quiet anyway, he said, and he was spending half his time with his feet up, catching up on his reading. The note asked her to get some ear drops around to Sonny Davies, whose dog had an infection.

There was a whole pile of similar notes, all asking her to take care of things Tom hadn't been able to do because he didn't know where things were kept anymore. When the office door opened, he looked up with the face of a man harassed.

"Is this a bad time?" Michael asked.

"Right now, anytime's a bad time," Tom replied. "You hire somebody just to take care of appointments and keep a check on invoices, and the next thing you know, she turns out to be a paragon of organization. She changes everything around and invents systems you remain ignorant of, and before you know it, she's taken over your whole professional life. Take my advice and beware of women like that. One day they're going to rule the world."

"I'll remember that."

"My nurse is off with a cold, in other words," Tom said. "I've just discovered I can't cope without her. To make matters worse, this has

been the busiest week I can remember. Murphy's law applies: Whatever *can* go wrong *will* go wrong."

"Sorry to hear it."

He waved a hand in careless dismissal. "It's my own fault, I guess.
I should've kept an eye on that side of things. Now I can never fire
her, no matter what she does wrong. It's a feminist plot."

"My guess is you wouldn't think of it," Michael said.

Tom grinned. "You're right. Rose is the best nurse I could wish
for. That's probably why I married her ten years ago. Now what's
the problem?"

"It's Cully's wing," Michael said. He'd brought her in on his fist,
hooded. She shifted position, her bell making a small sound.

Tom looked at him over the top of the reading glasses perched on
his nose. "Still giving her trouble?"

"I got a good look at her flight yesterday," he explained, then
described what he'd seen.

"Okay, let's take a look at her." Tom probed around the site of the
fracture, feeling gently at the joints on either side, his brow furrowed
in concentration. "No sign of grating," he observed. "The callus is
still there." He felt around the edge of her wing. "And I can't feel
any sign of inflammation." He let her go, and watched while Cully
flicked the wing back into position. He repeated this a couple of times.

"What are you looking for?"

"Any sign that she's uncomfortable. Does she ever carry this wing
lazily when she's at rest?"

"She did after I flew her," Michael said. "Why?"

"It can be an indication there's something wrong, but she seems
fine right now. How long were you flying her?"

"Just a few minutes."

"Okay, I can't tell much more from my exam," Tom said. "Let me
take some X rays."

He and Cully were gone for fifteen minutes, and when they came
back, Tom put the film up against a light box to examine it. There
was a smudge of darkness against the skeleton of Cully's wing where
the fracture had healed, and he frowned.

"Looks like a very slight infection there," he said, pointing at the
ulna.

"What does that mean?"

"Maybe nothing much. We'll try her on a course of antibiotics.

Keep the wing rested for a few days and see how she does. What you saw might just be some residual stiffness, but we'll take the cautious view, I think. When you start exercising her again, do it gently, and if there's any sign of her being in serious pain, bring her back."

Michael stroked Cully's breast to soothe her, talking quietly. She was nervous and tense after being handled for the X ray. After a few moments she started to relax a little at the familiar feel of the glove and the sound of his voice.

Michael had detected a note, a certain reserve, in Tom's tone. "If she's in pain, and I bring her back, what happens then? Will you operate?"

Tom took off his glasses and rubbed at the bridge of his nose. "I hate having to say this, but if the antibiotics don't do the trick, I don't think we have many options left. There's no operation I can do that'll help."

Michael considered this while Tom found something he needed to brush from his coat. "You're saying she'd have to be put down?"

Tom gave Michael a sympathetic look. "I could amputate, but I don't think you'd want that. I'm sorry, but all I can tell you is a bird like that wasn't born to spend her life crippled in a cage. It's not like you or me losing a leg. For her, flying is her life. It's what nature designed her for. I wish I could tell you something else."

Michael nodded vaguely, absorbing the truth of what Tom was saying. He just didn't want to accept that it might come to that. He took the antibiotics and drove home, thinking all the way that she would be fine, that she was a fighter. He couldn't envisage that in the end she would suffer an ignominious end, injected with some lethal potion.

When he arrived back at the house, he took Cully into the wood-shed and fed her, then waited for Jamie to arrive so he could tell him her training was called off for a few days.

18 FORTY MINUTES OUT OF LITTLE RIVER heading up into the Cariboo Mountains, the country road passes through a valley. A man from Victoria had bought some of the land around the small lake there twenty years earlier and had built a cabin that he used occasionally for fishing. When the man died, his brother had wanted to sell the cabin and the land. He'd had the idea of selling building plots around the shores of the lake, and every now and again a lawyer acting for him would send up somebody he'd managed to get interested in the scheme.

The latest was John Softly, an American taking a vacation from his hometown of Seattle, who'd looked up the lawyer because he was the brother of a good friend. They'd had dinner together, and Softly had remarked in passing how it would be nice to have a place up in the mountains where he could get away for a little peace and quiet sometimes; one thing had led to another, and before he knew it, he had an appointment to meet a real-estate agent in some town called Little River Bend.

Susan pulled over at the side of Falls Pass Road just before it crested the brow of a hill. They'd been climbing steadily for fifteen minutes, the road hemmed in by forest on either side, so there wasn't much to see. Whenever she brought prospective clients here, she always stopped at this same spot to give them their first view of the valley.

Softly looked about him with slight bewilderment. "What are we stopping for? Is this the place?"

"No, we're almost there. I just thought there's something here you'd like to see."

She sensed the American's reluctance. He was in his late fifties, soft and fat, and she guessed he wasn't relishing the notion of a long walk. "It's just a little way, over there by that tree," she assured him, pointing to a lone cedar at the edge of a clearing that went up to the brow of the hill. The tree was framed against a clear blue sky, which she knew would make the stop all the more worthwhile.

"Well, okay, then, I guess I can make it that far," Softly conceded, and hauled himself out. He was wheezing by the time they reached it. His chest rose and fell, sounding like an old bellows.

"This is it," she announced.

Below them the valley spread out, turning to the north at the bottom end. Much of its slopes were covered with forest, but down on the valley floor there were great areas alongside the narrow river that were open meadows. At this time of year the ground was covered with snow, but Susan described how it looked in the spring, when the snow was melting. The meadows would be rich with cotton grass, lit with flares of orange hawkweed, yellow goldenrod, and the bluebell-shaped flowers of Jacob's ladder. The lake itself was quite small, reflecting the sky.

"Wow," Softly commented after he'd taken a moment to absorb the view. "This really is something, isn't it?"

Susan pointed to the eastern shores of the lake, where forest gave way to lightly wooded ground. "You can see some cabins that have been built already. The people who own them come up here maybe two or three times a year."

She thought that Softly was imagining himself on the porch of his own cabin down there in the wilderness, drinking a beer on a summer's evening as the sun went down. Maybe he would get to know some of his neighbors, and they would meet up to go fishing or hunting sometimes, and later they would have a friendly barbecue at the edge of the lake.

"Shall we go down?" she suggested.

They went back to her car and drove down into the valley, where she pulled over by the side of the road close to the lake. Softly looked around and breathed in deeply.

"You know, I think it'd be really something to have a place up here. Somewhere to get away to."

She brought lots of people here who were taken with the quiet solitude. It was hard not to be, given the surroundings, and invariably she found them musing about the house they would build, picturing themselves and their families taking vacations. Usually they were from Vancouver, though one plot had been bought by an American from San Diego. What they had in common was that their lives were firmly centered in the city and they were affluent enough to be able to consider a place in the mountains they could escape to. They liked the idea of the wilderness setting, breathing clean air, fishing for their breakfast, communing with nature—so long as they had their microwave ovens and a supermarket within driving distance where they could stock up on beer and pizza.

When Softly had seen enough, she drove him back to the turnoff where they'd left his car, since he was heading back toward Williams Lake. On the way she saw what she thought was Michael Somers's Nissan, but she couldn't see anybody around.

Softly took a brochure with pricing details and said he'd give it some thought; if he decided he was interested, he'd get in touch with the lawyer in Victoria when he got home. He thanked her for taking the time to drive him up here, and as he drove away, she made a bet with herself she wouldn't see him again. Nine out of ten people she took to the valley went away and never came back. The lack of facilities deterred most of them in the end, once they'd had a chance to get back to their hotels. There were no restaurants or shops or golf courses or, in fact, any of the things most people wanted from a vacation spot. They simply decided that the wilderness was a nice place to look at on the way to somewhere else.

She checked the time and thought she ought to be getting back to town. Jamie would be back from school, and though Linda had said she'd meet him, Susan didn't want to be too late. On the way she passed the Nissan again, and on impulse she stopped and got out.

The snow-covered ground rose gently in a broad sweep toward a far ridge above the valley where towering rock cliffs rose vertically up the mountain. Michael was coming across the snow toward her, his falcon on his fist, and as he got closer, she raised a hand. He made a gesture back that might have been a wave, and she waited until he reached the roadside.

"I saw the car," she explained. "I thought it was yours."

"You just missed seeing her fly," Michael said. "I waited for Jamie, but he didn't come over."

"My fault. I had a client to see." She grimaced. "He's not going to be happy I made him miss seeing Cully." Michael smiled. "So how's her training going?"

The falcon was beautiful, she thought. It watched her intently with intelligent eyes, and she could understand why Jamie was so fascinated by her. Michael stroked her breast feathers with a gentle caress, then adjusted the straps on her legs. As he tended to her, Susan watched his expression, his eyes clear, a faint shadow of a smile around the corners of his mouth. She couldn't imagine how this man could ever have hurt anyone, and she knew suddenly that whatever had happened, it must have been an aberration.

"She's coming along," he said in answer to her question.

"What happens when you finish?"

"I'll release her."

He looked away from her, back toward the ridge in the distance, where the smooth white of the snow ended in a line against the sky. She had the feeling he was thinking of her flying up there again, and she detected a kind of wistful note in his voice.

"Today's the first time I've flown her since I was up here with Jamie on the weekend. Vet's orders. Her wing was giving her a little trouble." He frowned as he spoke, the lines around his eyes creasing.

"She's okay, though?"

"I hope so."

"Tom Waters is a good vet," she assured him, and he looked into her eyes, his frown smoothing away. "Listen, I feel like I should repay you. You've been good to Jamie. How about letting me cook you supper one evening?"

"You don't need to do that."

"I know," Susan said. "But I'd like to. How about tomorrow?" She sensed his hesitation. "I promise I'm not a bad cook."

"Okay, thanks."

She smiled. "That's great. Come by around seven?" She looked at her watch and said she had to be going. "I'm late already. See you then."

"Okay."

He raised a hand as she drove away.

WHEN SHE GOT back to town, the school bus had come and gone, so she went over to the diner to pick Jamie up.

"How'd it go?" Linda asked.

Susan put her thumb down. "By the time I've sold those plots, if it ever happens, I'll be a hundred years old." She looked around for Jamie.

"He's with Coop," Linda said. "He came in earlier, and I said you'd taken some guy to the valley, so he offered to pick Jamie up." She noted Susan's expression. "That's okay, isn't it?"

"Of course it is," Susan said. "I always get nervous when I think of those two together, that's all."

"They'll be fine. You worry about Jamie too much."

Susan made a wry face. "It's not Jamie I'm worried about. Listen, I better go and rescue one of them. I'll see you later."

Coop's cruiser was parked outside the station house. As she approached, Ben Miller came out the door.

"Hi, Ben, is Jamie inside?" she asked.

He nodded. "Coop brought him in about half an hour ago, Mrs. Baker."

"How are they getting along?"

"Well, it's sort of strained, I'd say."

Susan sighed. "Well, say hi to your wife for me."

"I will. Bye, Mrs. Baker."

She went inside, and when they both looked over, she could tell Jamie was relieved to see her. He got up and started getting his things together. Coop's smile looked a little pained.

"Hi there," she said brightly. "Thanks for this, Coop. You didn't have to."

"I thought he might prefer to wait here instead of the diner," he said.

He got up from behind his desk, which was strewn with an array of stuff that should have been just about guaranteed to capture any kid's interest. There were some crime sheets faxed over from Williams Lake and some wanted posters that had arrived in the mail, along with a set of handcuffs and a nightstick. Jamie didn't give any of it a second glance.

"How'd the sale go?" Coop asked as he began putting things away.

"It didn't," she said. She told him about the guy from Seattle.

Without thinking, she added, to Jamie, "I saw Michael with Cully. He said you could go over tomorrow after school."

The boy's eyes lit up. Then she saw the tightening ridge of muscle in Coop's jaw, the hurt in his eyes that he couldn't hide. She cursed her own big mouth, wondering how she could have been so thoughtless. At the door, she told Jamie to go ahead to the car.

"How was he, really?" she asked, though she had already imagined the scene before she'd arrived: Jamie impassive while Coop searched for something to engage him.

"He was okay."

She felt a tender sympathy for him. All his patient efforts were rebuffed. "I know how you feel," she said, laying her hand briefly against his arm. "He doesn't mean it personally."

"It's no big deal."

He walked her out, and she had the impression he was thinking about something. They stopped across from her car, and Coop watched Jamie getting in.

"Maybe we should go fishing or something," he said suddenly.

"Fishing?"

"Yeah, I know a guy who's got a cabin up around Quesnel, on the lake. I could get it for next weekend, I think. It might make a difference, you know, if it was just me and Jamie together for a couple of days. What do you think?"

She tried to picture them together and couldn't. Sometimes David had taken Jamie fishing for the weekend, and Jamie would be excited about it for weeks afterward. Coop was waiting for her reaction, but she could already feel his disappointment at her hesitation. Maybe it would be good for Jamie, she told herself. Maybe it was what he needed. She reminded herself that he was starting to come out of himself a little.

"Why not?" she said, trying to keep the doubt from her voice.

"I'll call this guy I know," Coop said.

She wondered how she'd break it to Jamie, and decided she would need to pick her time.

"I could come over tomorrow and tell him about it," Coop suggested.

It struck her she'd invited Michael over, and that if she invited Coop, too, it would be a chance for them to get to know each other. Instead of saying that, however, she said, "Maybe you should let me tell him. Let me pick the right time." She felt a stab of guilt, and made a show of looking for her keys.

Coop didn't seem to notice anything. "Okay," he agreed.

"I better get going," she said, turning away before he saw something out of place in her eyes.

MICHAEL WAS IN the den, sitting in the same chair his dad had always used, next to the old wooden desk, its surface scarred with a lacework of razor slits and hard pinhead-like globules of ancient glue. He ran his hand across the top and felt the rough texture against his palm. A person might wonder how a writing desk had come to be marked in this way, he mused. In fact, this was where his dad had spent countless hours in the evenings, drinking small shots of bourbon and working on his model ships.

Michael chose a book off the shelf and leafed through the pages. Mildew had marked the edges; the leather binding smelled of damp and mold. The pictures were all of seventeenth- and eighteenth-century tall ships, schooners and warships, some graceful, some blunt and heavy in their outlines, all powered by sail. Some of the pictures were still in good-enough condition to make out all the fine detail of the rigging and decks. His dad had built replica models to scale, from scratch and without any plans except those he'd devised himself. The work involved was immense, and the time for each one could be counted in the hundreds of hours. He would sit in this room, night after night, cutting and shaping pieces of wood with a hobby knife, joining them with glue and leaving his marks in the surface of the desk.

Michael had searched the house for the models, but they were definitely gone. He had no idea where. When he was growing up, he'd thought it odd that his dad's models were never displayed somewhere proudly instead of consigned to shelves or even the floor in his study. He never talked about them unless he was asked, and he didn't take trips to the ocean to see the real things when sometimes they came to Vancouver from England or the States, either restored vessels or replicas. He didn't have magazines on the subject delivered, or possess any other books about them except the few on the shelf from which he copied his designs. Michael had been wondering why.

He'd decided there was a reason, and he thought he knew what it was. It was because his dad had never really been interested in ships. He'd built the models as a means of passing time. They were intricate and detailed and gave him a reason to be alone in his den for long hours at a stretch. Anything might have served the same purpose. He might have read, or made puzzles. It was possible he'd chosen to make ships simply because he already owned the books; maybe they'd been left to him by a relative. It struck Michael that he would never know.

There was a quality of ineffable sadness about the knowledge of all those hours spent in the den, and contemplating it drove Michael out of the house. His mother had always said that his dad went in there primarily to drink, and over the years Michael had absorbed this as truth. He needed air and to escape his own thoughts, and so drove into town.

Outside Clancys, he hesitated for a moment, unsure about being among people who were generally hostile. He thought, fuck them, and went inside.

The place was busy and all the tables were taken, so he bought a beer and found a spot at the end of the bar where he could be inconspicuous. Nobody paid him any attention. Country music played on the jukebox, and people were dressed either like lumberjacks or cowboys. The atmosphere was noisy, the bar full of people starting to think about the weekend coming up and drinking beer without a thought for the working day ahead of them.

Michael finished his bottle and ordered another. He thought about Susan stopping to talk to him earlier in the day and how she'd invited him to supper. He couldn't remember the last time he'd sat down across a dinner table with a woman, and he was unsure what they would talk about. Would he tell her stories about what it had been like in prison? Would they dance around tricky subjects and keep the whole thing on a safe level?

"Is this spot taken?"

He came to with a start, aware that somebody was speaking to him.

"I just wondered if you were keeping this stool to yourself." Rachel Ellis smiled at him.

"Help yourself. Sorry, I was miles away." She had a warm smile, but there was a melancholy quality in her eyes. He asked if he could buy her a drink.

"I actually just came in for cigarettes."

She offered him one, and without thinking, he said he'd given up smoking when he was in prison. She cast him a quick appraising look as she lit up.

"Maybe I will have that drink. What are you drinking?"

He looked at his empty bottle and signaled the barman for another. "The same," she said.

They touched bottles, and he asked her polite questions about her kids and where she worked. When he mentioned her husband, she looked away for a moment. Her eye scanned the bar, and when she looked back, she caught him watching her.

"Pete comes in here sometimes," she explained.

"I knew him at school, I think. Pete Ellis, right? Biggish guy?"

She nodded slightly, her expression enigmatic. "Yeah, that's him."

He thought it strange that somebody like Rachel should end up with a guy like Ellis. He'd recognized the name the second he'd heard it. The only mental picture it formed was of a loudmouth kid who liked to push people around and get into fights. Maybe he'd changed, Michael thought, though since being in prison, he'd decided people rarely did, unless they had a powerful motivation. He studied Rachel as she fiddled with her beer bottle, her fingers restless. Maybe she'd been motivation enough, he decided.

She looked up. "Can I ask you something? Why did you come back here? Do you mind me asking that? I mean, I'm just curious." She regarded him steadily, as if his answer was important to her.

"It's a nice town. Quiet. I grew up here." He took a pull of his beer. He hadn't felt the need for a cigarette for a long time, but now he did. Perhaps it was because she was smoking, or because he was in a bar with a beer in his hand. "That's three reasons."

She didn't smile at his humor. "You don't have to tell me."

"I'm sorry, I guess I'm a little touchy. My social skills have gone all to hell." He grinned at her. "The truth is, there were a lot of reasons. Some were practical, because there was nowhere else for me to go, others were about getting things sorted out. I'm not even sure I could tell you exactly. It's something I'm still working on."

"I wasn't trying to be nosy."

"I know that."

"Will you stay here, do you think? I mean, it must be hard for you here. You could just go somewhere else. Who needs it?" She peered at him intently, and then suddenly, as if she realized what she was doing, she smiled, laughing at herself. "Don't take any notice of me," she said.

"It's okay. I haven't decided yet, anyway."

She thought about that, then emptied her beer and set down the empty bottle. "Sometimes I wish I'd gotten the hell out of this town. Thanks for the drink. I have to get home."

"Anytime."

"Maybe I'll run into you again, and it'll be my turn to buy you a drink."

"I'd like that," he told her.

She hesitated, and seemed on the verge of saying something else. "It was nice to talk to you."

He watched her go, wondering about their conversation. It seemed that her questions had more to do with something about herself than about him, as if she'd been looking for answers to dilemmas of her own. He ordered another beer, deciding it would be his last. On impulse he asked the barman if there was a phone he could use, and was directed to the rear of the bar.

He went back there with his beer and a pocketful of change. It was quieter, but there were still people drinking in the booths, and on one side of the room some guys were playing pool. For a while he watched them, considering what he should do. He leaned against the wall, then made up his mind. He had Louise's Boston number in his wallet, and after he'd fed change into the phone, he dialed and listened to the ringing tone. Then somebody picked up, and a voice at the other end said, "Hello?"

ELLIS WAS AT the bar when he saw Rachel come in and go to the cigarette machine. For a moment he thought she was looking for him, and he experienced a sickening horror that she'd come over and start asking what the hell he was doing in there drinking. He thought she must have noticed he'd taken twenty bucks out of her purse that morning without telling her. He could just imagine the sneering comments from Hanson and Red Parker if she confronted him. They'd say he was pussy-whipped and laugh about how he should run on home. It was a big fucking relief when she left again without the others noticing, but he wondered what she was doing talking to that Somers guy.

Ellis hadn't even seen Somers before that, standing in the corner where nobody would notice. He watched as Somers went back to the phone. Then Red saw where he was looking.

"Ain't that that guy Somers? What the hell is he doing in here?"

Ellis took a drink. "How should I know?"

"He's got some nerve." Red belched softly and put his glass on the counter. "Your round, ain't it, Ellis?"

Ellis waited for some smart remark about whether he needed a loan to pay for a couple of pitchers, but nobody said anything, though he thought he saw Hanson smirk a little. All the stuff about when he was coming into the money he'd talked about had finally lost its interest, which was one thing he was glad about. He ordered a round and fished in his pockets, counting out change and crumpled bills. After he paid he had about a buck and half left over, but Hanson still had to buy a round to even things out, so he had at least one more coming, and there was a pint of bourbon on the floor of his truck that wasn't finished yet.

He was drinking a lot, he knew that—more than he should, but he was going through a bad patch at the moment. It was bad enough that he had no work to speak of, but things at home were getting steadily worse. Rachel was acting strangely, going around so quiet all the time, like she had things on her mind. He wanted to ask her what they were, but he wasn't sure she'd want to tell him, or even that he'd want to know if she did. He thought maybe he should let things alone for a while. It was probably the best thing: give her some space and wait till she came around.

He'd got up to take a leak the other night and found she wasn't in bed; the sheets on her side were cold. He'd been halfway down the stairs when he looked over the edge and saw the glow of a cigarette in the kitchen. He'd stopped, wondering what the hell she was doing. She was looking right at him in the darkness, but he knew she didn't see him; her mind was somewhere else. He'd thought about going down and making some coffee, maybe sitting down and talking things out the way they had years ago. In the end, though, he'd decided he ought to just let things ride, and he'd gone back upstairs to bed.

He looked back toward the phone again, and Somers was still there. It still bugged him that Somers had practically stolen the gyr falcon from him. That two grand would have made a difference to the way things were—still would, come to that. It had preyed on his mind for a bit, and he'd thought maybe he should do something about it, but thinking and doing had remained for him two separate things. All the same, seeing Somers was a harsh reminder of all the shit he'd had to put up with, a lot of it Somers's doing. He wondered again what the hell Rachel had been doing talking to him, and it occurred to him that he wouldn't even be able to ask her, because if he did, she'd know he'd been in Clancys, and he wasn't about to open that can of damn worms.

"What are you looking so steamed up about, Ellis?" Red demanded of him.

"Nothing," he said. "Just that Somers guy, I guess."

"Yeah, well, what do you care about him?"

There was a note that Ellis didn't like in Red's tone, as if Red knew about the falcon and was trying to be funny about it, but then Red just looked past him at Ellen Tilley's ass.

"I wouldn't mind getting me a piece of that now," he commented, cupping his balls with a casual gesture.

"In your dreams," Hanson said. "Bill Tilley's got a pecker bigger'n two of yours put together, Red."

Ellis snickered, glad the subject had changed, but Red smirked at him.

"What the fuck are you laughing at, Ellis? At least my woman ain't sitting around bars drinking beer with jailbirds."

"What the hell is that supposed to mean?"

"Don't tell me you didn't see her in here before," Red insisted. "Shit, you went as white as a damn sheet there for a minute. She was just sitting over there with that Somers guy you keep staring at."

"Shut your mouth, Red," Ellis warned.

Red was happy to, since he'd already made his point and Hanson was looking into his beer as if there was something in there that was deeply fascinating to him. Ellis drained his bottle and told Hanson it was his round. That fucking Somers guy was starting to really get on his nerves.

IT WAS LOUISE. He knew her voice immediately, and hearing her took him back six years. The last time he'd spoken to her she'd been

terrified of him, huddled in the corner, clutching Holly to her protectively.

"My God, Michael, what have you done?"

Until right then, it hadn't seemed real. It was the horror in Louise's
eyes that shook him: She was scared. She was petrified. Holly was
crying, not understanding anything.

There was a big chrome-framed mirror on the wall, and in it he
saw this wild-eyed person, his shirtfront splattered with blood. He
was holding a gun, waving it indiscriminately. When he paused to
reflect on this sight, he wiped his hand back through his hair, and
he could still see the faint smears of red he'd left there earlier.

Louise had thought he meant to shoot both her and Holly. He
didn't know even now if that was true. By then he was way over the
edge, spinning into the abyss. He knew he'd never threatened her
directly. He'd only let the cops believe he was holding them hostage
because he was trying to decide if he should shoot himself. Only
himself.

The truth was, he would never know what he'd been thinking
about doing.

Across the miles there was a faint hum; it was a bad line.

"Hello?" Louise said again, her tone impatient.

He couldn't speak. There was a silence that must have lasted for
five or ten seconds but seemed longer. He could almost hear her
thinking, and then there was a soft click as she hung up and the line
went dead. A soft click.

It took a moment for him to gather his composure, then he turned
to leave. He put his bottle on a table and made his way toward the
door, and as he passed along the bar, he was aware of a group of
guys drinking beer, and one guy in particular who stared at him. He
had angry pale eyes, and his mouth was clamped tight. Michael
looked away, sensing trouble.

Outside, he was halfway across the street when the door opened
behind him, music spilling out, then fading again as it closed. He
reached the other side and looked back. Two men were watching
him. He turned and made for his car, fishing for his keys.

By the time he reached it, the men were gone. He backed out of
his spot and turned off Main Street onto the road that would take
him out of town. As he did, he could see a set of headlights following

him. For a half mile he told himself that it was just a coincidence, but then he decided he didn't believe in coincidences that hung back the way this one did. He thought about what might happen if somebody ran him off the road out of town, where there were no lights, or if he was followed all the way back to the house. People around here carried rifles in their trucks. While he was still within the town limits, he pulled over to the side of the road.

He watched the approaching lights in his rearview mirror, thinking at the last moment they would go by, but then an old battered Dodge came alongside and swerved dramatically, stopping at an angle right in front of his car, blocking his way.

He got out and walked around to the front of the Nissan; two men climbed from the truck. They were the same two he'd seen outside Clancys, one of them the guy who'd stared at him as he was leaving. He was the driver and the bigger of the two, squat and thick in the body, brown-gray stubble growing over a head like a medicine ball. There was something about his stance that struck a chord, but Michael couldn't place it. The other guy was thinner, with a scar beside his eye that pulled the corner down a little. It made him look mean, but there was an uncertainty evident in his posture that belied this.

"Is there something I can help you with?" Michael asked, focusing on the driver. He kept an eye on the other man, who hung back around the tailgate of the pickup, half concealed.

Ellis leaned against the Dodge's door and lit a cigarette. When Somers had left the bar, Ellis had told Hanson he was going, and if he wanted a ride, to shift his ass. He hadn't said anything about Somers until he'd pulled out behind him, then he'd passed over the bottle of bourbon that was rolling around beneath his feet.

"See who that is up ahead?"

Hanson had looked puzzled. "Who?"

"It's that Somers guy. The one killed his wife and kid."

Hanson had taken a swig from the bottle. "Shit, he didn't do that, Ellis. It was some guy he shot."

"Listen, the only reason he didn't kill 'em is the cops got him first. That's what I read."

"I didn't know you could read, Ellis," Hanson had said.

"Very funny." Ellis had reached over and grabbed the bottle. "I say we have a little fun. Show this guy we don't want his sort around town. Whaddya say?"

Hanson had shot him a nervous look, but then he'd grinned and reached back for the bottle.

He hadn't known exactly what he was going to do, he'd still been thinking about it when Somers had stopped. Now he pointed a finger and narrowed his eyes. "I remember you, Somers." He nodded, as if this had only just occurred to him. "Your old man had the hardware store. You used to work there."

"I remember you, too," Michael said. It had come to him just then who this was. As far as he could see, Ellis hadn't changed a hell of a lot since they were at school. The question he'd asked himself in the bar came back to him, how Rachel had come to marry a guy like this. But then he reminded himself that people who knew Louise had probably asked themselves the same kind of questions about him. He wondered if this was about him talking to Rachel in the bar.

"There's a lot of people around here ain't too comfortable having someone like you living in the same town, you know," Ellis said. He looked over his shoulder at Hanson. "He was always a strange kid when he lived here. Got that off his old lady, I guess. She was crazy as a fucking loon."

Michael knew that Ellis was just trying to provoke him, and he didn't react. He thought maybe Ellis was the type who needed something to spur him on, that if he wasn't challenged, he would just talk himself out.

"They say your old lady killed herself, Somers. That true, d'you think?" Ellis blew smoke and spat on the ground. He hated the way Somers just stood there calmly. He started to think about the way Somers had been talking to and smiling at Rachel, and her smiling back at him. Who the fuck did he think he was, buying a man's wife a drink like that? It wasn't enough he stole that damn falcon, which rightfully belonged to him, now he was sitting in bars with his damn wife, for chrissakes. Maybe that was why she'd been acting so strange lately—except she'd been that way for a lot longer than Somers had been around.

"Hanson didn't live around here back then," Ellis said, half turning to Hanson while he kept an eye on Michael. "His old lady was supposed to have taken a load of pills and killed herself. She was always taking pills and all kinds of stuff. You know what people say, though, don't you?"

"Listen, why don't you just move that truck out of the way, okay?"

Michael said. He knew what was coming, and he knew Ellis was only needling him, but Michael could hear the edge in his own voice.

Ellis heard it and grinned. "They say your old man let her die, Somers. They say he came back and found her and he let her die. I guess you and your old man were a lot alike."

Michael clenched his fists. It bothered him to hear this kind of talk, even after all these years. It hit a nerve, and he knew why. It was because he'd thought the same thing. There never was any explanation for his dad coming home so late that night, after a lifetime of routine. On Wednesdays he was always home at six. So why on that one occasion did he stay out until eleven? Maybe Ellis was right, maybe he had found her and left her to die. Along with being a drunk, his dad had killed his mother.

He started to feel a pulsing ache in his temples. It shot like a needle through the side of his head and lodged behind his eyes.

"Just move your truck out of the way, Ellis," he said. He started to turn around to get back into his car. Back along the road he saw the lights of a stationary vehicle, and he wondered if there were more around like Ellis.

"Hey, Somers, who said you could go?" Ellis demanded. He hated the way Somers just fucking dismissed him, as if he was nothing to be concerned about. People had been treating him like that all his damn life.

Michael heard the belligerence in Ellis's tone. The ache behind his eyes was getting worse, and he just didn't need this. He should never have gone into town, it had been a dumb move.

"Listen, I'm leaving," he said, raising his palms outward. "I don't want any trouble."

"What you want and what you're gonna get ain't the same thing," Ellis told him. He looked to Hanson, who'd quietly slipped his hand over the back of the tailgate.

Michael knew he wasn't going to get away so easily. He felt weary of all this, and allowed his anger to harden, actually welcoming a fight, a chance to hit back. "Listen, Ellis, let me tell you something now," he said quietly. "I don't have to listen to this kind of crap, so why don't you and your shitkicker buddy over there just climb back into your truck and get the fuck out of my way."

He was ready for them if they weren't going to give him a choice. Ellis might be solid, but he had a fat gut. It wouldn't take much to stop him. The guy behind the truck was nervous-looking; he wouldn't stay to fight on his own. One thing Michael had learned in prison was how to take care of himself, out of necessity, and there had been plenty of time to kill in the gym every day.

For the first time, Ellis showed a flicker of uncertainty. Then his mean stupidity took over and he started forward. Out of the corner of his eye, Michael saw the guy at the back of the truck reach in and come out with something that looked like an ax handle.

A sudden howling whoop sounded loud close by, startling them all. Then they were bathed in light, and a second later Coop's four-by-four pulled up, the blue light flashing momentarily. Coop sat behind the wheel, his arm resting on the door, and looked them over with a nonchalant sweeping glance.

"Ellis." He nodded and looked to the other man. "Hanson. Anything I can help you with here?"

The tension eased, and when Michael looked, the ax handle Hanson had been hefting a moment earlier had vanished.

"We were just talking, Coop," Ellis said.

Coop looked at him silently, then gestured toward Ellis's truck. "That's kind of careless parking, Pete. Could be a danger to somebody there."

Ellis looked at his truck but he didn't move. "I guess you're right."

"I could tow you back into town if there's a problem."

"There's no problem." Ellis shifted his feet uncertainly, then spat on the ground. "We'll be going," he announced. He shot a final resentful stare at Michael, then he and Hanson climbed back into the truck. He backed up and swung around, then headed toward town.

Michael watched the rear lights dwindle, aware of Coop's silent scrutiny. "I'm glad you came along," he said. The pain in his head was subsiding.

Coop nodded, almost imperceptibly. "It's my job."

"Well, I'm grateful anyway," Michael said.

"I better follow them. Make sure they don't get into any more trouble." Coop made as if to leave, then paused. "I hear Jamie's been helping train that falcon of yours."

"That's right."

Coop looked as if he wanted to say something else, but then appeared to change his mind and said good night.

Michael watched as Coop turned around. The vehicle he'd seen earlier was gone, and he guessed it had been Coop back there. It made him wonder why he'd taken his time to intervene, as if he was waiting to see what would happen.

COOP DROVE INTO town and found Ellis's truck where he'd expected it to be, parked across the street from Clancys. Ellis was alone now, sitting in the dark, drinking from a bottle. Coop thought he could have just allowed whatever was about to take place back there to happen. He'd considered it, and that bothered him. He asked himself if his dislike for Somers was rooted in who Somers was, or if it was about Jamie. If he was honest with himself, he knew the answer. The truth was, he'd be happy to see Michael Somers just get the hell out of Little River. He had a feeling that if that were to happen, it would be the best thing for everybody.

He went over to Ellis's window and rapped on it.

Ellis gave a start. "Jesus, Coop, what the hell are you trying to do?"

Coop indicated the bottle Ellis was holding. "You shouldn't be driving, Pete. I would have thought you had enough problems without causing any more for yourself."

"Yeah, well." Ellis looked at the bottle and screwed the cap back on. "I was going to walk home anyway," he said.

"So what was that all about back there?" Coop asked. He was curious to know the answer. Ellis had been drinking a lot lately and getting loudmouthed with it; Coop knew that, but he didn't know what ax Ellis had to grind with Somers. Ellis wasn't exactly the type to get all righteously worked up about what Somers had done; he had too many problems of his own making to be worried about taking care of other people's.

Ellis didn't answer right away. Then he muttered something that Coop didn't catch.

"What was that, Pete?"

"I said, he cheated me, dammit!"

Coop saw the flare of irrational anger in Ellis's bloodshot eyes. "Cheated you out of what?"

"Out of two thousand bucks, that's what."

"Somers did?" Coop decided Ellis was drunker than he'd thought. He doubted Pete had ever seen two thousand dollars at one time, let alone allowed himself to be cheated out of such an amount. All the same, he was intrigued. "How did he do that?"

"That damn falcon he's got. I spent days walking around up in those mountains looking for that thing. I saw it before he even arrived here, dammit. It shoulda been mine. Had a guy all lined up was gonna pay me cash on the nail."

Then Ellis shut up abruptly, looking away as if he thought he'd said too much.

Coop pondered what Ellis had said, wondering if it was true. After a moment he said, "Pete, you know, if a guy cheated me out of that sort of money, I don't think I'd do what you were going to do tonight."

Ellis looked at Coop out of fogged eyes, trying to see what he was getting at.

Coop leaned in close. He could smell the booze coming out of Ellis's pores. "What I'd do is go get the damn bird back. That would be the smart thing, don't you think?"

19 THE STORE WAS STARTING TO LOOK DECENT again. Michael had traced the damp patches to a leak in the roof where rain had seeped in and found its way down to the ground floor. With the leak mended, he'd hacked away the damp plaster and replaced sections of the board underneath, then replastered over the top. The result wasn't perfect, but unless you were looking for the repair, you wouldn't see it. The holes in the floor had also been fixed. He'd taken up the boards and cut them off evenly, then fitted new sections in. The result left a patchwork finish, but he thought that by the time he had the whole thing sanded and restained, it would be as good as new. He'd drawn up a plan of where he was going to put new counters and the fixtures he was going to build. All he'd need to do after that would be to paint the place, and it would be finished. It would look just the way he remembered it had when he'd been a kid, he thought.

That morning he'd gone over to the real-estate office to tell Susan he wanted to finish the new counter he'd been building. "When you pick Jamie up from the bus, why don't you drop him off with me? We can go straight from here to train Cully, then I'll drop him back at your place later."

"Okay," she'd said. "You haven't forgotten about supper tonight?"

"Around seven, right?"

He'd paused to look at the pictures of property for sale, comparing the prices with what Carl Jeffrey had offered for the house. "Business good?" he'd asked.

"It's quiet right now, but things will pick up in a month or so. Are you thinking of selling?"

"Just curious."

Later, in the afternoon, Susan dropped Jamie off. While Michael finished fitting on the new countertop, Jamie sat on a box and sketched Cully, who was perched on one of the fixtures Michael had built. When he was finished, Michael glanced over the boy's shoulder. The drawing was just of Cully's head, and had captured something of her regal bearing, her sharp proud look.

"That's good." Jamie looked back quickly, startled that Michael was standing there. He closed up his pad and turned away.

Michael sat down, wiping his hands, looking around at his handiwork. It was funny seeing Jamie there. The way he sat, his expression impassive, giving no clue to what he was thinking, made Michael think he himself must have seemed that way at that age.

"This was my dad's store," he said. Other than a brief glance in his direction, a flicker of interest, barely discernible, Jamie gave no indication he'd heard. He went back to watching Cully as she stretched her wings up above her back. Abruptly she started flapping, disturbing the air around them, her feet gripping the fixture for purchase, then she settled again. She was hungry, eager for exercise. Michael rose and started getting his things together, and apropos of nothing except that it was a change to think aloud, he started talking.

"I used to work here after school. I'd sit on a stool at the end of the counter over there." He pointed, picturing the scene as if it were yesterday. "My dad would be fiddling around with stuff, serving customers, writing himself reminder notes, and I'd be doing schoolwork, or maybe sometimes I'd unpack a delivery. I'd watch him when he didn't think that I was." He paused, lost in reflection for a moment. Jamie appeared to be paying him no attention.

"He used to talk to me while he worked," Michael said. He'd forgotten that until now: the way his dad had carried on this one-sided conversation, telling him who'd been in that day, what they'd bought, the chats he'd had with people about what was in the newspapers—all kinds of stuff that Michael had barely listened to most of the time. But it was always there, this background noise that had been comforting in a way. Something familiar. It struck him how quiet the store was now.

"He worked here most of his life," Michael said. "Until he died."

Maybe it was something in his tone, but he looked over to find Jamie watching him. Just for a second their eyes met, then Jamie looked away again. There had been something in his expression, something questioning, but it was fleeting.

Michael picked up his gear and put on his gauntlet. "Okay, let's go."

They pulled over at the regular spot high up on the road to Falls Pass, and Michael took Cully out of the back of the Nissan. With his free hand he crushed one of the pills Tom Waters had given him and sprinkled the powder onto a piece of meat, which he folded and offered to Cully. She seized it and swallowed it whole.

"Antibiotics," he explained to Jamie. "Don't worry, she'll be fine," he added when Jamie looked worried, though he was less confident of that than he let on.

He stroked Cully's legs, gently brushing her toes. She arched her neck and peered with interest at his finger, then decided she would tolerate him and roused her feathers. She was more interested in the wide-open landscape and the sky, turning her head sideways to watch a duck fly overhead toward the ridge in the distance. It was heading toward the lake, and Michael had noticed that this seemed a regular route. Another flew overhead, and they watched until it was just a smudge against the sky before it dropped down to the valley below.

Cully turned her head to tug at her tail feathers, working her beak along each one in turn.

"You know what she's doing?" Michael said, and Jamie looked at him questioningly. "She's preening herself. She has an oily coating on her feathers to repel water so that when it rains she doesn't get wet, it just runs away. That's why we only stroke her breast, never her back or wings, so we don't wipe it off."

As they watched, she worked methodically, running her beak along the shafts of each wing and tail feather, spreading oil from a gland at the base. The action also worked like a zipper, straightening and aligning the filaments of each feather so that in flight the air would stream across their surface, giving her lift when she wanted it. Each feather was a masterpiece of natural design: light, yet incredibly strong, each filament sitting snugly against its neighbor.

Michael planted the block perch in the snow, leaning his weight on it until he felt it bite firm. As he stood, he took off the gauntlet and passed it to Jamie.

"Same as last time, okay?"

Jamie barely hesitated, then pulled the glove on. While Michael tied a piece of meat to the lure, Jamie bent down and took Cully up from the perch. She stepped back and found her footing, and as Jamie stood, she roused her feathers again, then laid her plumage sleek against her body, her eyes fixed on the lure.

"Take her jesses off as I walk back," Michael said. He held the lure in front of his body so that it was out of Cully's line of sight and started to walk away. The snow was unblemished, stretching around them in a sheet of pure white to the cliffs half a mile away. A pair of tracks cut a line back to the Nissan. Each step broke the frozen crust of the snow, crunching audibly, the sound mixing with Michael's breathing. He stopped fifty yards away.

"Ready?"

There was no reply, and he grinned at his mistake. Glancing over his shoulder, he saw Jamie, looking small, with Cully on his fist, her head level with his. As Michael turned he called her name and started swinging the lure. Out flicked her wings, brushing Jamie's face as he ducked away, then she was off, pushing Jamie's arm down with the force of her launch. She skimmed the snow with her wing tips as she made a line toward him. He'd been practicing with the lure the last few days, and now, as she drew close, he swung it smoothly in an arc parallel to the ground in front of him as he turned in to her path. At the last moment he pulled the lure in and she went on, rising into the clear cold air. For a few seconds he watched her rising, the sun on her back, the sky vast and open before her. Looking back, he saw Jamie's expression, pinched with worry, but this time Michael was confident. Cully was turning even before he called her.

He scrutinized the pattern of her flight. Once again, the flutter and correction was apparent, which dampened the moment, but then he peered hard and thought maybe, just maybe, it had improved a little. There was no time to ponder. She straightened and came in again, and when she was close, he threw the lure out for her to catch. He mistimed his throw slightly so that the lure landed before she reached it, but she came down with her wings thrown back, her tail fanned wide, and landed gracefully. When he had the timing down pat, he figured, she ought to be able to grasp it while it was still airborne.

Michael decided to take a break before he flew her again, so they walked to the ridge and looked out at the view. The ground fell away steeply, then leveled out like a broad snow-filled shelf before dropping down to the edge of the forest. Far beneath them, on the valley floor, a river fed a small lake in which the mountains on the other side were reflected in a perfect mirror image. Across the valley, a hawk rode a thermal in high lazy turns and issued a plaintive cry. Cully cocked her head, and when she found her distant cousin, she watched with bright interest.

When they flew her a second time, she made two passes at the lure before Michael let her catch it, and this time he threw it high so that she turned and seized it midair. When she landed, he watched to see if her injured wing would trail on the ground again, but this time, though she flicked it once or twice across her tail, the wing stayed in place.

He let Jamie carry her back to the Nissan, and when she was in, he closed the door and caught Jamie's eye. They grinned at each other, and for that moment no words were necessary.

SUSAN HAD MADE a beef casserole, simmering the meat in wine and its own juices, flavoring it with onions, beans, a handful of herbs, and garlic. She tasted it and added more seasoning. Fresh broccoli was in a pan of water just waiting to be heated, and there were dried noodles she was going to cook just before serving, then toss in butter and black pepper. A bottle of merlot was open to breathe a little. Outside, it had become dark. She stepped into the TV room, where Jamie was doing schoolwork.

"I'm going upstairs to get changed, okay?" She looked over at what he was doing. "What are you writing? Can I see?"

He showed her. It was an essay for his English class, all about Cully. She read how he'd held her on his fist, and how Michael had then called her to the lure.

"You held her yourself?" she said, surprised and faintly alarmed. There was no doubt Cully was beautiful, but she also had sharp talons and a lethal-looking beak.

He grinned at her, his whole face lighting up. Bending down, she kissed his head. His hair smelled of shampoo and his own boyish scent, clean and childlike and carrying echoes of when he was just a baby at her breast. She loved the texture of his hair, like satin against her skin. He let her hug him, then squirmed free, still grinning. Her eyes filled with inexplicable tears, and she wiped them away.

"I have to get ready. Michael will be here soon."

His expression clouded for a second, then it was gone and he went back to his work.

She took a shower, letting the hot needles of water pound her skin, then dressed in jeans and a shirt. She tied her hair back and put on a little makeup, noticing that she carried a high flush in her cheeks that might have been from the shower.

Michael was on time, knocking on the door just after seven. Susan went through from the kitchen to let him in, checking in the mirror on the way to make sure she hadn't wiped flour on her face or something. She still looked flushed, but she guessed it was from the heat of the kitchen. When she opened the door, he was standing on the porch holding a bottle of wine, wearing jeans and a dark blue sweater that was almost the same color as his eyes. He appeared freshly shaved, and she could smell a subtle cologne. His thick hair was brushed, but it was still unruly.

"Hi. Come on in." She took the wine he offered her and showed him where he could hang his coat. While she fetched some glasses, he poked his head into the TV room and said hi to Jamie, getting only a brief glance in return.

Susan noted Michael's slightly puzzled response as she gave him some wine. "He's like that with people who come to the house." She shrugged.

"I thought he was loosening up a little," Michael said.

"Maybe he sees things differently when you two are out with Cully. He's writing a story about her, by the way, for a school project. He's pretty absorbed with her, I guess you know that."

"I'm pretty absorbed with her myself," Michael said, and smiled.

His eyes wandered around the kitchen. He seemed to be taking it all in, his gaze resting here and there. She felt a slight awkwardness in the situation that probably came from both of them. "I need to check how dinner's coming." She stood over her pots, keeping her hands busy, sipping occasionally at her wine while they chatted inconsequentially about her business, where she was from, how long she had lived in Little River. He maneuvered the conversation so that they never talked about him, it seemed to Susan, or maybe it was just that he asked more questions than she did.

"How long is it since Jamie has spoken?" he asked as she refilled his glass.

"Ever since his dad died. I guess you know all about that. It was an accident; it happened around a year and a half ago."

"I heard something about it. Tom Waters mentioned it."

She went back to her pots. It seemed that there was a break in the flow of conversation, as if he were leaving it to her to decide if she wanted to tell him more. "According to the psychologist Jamie was seeing," she said at last, "he's blotting out what happened. Not talking is a way of avoiding having to face it. He was with David that day. I guess the shock was too much for a kid his age."

"He's still seeing a psychologist?"

"Not right now. We're kind of taking a break." She let a moment pass. "You know, I haven't seen him so excited about anything for a long time as he is about is about Cully. I can't tell you how it felt to see his face when he got home today. He looked as if he had a million-watt lightbulb behind his eyes. I wish there was something more I could do to thank you."

"You don't have to," Michael said. "Besides, to tell the truth, I like having him around."

She wondered about that, whether she ought to seize his remark as an opening. "It must get lonely over there," she said, not quite achieving the casual tone she'd tried for. She gave a nervous little laugh. "I mean, I know how it must have felt coming back here . . . I mean, with all the talk . . ." She trailed off uncertainly. "Listen, you don't have to talk about it if you don't want to."

"It's okay. You're right, it does get a little lonesome at times."

"Can I ask you something?"

He hesitated, looking wary, but then nodded. "Okay."

"Why did you come back here?"

He sipped at his wine, avoiding her eye, and she could tell he was thinking about how to answer her. "I had nowhere else to go," he said eventually.

She felt rebuffed, and a flush of heat rose to her face. It was a pat answer that obviously had nothing to do with his real reasons, reasons he obviously didn't want to talk about. "I'm sorry. It's really none of my business, is it? Listen, I'm going to get Jamie upstairs. Just relax, and we'll eat when I come down. Make yourself at home." She left the room before he could say anything.

Once she had Jamie in bed, she told him he could read for a while; then she went into the bathroom. She splashed water on her face and dried off, staring at her reflection. She didn't know why she felt the way she did, nervous and awkward, why she'd felt the need to hurry from the kitchen. When she went back down, she took a breath and smiled as she walked into the kitchen. He was standing by the window, looking at her copper pots hanging from the ceiling.

"Okay. It's just a casserole," she said, downplaying her efforts. "But there's plenty of it, so I hope you're feeling hungry."

"It smells good."

They sat down to eat, their conversation more stilted than before, as if they were both uncomfortable with the situation. Eventually, he put down his cutlery.

"Look, I didn't mean to cut you off earlier. I'm not used to talking about myself."

"That's okay. I understand."

"No, it's not okay. You asked me why I came back here, and the truth is, the things that landed me in jail started here, when I was a kid. I thought coming back here might help me to understand some of them, and myself, and maybe help me to put it all behind me."

Susan thought about that for a second. "And is it working?"

He frowned, toying with his glass. "I don't know."

She decided to take a chance, now that he was sort of opening up. "Can I ask you something else?"

He half smiled. "Sure."

"What were you thinking about when I came in the room earlier? You were looking at those copper pots, and you had this funny kind of expression, I don't know, maybe wistful or something."

He shrugged, smiling again. "It's nothing, really. I was just thinking about how the light gleamed in them, kind of deep and soft. Warm. I always thought of copper pans like that, as a homey thing." He gestured about the kitchen. "This room is like that."

She wondered what he was comparing it to—maybe the hospital he'd been in, or prison, or the house where he lived now. He had a far-off look in his eye, as if he was thinking of something else. He finished his meal and put down his fork.

"The food was terrific. Thank you."

She'd hardly noticed her own, eating without tasting. "There's more."

"Thanks, but I'm full, really."

He rose with her as she started to clear the table, and though she told him to relax, he insisted. He helped her prepare dessert, a fruit salad for which she whipped up a little cream. While she did that, he made coffee. As they moved around the work space together, they brushed against each other, and she could smell his cologne. Her heart was beating a little too fast, she thought, and there was a slight tension in the air, or was it her? He seemed relaxed enough, maintaining his slight reserve.

Over coffee, she told him about David, about how she'd come to be in Little River. "It was never what I planned," she finished up. Talking about David made her feel a vague unease, and her eye went to his picture, pinned to the bulletin board on the wall. Michael followed her look. "Did you know him?" she asked, realizing suddenly that they were around the same age and would have gone to school together.

"Not really," he answered.

A silence fell over them, each reflective, and when he finished his coffee and said he ought to be going, in a way she was relieved. She felt suddenly like being alone. On the porch, he thanked her for the meal.

"Anytime," she said, and closed the door.

WHEN HE GOT back to his house, Michael sat on the porch, nursing a whiskey and thinking about how much Susan's kitchen had reminded him of what he'd missed in his life over the past few years. A home. A family. But it also brought darker thoughts to mind. Once he'd had those things, and it had ended with him waving a gun while his family cowered in terror. He stared up at the sky, at the deep black infinite space lit with distant stars, and felt its emptiness surround him, felt no more significant than a speck of dust.

20 ELLIS LEFT HIS TRUCK OUT OF SIGHT, back in the trees, and walked the last half mile or so to where Michael's Nissan was pulled off the road. By the time he reached it, he was wheezing and breathless. He had a headache that made him wince and a thirst he couldn't quench. When he'd stopped at the gas station earlier to buy a packet of aspirin, he'd grabbed a can of Coke; now he wished he'd bought a couple more while he was at it. He'd chewed half a dozen of the aspirin while he drove, washing them down with the Coke, but they hadn't done him much good. Now he was sweating inside his parka, and every so often he felt as if his stomach were rising up into his throat. He leaned against the Nissan to get his breath, spat into the snow, and swore softly.

He looked toward the ridge: Somers and the Baker kid were out there. He couldn't tell what they were doing until he looked through his glasses, and then he could see the falcon. It was flying around in a high, wide circle, then coming in toward Somers, who was swinging something on a line. After watching for a while, Ellis dropped the glasses. He guessed that whatever they were doing they'd be there for a while, and he started back toward his truck.

A WEEK EARLIER Ellis had woke with a hangover thinking about what Coop had said the night before: "What I'd do is go get the damn bird back." Those had been his exact words. Ellis was trying to figure out if he'd heard him right—and if he had, then what the hell was going on? He thought he must have got it wrong somehow, but the more he thought about it, the more he knew he hadn't. One thing was for sure: Coop sure as hell wasn't doing him any favors because they were such great buddies or anything. He must have had his own reasons for saying what he did, but Ellis couldn't think what the hell they might be.

He was considering it that morning while the kids were getting ready for school, and he was so absorbed he didn't even hear them leave. Rachel came back into kitchen and put on some fresh coffee, then asked him if he was planning on going to the yard.

"Yeah," he said. She was standing at the counter, watching him.

"What're you thinking?" she asked.

He couldn't tell her about Coop, of course, so he said it was just work. She didn't say anything, just watched him steadily over the rim of her cup. He wondered if she'd been up again in the night, smoking cigarettes in the dark, thinking about whatever was on her mind.

It worried him when she became thoughtful these days. Sometimes he felt like he didn't exist, like she was off someplace in her mind. She was a lot smarter than he was, he knew that. She probably thought that if she hadn't married him, she could have done something better with her life than get saddled with kids and a whole lot of bills to worry about. But no. He knew how much she loved those kids. She'd do just about anything for them.

She turned away, saying she had to get ready for work, and he watched her wash up the breakfast dishes. She was wearing a robe over her nightgown, and when she moved, the material stretched over her hips. It had been a long time since they'd lain together on the big bed upstairs. That was one place where things had always felt right for them, no matter what else was going on.

Sometimes when he'd been lying between her legs, he'd look down at her face as he moved inside her. Her eyes would be closed, her mouth a little bit open so he could see the tips of her teeth, and she'd be kind of smiling in a way that made him think of some sleek cat that had found itself a warm place to lie after a big bowl of cream. He couldn't remember the last time they'd had sex, the last time the old springs had creaked underneath them and she'd slid a pillow under her butt to raise up her hips.

He got up and stood behind her at the sink, and she knew he was there. He felt her stiffen, but she just went on with what she was doing. He wanted to reach around her waist and hold her, but in the end he didn't touch her. When he left, he called out that he would be late. But he didn't know if she'd answered him.

The day after that, Red Parker had said he needed someone to help him with a load he was taking to Calgary. Red had asked Ellis if he wanted to make a few bucks if the yard wasn't busy, and not being in a position to refuse, Ellis had gone along for the ride. As it turned out, they'd been gone a week; Red had picked up some work while they were in Calgary, and they'd taken a couple of days to get back. Ellis had spent the last of the money he'd made in a cowboy bar in Williams Lake, though he couldn't remember much about the night except for a couple of women who'd sat at their table drinking with him and Red until the money had run out. Soon as they knew that, those girls had been up and gone in a snap.

Now that he was back again, and broke, Ellis had turned his thoughts again to Michael Somers and the falcon.

WHEN HE GOT back down to the road into town, Ellis turned off when he reached the Somers place. He took his time looking around, since he knew he wouldn't be disturbed. Out back in the woodshed, a perch had been rigged up. Judging from the white splashing on the ground, Ellis guessed that this was where Somers kept the falcon. He noted that there was no lock on the door. While he was there, he had a look around the rest of the house, climbing up on the porch and peering in the windows. The rooms he could see had a kind of un-lived-in look. The furniture was old, and everything was in place as if somebody had walked out years ago and never come back.

When he'd seen enough, Ellis got back into his truck and headed to the yard. He made a call to Prince George and waited until Tusker picked up the phone.

"This is Pete Ellis," he said.

"I'm busy, Ellis, you'll have to call later."

He could sense that the son of a bitch was about to hang up on him and said quickly, "If you don't want that gyr falcon, I guess I can sell it to somebody else."

There was a short silence while Tusker thought about it. "Are we talking about the falcon you were going to bring me weeks ago, Ellis? Is that still the same bird?"

Ellis allowed that Tusker was entitled to be a little doubtful after the way things had turned out, but he guessed that if Tusker wasn't interested, he really *would* have hung up.

"This time I've got it."

Another pause. "You actually have, Ellis? Because you know I've got better things to do than this. I already made myself look stupid to a client once. I don't want to do that again."

"I said I had it, didn't I?" Ellis said.

"All right, then. It's definitely a gyr?"

Ellis didn't even respond to that. "So, are we talking about the same kind of money?" he asked instead.

"Fifteen hundred."

"We agreed on two thousand."

"That was then," Tusker said. "I incurred expenses."

Ellis gripped the phone hard until his knuckles were white. People like Tusker were always jostling for an edge, always looking to make an extra buck out of somebody else's work. He wondered what kind of expenses Tusker had that amounted to five hundred bucks. Maybe a phone call or two.

"Fuck you," Ellis said.

"Wait a minute."

"What?"

There was a pause, then Tusker said reluctantly, "I guess I could make it seventeen hundred." Ellis thought about it, and Tusker added quickly, "You put me to a lot of trouble last time, Ellis."

Ellis gritted his teeth and thought, What the hell. He agreed to deliver the falcon the following day.

It was strange, though, when he thought about it. The money wasn't going to change his life, he knew that. It was going to take more than seventeen hundred bucks just to pay off the bank loans. But it wasn't about just the money anymore; maybe it never had been. It was about doing something right for once in his damn life. It was about proving something to Rachel. He could still take her out, they could have dinner somewhere and they would talk and maybe somehow they'd get back to where they'd started from. He was pretty sure everything would work out if they could just do that.

If he showed her he could do something right, if he gave her the money and said she should do what she thought best with it, and if he told her he wasn't going to drink anymore, well, that would change things, wouldn't it?

 STANDING ON THE PORCH OUTSIDE THE
house, Michael felt a shift in the air. It wasn't
getting so cold at night, and the days were
getting longer. Though there was still plenty of snow on
the ground, no more had fallen for several days. The
weather reports said that in the south, spring had arrived early.
Around Little River spring was still a month or so away, but there
was a feeling of expectation in the air. Beneath the snow and the ice,
in the frozen ground, a stirring of new life had begun, a gathering
of energy, buds getting ready to break out when the time was right.
When the snow melted, the high tundra would be the home of purple
fleabane, red Indian paintbrush plants, and yellow ragwort.

The day had dawned with a clear sky. There was warmth in the
sun, and in the woods around the clearing, snow melted and dripped
from the branches of trees.

High up on the road toward Falls Pass where he would drive later
with Jamie, it was colder, the breeze still carrying a sharp winter
bite. Cully had flown to the lure for a week, and now she could make
a dozen or more passes before her wing started to show signs of tiring.
The course of antibiotics was finished, and now there was nothing
more Tom Waters could do. He'd examined her again and said he
thought the infection had cleared, but maybe the injury had left her
permanently weakened. He didn't know if she retained the strength
and agility to survive in the wild.

Later, as Michael and Jamie crossed the snowfield toward the ridge,
Michael was thinking about what lay ahead, and he was worried.

Cully had to prove that she was capable of hunting before he could contemplate releasing her, and before that test he had to persuade her to do what the books called "stooping." Jamie had picked up on his mood and cast him anxious glances as they prepared to fly her.

"We're going to try something a little different today," Michael explained. He described that what they'd been doing so far, having Cully chase the lure at relatively low levels, wasn't always the way she would hunt in the wild. "Sometimes she'll ride the thermals high up, waiting for an opportunity. When she dives, that's the stoop; she'll close her wings up like this." He made a V shape with his hands. "When she comes down, it'll be fast. That's what we have to get her to do today."

Jamie listened, but his expression remained puzzled. Michael hesitated, unsure of how much he should explain, but he reasoned that Jamie had come this far with him and had a right to know what risk this entailed for Cully. "I don't know if her wing will stand it," he went on. "Do you know what G force is, Jamie? It's the gravitational effect a jet fighter pilot experiences."

Michael saw that Jamie had some idea of what he meant but was trying to understand what this had to do with Cully. Michael tried to explain, repeating what Frank had told him, that the G force effect a falcon experiences in a full stoop, at speeds of over a hundred miles an hour, would kill a man. The final part of her training entailed hiding the lure as she came by after the first pass, the idea being that she would then rise and circle, waiting for her meal. He had to keep the lure hidden while she gained height. She might find a perch on the cliffs half a mile away, or just land in confusion on the snow, but if she did either of these things, he had to try again until eventually she got the hang of it, following her natural instincts. When she was high enough, he had to show her the lure and call her; then she would stoop, imitating the way she would hunt in the wild, eventually throwing out her wings as she neared the ground to suddenly change direction and catch the lure. That was the moment when the pressure on her wing would be at its greatest and, in Cully's case, the most dangerous. In falconry terms, this was known as training a bird to "wait on."

Cully's survival depended on this.

She gave no sign this was anything but a normal day's training for her. When Jamie had her on his fist, she bit impatiently at the glove and roused her feathers, eager for her meal. Michael made sure Jamie had hold of her jesses tightly before he took off the leash and swivel. He'd explained a dozen times how important it was that she didn't take off trailing her leash. All Jamie had to do now was quickly thread the jesses through their eyelets.

"Ready?"

Jamie stared at him, hesitant, unsure.

"She has to be able to do this," Michael said.

Jamie looked fearful, understanding what was at stake, and he took a step backward, half turning as if to shield Cully.

"Look at her, Jamie," Michael urged.

Cully stood square-footed and turned into the breeze, her wings held partly open, fluttering from her body.

"She's ready," he said, and they could see that she was. Her eyes were fixed on the sky and on distant points of the landscape. Her fate was her own, and they could only be spectators. Michael was her custodian but he didn't own her—that was how it had always been. He tested her hunger one more time with a scrap of meat that she snatched eagerly, then he started to walk away.

At forty yards or so he turned and swung the lure, and as he did so, he called her. She came to him, making a halfhearted feint at the lure, knowing she wouldn't be allowed it yet, and then began to rise. She started to turn, but he had coiled the lure and put it away in the bag at his side. She came around and, having nothing to pursue, settled into a glide, passing overhead, waiting.

HIGH IN THE air, the breeze is stronger, and it makes a crisp stream-lined sound as it passes across Cully's feathers. She is aware of the sound and of the power that she can tap into with a subtle shift in the angle at which she holds her wings. There is some instinctive recognition of its feel and texture that is pleasurable to her. With each sweeping wing stroke she feels the stretch and contraction of the large powerful muscles across her back and breast, and as she rises, she tucks her feet beneath her tail.

When she turns, the figures below are as clear to her as if they were close enough to touch. She is able to resolve detail ten times more clearly than a man. She's already at 150 feet, but she can see the color of their eyes, the rhythm of muscle movement beneath the exposed skin of hand and face. For a moment she falters, unsure what to do when she can't see her meal. To save energy, she hangs on the air, letting the updraft carry her while she waits to see what will happen. The thermal she has found carries her higher, and she turns in a circle to stay within its light grasp. When she feels its effect lessening, she flies until she feels the upward lift of another current, then she circles again, allowing herself to be carried aloft.

Beneath her, the broad white slope is punctuated only by the two stationary figures she has come to know. She trusts them, and has come to accept the strange world of sights and sounds she has lived in. Sometimes when she is in the air she feels the call of old instincts, and now, as she circles, she looks northward across a landscape of valleys and mountains toward distant peaks. Something pulls her in that direction, but then, too, there is a pull earthward. She feels a bond with the tall figure now far below and half a mile distant. His face is turned toward her, pale against the dark of his body. She is above the cliffs now, at fifteen hundred feet, and as she passes over the ridge, thermals rising from the valley carry her higher and farther afield.

She turns her head, surveying the landscape, and looks back to the figures on the ground. She is hungry.

MICHAEL WATCHED WHILE she drifted higher and farther away. A tight ball of apprehension had settled in his stomach. Jamie had come closer, his face pinched and white. He kept looking from Michael to Cully as she drew away from them, becoming just a dark speck against the clear sky, and Michael could feel the boy's silent plea for him to call her back.

There was a temptation not to. He could just watch her while she drifted far across the valley. Hunger would distract her; she'd see a rabbit or a pigeon and vanish, and he'd never know what happened to her. He could convince himself that she survived, and whenever he thought of her afterward, he could imagine her flying free somewhere high above the mountains. It was a momentary fantasy, fueled by the fear of witnessing what might happen next.

When she had drifted above the valley and was two thousand feet in the air, barely visible if he took his eyes from her for a moment, he produced the lure and called her. He could feel his heartbeat, the rushing of blood coursing through his veins, the tightness in his throat. He was afraid he'd left it too long, that she wouldn't hear him, wouldn't see the lure, wouldn't want to return. He had lived with her too long to lose her now. Though he was afraid for her, he had a greater fear, he realized; that of never knowing her final fate. Her success would be his as well, and if her wing gave out under the pressure, though he felt sick at the possibility, that, too, he would share. He felt such a powerful swelling of emotion, such a long-forgotten feeling, that it took him a moment to understand what it was. It was the opening up of his heart and soul to another creature.

While he watched and sent a silent prayer out to her, she folded back her wings and dropped.

SHE IS THE perfection of aerodynamics as she hurtles earthward. The sound of rushing air builds to a low whistle. Her path is straight and true, her direction faultless, as she gathers speed so quickly that she is a blur in the sky. In her wing there is a tremor where there has been an injury, a faint stiffness that she feels at times, but if she senses there is a risk to herself, she pays it no heed because this is how she lives. There is no possibility of compromise. She is a gyr falcon, without peer in the air, and her life is marked out in absolutes. She will survive as nature designed her, in full beauty and grace, or she will perish unbowed. She gives no quarter when she homes in on her target, and she expects none. Below her, the small dark figures rush closer.

AS SHE STOOPED, a portent of disaster clung in Michael's mind: the horror that her wing would snap, that it would flutter uselessly, whipping in the wind as she corkscrewed earthward. He could see an imperfection in her flight, a slight twisting out of alignment.

She altered the angle of her dive at a hundred feet, swooping in a perfect crescent, and on cue he released the lure so that it spun into the air. At the apex of its upward momentum Cully seized it, and with half a dozen strokes she carried it to the ground and landed in a soft swirl of snow. She stood erect, her beak open, panting and recovering her breath, then mantled her wings protectively and began tearing at her meal.

Michael exhaled, a long slow release of pent-up tension.

When he could trust his voice, he turned to Jamie, his eyes stinging. "I told you there was nothing to worry about, didn't I?" he said.

Jamie broke into a wide smile.

"I guess that's about how I feel, too," Michael said.

DRIVING HOME, HE was thoughtful. "You know," he said to Jamie eventually, "I thought about just letting her go for a little while up there." He wasn't sure how exactly to phrase what he wanted to say. He had Jamie's attention, but the boy was wearing the perplexed frown that was becoming familiar as a sign he didn't fully understand something. "I mean, I was afraid of calling her back because of what might happen. It felt like it would be easier to just let her go, to pretend everything was okay. I don't think that would have been the right thing to do, though, do you?"

A silence ensued, and then after a while Michael said, "I guess sometimes we just have to make the hard choices, no matter what that means we have to face."

Jamie turned away and looked out the windshield, and Michael wondered if there wasn't a lesson out of this day for himself.

ELLIS PARKED HIS truck in the trees off the road where it wouldn't be seen and made his way down the track toward the house. There was a moon to light the way, casting shadows across the clearing. He stopped above the house and listened. There was no sound, no lights; everything was still. All he had to do was go around to the woodshed. He was wearing gloves to protect himself from the falcon, but he figured it would be sleepy and that if he was quick enough, he ought to be able to grab hold of it and just break its neck nice and cleanly. There wouldn't even be a gunshot wound for Tusker to worry about.

Ellis hesitated, a hint of misgiving arising to trouble his mind. He didn't know exactly why he felt the way he did, except that maybe it had something to do with Rachel coming by the yard again that afternoon.

"I think we should talk," she'd announced, standing suddenly in the doorway.

At the time he'd had his feet up on the desk; since there was little

else he had to do, he'd been taking a nap. By then his headache had
subsided, and though he still generally felt like shit, he was buoyed
by his call to Tusker. It had surprised the hell out of him seeing
Rachel there, and following right after his surprise had come something else when he saw the expression on her face. It was because
she'd been watching him sleeping, and when he'd sensed her presence
and opened his eyes, he'd caught her off guard. She'd been looking
at him like he was some stinking old dog that couldn't control itself
any longer, couldn't rouse itself to go outside, and was asleep by the
fire. Like she was facing up to the fact that it would be kinder to
call the vet to come over and put it to sleep, or to just take it into
the woods with a rifle. It had shocked him, to understand what she
thought of him.

"I was just taking a break," he'd said.

She'd come inside and closed the door, not meeting his eye while
she rearranged her expression.

"Want some coffee?" he'd asked. He'd got up and gone to the stove,
wondering where the hell the coffeepot was, then remembering he'd
put it under the desk after he'd taken a leak in it earlier because he
didn't want to go outside.

She'd shook her head and sat down.

"Not working?" he'd said. He'd put a log on the fire and tried to
smooth his hair a little and straighten himself out.

"I asked for a couple of hours off. I didn't want to do this at home,
not with the kids around."

Ellis hadn't liked the way she'd sounded, serious and heavy with
what he felt were likely to be unwelcome recriminations. It had
struck him that he'd allowed things to go too far, and now she'd come
to tell him that she was leaving. He'd known he shouldn't be surprised; things always went against him, like he was constantly swimming against the tide. If he were one of those guys who believed in
people living more than once, he'd think he must have done something particularly bad in one of his other lives and that this was all
just so he'd suffer and know what it felt like. The trouble was, he
didn't believe in any of that stuff. It would be nice to think that
sometime he'd get another shot and then things would be different
because he'd paid his dues, but it was just a false hope. What you
see is what you get. He'd tried to picture his life without Rachel. She

would take the kids, and who would blame her? He'd end up some bum living in an old railcar, drinking cheap liquor from a brown paper bag.

"Listen," he'd said, "I'm glad you came by. I wasn't gonna say anything until later, but now that you're here, I may as well give you the good news."

"Pete, listen. We have to talk."

She hadn't even heard him. As he'd looked at her, he'd known she was absorbed in the speech she'd worked out in her head and didn't want to be distracted from it. Her face had been set, but she hadn't looked him in the eye, so he'd known she didn't quite hate him yet.

"I don't think I can go on like this anymore, Pete," Rachel said.

"I'm trying to tell you, Rachel, everything's gonna change now. I had some luck. I got a break finally." He'd gone on, talking over the top of her. He must've sounded like he was babbling, desperate, and she'd stopped then and peered at him. He'd guessed she was wondering if he was drunk.

It had occurred to him then that he hadn't been home since he'd got back from Calgary.

"How'd you know I was here?"

She'd given a little shake of her head, like it was hard for her to keep up with his train of thought.

"I'm gonna get some money. Tomorrow," he'd told her, not waiting for her to answer him. "Things are gonna be different then. I mean, I need to stop drinking. I know that. Thing is, it's hard for a guy like me, Rachel. You don't know how hard it is sometimes. I never had a fucking chance, every thing I touch turns to shit. Except for you. You're the best thing there is, and I know that. I've got this money coming, I mean it's not a fortune or anything, but it's almost a couple thousand. It'll pay some of the bills. We can get started again, the way things used to be. I need you."

He'd said the last part quickly, sensing she wanted to interrupt him. He'd wanted to stop her from saying whatever was on her mind. He'd known how pathetic he must have seemed. He was dirty, unshaven, and he probably stank.

She'd fastened her eyes on him. Seconds went by, and he'd felt her resolve fade away. Then she'd sounded suspicious.

"Where's this money coming from?"

"Just a deal me and Red did in Calgary. It was lucky."

She'd looked at him as if she was weighing it up, deciding whether or not to believe him.

He'd known that it all rode on that moment. Somehow, if she believed him, it might all work out, but if she didn't, that was the end of it. It seemed stupid that his life could rest on this one thing. In the end, she'd just kind of nodded sadly. He'd tried to get her to stay awhile so they could talk. He'd wanted to explain to her all his plans about the future, but she'd just looked at him as if she was dog-tired and said she'd see him at home. In truth, he'd been kind of relieved. She'd unsettled him, the way she'd looked at him. He hadn't known, really, what had been going on in her mind, but he'd thought she'd given him some kind of a chance, maybe a day or a week. He'd just hoped she never got to hear about how he'd come by the money. Somehow he'd thought that might change everything.

Thinking about it now, on Somers's property, Ellis wasn't sure what to do. He had this feeling that if he went ahead with what he was planning, he was crossing some kind of line, that there would be things he'd have to live with as a result. Down below, the house remained quiet and still. He didn't understand why he was holding back. He didn't owe Somers anything, that was for sure; the whole fucking town would've been glad if he'd never come back. Even Coop had his own agenda here, for chrissakes. Nobody was ever going to blame Ellis for what he was doing if it ever came out. And the falcon—well, that was his, anyway, by rights. He still couldn't make the idea sit easy in his mind. He kept thinking about Rachel, what she'd say, but he was caught between a rock and a hard place now. Somehow he had to get the money, and he was damned if he could think of any other way. He started down, creeping around the rear of the house.

IN A DREAM, Michael was speaking with his father. He was showing him around the store now that it was almost fixed up, restored to the way it had once been, and then they were looking out a window together. Across the snow they watched a man and a boy flying a falcon. He was telling his dad how he'd found the falcon, then he was telling him about the boy and his mother, who lived in the house through the woods. All the time he talked, his father looked out the window at the man and the boy, then at last he turned toward Michael and smiled.

He woke, the bedclothes twisted into knots around his legs, and sat up in bed. The dream that had been so vivid just moments before receded and became vague, the emotions he'd felt so clearly were almost forgotten, vanishing back into his subconscious mind. He got out of bed and went to the window, aware that something outside had woken him. Looking down across the clearing, he saw darkness chase the gray light of the moon across the snow as clouds gathered overhead. A pair of fiercely amber eyes shone from what he thought was a point midway across the clearing, perhaps a few feet from the ground. Nothing more was discernible except these bright points of intelligent light that he felt were staring up at him. He went downstairs and opened the front door to step onto the porch, a little warily, his heart thudding in his chest. The darkness before him was empty, but then a sound from around the back of the house reached him, like a door opening, old hinges squealing.

A rising wind rattled the bones of trees as he rounded the corner, and the moon appeared through thin cloud, casting soft light on the squat shape of the woodshed. A figure moved in the doorway, a solid shape in the dark.

"Hey, who is that?" Michael called out, suddenly alarmed.

The moon vanished again and plunged everything into darkness, but Michael heard something moving, stumbling, going back along the rear of the house. He hesitated at the corner, torn between pursuit and returning to the woodshed, unsure if Cully was still there. Fear and dread quickened his heart as he looked inside, but she was there: safe, unharmed, a pale shape. When he went closer, she stepped onto his fist when he offered it.

Outside, he heard the faint sound of an engine growing fainter, then all was quiet and there was only the wind in the trees. From then, he decided, Cully would stay in the kitchen, with the door locked, and he took her with him to rig up a perch.

It wasn't until the morning that he found animal tracks in the clearing, and he remembered those eyes he'd seen, which for a while he'd thought must have been a dream. The tracks looked like those of a big cat. In an Indian legend he'd heard somewhere, a mountain lion contains the spirit of a dead person.

He shook his head. Crazy.

22 "HEY," SUSAN SAID, REACHING OVER TO mock-thump Jamie's arm. "You look like you're going to a funeral."

She rolled her eyes and thought, Damn, terrific choice of words. Jamie, however, didn't appear to have noticed. She wondered if he'd even heard her. Since she'd told him that Coop was taking him fishing, he'd shut down on her.

"Come on, it's just for a couple of days," she'd said. "You'll have a good time."

Evidently he hadn't seen it that way. He mooched around the house, sullen and uncommunicative. It startled her to think how quickly she'd been able to forget what he could be like. She'd got used to seeing him come home excited, his eyes shining after being with Michael and Cully. It even seemed as though he was starting to come out of himself more, and maybe she'd allowed herself to nurture a seed of hope. Once or twice she'd caught herself daydreaming that he might speak again. Sometimes on the way home she imagined opening the door and he'd be there and he'd say hi and she'd smile and say hi back and go on through to the kitchen. Then it would hit her and she'd stop dead in her tracks, her heart thumping. She'd turn around and Jamie would be grinning at her, and she'd sweep him into her arms, laughing and crying at the same time, and . . . and life would be a fairy tale, she thought. Which it never was. It was just a daydream. She looked across at him and he was hunched down into himself, as remote as ever.

When they arrived in town, she pulled up outside her office and switched off the engine. They were a couple of minutes early, and Coop hadn't arrived yet. She smoothed Jamie's hair, a reflex action he responded to by brushing her hand away irritably.

"Listen, Jamie, I want you to be nice to Coop," she said. "He really thought you'd have a good time. He's doing this for you." She lapsed into silence for a moment, uncertain whom she was trying to convince. "Listen, Cully will still be there when you get back." She had spoken to Michael, just to let him know Jamie would be away for the weekend. He'd looked at Jamie, who had wandered off and was kicking the porch step with a monotonous thud. She'd thought he was going to make some comment about how Jamie seemed less than enthusiastic about the idea, but then he'd gone over and spoken to him, though she couldn't hear what he'd said.

"I just told him I'd wait until next weekend before I take Cully hunting. I think he thought he might miss it," he'd explained.

"Hunting?" she'd said.

"Her training's over. All she has to do now is show she can still catch her own food."

"Oh." She'd nodded, not sure at first why the idea made her uneasy. "What happens then?"

"I let her go, I hope."

She'd looked across at Jamie then, and wondered if he knew. She'd thought Michael understood what she was thinking when their eyes met, but he hadn't said anything.

Susan looked at her watch, wondering where Coop was. From down the street she could see John Heelman's truck coming toward them. It stopped, and John got out to climb a ladder so he could string lines across the street from which later he'd hang the winter festival decorations.

She pointed him out to Jamie. "This year we'll have a great time," she promised, knowing she sounded as if she was trying to make it up to him.

Privately, she thought how quickly time had passed. It was hard to believe a year had gone by since the last festival, the first they'd spent without David. It had been a hard time for them both. Any celebration or anniversary had seemed like a reminder. Now her primary feeling was one of mild panic. What had changed in a year? Where would they be next year?

At that moment, Coop's truck pulled alongside her own, and he climbed out to greet her. "Everything okay?"

"I guess so." She glanced back toward Jamie.

"How is he?"

She shrugged. "I don't know. I tried talking to him. Listen, Coop, I hope you know what you're doing here. I'll understand if you want to change your mind."

Coop smiled. "That bad, huh?"

"He's not in what I'd call a terrific mood."

"Maybe he's worried about my cooking."

She smiled at his joke. "Maybe."

"Well, he'll be okay once we get going," Coop said confidently. He went around to Jamie's door and opened it. "Let's go, Jamie. We've got to get moving if we're going to eat fish for supper."

Susan got Jamie's things out of the car and transferred them into the back of Coop's truck. She kissed Jamie good-bye, and as they pulled away, she raised her hand, but he didn't respond. She saw him watching her through the window, his face getting smaller as they drove down the street. When they turned the corner, she felt suddenly alone.

THE HOUSE WHERE Rachel and Pete Ellis lived was on the western edge of town. It was a two-story weatherboard place with a garden and a garage. Once, Rachel had loved it. Much of her spare time had been spent planting the garden or scraping and painting, planning how the house would look when the rotted railings on the porch were replaced, the foundations reblocked, and all the windows and doors rehung. At first they'd lived in one room and the kitchen, the rest of the house being uninhabitable. Then, room by room, they'd gone through and done the worst of the repair work. When the baby had arrived, that had slowed down progress. She hadn't minded, though. Finishing the house became a dream she could hang on to, a vision she could take out and look at now and then, when the lumberyard and the kids took up less of her time.

She sat on their ancient bed and looked at the walls. Parts of them were papered with an old, long-faded pattern; other places were bare, with smoothed gray patches of stopping compound spread over the board. The whole house was the same: unfinished, tottering between neglect and good intentions. Nothing had been done for a long time. They had started with determination and ended with disillusionment.

She should have told Pete she was leaving when she'd gone to the yard to talk to him, she decided. While he'd been away in Calgary, she'd had some time to think, to really think clearly, and she'd built a resolve based on the knowledge that if she didn't go, Pete would drag her down with him. She had managed to feel determined by the time she got to the yard, and when she'd opened the door and found him asleep in the chair, unshaven, snoring with his mouth open, and the place reeking of liquor and stale unwashed clothes, she'd been momentarily appalled at herself for having waited this long.

In the end, she hadn't had the nerve to say she was leaving him. She'd been afraid of how he might react, had thought that when he saw she was serious, he might even get violent. However, she'd been prepared for that. Instead, though, he'd taken her by surprise. He'd guessed why she was there and then hadn't given her a chance to talk, telling her how he was going to stop drinking, how they'd make things all right again, that he needed her. If he hadn't said he needed her, she might not have listened, but he'd sounded naked and bleeding and she wasn't made of stone. They had been married for a long time, and once, she had loved him despite his faults. She had always known his weakness, but she'd accepted him anyway, and she was plagued with a feeling of guilt now that she was planning on abandoning him. Still, she knew her feeling wasn't rational. Hadn't she tried to make their marriage work? Didn't she owe herself another chance?

Maybe her guilt had a sharper focus because all the time Pete had been away and she'd been thinking about what to do, she'd kept remembering what it had been like talking to Michael Somers the night she'd met him in Clancys. For the first time in a long while she'd felt that she wasn't just Pete Ellis's wife, struggling to pay bills and feed the family. She'd experienced the heady rush that comes from being attracted to somebody and sensing that the attraction is mutual. She'd felt the way she had when she was younger, when she'd known men looked at her in a certain way and her whole life had been ahead of her.

She told herself she'd been crazy to listen to Pete. All that stuff about how he had some money coming from a deal he and Red had done in Calgary—she was certain that this was just hot air. All the same, he'd talked as if there really was something in it, as if this deal would somehow allow him to drag himself out of the hole he'd dug for himself. She hadn't necessarily believed he'd stop drinking, that he'd get himself together, and she'd found his begging pitiable, but still, she'd backed down. Outside, taking deep breaths, she'd gone over in her mind everything he'd said. He felt sorry for himself, he thought he was being victimized, and that was what she couldn't stand. He believed that his failure was the result of a conspiracy against him; he wouldn't accept that it was due to his own shortcomings. She knew he'd never change, that this money was just another fantasy, because he was *always* looking for the magic solution. She'd almost gone back in, vowing to stick to her earlier resolve, but her sense that he was on the edge had stopped her. Everything about him—his tone, his appearance, his beseeching, desperate, bloodshot eyes—made her think that if she pushed him he would fall. It had scared her a little, and she'd wondered if he might do something terrible.

Since then, he'd called once to say he had to go away again with Red Parker. That was two days ago, and she hadn't heard from him since. She'd known from his voice that his deal, whatever it was, hadn't worked out, and that he just couldn't face her. Unable to comfort him, she'd hung up.

She went to the mirror and held up the dress she'd bought earlier that day in Williams Lake. It was black and reached midthigh. Simple but flattering. She knew she looked good in it.

That morning, she'd called information for Michael's number, and he'd picked up after the third ring. When she'd told him who it was, he'd seemed surprised and puzzled.

"I just thought you probably don't get out much," she'd said, trying to sound as if her words weren't rehearsed. "Pete's away at the moment, and I thought you might like to get something to eat, have a drink, you know?" She'd given it a moment. "It's okay if you don't want to, it was just a thought."

There'd been a pause, then he'd said, "What did you have in mind?"

She'd spoken quickly, rushing to get the words out before her nerve failed her, before the thumping of her heart got so loud it drowned them out. "There's a place toward the highway, the Red Rooster? Don't be put off by the name, it's better than it sounds."

She'd given him directions, and if he'd wondered why she'd picked a place so far out of town, he hadn't say anything. When she'd hung up, her hand shook with the faintest tremor.

Even now, holding up the first new dress she'd bought in years, she wasn't sure what exactly she was doing. Maybe she just wanted to spend some time with somebody who wasn't exactly a stranger but who felt as if he wasn't from this town, either—someone who wouldn't look at her and think of her just as Rachel Ellis who was married to a bum and a loser, who wouldn't pity her and try to hide it, who wouldn't notice the first signs of premature aging in the lines around her eyes. She just wanted to know what that felt like.

She ran a bath, pouring in a fragrant oil, and waiting for the tub to fill, she laid out the new underwear she'd also bought that day. She'd put it all on her credit card—the amount she'd spent bothered her, but she tried to put it out of her mind. She could worry about how she'd pay for it later, she told herself. For now, she wanted to forget about her life. The kids were with friends, it was anybody's guess where Pete was, and she had the house to herself. She went downstairs and poured a glass of wine to drink while she soaked in her bath.

THE RED ROOSTER looked more restrained than its name suggested. It was a few miles off the highway and had once been a sprawling settler's home. It was surrounded by landscaped gardens and a parking lot. Michael had imagined some bright neon rooster strutting the roof, a place where hamburgers were the chef's special and a jukebox played in the corner. Instead, as he drove in he couldn't see how the place had earned its name. There *was* a neon sign, and it *was* in red, but it was simply the name of the place written in understated flowing script and placed discreetly above the door.

It was ten minutes before eight. The host checked off the reservation, then showed Michael where the bar was. The restaurant was busy. The lighting was low, and music played at a level just below the hum of voices. Michael took a seat at the bar and ordered a beer. While he waited, he reflected on Rachel's phone call that morning, and as then, he was unsure about what to read into it. He'd been surprised by her call, but once he got past that, he knew he was going to accept. He didn't want to think too closely about what his motives were. Just having her company was reason enough.

He stood up as she approached. She was wearing a simple black dress beneath which her body moved fluidly, the material softly caressing her hollows and curves as she walked. She smiled, and her eyes were soft and dark in the subdued lighting.

"Sorry. I'm a little late," she said.

"I only just arrived myself. Can I get you a drink?"

"Maybe some wine," she said, sitting down.

With their drinks in front of them, Rachel produced cigarettes and lit one. "You don't, do you?"

"I gave up."

"That's right, you said."

She smiled at him and sipped her wine. She was feeling just a fraction heady from the couple of glasses she'd had before she left the house, which was just as well—otherwise, she might never have come. In the parking lot, she'd sat for a minute in the dark, feeling nervous and exhilarated.

"By the way, thanks for asking me here," Michael said. He looked around, making admiring noises about the place. The fact was, they were uneasy in each other's company, but he didn't know if it was because of him. It had been so long since he'd been in a restaurant with a woman, and he was keenly aware of the unfamiliarity of the situation.

Rachel smoked with quick nervous gestures, stubbing cigarettes out with sharp jabs when she'd just lit them; then, when the bartender replaced the ashtray, she'd light another.

"I hate smoking," she said.

She knew that the way she was acting was affecting them both, but she couldn't stop herself. She didn't know what she was doing here, and she thought maybe she ought to tell him it had been a mistake. Her dress was making her feel conspicuous now; she was aware of his eyes drawn to her as they talked, flickering over her body. He wasn't staring or being obvious, but she could feel his interest all the same. Before she could act on her thoughts, they were shown to their table, and that felt better. Her hands had something to do, though she barely tasted the food. He was so different from

Pete. He looked younger, for a start, and his eyes, though they were serious and kind of distant, touched her in some way when he smiled. She wanted to reach across the table and put her hand to his cheek, to feel the texture of his skin.

They talked a lot about the past, about school and people they remembered, and she told him what had happened to some of them. Over dinner they grew more relaxed in each other's company. He was, she realized, as nervous as she was. This was a situation neither of them was used to. She asked him about what had happened in Toronto, how he'd come to be in prison. She didn't want to dwell on it, but it would have been unnatural not to mention it.

"If you don't want to talk about it, that's fine with me," she told him.

"There's nothing much to tell that you probably don't already know." He shrugged. "I had a kind of breakdown, and I let things get out of control. I lost my perspective on reality, as my friend Heller used to be fond of saying."

"Who's he?"

"A shrink. It's all in the past. How about you, anyway? I know you're married and you've got two kids. What else is there to know about you?"

"Nothing much," Rachel said.

Michael shook his head emphatically. "Don't put yourself down. You've got a family. Your kids are growing up happy and healthy; that's a lot to be proud of."

"You sound as if you really mean that," Rachel said, surprised at the emotion in his voice.

"I do mean it."

"I guess you're right. I suppose I wish I hadn't had them when I was so young, that's all." She swirled the wine in her glass. "Maybe I just wish I hadn't gotten married when I was so young. Sometimes I feel as if I've just let my life drift by. I mean, I love my kids more than anything, don't get me wrong." She hesitated. "I don't know what I mean, exactly."

He didn't say anything, but smiled in understanding.

"I guess we all have our regrets, right?" Rachel said. "Can I ask you something? Do you miss your daughter?"

He nodded, his eyes clouding as if the room had become darker. "I think about her every day. I'm not sure I'd say I miss her so much, because I don't know her, but I miss what could have been. Sometimes I think what I feel is like grief for the dead. I wish things hadn't happened the way they did, and that we were still together, but that's futile, isn't it? She's lost to me now. The same way her mother was before everything blew up."

His voice held a taint of bitterness, she thought. "You blame yourself, don't you?" she said at last.

"Who else would I blame?"

"I don't know. Maybe blame isn't what you should be thinking about." She reached across the table and put her hand on his. It rested there a moment before she withdrew it. "You could still see your daughter, couldn't you?" she said.

"She has a different life now. She wouldn't even remember me."

"Your wife wouldn't have told her about you?"

"I don't know. I didn't want her to write or visit when I was in prison. I cut myself off from them. I don't know what Holly knows."

"She's still your daughter. Children are forgiving; they're not at all like us. Not like the people around here," Rachel said.

"I suppose I think it's better this way. Better for Holly."

"Better for her not to know her father?"

"She's better off without a crazy father."

Rachel felt slightly shocked that he'd say something like that, and she could tell that he meant it. "You haven't forgiven yourself, have you? You had a breakdown, you said it yourself, and it was a long time ago."

A waiter came to clear the table, and for a few moments they didn't speak. "Look, do you mind if we change the subject?" Michael said when they were alone again. "I appreciate what you're saying, it's just I'd rather talk about something else." He'd felt a dull ache start up in his temples, which he absently massaged. He sensed that Rachel had problems enough of her own without being saddled with his. He imagined that anybody married to somebody like Pete Ellis had to have a few regrets.

"What?" Her voice interrupted his thoughts.

He realized he'd been drifting. His headache subsided. "Sorry?"

"You had a funny kind of expression then. What were you thinking about?"

"To be honest? I was just thinking about you. About what you were saying earlier, about getting married young."

"You mean, you were wondering why I'd marry someone like Pete?"

The directness of her question took him unawares, but he admitted she was right. He wondered if she knew about Ellis and his buddy coming after him the night he'd met her in Clancys, and he guessed that she didn't or she would have said something. "You just seem like very different people."

She gave an ironic smile. "When I met Pete, he was just out of the army. It's probably hard for you to appreciate, but he was different then. He wanted to make something of himself, and he was kind of sweet." She was hardly able to reconcile Pete as he was now with how he'd been then. It seemed like a lifetime ago that she'd decided she loved him. "I was young. If I'd waited, got to know him better, I might have seen his weaknesses, but we never do at that age, right?"

"Not even at our own," Michael agreed.

"People change. They become whole different people," Rachel said. "Makes it hard for marriages to last a lifetime when that happens, don't you think?"

"I'm not the person to ask," he said.

"I'm sorry. I was just thinking about myself."

"Don't be sorry. It's true, anyway."

He'd felt it that night in Clancys, that she was unhappy and looking inside herself for answers, but he knew now that she hadn't found them yet, that asking him here had been part of her search.

She looked at him across the table. "What are you thinking about?" she asked.

"Nothing," he said. He couldn't tell her he was wondering what it would feel like to hold a woman again, to feel the softness of her skin, the warmth of her body, to hear his name spoken with tenderness and passion.

They had finished their meal. Rachel said, "We could leave. I could come back to your house if you like." She thought her voice sounded unnatural, but she held his eye. There was a tremor in her throat, and she kept her hands clasped on her lap so they wouldn't tremble.

"I'd like that," Michael said.

OUTSIDE, THEY WALKED across the lot together, pausing as Michael pointed out his Nissan.

"I'll follow you," Rachel told him. Headlights swung into the lot, sweeping over them, and a truck stopped by the side entrance. She saw Ted Hanson get out and go around to unload something from the back, probably a deer he'd shot and sold to the restaurant. She turned her face away and hurried on before he saw her.

It had begun to snow very lightly. Michael drove with the window down, even though the cold air numbed the side of his face and snowflakes drifted inside. Every now and then, he looked in the rearview mirror to make sure her lights were still there. Now that he was alone and had time to think, he didn't know if this was the right thing to be doing. He found himself thinking about Susan.

When they reached the house, they stood on the porch for a moment, looking out across the clearing. She was shivering inside her parka, and he put his arm around her and drew her close. Her arms went around him in response, and she rested her head on his shoulder.

A shape flitted in the air, and he thought it was the owl he sometimes saw hunting its territory. As if in answer to his thought, it hooted from among the trees. The light snow that had been falling began to drift in the breeze.

They went inside, and Michael poured them both a drink. He stoked the fire, threw another log on, and turned out the lights except for a lamp in the corner. They sat in chairs, watching the flames cast flickering patterns and sparks shoot up the chimney.

Rachel sat with her legs curled up beneath her, holding her glass in both hands. The light from the flames emphasized the dark yellow in his hair, she thought, and caught the blue of his eyes. He was strong; his arms around her had wakened feelings in her, warmth in her belly and breasts. She wanted to let herself go, to stay with him for the night. She felt that then she might know for certain what she should do about her life, and yet she also felt reluctant. She knew what her decision would be if she slept with Michael; it would be like closing a door, a confirmation that what was past was irretrievable, because then she could never stay with Pete. She couldn't cheat on him.

"Can I have another drink?" she asked, breaking the silence that had fallen over them.

He brought the bottle over, and she arranged cushions on the floor. He sat with his back against a chair and let her lean against him.

"Can we just talk for a little while?" she said.

Michael pulled her close, feeling her warmth, smelling her hair, and watched the flames.

STANDING AT HER kitchen window that evening, Susan watched the snow falling outside. It was very light now: She could watch individual flakes as they floated to the ground. Earlier, she'd gone outside to watch the sky as the light faded, but the clouds were too thick for her to be able see anything and she'd come in again. She sipped at the glass of wine she'd poured from a bottle she'd opened fresh, wondering how Coop and Jamie were faring in this weather. It was supposed to be worse up where they were. She smiled, imagining them in a Denny's eating hamburgers and fries before going back to a motel to watch TV all night. Maybe Coop should have waited until spring, she thought.

She couldn't remember the last time she'd had the house to herself, and thought it had to be when David was alive and had taken Jamie away for a couple of days. The house was silent; she realized it was the absence of the TV blaring in the other room that she noticed. Otherwise, nothing much was different. Her son moved around the house like a ghost sometimes, unnaturally quiet.

She finished her wine and poured another glass, looking vaguely at the refrigerator and wondering what she could make to eat. She felt hungry but didn't want to cook. The wine on an empty stomach was making her light-headed. She decided to put a frozen pizza in the oven, then went to a cupboard where she kept a pack of cigarettes for emergencies or times when, like this, she just felt like smoking. She lit one and inhaled, hating the taste and the nicotine rush but perversely enjoying it, too.

She considered putting on some music, unsure that she wanted silence, but couldn't quite decide. She wondered what it would be like to have a house full of kids, running around making all kinds of noise. A few years ago, she and David had started trying to get pregnant again. After he'd died, she'd grieved for a daughter she'd imagined in every detail who would now never be born. Of course, she was still young enough to have children.

The pizza tasted bland, like processed everything, and when she tried to liven it up with herbs and pepper, then a little chili sauce, she overdid it and ruined it. It went in the trash with barely a slice out of it, and she smoked another cigarette. Outside, it had become dark, with no moon or stars. She couldn't see ten feet beyond the window. She wondered what somebody might think looking in on her, framed in the bright, warm window. Would a stranger wonder about her life and why she stood getting drunk and smoking alone? Would he think she was beautiful, or wonder what she looked like naked? She shook her head a little, bemused at herself.

In the afternoon she'd been busy for once, because she'd sold a house to a couple moving here from the city and they'd wanted one last look around. Later, she'd gone over to the diner and watched the winter festival decorations being put up, transforming Main Street. On the last night of the festival there would be a dance in the hotel; it was an annual event, the only real event in the town. Almost everybody would go, and she'd agreed to help with the arrangements. She'd spent the last hour of the afternoon making lists of things to do and buy and wishing she could be home to enjoy the quiet time she'd been given. Only now that she had her wish, something was wrong. It was too quiet and she was feeling melancholy.

She thought she might run a bath and soak, then have an early night. She could light a candle and carry the wine upstairs, but she saw that the bottle was empty. David's picture looked down at her from the bulletin board. He was grinning, but half his face was hidden behind a reminder note to pick up some yogurt. It occurred to her that if she didn't want to be alone, she could go out somewhere, but she was too drunk to drive. Still, she found herself getting her coat and pulling on boots to take a walk in the fresh air. When she opened the door, Bob looked up from his basket, then flopped back down again when he felt the cold. Outside, the air was still and the snow had stopped falling.

She stood on the porch, and her thoughts turned toward Michael. It was like pushing open a door that had already been open a crack, letting it swing wide without resistance, and his image entered her mind as easily as if he'd stepped into a room where she was sitting. She'd been dwelling on the fact that he'd soon be finished training Cully, and though she wondered what that would mean for Jamie, she admitted that she also wondered what it might mean for her.

She wondered if he really intended to open that store, recalled the way he'd looked at the pictures of property for sale on her office wall and asked how business was. Did that mean he would leave? She reacted to the thought, inside, and knew she didn't want that to happen.

She went through the woods, refusing to pause and think about where she was going or what she'd do when she got there. When she reached the edge of the clearing, she stopped. A dim light came from inside Michael's house. She was beginning to feel cold, and the air had sobered her a little. Just then the front door opened and he stepped out onto the porch. She watched him as he stood there. She didn't move, staying close to a tree, afraid that he would see her. He was too far away for her to see his face, but she could imagine his eyes, the way she could see his loneliness in them.

The wine had made her bold, and she decided she would just go and talk to him. As she stepped out of the trees into view, he saw her and froze, peering at her in the darkness, and she wondered if he could tell who it was. As she took another step closer, a greeting forming on her lips, another figure appeared in the doorway behind him, silhouetted in the dim light.

FOR A MOMENT Michael thought he was seeing a ghost, a spirit. He didn't move, surprised and yet accepting, and then he felt it was only a person. Peering into the night, seeing only a dark shape, he wondered who it could be, and thought that whoever it was had been watching him. He could feel that now, and he realized it had to be Susan. Before he could think anymore, a shadow fell across his own and Rachel stood behind him. She stepped close and arranged herself and the blanket she was wrapped in around him.

"What are you doing out here?" she said quietly.

He closed his eyes, and when he opened them, the figure was gone. He wondered if he'd imagined it. "You fell asleep. I didn't want to wake you," he said.

"I'm sorry, it must have been the wine. I didn't mean for it to happen like this."

"It's okay," he said, turning to her.

"Anyway, maybe now wasn't the time for either of us," Rachel said, and she looked beyond him to the clearing.

He wondered if she had glimpsed the figure, too, but when he looked at her questioningly, she just smiled faintly and went inside. Before he followed, he looked back to the trees, but if Susan had been there before, she was gone now.

23 THE SOUND OF A VEHICLE COMING DOWN toward the house woke her, and Susan opened her eyes to sunlight coming through the window. Her mouth was dry; and when she moved, sharp pains shot through her temples. A heavy, dull ache settled in the back of her head.

She made it to the window and saw Coop's truck outside, and Jamie getting out. For a moment, she was confused about the time. The clock said it was almost noon, which meant she'd slept really late, but she still couldn't figure out what they were doing back so soon. She hadn't been expecting them until late in the afternoon.

She pulled on a pair of jeans and hurriedly brushed her hair, briefly horrified at the way she looked in the mirror. She opened the door to see Coop putting Jamie's things down on the porch.

"Hey, I wasn't expecting to see you guys until later." She tried to sound happily surprised, but her voice came out like a croak.

"We decided to come back early. The weather wasn't so good," Coop said.

She looked from his set, enigmatic expression to Jamie, who hung back and avoided looking at her, and guessed there was more to it.

"Go and get washed up," she told Jamie. "Then I'll fix you something to eat."

He went past her, head down, and she waited until he was out of earshot.

"So what really happened?"

Coop scratched his head. "Well, we got to the cabin okay, and everything was going fine. I mean, Jamie wasn't acting like he was having the time of his life or anything, but he was fishing anyway. I thought he might ease up a little once we got the barbecue going. Only there was no food to cook."

"What do you mean? You forgot to take the food?"

Coop looked uncomfortable. "I don't think that's what happened."

Susan tried to read what he meant, but her head was still hurting and she was finding it hard to think. Memories of the night before were starting to crowd her mind. A bottle of wine, a whole bottle, on an empty stomach.

"You okay, Susan?"

She focused her thoughts. "Sure, I'm fine." She managed a smile. "You were saying about the food?"

"It was right there when we left. I packed everything away in the cooler. There was steak and potatoes, some ham, eggs, coffee, everything."

"Maybe you forgot it," she suggested.

"The cooler's still there in the back of the truck, but it's empty."

This was just getting too hard for Susan to follow. "What are you trying to say?"

"Only thing I can think is that when we stopped for gas on the way, Jamie must have got out while I was in the store."

Finally she saw what he was getting at. "Jamie dumped the food? Oh God, Coop. I'm so sorry." She took his hand. "Come inside, I'll put some coffee on."

SHE DID HER best to make it up to him, but she could tell he was hurt. She cooked some eggs and sat with him at the table, and he told her that they'd spent the night in a motel. He hadn't seen any point in staying after that, so this morning they'd driven back.

She was angry with Jamie that he could do something like that.

"Don't take it out on him," Coop said. "It's no big deal."

"It is, though," she said. "What am I going to do with him?"

"He'll come around. Give him time."

She could hardly believe his patience; she didn't know why he persevered when all his efforts met with the same response. Except, she reminded herself, she *did* know why.

"So what did you do all by yourself?" Coop asked her.

Her smile faltered. The empty wine bottle was still on the counter, and she knew what she must look like. "Nothing much," she said.

Suddenly she saw herself standing on the edge of the clearing while Michael looked across at her from the porch; then a woman appeared behind him. Jesus, what had she been thinking?

"Susan?" Coop looked at her worriedly. "You look sorta pale, you know."

"I'm okay. Just a headache."

She couldn't meet his eye and stood up to clear the table, feeling heat rise in her face. She felt humiliated. For an instant she clung to the idea that Michael might not have recognized her, though that was a faint hope. Even if he hadn't seen at first that it was her, he would have worked it out eventually. He would wonder why she'd been there. How many reasons could there be?

She thought about having to face him again, and her headache got worse. Vaguely she wondered who the woman had been.

"I guess I should be going." Coop got to his feet.

She turned to face him, trying to compose herself, though she didn't think she was doing a very good job. He looked at her strangely, and she thought he could read her thoughts.

"I'm really sorry, Coop," she said again as she went with him to the door.

"It's no big deal," he said. "He can't hold out forever."

The implication in that bothered her, but she couldn't face thinking about anything right then. She waved as he went, then shut the door and leaned against it, her eyes closed.

She felt that her life had drifted from her control, and she didn't know what she was going to do about it.

PART THREE

THE FIRST WEEK IN APRIL, THE STORE
was finished. The floor had been sanded and
stained, and successive coats of polyurethane
lent a deep luster. The walls were all painted, and the
sign outside had been taken down and a new board put
in its place, dark green but otherwise blank. The counter ran along
the back wall as it had when Michael was a boy; the shelves and
fixtures he'd built were all empty and waiting.

There was no money left to buy merchandise. Michael took a trip
down to Kamloops and saw a wholesaler there who agreed to supply
opening stock on sale or return so long as Michael could pay for it
all up front. So Michael went to a bank in Williams Lake and took
out a mortgage on his house, and midweek, a truck pulled up to the
store loaded with cartons. As he helped the two guys unload, Michael
was aware that people were stopping across the street to stare, and
when he went into the diner to buy the guys a late breakfast, the
place went quiet.

The driver, whose name was Walt, looked around in puzzlement,
picking up the turned-away looks and the muttering.

"Small towns," Michael said. He shrugged.

"Yeah," Walt agreed uncertainly.

When the unloading was finished, it took Michael three days to
check everything off against the invoice and display it all on the
shelves and fixtures. When he was finally done, he put up some signs
in the windows, which were still blanked out with paper, announcing
the grand opening.

When everything was ready, he locked the door behind him and drove to the church on the edge of town. After he'd pulled over, he sat behind the wheel and drank a beer from the six-pack on the seat beside him. He'd grown up disliking and resenting his dad, believing everything his mother had told him over the years. He was a drunk who'd wanted to leave them when Michael was young, she'd said, but she'd shamed him into staying. Ever since she'd died, he'd wondered if his dad had really found her that day and left her, the way some people had said. For that, and for everything else his mother had bitterly nurtured in him, he'd left Little River Bend meaning never to return and vowing that whatever happened in his life, he'd never screw his own kids up the way he'd been screwed up.

As he'd come to realize over the years that his mother had been crazy, it had, as if by osmosis, also seeped into his awareness that maybe his dad hadn't been everything she'd tried to make him out to be. As Michael had tried to assimilate that notion and started to wonder if cutting his father dead all those years had been an injustice, his own madness was budding, and when his dad died before any of the mixed-up quagmire of his emotions could be resolved, he'd lost control and fallen into the abyss. He wasn't sure what he'd been looking for when he'd decided to come back; maybe it was just that he needed to look his demons in the eye. He accepted now that he could do no more. He would never know for sure all of the answers to the questions he had, and all he could do was accept that. Perhaps initially he'd been looking for a neat package to explain himself, a set of actions and reactions, but now he knew it would never be that simple.

He finished his beer, and in the fading light he went across the road. Back in the corner, beneath the old tree, a figure emerged from the landscape of headstones and angels, and as they met on the path, she looked at him briefly, meeting his eye. She was an elderly woman, with fine wrinkled skin and bright eyes, her white hair pulled tight beneath a hat. For an instant he thought she was going to stop and say something, but then, with her head down, she went on, and he watched her retreating back.

He stood beside his parents' grave, and though he'd thought he might say something, he didn't. At different times he'd felt angry and bitter toward them, individually and together, but now he just felt regret. After a while he turned around and drove back into town.

In the dark, the lights of the decorations for the forthcoming festival gave Main Street a celebratory air. The posters were all over town, advertising the sled races and market day, the cooking competitions and woodsmen's events. The highlight was to be the supper and dance at the Valley Hotel. Michael went past the store and turned off toward home, but on the way he took a short detour and pulled up outside Susan's house. He hadn't seen her for more than a week, not since the night Rachel had been at his house.

He pulled up and killed the engine, and from inside the house he heard the dog barking. When he knocked at the door, he had to wait only a second or two before Susan opened it.

"Hi. I was on my way back from town," he said.

There was a mixture of things in her expression, but they shifted and fled before he could interpret them, and her face set, giving nothing away.

"I wanted to tell Jamie that I'm going to take Cully hunting on Saturday. I thought he'd want to come along."

"I'll tell him," she said. "I know he'll want to go."

She was being polite but distant with him, and he had the feeling she wanted to end their conversation as quickly as she could and close the door on him. Ever since that night, he'd wanted to come over and say something to her, but quite what he didn't know. At times he was uncertain even that it had been Susan in the clearing, and what, if it was her, she'd been doing there. Faced with her cool reserve now, he was at a loss for something to say that might bridge the gap between them; he wasn't even entirely sure why he wanted to, what he thought it might lead to. Perhaps for a while he'd allowed feelings for her to grow in him almost unnoticed. He felt that she'd taken root in him, and at night he thought of her while he sat alone in the house in front of a fire. He mused about what might have happened had Rachel not been at his house that night. Now, though, all he saw in her expression was something like discomfort at his presence.

"I have something on the stove," Susan said, breaking into his thoughts. "I better go." She made as if to close the door

"Wait," he said quickly. "I saw there's a dance at the hotel in town this weekend, and . . . well, I wondered if you'd like to go. With me, I mean." It hadn't come out the way he'd planned; he was out of practice and unsure of her. "What I'm trying to say is, I'd like to take you."

Her expression was blank for a moment, then she said, "I can't. I'm sorry. Somebody . . . I mean, Coop has already asked me."

He tried to keep the disappointment from showing in his expression. "It doesn't matter, then. It was just an idea," he said. He thought again that perhaps he'd been wrong about seeing her in the clearing, or misinterpreted her presence. He'd always wondered if she and Coop were involved, and perhaps in the end it was better to believe that they were. Maybe she and Jamie simply represented something Michael had lost, something he could never regain. As he retreated down the steps, she said something he couldn't quite hear, and he turned back.

"I said, 'Good luck.' I hope everything goes well with Cully. I'll tell Jamie you came by."

"Thanks." He went to his car as the door closed behind him.

25 SUSAN SAT AT THE COUNTER, HER SEAT swiveled around so that she could see across the street. The paper was gone from the windows of Michael's store, revealing displays and special offers. The sign above the door was freshly painted.

"I haven't seen anyone go in there for an hour," she said.

Linda sat beside Susan to take a break. "Nobody's been in there all day, from what I've seen," she said.

"And they won't, either," Carl Jeffrey butted in as he took a seat. "Let me have a piece of that blueberry pie and some coffee, Linda." Linda rolled her eyes and got up to fetch his order.

"You sound as if you're pleased about that," Susan said to Carl.

Carl shrugged. "It's not a case of being pleased or otherwise, Susan. I'm just stating a fact. I could've told him right from the start he was wasting his time." He took a mouthful of pie. "Mind you, I didn't think he was going to make it so hard for himself. What the hell does a town this size need with two hardware stores?"

Susan frowned. She didn't particularly like Carl; he was just too smug for her taste. There were plenty of others like him, the businessmen and their wives who liked to think they ran the town, sitting on all the council committees, making a lot of noise about moral values and keeping Little River a decent place to live. And yet it was well known that Carl had been seen with a waitress from the truck stop on the highway, and that his car was sometimes parked around the back of the Sunset Motel.

All the same, he was right, she admitted. She couldn't understand why Michael had decided to sell hardware, of all things, when there was a store just down the street that was part of a big chain and could afford to sell its merchandise cheaper. It didn't make a lot of sense.

"He should've taken what was offered when he had the chance," Carl commented. He wiped his mouth with a napkin and stood up to find his wallet. "It was a fair price. More than fair."

"He had to make a living," Susan pointed out, "since nobody would give him a job."

"Yeah, well, I guess that hasn't changed," Carl said. "The only thing that's different is that now he's going to get less money for that store than he would have if he'd sold when he had the chance."

"But he's fixed it all up," Susan said.

"That's not the issue." Carl put some money down on the counter. "It's about market forces, Susan, you ought to know that. Things change; he's got a mortgage now—and no income, by the look of it. That sorta reduces his negotiating power, I'd say."

"You mean, it gives people a chance to take advantage of him," Susan said.

"Hey, what are you being so defensive about?" Carl wrinkled his brow. "What's he to you, anyway?"

"He doesn't have to be anything to me, does he? He's just my neighbor, and I don't see why anyone should want to take such obvious pleasure in somebody else's bad luck, that's all."

"Luck's got nothing to do with it. He brought this all on himself. Anyway, I have to go. Good pie, Linda."

Susan watched him go, his suit jacket stretched across his broad back. "Asshole," she muttered.

Linda grinned. "He may be an asshole, but you have to admit he's got a point. It was a pretty dumb idea to sell hardware."

"Yes, I know," Susan admitted. "That doesn't mean I can't feel sorry for him." She slid off her stool. "I should get going, too. I'll see you later."

Back in her office, she sat behind her desk fiddling distractedly with a pen. After a while she got up and went down the street, pausing briefly to look in the window of Somers Hardware before she went inside. Michael was leaning against the wall behind the counter, reading the newspaper. He looked surprised to see her. She picked something up at random and went to the counter.

"I'd like to buy this, please," she said.

He looked at it. "You want a wrench?"

She hadn't even looked to see what it was. "That's right. How much is it?"

She met his eye and felt her cheeks starting to heat up. She'd done her best to avoid him since the night she'd humiliated herself outside his house, determining that the best way to handle it was to pretend it had never happened.

"It is for sale, isn't it? I mean, this is a store?"

"Sure." He looked around and got a bag. "There's no charge."

"That's not a good way to make money."

"You're my first customer. That means you get your purchase free."

She didn't know what to say. "It'll get busier when people realize you're here."

He smiled. "I don't think so."

His attitude was perplexing. She'd thought he would be angry and bitter—disappointed, at the very least—but she didn't detect any of those things. In fact, he seemed amused by it all in some private way. She insisted on paying anyway, and eventually he took her money.

"Thanks for the wrench," she said at the door.

"My pleasure," he said.

IN THE DINER, Linda watched Susan leave the store and return to her office. She poured Coop some coffee and guessed that though he was pretending not to look, he'd seen Susan, too.

"So, what's new, Coop?" she asked brightly.

He sipped at his coffee. "We're busy, you know. Getting ready for the weekend."

"How's that young guy working out, what's his name?"

"Miller."

"That's right. Miller."

"He'll be okay, once he stops quoting the rule book at me."

She left him to take an order, and when she came back, she saw he was looking over at Somers's store, and she wondered what he was thinking. There had been a certain note in Susan's voice when she was defending Michael Somers to Carl Jeffrey, and it struck her that it wasn't the first time she'd heard it. She knew that Jamie had been spending a lot of time with Michael and his falcon, and she thought that Coop hadn't been his normal self lately. None of it added up to anything specific, but she had a feeling about it all. Three months ago, she would have bet that Coop and Susan would end up getting married, once they both stopped skirting around the edges of things. Now she wasn't so sure.

She sat down next to him and lit a cigarette. "Are you taking Susan to the dance?"

He nodded. "Yeah."

"You don't sound too happy about it, Coop."

"I've just got some things on my mind, that's all."

That much she could tell. He seemed preoccupied, and the way he kept looking over to Susan's office, it wasn't hard to guess what with. She could picture Coop and Susan together. She knew Susan had her doubts about him, but maybe that was because she made comparisons to David; if she was ever going to move on, she had to put him behind her. Coop was a good guy, all things considered. He had his faults, but then, who didn't? One thing was certain, and that was that he loved Susan and would be good to her and Jamie. Plus, he wasn't a bad-looking guy. There were a lot worse around, that was for sure. Coop's problem—and his undoing, she thought—was that he needed to speed things up a little.

"Can I offer you some advice, Coop?" she said.

He looked at her uncomprehendingly. "What kind of advice?"

"You can tell me this is none of my business if you like..."

His expression became guarded. "I probably will, then."

She smiled at him. "Listen, don't you think it's about time you sorted things out with Susan?"

He considered her question for a moment, his eyes giving nothing away. "If I did think that," he said slowly, "how do you think I might go about it?"

"Well, you could just figure out what it is you want to happen, and then just ask."

He nodded slowly. "You mean, I should ask her to marry me?"

"That's the way these things usually happen."

She saw the uncertainty in his eyes and wondered how else he thought he might resolve things. He was thinking hard about what she'd said, and she could feel him weighing it up, perhaps trying to think how he would go about it. She guessed he'd never talked to anybody about this before.

"Coop," she said, wanting to help him out, "what's the worst thing that could happen? She might say no, right? But wouldn't it be better to know that now?"

"I've never wanted to rush things," Coop said.

"Which I think was the right thing to do at first," Linda agreed. "But sooner or later, you just have to take the bull by the horns."

Coop thought about that, and nodded as if she was confirming something he'd been thinking himself.

"Maybe you're right." He got up. "Thanks for the coffee."

"Anytime," she said.

She smiled to herself as he left and wondered if Susan would thank her for what she'd just done. When she got up, Pete was watching her out of the corner of one eye while he scraped down the grill.

"What?" she said.

He looked away. "Hey, I didn't say a word."

COOP WENT BACK to the station house and sat down at his desk. Miller was writing up a report.

"Listen, we need to get something sorted out for the weekend," Coop said. "It can get a little rowdy during the festival." Miller looked at him blankly. "I mean, we need to figure out who's on duty when," Coop explained. "You might want to spend some time with your family."

"The kids want to see the sled racing," Miller agreed.

Coop wondered how somebody so young had come to have kids when he wasn't much more than a kid himself. He'd mentioned it once, and Miller had said that he and his wife had decided to have them early so they would be young with them. Like everything else, Miller seemed to have had this all worked out and planned. Unlike his own life, Coop reflected, which lately had seemed to be going nowhere fast.

"If there was something you particularly wanted to do, maybe we could work our shifts out around that?" Miller suggested.

"There's the dance," Coop said. "Think you could manage things around here on Saturday night by yourself?"

"Sure."

Coop had his doubts. The festival was a time when people had more to drink than they were generally used to and occasionally it meant there were fights to break up outside Clancys. Still, he reasoned that he'd just be at the hotel if he was needed. He thought back to what Linda had said in the diner, which echoed his own ideas if not exactly in the same terms. Things with Susan didn't seem to be getting any further ahead. If anything, he'd seen less of her lately, and when he did stop in at her office or meet her in the diner, she seemed slightly remote in some indefinable way. The weekend fishing with Jamie hadn't exactly worked out, either, and Somers was still around, and so was his damn falcon, despite the talk he'd had with Ellis. Coop decided Ellis must have been too drunk to remember, or else in the end he hadn't had the balls to do anything about it.

Coop tried to picture himself asking Susan to marry him. Now that he considered it, it seemed like one way to settle things. Maybe if she understood how serious he was, she'd see things in a different light; she might stop holding on to the past and think about what was really the right thing for her and Jamie. The more he considered it, the more it seemed he could make her understand that getting married would probably help Jamie to set himself straight. He'd see that there was no point anymore in pretending that what had happened hadn't happened, and sooner or later he'd come around. Coop knew how important that was to Susan. All he had to do was ask her.

And the dance, he thought, would be the ideal time.

EARLY IN THE MORNING, THEY CLIMBED
the open slope toward the ridge. There, they
paused to view the lake in the valley, surrounded by dark green forest, its surface placid and ice
blue. Back the way they'd come, the sky was empty.

A few days earlier, Cully had been waiting on, high above the
cliffs, when a lone duck had come across the slope a hundred feet in
the air, heading for the valley and the lake below. Michael had
watched it approach, wondering if Cully would attack it, but the duck
must have seen her and had veered away across the forest. He hadn't
wanted Cully to chase it—he was afraid he might lose her—so he'd
begun swinging the lure and called her down. But it had given him
an idea.

He knew that the ducks generally came by at intervals, either alone
or in small groups, and his plan was to wait until the first of them
had passed over before putting Cully up, in the hope she could am-
bush those that followed. He had to wait an hour before at last a
single bird appeared. He and Cully watched it grow larger as it approached; then it flew above them, its wings making a soft whirring
noise.

Cully watched it pass, curious but no more than that. Michael was
concerned by this, because he'd read that occasionally a falcon trained
to fly after the lure will no longer be interested in the more difficult
task of catching her own prey. This was unlikely in a wild bird like
Cully, but there was also the possibility that maneuvering in the air
was more difficult for her because of her injury—perhaps she would

take the easier option in the end. Either way, there was little he
could do. He'd trained her hard over the past week, making her pass
repeatedly after the lure until she was visibly tired. Her wing still
worried him. Sometimes when she turned there was a distinct waver
in her flight, and occasionally when he tossed the lure high, she
missed her catch.

He turned to Jamie and said, "This is it. Are you ready?"

The boy nodded. Michael removed Cully's leash and jesses, then
raised his fist into the breeze so that she could feel it flow across her
feathers. Her softly inquisitive eye sharpened with purpose and she
took to the air, rising rapidly on her long pointed wings.

"Good luck, Cully," Michael murmured.

Without thinking, Michael rested his hand on Jamie's shoulder,
and together they watched Cully circle, gaining height as she found
a thermal to carry her aloft. In the distance, two small shapes appeared, headed on a course toward the lake: a pair of ducks, unaware
of Cully's presence. She was high above them, out over the valley
perhaps a quarter of a mile distant, when as they flew over the ridge
they sensed danger and abruptly separated, descending to find cover.
The lake, however, was a mile away.

Cully seemed oblivious to the opportunity. She couldn't have failed
to see them, but it seemed to Michael as if she were waiting for the
lure. Intense disappointment washed over him. Since the day he'd
saved her, this was the moment he'd looked forward to: the time
when she would become again what nature had intended her to be—
a wild and free predator, the largest, swiftest, most beautiful of her
kind. Any conflict within him had vanished. His attachment to her
paled beside his desire to see her prove that she could survive again
on her own.

"No lure, Cully, not this time," he said under his breath, tightening
his grip on Jamie's shoulder, willing her to strike. Jamie didn't notice,
his attention riveted above.

The two ducks fled, quickly losing height, and it seemed certain
Cully had missed her chance. Michael began reaching for the lure,
thinking he would call her down and they would try again later,
when abruptly she changed direction, breaking her soaring pattern.
She began to fly with rapid strokes.

In his mind Michael was with her, up high in the cool air. He
imagined her view of the ducks below and could see the green and

brown markings on their backs and wings as they passed underneath, flying in a separating formation. He was with her as she fixed her focus on the one farthest from the trees and adjusted her position.

Her wings closed, and she turned earthward. As she began her stoop, the soft passage of air across her plumage became a rushing torrent. The sound it made grew to an insistent hurricane as she gathered speed.

She was perfectly streamlined, her shape honed and perfected by millions of years of evolution, the perfect predator, fast, agile, sleek with deadly grace. In command of her element she fell, armed with talons that could deal instantaneous death.

The gap between Cully and her target closed in the space of a few seconds. The duck, aware of the danger, abruptly changed course, turning at right angles, it seemed, banking at the last moment.

Cully turned in the same instant, a slight tremor in her flight. For a split second the two birds seemed to merge, but Cully passed beyond, still moving with incredible speed. Michael knew she'd missed, though it must have been by no more than inches.

The duck turned again, making a dash earthward, seeking cover. Cully came around and rose above it, pursuing from behind, her speed increasing. The duck was headed for a patch of rocks and bushes where it meant to hide, and though Cully was faster, it seemed certain she'd waited too long. Then suddenly she was above the duck, her wings folded, and this time when she fell, she didn't miss.

They saw her strike, a cloud of feathers, and the duck dropped limply to the ground, where, a moment later, Cully landed.

Neither Michael nor Jamie moved. No more than a minute had passed since Cully had begun her stoop, but it seemed longer. Michael's heart was beating as if he'd run a mile at full pace, and his system buzzed with adrenaline.

He grinned at Jamie, then let out a whoop. "All right!" Jamie's face split into a grin from ear to ear, and they both started to run across the snow, their feet sinking so that they sprawled head first in their haste and reached her breathless and panting. She mantled her wings as they approached, watching them warily. Already she was busy plucking her prey, standing with one foot on its breast; the surrounding snow was littered with downy feathers. Side by side, Michael and Jamie sank down on their knees and watched her feed.

On the walk back, Jamie was subdued, kicking his feet in the snow.

Now that the excitement had worn off a little, Michael guessed Jamie
was thinking about what came next. On the way up here, he'd explained that if Cully proved she could survive, they were going to
have to let her go. Maybe only now was Jamie really absorbing that,
Michael thought. After a while, Michael stopped, and when Jamie
noticed, he looked around questioningly.

"You're thinking about what I said earlier, right?" Jamie looked
away, then nodded slowly. Michael could see that the boy was holding
back tears, and he struggled for the right thing to say.

"Listen." He pointed back the way they'd come, toward the wide-
open sky and the ranges beyond the valley. "That's her world. That's
where I first saw her, and it's where she belongs. I know you want
to keep her, and a part of me does, too." He shrugged helplessly,
unable to think of anything that was going to make Jamie feel better.
"The thing is, Jamie, I never told you this, but I made a pact with
her. The first night I had her, after I brought her back from the vet,
she was weak and hurt and I thought she was going to die. She
wouldn't eat anything, and it was like she'd decided she wasn't going
to go on living if it meant being shut in a woodshed, having these
jesses put on her legs. So I made her a promise. I said that if she
would just eat and get strong, I'd help her to get well again, and
then, when she was ready, I'd let her go. Well, now it's time I kept
my promise. You wouldn't want me to break it, would you?"

Jamie turned to Cully, standing on Michael's fist, her crop stuffed
with the rich dark meat of the duck. She gazed back at him, then
flicked open her wings and held them there in the breeze for a second,
her sharp eye turned to the mountains in the north. Eventually Jamie
shook his head and turned away.

27 DURING A WEEK OF TRADING, HE HAD taken in a total of fifty-six dollars and twenty-two cents, from three customers. He'd spent a lot of time recalling the hours he'd worked in the store when he was growing up. It was the only place he'd been alone with his dad, and he saw now why his dad had wanted him there. Despite the fact that they hardly ever talked about anything, they had at least been together. Maybe his father had hoped that someday things would change, or maybe he'd just been content that he got to spend some time with his only child.

Midmorning, he was just getting off the phone with his supplier in Kamloops, who'd been both sympathetic and pragmatic. He hung up as the door opened and a woman entered. She stood at the threshold, looking all around, a kind of wistful smile on her face. After a while, he recalled that he'd seen her before, at the cemetery a week ago.

She met his eye, and her smile deepened. "It looks just the way it did when your dad was alive," she said. "Except that it was never so tidy, of course. Did you plan it that way?"

"The tidy part, or the other?" he said, surprised at her question.

"The other."

Michael looked around. "I guess I did," he admitted.

"I thought so." She came over to the counter and put her bag down. Her voice was strong, and she walked with a straight back despite her years. "Did you really think it would work?"

He hesitated, then shook his head. "No."

She seemed pleased at his answer. "I hoped you'd say that. I wouldn't like to think you'd wasted all that time and effort, not to say money. I take it you haven't? Wasted it all, I mean."

"No, it's not wasted."

"I'd like to ask you why you did it. Would you think that's none of my business if I did? You can say so if you like."

Michael looked at her carefully, thinking back to when they'd crossed paths in the cemetery. Now she was in the store. He began to think that maybe it *was* her business. "Did you know my father?" he asked.

She smiled and extended her hand. "I'm Eleanor Grove, not that it will mean anything to you. And you, of course, are Michael."

"That's right." He shook her hand.

She studied him carefully. "I'd still like to ask you why you opened this store."

He looked around at the bright lights, the full shelves, the wooden floor. "It was just something I needed to do," he said. "How well did you know my dad?"

"About as well as it's possible to know somebody. Would you like to hear about it?"

Michael opened the counter and pulled up a stool for her. "How about some coffee?" he asked. "I don't think we're going to be disturbed."

Eleanor told him she'd met his dad when Michael was quite young, perhaps four or five. "We didn't plan to fall in love," she said. "Sometimes these things just happen." There was no note of apology in her tone, and the way she looked at him made him see he shouldn't expect one. The affair had continued until the day his father had died, she explained, and throughout that time they'd loved each other.

"I wanted your dad to leave your mother when you were young," she told him. "I expect that shocks you, or else you dislike me for it."

"I might have once," he answered.

She raised an eyebrow slightly. "You know, you're not at all what I expected."

"What did you expect?"

She gave a small apologetic smile. "Perhaps I expected somebody less sure of himself."

"You mean, a little crazy? Like my mother?"

At that, Eleanor became serious. "John should have had your mother committed, you know. I always told him that."

It was strange hearing his dad referred to by his first name. His mother had always said "your father," in a way that conveyed her warped prejudice.

"There's something I'd like to ask you," Michael said. "Why didn't my dad leave?"

Eleanor looked surprised. "You don't know? He wouldn't leave because of you. He tried to once, and told your mother he was taking you with him. He wanted her to get treatment, but of course she wouldn't."

Suddenly it all seemed simple, and he wondered why it hadn't appeared that way when he was young. "Did my mother know about you?" he asked.

"I think she suspected," Eleanor said. "She was determined that John wouldn't leave, and she used you to make sure he never did. She turned you against him before you could understand what was happening. John was afraid that if he left you with her, she'd make sure he never saw you again. Your mother knew he wouldn't commit her, you see. She was certainly deranged and unstable, a very manipulative person, but she was aware of what she was doing." Her voice had become tainted with a bitter edge that she couldn't hide. "I'm sorry, I shouldn't talk about your mother like that."

He waved a hand in dismissal. "It's okay, I think I'd worked it out myself anyway."

Suddenly his life seemed clearer. Maybe he'd always known, at least subconsciously, that the way he'd felt about his dad was the result of his mother's manipulation. In his teenage years, he'd thought his mother crazy and his dad remote; he thought that he came from a loveless family. He'd been too screwed up by then to recognize the ways his dad had tried to reach out to him.

"You know, I never saw him again after my mother died," Michael said.

"Of course," Eleanor said.

"I felt guilty about that, deep down. I didn't know if I loved him or hated him, but I was pretty sure he had never loved me. I think it was only when I heard he was dead that all this stuff I'd buried started coming out. I started thinking about this store a lot: how I'd worked here over the years after school, the two of us in here together. After he died, I guess I knew I'd never be able to reconcile myself with him."

"And you had a mental breakdown?"

"Something like that. I mean, it wasn't that simple; there was more to it."

He looked around at everything in the store. Fixing the place up had been a way of turning back the clock, he supposed, or maybe a physical expression of a need he still had to connect with his dad. Perhaps it had worked. He imagined his dad continuing on in the store after he'd left, and a question occurred to him.

"How come you didn't marry each other after my mother died?" he asked Eleanor.

She smiled sadly. "We used to see each other every Thursday and on Saturday afternoons, that was our time. We kept it that way right up until John died. You see, I married, myself, eventually, once I knew John would never leave your mother. I won't go into that, but it never changed anything between me and your dad."

Once again there was no apology in her tone. Michael saw how much this woman and his dad must have loved each other.

Eleanor stood and said she ought to go. He walked her to the door, where she asked him what he would do now.

"I'm not sure," he told her honestly.

"But you won't stay here?"

"No, I won't stay here." Something occurred to him. "Dad used to build these model ships. Did you know about that? He spent hours on them."

She nodded. "He burned them all. Built a big fire in the garden and set light to them."

They were both silent, each contemplating the pathos of that act. All those wasted hours. There was still one question Michael needed to know the answer to, and he couldn't let her go without asking.

"The night my mother died," he said at last. "Was he with you?"

She looked into his eyes for a long time, then finally said, "No, he wasn't."

"Do you think my mother intended to kill herself?"

"No," Eleanor said. "I think she was afraid she would lose both you and your father, and that was the only way she knew how to deal with it. It just went wrong."

"Because Dad wasn't home at his usual time. He was always home except on Thursdays, when he was seeing you."

"I know what people said about him," Eleanor told Michael, "but I never believed it. I never even asked him."

Her eyes held his a moment longer, and he knew that was the only answer he would ever get.

"I feel him here, you know," she said.

Michael looked around the store. "I know. So do I," he said.

She smiled. "He loved you very much. He always thought it was the greatest sin of his life, to allow your mother to destroy what there should have been between you. He never blamed her. Only himself." She took a final look around. "And he never blamed you, either, for never coming back here. He wanted you to, of course, just to visit. He wanted to meet your wife and his grandchild, but he never said a word against you. Remember that."

She left, closing the door behind her.

SUSAN WAS WORKING when the door to her office opened. She looked up, and there was Michael. Her thoughts scattered, and she felt the blood rush to her face, which made her angry more than anything. Dammit, why did she have to think of that night every time she saw him? She'd had too much to drink, that was all. She'd been feeling sorry for herself and lonely without Jamie there, and she just hadn't been thinking. Maybe it would be better if she just came out and told him as much. Then she could just forget about it.

"What can I do for you?" she asked.

"I've decided to sell," he said. "I want to put the house and store on the market."

It took her a moment to absorb what he was saying. "You mean, you're leaving? I mean, already? You only just opened, I'm sure if you give it time..."

"It's not that. There's nothing here for me now. You won't need to sell the store as a going concern; the place I got the stock from will take it back for a five percent fee, and the building ought to fetch a decent price. You might try Ron Taylor. I think he was interested at one stage."

She nodded dumbly, still struggling to take in everything he was saying. She felt as if something was collapsing inside her, and in her mind's eye she saw his house standing empty and silent. She would look out her bedroom window across the woods, and there would be no smoke rising from the chimney. Michael would be gone, but she and Jamie would remain; their lives would go back to their previous rhythm. The prospect seemed bleak.

"What abut Cully?" she asked suddenly.

"Jamie and I are going to let her go tomorrow."

"Tomorrow? So when were you hoping to leave? I mean, things don't start picking up around here for a few more weeks yet. It could take a while for the house to sell."

"I won't wait for that. I'll let you have a forwarding address as soon as I can. Could you mail the forms to me, whatever I need to sign?"

She was stunned that he would be gone so fast. A sudden irrational anger rose in her. She wanted to ask him who the hell he thought he was to arrive in her life, in Jamie's life, the way he had? And then to just up and disappear when he felt like it, just like that. She thought about how Jamie was going to be without Cully, pictured him sliding back into his insular state. She felt unbidden angry tears she didn't want him to see pricking her eyes. The humiliation of going over to his house that night returned with force, sweeping over her so that she felt heat rising to her cheeks. She just wanted him to leave, to get out so that she could be alone.

"Fine," she said, and abruptly held out her hand. He looked surprised. Then they shook briefly, businesslike.

"I'll leave the keys in my mailbox," he said.

She watched him go out to his car and drive past her office along the street, which suddenly appeared gray and empty.

28 MAIN STREET WAS AGLOW WITH COLORED lights strung across the street, giving the night a festive air. Michael parked across from the diner, noting that traffic was barred from going farther. Stalls that had been set up earlier in the day were closed for the night, but there were still a few families milling about, eating hot dogs and getting ready to go home. Music came from Clancys back along the street, and in the other direction the hotel was decorated with multicolored lights strung across the front and a banner proclaiming the annual winter dance.

It was a cold night, a reminder that spring hadn't really arrived yet, and Michael turned his collar up, his breath appearing in frosty clouds in front of him while his feet crunched on snow. The bar door opened, and the sound of music swelled and spilled with the light onto the street. He stood aside to let three guys stagger out drunkenly, then went in and bought a beer. The place was busy with people who'd been drinking for most of the day; in the press of bodies and the noise of music and voices, nobody paid him any attention. He found a table in the corner by the window, awash with beer and cigarette ash, and sat down. He gazed outside without taking anything in, thinking instead about everything Eleanor had told him. For the first time in as long as he could remember, he didn't feel as if something lay coiled tightly at his core. This had all happened gradually, a result of coming back to the town, of living in the old house, and of fixing up his dad's store, but he also saw that it had as much to do with something he had discovered in himself through Cully. The prospect of releasing her in the morning felt like a natural resolution, the ending he'd hoped for, but it also saddened him. He knew that he was going to miss going up into the mountains with her, watching her fly against the wide-open sky. He was also going to miss Jamie, and thinking of him—quiet, sometimes solemn—he frowned.

"You look like you could do with some company."

He looked up at the sound of the voice. Rachel was there. "Does it show?"

She pulled up a chair and sat down. "Just a little. I came over with Alice, she works with me at the store. Are you going to the dance?"

"I don't think so."

"You don't know what you're missing," she said with faint irony. "It's the major event of the year." She reached into her bag, found some cigarettes, and offered him one. "That's right, you quit." She lit one herself.

Michael watched the flare of the flame in her eyes. It was the first time he'd seen her since the night they'd had dinner. "So how've you been?" he asked.

"You mean did I decide what to do about my marriage?"

She'd thought when she'd arrived home that morning that she would stay and that somehow she and Pete would work it out. Maybe it was because she'd had a chance in some small way to see what it would be like without him and she hadn't taken it, which meant she really didn't want it. That feeling had lasted a day, until he'd come home from wherever he'd been with Red Parker. He'd already spent whatever money he'd made and within ten minutes they were arguing. The fight had finished with him thrusting his finger at her face and telling her to get the fuck off his back; then he'd swept his arm across the supper dishes on the table and sent them all crashing to the floor.

"I can't help him anymore," she said. "He's too angry and bitter with everything now, and I think I need to take care of myself."

"I'm sorry."

"Don't be," she said. "I should have done this before. How about you? I saw a sign in the store saying you were closed. I had the feeling it was permanent."

"It is."

"You're leaving?"

"On Monday."

Rachel nodded thoughtfully. "You know, I've thought about what happened at your house that night—or, should I say, what didn't happen." She smiled and hesitated before going on. "I wanted to call you, but I didn't. Do you know why?" She didn't wait for him to answer. "I kept thinking about that night, and I decided that if you'd maybe said the right thing, kissed me maybe, I would have stayed with you. But you didn't."

Michael didn't know what to say. "You're a beautiful woman, Rachel, it's just that—"

She put her finger against his mouth to stop him. "Don't say any more. Maybe if this had been some other time..." She smiled to herself. "There was somebody out there that night, wasn't there?"

"I don't know."

She regarded him skeptically. "Come on. Was it Susan Baker?"

He was surprised at that. "What makes you say that?"

"Woman's intuition. Look, whatever's going on between you two, it's none of my business—"

Michael interrupted. "There's nothing going on."

Rachel put out her cigarette. "Well, like I said, it's none of my business." She looked around at the bar, seeing everybody drinking and having a good time. "I'm going to go. I'm not in the mood for this." She leaned over and quickly kissed him, then stood and picked up her bag. "Look, I'm going to say this whether it's my business or it isn't. We don't get too many chances in this life, and I think you've already used up a few of yours. Just think about that, okay?"

He smiled at her. "I will."

"Good luck, then."

"And to you."

Rachel raised a hand, gave him a final sad smile, and walked out the door, leaving him to think about what she'd said.

COOP WAITED AT the station house for Miller to arrive. He was sitting at his desk, holding a small velvet box that held a ring he'd inherited from his mother. He opened the lid, turning the box to catch the light. The ring was a solitaire diamond, a small, intricately shaped crystal.

At that moment it was just a piece of jewelery, he thought, but with a few words it could change his life. He tried to imagine how he would feel if Susan were to wear it.

He thought it strange that the sum of all his hopes could be represented by an object so small. As the door opened, he flicked the box shut and palmed it into his pocket.

"Sorry I'm late," Miller said.

"No problem." Coop got to his feet. "I'm going to go home and get myself changed before I go over to the hotel. Everything quiet out there?"

"At the moment."

"Yeah, well, I doubt it'll stay that way. Just keep an eye on Clancys. I saw some guys in there earlier, drinking like they hadn't seen beer for a year."

"You think there'll be trouble?"

Coop shrugged. "There's always someone who'll start something, you can be sure of that. You know where I am if you need me."

"Sure, Coop. Have a good night."

"Thanks." Coop paused at the door, hesitating over his words. "Listen, Miller, don't come for me unless it's urgent, okay?"

"Okay."

As Coop drove home, he saw Susan turn the corner onto Main Street in her Ford, on her way to the hotel, where he'd arranged to meet her; she didn't see him. He caught just a glimpse of her, with her hair falling around her shoulders, and it made his heart jump in his throat. He kept going, pondering his nervousness. He felt like a school kid working up the nerve to ask for his first date, only the feeling was magnified about a thousand times.

At home, he turned on the kitchen light and got a bottle of bourbon from the cupboard. Pouring himself a small measure, he tossed it back in one swallow, savoring the sudden raw hit of liquor in the back of his throat. Then he went through to the bathroom and turned on the shower.

SUSAN SAT IN her Ford outside the hotel, trying to muster the will to go inside. People were arriving constantly, husbands and wives all dressed up, women with hair and makeup fixed with more care than they'd probably taken since the dance the year before. Susan smiled to herself, looking down at what she was wearing: a simple black dress she'd bought years ago and worn maybe half a dozen times. She glanced at the time and thought that Coop would be along soon; then she wondered about Michael and what he was doing. After he'd left the office, she'd sat down and stared blankly at her desk. Her anger had dissipated as quickly as it arrived, and she was left feeling numb.

Up and down Main Street, colored lights swung on their lines in the breeze. From where she was sitting in her Ford, she could see the bank and the grocery store; farther along were the diner and her office. A couple walked by, and when they saw her sitting there, they waved. It was Sally Crane and her husband, Alan. They had two kids, a boy and a girl, whose faces Susan could clearly picture, and if she thought hard enough, she would probably be able to remember their names. She didn't know whether this made her feel good—that everything was comfortingly familiar—or whether she felt oppressed by it all.

She decided it was time she made some decisions in her life. She realized that Michael's coming to Little River had changed her, snapped her out of the lethargy she'd been in for so long. She thought that maybe her feelings for him had something to do with viewing him as an escape. Maybe because Jamie had responded to Cully, she'd allowed herself to be caught up in the emotions that had awakened in her, but perhaps what she *really* ought to see was that she couldn't allow either herself or Jamie to slip back into their old selves. She had to make decisions; they had to go forward with their lives. She couldn't simply wait around any longer and hope that somehow things would just get better. Either she was going to up and leave Little River or she was going to stay, but either way it would be her decision, it would be what she wanted and thought was best for them both. If she stayed, maybe she would put things on a different footing with Coop. Settle that one way or the other, and Jamie would have to accept it, whatever she decided there, too. It was time she got a little tougher with him, made him see he had to start dealing with life.

With these thoughts in her mind, she got out of the car and crossed the street, entering the hotel with a new resolve, one she intended to stick to. As the music reached her and people said hello, she saw Linda and Pete Kowalski across the room and made her way toward them, thinking that tonight she might as well have a good time.

COOP KNEW THAT people were watching them. He'd never seen Susan look more beautiful than she'd looked as he'd come through the door. Her hair shone in the light and, when his fingers brushed against it, felt like satin. As they danced, he could smell her perfume, could feel her body moving against his through the material of her dress, and he was on top of the world. He felt the good-natured envy of guys he knew, and the other type of envy from one or two of the women. As he held her and they glided across the floor to a slow Crystal Gayle number, his hand rose high on her waist and brushed the cool flesh of her back. He allowed his fingers to rest there momentarily, against the ridge of her spine, and at his touch she looked at him and smiled. The words almost fell out of him then, in a rush.

The ring was in its case in his pocket. As they danced, he was aware of her hand resting on his shoulder, and he thought back to the times they'd kissed and he'd felt her start to respond. Each time she'd pulled away, as if she was suddenly scared of letting herself go. He thought maybe that was the trouble, that she was just afraid. Once she saw the ring, he thought, she'd know how serious he was, and maybe then she wouldn't be scared anymore.

When they caught each other's eye here and there, she smiled at him, her soft dark red lips parting to reveal the tips of white teeth, and though there was warmth in her expression, he could tell she was a little distant as well. There was a brief moment when she looked through him and off into some inner distance. He wondered if she was thinking of the past or the future, or of something else.

Sometimes it was best not to know everything about people, or to question all they did, because everybody had private spaces where the doors stayed locked and it was best for others not to go. He loved her, that's all he knew. He wanted to marry her and be with her and raise Jamie, and if he couldn't be the boy's father, he could at least be his friend, and one day Jamie would understand that and would stop fighting him.

The music stopped, and couples moved back toward their tables.

"Shall we get a drink?" Susan asked.

Coop led her back to the table, and she asked for a glass of wine. Going to the bar, he met Linda, who paused as she squeezed past him and put her hand on his arm.

"How're things, Coop?"

"Fine," he said, and she let him go, smiling encouragement. Back at their table, Susan thanked him when he brought her drink. It was only her second, and she was taking it slowly.

He sat down beside her and saw she was looking at the new clothes he was wearing.

"Have you been shopping, Coop?" she asked.

He shrugged. "It's no big deal. I was in Williams Lake."

"Oh? What were you doing there?"

"Just some police business."

He watched the dancing couples. The hotel was packed with people now, as if half the town was there. He was pleased she'd noticed the way he was dressed. The fact was, he'd gone over to Williams Lake first thing in the morning just because he thought he should make some kind of a special effort.

"By the way, I like your dress," he said. "You look terrific."

"Thank you." She laid her hand on his arm, just briefly.

Al Taylor came over and Coop got up to talk for a minute, though Al's conversation never got much beyond the bad times he was going through with his business. Coop half listened to an account of the latest disaster. George Pederson took the chance to sneak in and ask Susan to dance, and she went with him. Coop half watched them as George hammed it up on the dance floor, twirling Susan and catching her around the waist again. One thing about George, he could dance; he was as light on his feet as any man Coop had ever seen. He was glad Susan seemed to be having a good time. At one point she looked over and flashed a sympathetic look as Al went on bending his ear.

Coop got his chance to dance with her again after Al left to find himself a more attentive audience. She seemed happier now than when he'd arrived; the faraway look in her eye had gone. As they got back to the table, dinner was being set out. He asked if she was ready to eat.

"Now that you mention it, I'm starving."

"I'll get you a plate. Little of everything okay with you?"

"Not too much potato salad." She patted her stomach.

While Coop waited in line, he decided that after they'd eaten he would ask her outside for a walk. He felt for the ring in his pocket to make sure it was still there. Suddenly he didn't feel hungry anymore, and there was a tight nervous feeling in his throat. When he got back to the table, Susan looked at her own piled plate and his smaller one and raised her eyebrows.

"What are you trying to do to me, Coop?"

"I had something earlier," he said, but his voice must have sounded strange because she gave him an odd look.

"You're okay, aren't you?"

"Sure, I'm fine."

Linda and Pete arrived at the table with their food and a bottle of wine, and while they ate, the Saunderses joined them. Coop couldn't keep his mind on the conversation, half watching Susan eat every mouthful.

"What do you think, Coop?" Craig Saunders said, halfway through some discussion Coop hadn't been following.

"About what?"

"Jesus, about the game, weren't you listening?"

"Sorry." He shrugged and started to get up, deciding to go to the men's room and splash some water on his face.

"Coop, are sure you're okay?" Susan said, her expression creased with concern.

"I'm fine. I'll just be a minute."

In the men's room he looked at himself in the mirror. He did look kind of strained. He splashed water on his face, which did nothing to relieve the churning, queasy sensation in his stomach, and straightening up from the basin, he examined himself again while he dried his face with a towel. He took the ring out of its box, turning it in the light. He wondered how Susan was going to react when he showed it to her. He didn't know if he should ask her to marry him first, then show her the ring, Or let her see it first, then ask her. He couldn't decide.

He'd practiced what he would say. He'd tell her he loved her, which he'd never said before. Then he'd tell her he always had and that he had something to say, and would she please just listen to him for a minute because he wasn't sure how to say it. Then he'd launch into how he knew she'd loved Dave in a way she might never feel for him, and that he understood that and respected it and didn't want to take Dave's place but hoped she might feel for him in a different way. He'd talk about Jamie and how he wanted to be a friend to him and maybe someone Jamie could talk to, even though he wouldn't be his real dad. Then he'd lay out the kind of future he saw for them in Little River, building up to the big moment.

Suddenly it all sounded confused in his mind, and he knew that come the time, he'd probably forget all about it and just stumble over whatever words he could find. He took a deep breath and put the ring back into his pocket. As he made his way back to the table, the band started up again, and before he got there, he saw Pete Kowalski ask Susan to dance. He didn't know if he could stand to wait any longer and thought about just cutting in, but then Linda made a prompting sound in her throat.

"How about making a woman feel she's not just a piece of the furniture?"

"Sure, it'd be my pleasure." He offered his arm and led her to the dance floor.

"Things on your mind, Coop?" she asked as they found a space.

He shrugged and glanced toward Susan and Pete. "You know," he said, feeling Linda studying him.

At the end of the song, he took Linda back to their table. He turned around, expecting to see Pete and Susan coming back too, but they were dancing to the next number. Linda raised her eyebrows at him and smiled.

"Relax, Coop, she isn't going anywhere."

He lost sight of them among the press of people, and when the music ended, Pete came back alone and said Susan had gone to the ladies' room.

"Think I'll have a beer," Coop said, avoiding Linda's eye. Excusing himself, he made his way to the bar. A few minutes later Susan came looking for him. He asked her if she wanted a drink.

"Okay, that would be good. I'm thirsty with all this dancing," she said.

"How about a beer?"

"A soda's fine."

They stood at the bar, where there were fewer people, and Coop tried to think of a way to ask her to take a walk with him. Now that he had the chance, it seemed like an odd request, as it was so cold outside. He felt in his pocket for the ring, wondering if he ought to ask her right there in the hotel, maybe out in the lobby, where it was quiet. He imagined somebody passing by and overhearing them and decided it was a bad idea.

"You're quiet tonight."

He realized she'd spoken. "Am I?"

"Is everything okay?"

He twirled his beer bottle in his hand, trying to think of what to say, and found himself suddenly tongue-tied. "I guess there *is* something on my mind," he said at last.

She waited for him to go on, watching his face with her wide green eyes.

"The thing is, I sort of wanted to talk to you," he continued.

"Okay," She said hesitantly. "Here I am."

Coop looked around. "Not here. Can we go outside for a while?"

"Outside?" Her eye went to the door.

He heard the uncertainty in her tone. He drained his beer, and as he did, the band came to the end of a song and one of the musicians announced that he wanted everyone up on the floor forming lines. It was a tradition for everyone to join in at this point in the night, something that had started years before and become a kind of symbol of town unity. The guy on the stage was waving people up and directing them to join this line or that, calling out to stragglers at the back. Somebody called for Coop and Susan to hurry up.

Susan shrugged, smiling sympathetically. "Guess we'll have to talk later."

The music started. Coop tried to keep his eye on her through the throng of people. In the end he resigned himself to waiting until this dance had finished. He thought he might as well get into the spirit of things, look as if he was having a good time.

The dance finally ended, and people headed back to their tables. Coop looked for Susan, but instead he saw Miller signaling to him from the door. Coop shook his head, believing he had to be jinxed.

"I'm all yours," Susan said, appearing at his side. Then, seeing his expression, she followed his look. "Is that Miller?"

"I better go see what he wants," Coop said reluctantly.

"Go ahead, I'll be fine."

He told her he wouldn't be long and made his way to where Miller was waiting.

"This better be good," Coop said.

RACHEL WAS SITTING IN HER DARKENED
room, looking out the window. On the bed
were the clothes she'd worn to meet Michael, strewn where she'd found them when she got
home. Most of the rest of her things had been pulled out
of drawers or torn from hangers in her closet. She'd tidied some of
it away, but the sight of everything scattered about, and what it must
mean, had dealt her a tricky blow. She didn't know how to feel, and
couldn't muster herself to think of a way to deal with the situation.

She heard Pete's truck pull into the drive and saw the lights go
out. He must have sat out there for a while, because it was ten
minutes or so before she heard the door. Then it was another five
before she heard his tread on the stairs.

She didn't look around, but she could sense him in the doorway.

"Where've you been?" she asked.

"I went for a drink," he said.

There were currents in his tone. He was uncertain about what he'd
found, she thought, or maybe he wanted to be, and maybe he was
afraid, too. She felt sorry for him then. He was angry, too, she felt
that.

He came into the room and sat down heavily on the bed. His
weight made the springs creak. It was an old mattress. Once, she'd
hoped they could get a new one, a whole new bed. Pete had said
he'd miss the old one, that they'd had a lot of good times in it. Well,
that was true enough, but it had been a long time ago.

He breathed beery fumes. She thought he wasn't going to say

anything and was starting to imagine he'd fallen asleep, but then she realized he was only thinking.

"Don't you wanna know about your clothes?"

She let his question hang for a while. She could virtually see it in the air, the words all spelled out for her to examine. Even now she thought that if she said the right thing, he might let it slide. He might just choose to believe whatever she told him. She turned around to face him.

"They're new," she said.

He looked at her as if she was crazy. She might have been imagining it, but she thought he looked as if he couldn't believe it. He shook his head.

"No kidding? I guessed that." He got up abruptly and started to look for something, and when he didn't find it right away, he started to toss things around the room. He picked up her dress and threw it at her.

"You think I don't fucking know that?" he yelled.

The dress had wrapped around her neck. She thought he'd wanted it to be something more solid, maybe a chair or something heavier. He was panting like a thirsty dog. Rabid animals got thirsty, she remembered hearing somewhere. He was looking at her out of pained angry eyes, and she felt sorry for him again.

He saw something on the floor and picked it up. He held it right in front of her face with a flourish. "See! You see what this is? It's a goddamn receipt is what it is." He opened it up. "It's for the dress. Sixty-five dollars for a dress!"

He balled it tight, as tight as he could, and threw it at her from a foot away. It hit her below the eye, and she was surprised how much it hurt. It was like a slug. If it had hit her in the eye, it could have done some real damage.

He found another one on the floor. He must have thrown them there earlier when he was going nuts looking through her closet.

"This one's for the shoes. Thirty-six dollars for shoes." He held up one of her new black pumps. The heel and the whole style made it obviously a shoe for going out in, a shoe for maybe meeting somebody in a restaurant.

He threw it across the room at a picture, and when the picture didn't break, he went over in a rage and ripped it off the wall.

"What the fuck for? Just tell me that!"

"Pete—"

"Don't fucking 'Pete' me!"

His cry was full of rage and anguish. It changed the way she thought, shook her out of some lethargic state she'd sunk into. She suddenly saw what ought to have been obvious a while ago. Now that it was in front of her, she couldn't understand how she'd missed it. He'd lost a little of his mind. He was literally slightly crazy. She was glad the kids weren't at home.

It had happened slowly, she thought. He'd always been a little tense. She'd understood early on in their marriage why he'd been a bully at high school. He was basically insecure. He had no self-respect—that was something his dad had beaten out of him a long time before. He thought he was no good.

She got up and went to him. "Listen, Pete—"

He shook her hand off violently. "Why did you buy the clothes, Rachel?"

"Look, I can take them back," she said. "It was a stupid thing to do."

She knew she couldn't return them, but she just wanted to say anything that would calm him down. She was concerned now, not for herself, but for him. She should have seen what was happening to him. The business failing had sapped away his self-confidence little by little, changing him.

He took her by the shoulders and put his face up close to hers. He stank of beer.

"I want to know why you spent all that money on clothes," he said.

He seized her arm and dragged her across the room. His grip was hurting her, digging into her flesh. He pulled her along like a floppy doll, and then he bent down and picked something up. She didn't know what it was until he shoved it in her face.

"How much did these cost?" He rubbed the material of the panties between his fingers, leering in a way that frightened her.

He shoved them back in her face, grinding them into her as if he were trying to rub out her features. She opened her mouth, struggling to get away, and he shoved them down her throat, pushing until she gagged.

"Who were they for, huh?" He was yelling, spitting. "Do they look good on you? Do they feel good? Tell me!"

She tore herself away from him, sputtering, pulling the panties out of her mouth.

"Please, Pete! Nothing like that happened!"

She wanted to calm him down. She *had* to get him on an even keel. She had to help him see it was okay about the business, that everything was going to work out. She wouldn't leave him, she couldn't. Because if she did, there was no telling what might happen.

He shook his head. He shook it back and forth, back and forth. As he did, he came toward her and she stepped away.

"Put them on," he told her.

"What do you mean?"

He picked up the panties and threw them at her. "Come on, I want to see them on you. I bet they feel real smooth, huh? Sexy, I bet. Put them on."

"Pete," she pleaded. "Don't do this. Let's just calm down here——"

"I said put them fucking on!"

She stopped, shocked rigid. She could see the thick vein in his neck pulsing, and the one in his forehead standing out. His hand shot out so fast she didn't have time to move, and the sound of him hitting her face was loud in the silence of the room. Her head snapped around and tears sprang to her eyes. She turned back to him, tasting blood.

"Put them on," he said quietly.

Slowly she undressed. She fumbled with the strap on her bra. He stood in front of her and watched her every move. There was nothing sexual in his gaze, just anger. She felt humiliated and caught sight of herself in the mirror, her hair disheveled and blood on her lip, her attitude cowed. Finally she put the panties on and stood before him with her arms across her breasts.

She knew what would happen next. She tried to stop him, tried to tell him that if he did this, they might never get past it. It was no good, though, and after a while she just lay there and endured him raping her. She knew what it was all about. It was about him proving himself. She cried into her pillow while he lay on her and brutally fucked her, and she wondered if things would ever be right again.

30 COOP HAD BEEN GONE FOR AN HOUR, AND Susan was feeling tired. The place was emptying out a little, and there were fewer people dancing. She caught Linda's eye across the table. "I think I'm going to leave soon," she said.

"Isn't Coop coming back?"

"Maybe he got caught up. I'll have a look by the station house."

Outside, she paused by the door. She wrapped her coat tight, took a deep breath of icy air, and looked up at a clear sky. She thought about Coop, recalling his distracted manner during the evening, then his asking her to take a walk outside. She wondered what that had been all about.

She began to walk toward her car, and as she drew closer, she could see there had been some kind of commotion at Clancys. A small knot of people were milling about outside, some of them drunk, and someone was cleaning up broken glass. Whatever had happened appeared to be all over now. As she crossed the street, a figure came toward her from the shadows, and for a moment she thought it was Coop.

Michael stopped when he saw her. For most of the night he'd sat with an untouched beer, thinking about leaving, thinking about Susan. An hour ago he'd left the bar to go home, but he'd seen Susan's Ford and guessed she was at the dance, and while he lingered in the dark, he saw Coop go past, heading toward Clancys, where it sounded as if a fight had broken out. Then he'd waited, uncertain what he should do. As he watched her draw closer, he knew he felt something he'd been holding back for a while, something he hadn't dared admit to himself. He was certain she'd been in the clearing that night, and he knew that if Rachel hadn't been there, something would have happened between him and Susan. Rachel's words came back to him. She was right: He had used up his share of chances. Was he going to let go the last one he might ever have?

He stepped forward to meet her. "Hello," he said.

Her step faltered, and for a second he thought she'd pass him by. She stopped. "Hello."

"How was the dance?"

"It was fine." She looked back toward the hotel. "Coop had to leave."

"Oh, right. There was trouble at the bar, I think." She looked beyond him, refusing to meet his eye.

"Well . . ." She started to go past him.

"Look." He put his hand on her arm, and for a moment they were both looking at it. He let it drop.

"There's something I've been wanting to say." He wasn't sure how to go on. Her face was a mask giving nothing away, and he was unsure of his ground.

"Go on," she prompted.

"The night I saw you. In the clearing."

Her mouth tightened, and he got the impression she didn't want to be reminded of that. He went on quickly.

"The person you saw . . ." He looked for a way to make this better than it was going to sound. "The thing is, she was just a friend."

"You don't have to explain anything to me."

"Wait." He stopped her again and felt her bristle. "Why did you come over that night?"

"It doesn't matter," she replied brusquely.

Michael let go of her arm, but she didn't leave. For what seemed like a long time they stood apart, searching each other's expressions. He didn't know what she was thinking, and wasn't certain of himself, but neither of them moved. He looked at her closely, at the shape of her eyes and the shades of green they contained, at her wide mouth and soft full lips. Her face was more familiar to him than he'd known. He'd absorbed more of her detail than he'd thought. He could smell her scent, and a streetlamp threw light and shadows onto her hair. Her coat had fallen open, and he saw her shiver, saw her breasts rise with her breathing, and what he wanted more than anything he had ever wanted in his life was to hold her.

Susan saw his intention in his eyes before he moved. She sensed his need, and it wakened in her a yearning loneliness she'd kept buried for too long. His hands fell to her waist, and for just a brief moment she resisted.

She flinched, staring at him. He bent to kiss her and she turned her face up to meet his, and then nothing else registered except the feeling of him holding her, pressing his mouth and body against hers.

IN THE DARKNESS across the street, Coop watched unseen. His fists were balled, anger and hurt ripping his insides to shreds. He knew he'd been kidding himself all along, that Susan had never really felt anything for him. But it might have worked out. Sometimes people grow to love others slowly, and maybe that's what would have happened if he'd had a chance. Jamie would have come around in time, and she would have, too. Somehow he knew that's what this was all about. She was so worried for Jamie that she was confusing her emotions. He didn't see what else it could be. Somers was a jailbird, he'd gone crazy and shot somebody, so how could Susan go for him if he hadn't turned her head, getting Jamie all tied up with that falcon of his. He thought maybe he ought to go over there and do something about it, make her see she was making a hell of a big mistake. He had to struggle to remain where he was, knowing that getting into a fight wouldn't solve anything. It might give him some brief satisfaction to smash his fist into Somers's face, but it wouldn't get him anywhere with Susan. What he had to do was keep calm and think things through. He had to figure out a way to talk to her calmly and make her see what was happening, that it was all wrong.

He stayed hidden in the shadows, and when they'd gone, driving away in their separate cars without either of them seeing him, he smashed his fist violently into the door he was standing by. He felt his knuckles crack, the tight skin split and erupt, smearing blood across the wood. Pain flashed bright like a flare in his brain and focused his anger, his hurt, and he turned and slowly walked back to the station house.

Miller looked up from his desk, where he had begun writing out

a report on the brawl that had broken out at Clancys, and was surprised, then puzzled, to see Coop back again. "I thought you'd gone
back to the hotel," he said.

"I changed my mind." Coop went to his desk and sat down. "Listen,
it's all quiet now, why don't you go home?" he said.

"I was going to get this report done." He saw Coop's fist, shredded
skin and blood beneath a hastily wrapped handkerchief that he was
now unwinding. "Shit, did that happen back there?"

"Yeah," Coop said. "Listen, the report can wait. Go on, I'll finish
up here."

Miller got up hesitantly. "Well, okay then."

Miller stopped at the door, suddenly unsure. Coop looked as if he'd
been poleaxed or something, he had a different look about him, sort
of glazed but like he was struggling to hold some deep emotion in
check. Miller wondered what had happened after Coop had left Clancys.

"Listen, Coop, I don't mind hanging around—"

Coop waved him away. "Go home."

Miller hesitated a fraction longer, then shrugged and grabbed his
coat. "See you in the morning," he said, but Coop didn't answer.

Coop waited until he was alone, then went to a cabinet where he
kept a bottle of bourbon. It was mostly full, hardly touched in the
time it had been there, which was longer than Coop could remember.
He sat down again and took the velvet box from his pocket and
opened it. He stared at the ring while he poured a drink, then he
put the ring down on the desk and swallowed a half glass in one go.
He poured another. There were points of light like miniature stars
in the diamond, winking in the dim light.

Coop snapped the case shut and threw it into the back of a drawer.

"Please . . ." Her voice was a murmur, just a movement of her
lips. She didn't know what she was asking. Their lips brushed, then
he pulled away.

They hadn't spoken much since arriving at his house. All kinds of
things had gone through her mind on the way, doubts, anxieties, but
she pushed them aside. Inside they were awkward in each other's
company and with the situation.

"Would you like a drink?" Michael offered uncertainly. "I think I've got whiskey somewhere, or bourbon?"

She shook her head, looking around the living room. The furniture was old, the air faintly musty. Michael guessed what she was thinking.

"I don't use this room much." He lit a fire, more to give himself something to do than anything else, while she sat on the couch, shoulders hunched and knees drawn tightly together, hugging herself for warmth. Flames flickered and caught, and he stood up.

When he'd met her in the street, he'd been certain of what he wanted. He wanted to hold her, feel her warmth and reassuring presence. He wanted her softness, her arms around him, her lips against his ear, whispering, her legs around him drawing him close, his face in her hair, inhaling her sweet female scent. Now it seemed they were stalled. She was wrapped in herself as if she was drawing away, unsure of him. He wondered if she was thinking about him leaving, unsure why she was there and why he wanted her.

She met his eye and gave a wan smile. There was a gap between them that neither was sure how to bridge. Each sensed the other's need, and perhaps that was their stumbling block. Perhaps each needed somebody who wasn't weighed down with uncertainty.

Neither of them moved, and a minute went by, feeling like an hour. Then at last Susan stood. She'd been thinking of David, and his image had become grainy, his smile dissolving as he receded into her memory, where she would now hold him. She took both of Michael's hands in hers. She searched his eyes, saw his need, her own rising in her breast. The touch of a body, a body she could love.

"I haven't done this for a long time," she said.

"Me neither." He half smiled, ironically.

"I want you to know something," she said, holding his eye. "This means something to me. It's not something I do lightly."

He nodded, and silence crept over them. Eventually he said, "If it makes a difference, I love you." He watched her reaction, and in the quiet stillness of the room he felt a heavy weight he'd been carrying around lift away from him. "It's been a long time since I've said those words."

She smiled slowly, reached up, and kissed him softly. "Where's your bedroom?"

He led her upstairs, and they stood together beside his bed. The door was closed, and it was very dark, so dark it was like being folded into something almost tactile.

For long minutes they held each other without moving. Only now did she know how lonely she had been, and she knew he understood that better than anyone. It felt as if they could just stand there for all time, just letting that emptiness melt away from each other, just so they could feel another human breathing, another heartbeat, the smell of skin and hair and some huge swell of emotion welling from deep within. She felt tears running across her cheeks, which perplexed her because she didn't feel sad.

She traced her fingers across his back, and moved apart from him to raise her mouth to be kissed. Their lips brushed, hesitant at first. Then their mouths met, and she felt his need like hunger and her own, too.

"Wait." She stood back so that there was space between them, and in that absence of touch there was pleasure in denial. She could barely make out his shape in the pitch-black of his room, but she sensed that his eyes were closed. She reached toward him and, when he moved, laid a restraining hand against him. She wanted to remove his clothes, to feel him naked. There was something ritualistic about it that felt right. It had a meaning beyond merely being erotic, and he was unresisting, as if he sensed what she was feeling.

She closed her eyes, doing everything by touch. Her fingers brushed softly, trailing across his body. She took off his shirt and unbuckled his belt. When he was completely naked, she placed her hands against the sides of his head. She felt his hair, its thick wavy texture, then moved across his forehead and eyes, probing the hollows and planes of his features. She put her finger between his lips. When she moved across his chest and sides, she counted his ribs beneath lean hard flesh. She could feel his musculature beneath her fingertips. They skimmed across his belly, brushing against his erection. She was mapping his being, committing him to memory, taking sensual pleasure after the long absence of touch. She touched every part of him, making currents of air as she moved around him, her hands caressing, leaving, caressing again. Her fingers glided over his shoulders and along his arms, and she raised his hands to her mouth.

She slid her hands across his buttocks, then put her arms around him and held him. He shivered at her touch. She knelt in front of

him so that she could explore his thighs, then moved down his legs
to his feet, tracing each toe and then resting her face against his
belly. He was absorbed in her cells and nerves and captured in the
impulses in her brain.

When she stood, she guided his hands to her clothes.

He undressed her as she had him, by touch. Though he couldn't
see her, it was like unwrapping some precious gift, and in his mind
he transformed what he touched and felt into an image of her that
was more real than mere vision. She reacted, her flesh rippling almost
undetectably, nerve endings shivering. When her dress fell from her
body, he heard the soft sound it made. He gathered her hair from
her forehead so that it fell down her back, leaving her shoulders
naked except for the thin straps of her bra. He explored the delicate
bones that ran from her neck to her shoulders, where the skin
stretched tight, forming deep hollows beside her throat. Gently he
pressed his thumbs there, thinking that if there was light, he'd see
deep accentuating shadows. He slid the straps across her shoulders,
pushing them down her arms, and reached around to unfasten the
clasp.

Her breasts were soft and full. Rolling his thumbs across her nip-
ples, he felt them grow hard, and he brushed them with his mouth
as he knelt to take off her panties. They were cut high on her thigh,
and he traced their outline across her hips and buttocks. He touched
her belly, then his hand rested against the soft swell at the junction
of her thighs. He guessed that she shaved herself and imagined her
performing that intimate task. She stepped out of her panties, and
he rose and guided her toward the bed.

Naked and shrouded by darkness, they lay down together side by
side, the mattress giving way beneath them, only their arms touching.
They kissed and moved closer, pressing belly and thigh, her breasts
against his chest, their arms wrapping around each other. He wanted
the moment to last forever. Her full wide mouth enveloped him in
softness, and he felt he wanted to be sucked inside her and held there,
cherished and safe. At the same time, he felt that her need was equal
to his own, and he rolled above her, supporting his weight on his
elbows, wanting to give back what he felt.

She could feel and hear the rush of blood in her ears and the
quickening sound of his breathing, in time with her heart. They
kissed slowly, then more hungrily, their mouths devouring each other

while their hands explored. She parted her thighs and wrapped them around his back, and he held himself on one elbow and slipped his free hand across her buttocks and between her legs. She reached down for him and they rubbed and caressed each other, fingers and wetness and hard flesh becoming entwined and confused.

She wanted him inside her, his weight on her, to hold the intensity of the moment. It was physical and emotional. She rolled across him and took him in her mouth and felt him shiver. Then he turned her over onto her back, holding her thighs apart as he lay down to kiss and taste her. She made a sound and shuddered, her hands gripping his hair, the taste of him still swarming in her mind. Pulling him urgently, she sought his mouth with her own as he slipped inside her, molding them together. They moved smoothly, without haste, his weight bearing down and through her, and his mouth sought the nape of her neck, her breasts, and as they rocked in each other's arms, each felt the other rise toward a climax.

They lay in the dark, their skin touching in places, breathing softly, their eyes closed, partly together, partly awash with memories. He kissed her again, and when she responded, he began to caress her, and this time when he was inside her, she kept him there for a long time. They moved slowly, then quickly, then rested, absorbed in each other's heat until they could begin again. She felt tears and tasted their salty flavor, felt their wetness against her cheek, and she wasn't sure from which of them they had come, or if from them both.

Eventually they slept, their arms around each other.

31 SOMETHING WOKE MICHAEL IN THE MORN-
ing, and he lay still for a moment, getting used
to everything, wondering what the sound had
been. He could see the sky through the window, pale ice
blue with the sun still low. He was lying on his side, and
he could feel Susan curled up against his back. When he rolled over,
she muttered something sleepily and draped her arm across his chest.

He thought he might have dreamed the feelings she had evoked
in him. Being with her had felt both sexual and nurturing, and he
understood why nature was always referred to in the female gender.
He kissed her. The scent of her hair and her skin lay over him, and
the smell of sex in the early morning. Her hand trailed across his
belly, making him shiver, and she gripped him and mumbled something into his chest.

He heard it again, the sound that had woken him, a sharp crack
against the roof and then a skittering noise. It repeated itself.

"What's that?" Susan opened her eyes and propped herself on one
elbow.

Michael went to the window. "It's Jamie."

He was standing outside, throwing stones onto the roof. When he
saw Michael at the window, their eyes met for a moment, then he
turned away sullenly and scuffed his feet in the snow.

"Oh God, I should have remembered." Susan got up and began
pulling on her clothes. "I better talk to him."

Michael dressed, and while Susan went outside, he went to the kitchen to make coffee. He could see them out the window, Susan crouched down talking to Jamie, holding his shoulders. He was avoiding her eye, refusing to respond. She brushed a strand of hair from her face and paused, frowning with consternation. Standing up, she put one hand on his shoulder. Looking toward the house, she saw Michael at the window and shrugged hopelessly.

They drank their coffee while Jamie hung around outside, refusing to come in.

"Don't worry, he'll be all right," he assured her.

She managed to smile, but there was something like doubt in her eye. Or maybe it was simply uncertainty. They hadn't talked about what they would do; all she knew was that he was leaving. He held her hand and squeezed.

"I love you," he told her. He held her eye, wanting her to know how certain he was. She didn't say anything for a moment, looking deeply and searchingly, then she nodded slowly and smiled.

"And I you."

He finished his coffee. "I want to release Cully this morning. I'll take Jamie with me, and when we get back, we'll decide what happens next."

"Okay."

He went to Cully and she greeted him by bobbing her head, her feathers ruffled with contentment. He offered her a piece of meat, which she took with less enthusiasm than normal. He had half a rabbit carcass in his bag that he he was going to give her later, before he let her go, and the night before, he'd fed her twice her normal ration. He was confident that she wouldn't need to kill her own food for a few days, which would give her a comfortable margin to get used to being free and having to hunt again.

Outside, Jamie was waiting in the Nissan, and Susan stood at the door. Michael put Cully on her perch in the back. "We'll be a couple of hours," he said.

"Good luck," Susan said.

As they left, Michael returned her wave, but Jamie ignored her, resolutely staring out the window.

As they drove through the forest, following the winding road up through cold dark canyons of trees, Jamie wouldn't look at him. He was turned away, hunched in on himself, and Michael didn't know what to say. He could almost feel the things going on in the boy's mind. It would be a whirlpool of confusion and hurt. The silence hung heavily over them until they came out from the trees and, shortly afterward, pulled over.

"Wait, Jamie," Michael said as the boy started to get out. He didn't want it to be like this when they let Cully go. "Listen, I think I know how you feel about this. You think I'm taking your dad's place, right?" He tried to put himself in Jamie's position, to understand what was really going on in his mind. He wondered what had really happened to make Jamie shut down the way he had, to decide he wasn't going to speak anymore, to resent anyone that tried to get close to his mother. He saw the boy and could picture the man, knowing firsthand how things that get locked in tight for too long become twisted. Was Jamie going to end up full of confusion and hate? Would he turn it outward someday, maybe against his mother, or turn it against himself in destructive self-loathing that would destroy his life? It was all too possible.

Michael put his hand on Jamie's shoulder, and when the boy tried to shrug it off, he kept it there. "I want you to listen to me, Jamie. You can't go on like this forever. I think you're trying to keep things just the way they were, aren't you? That's why you don't speak, that's why you don't want your mother seeing anybody else, am I right?" Jamie stiffened and then reached for the door handle to get out, but Michael leaned past him and held the door to.

"Just listen. Just give me a minute, okay? You want to help me let Cully go, don't you? Come on, just a minute."

For a moment they didn't move, Jamie still tense with his hand on the door, then slowly he let go. He turned and stared out the windshield, still refusing to look at Michael, who thought that was the best he was going to get. Now that he had Jamie's attention, he was unsure what to say.

"Look, Jamie, I don't know what happened the day your dad died, but my guess is you loved him a lot, and you miss him. You should hang on to that feeling. If you carry on like this, not thinking about him, you know what's going to happen? You're going to start to forget what he was like. I know what I'm talking about. For a long time, I shut my dad out of my mind—for different reasons, maybe, but I shut him out all the same. And you know what? It was the worst thing I could have done. It cost me a lot of pain, and it cost people I loved a lot of pain, too. That's why I came back here, to this town, so I could remember my dad again. I found out a lot of things I'd forgotten, a lot of things that would have been a comfort to me when I was younger, if I'd remembered. Don't do the same thing I did, Jamie. Don't shut it all in, not remembering what your dad was really like. Whatever happened that day, you have to face it, and you have to face up to the fact that your dad is gone. It's the only way you're going to be able to feel him again."

Michael knew that Jamie was listening; he just didn't know how much of what he was saying was getting through. He didn't know either if what he was saying made any sense. Glancing toward the rearview mirror, he saw Cully in the back of the Nissan, standing square-footed, strong and sleek, her eye fixed on the mountains outside.

"Jamie, look at Cully. You remember the day she stooped the first time, when I was so worried about her wing giving out? She must have felt the injury then, it must have hurt her to do what she did, but she never faltered." Jamie looked at him slowly, his brow furrowed, then he turned a little in his seat and looked back at Cully. "What I'm saying is that we have to be like her. Don't you want that? Look at her, she's not afraid of anything."

He could think of no other wisdom to offer. He got out and went around to Jamie's door and opened it. "Come on. Let's send her back where she belongs. Up there." He swept an arm, indicating the sky, and when Jamie got out, Michael put his hand on the boy's shoulder again and squeezed it briefly.

RACHEL WOKE EARLY, as the sky was beginning to lighten. She was in bed, exactly where she'd cried herself to sleep, curled up with the blankets pulled around her. Pete had gone in the night. She'd heard him go down the stairs after he'd got up from her, and then she'd heard the sound of his truck backing down the drive with its wheels spinning.

She rose and went into the bathroom. She looked a mess. Her eyes were red, her mouth was bruised where he'd hit her, and when she brushed her teeth, her gums were tender. She felt her teeth gingerly, hoping he hadn't knocked any loose, then took a shower. The hot water made her feel a hundred times better. She let the stinging jets scald her skin, scrubbing herself hard and washing her hair vigorously enough to make her scalp ache. Afterward she dressed, put on some makeup, and went downstairs to make some coffee and think.

Despite everything, she was worried about Pete. It amazed her that she could still feel that way, but there was a part of her that couldn't just abandon him. She didn't love him anymore—whatever had been left of that had finally died—but neither did she hate him. She pitied him and knew that he wasn't bad but weak, and he was still the father of her kids. She was afraid of what would happen when he realized what he'd done, afraid he might not be able to live with himself.

She picked up the phone and dialed the yard, and the phone rang endlessly. It didn't mean he wasn't there; he could be passed out in the office. She didn't know what he might have done after he'd left the house; he might have had some booze in the truck or gone to some bar to drink himself into a stupor. Or he might just be letting the phone ring because he'd know it was her. She wanted to think that was so, but she had a bad feeling in the pit of her stomach. Across the miles of wire she could sense he wasn't there, and in her mind's eye she saw the untidy little office with its cheap desk and dirty windows, and it was cold and empty.

She hung up and tried to think where he might have gone. She tried Red Parker's place and let the phone ring and ring until he answered, his voice grouchy at being woken so early.

"Yeah?"

"Is Pete there, Red? This is Rachel."

There was a pause. Either he was getting his scrambled thoughts together or considering what he ought to tell her, she couldn't tell which.

"He's not here."

"Have you seen him?"

"Not since last night."

She had a feeling Parker was holding something back. "Listen, this is important. I'm really worried about him," she said.

He must have picked up something from her tone that made him think, because he hesitated for a good long while.

"Please. If he's there, just tell me. I just need to know he's okay."

"He was here, but he ain't now," Parker said. "Turned up late last night, after he'd been home. He was talking crazy stuff, I don't know—rambling, I guess. Anyway, he stayed on the couch, but I

don't know where he is now 'cause I'm looking at the couch and he
ain't on it."

It crossed her mind to wonder what Pete had told Parker, whom
she didn't like. It made her skin creep a little to think that he might
know what had happened.

"Can you see if his truck's still there?" she said.

Parker went away and eventually came back on the line. "It's
gone."

"Have you got any idea where he might be now? Did he say
anything?"

"I don't remember that well."

She sensed he knew something, and this bothered her. If he knew
where Pete was, why didn't he just tell her? She calmed herself,
trying to make herself think clearly.

"Listen, you have to tell me. I think Pete's a little strained at the
moment. I think he needs help. I'm scared he might do something."

Parker was quiet. She thought he had to be considering what she'd
said, deciding where his loyalties lay.

"Listen," she said. "Where were you last night? Before Pete came
home."

"Out at the Forester," Parker said.

She knew the place, a tavern along Maple Road she never went
near because it was kind of rough.

"Did something happen there? Did something happen to Pete?"

She was thinking about her clothes and the wrecked bedroom. Pete
had trashed her things and then gone out drinking. She wondered
why he hadn't stayed out all night, or at least until the tavern had
closed. She thought something else must have happened.

"Pete talked to Ted Hanson, that's all I know. Then he started
going nuts. He wouldn't say what the hell happened."

It took a moment, and then she knew. She pictured Hanson outside
the Red Rooster and realized he must have seen her as she'd left
with Michael, and with that thought another occurred to her. She
hung up the phone, stunned. Suddenly it wasn't Pete she was worried
about. She ran outside and got in her car.

SUSAN WAS GETTING ready to go over to her house, thinking that
Wendy would be worried because she'd been out all night. She heard

a car coming down the track and thought it must be Michael returning. They'd been gone only fifteen minutes, but maybe he'd forgotten something—or else they might have come back because of Jamie. She was worried about him, what he was thinking, and she wasn't sure she should have let them go off together.

She went outside as an old Honda skidded down the track and stopped in a flurry of snow and dirt. The driver's door flew open, and Susan recognized Rachel Ellis and wondered what she was doing here. The two of them stared at each other, each working out what the other signified. Then the way Rachel looked set off alarms in Susan, though she didn't know why.

"Is Michael here?"

"What happened to you?"

They'd both talked at once, Susan belatedly seeing the bruises on Rachel's face. She guessed it was Rachel she'd seen at the house that night, something she couldn't begin to figure out. Rachel's hand went automatically to her discolored eye.

"Please," Rachel insisted, "do you know where he is?"

Susan went to her, putting aside all the other things that were buzzing in her head. "What is it?" she asked.

Rachel took a breath. "It's Pete, he thinks . . . He's not himself right now, and I'm worried."

"What does he think?" Susan didn't understand.

"I don't know where he is," Rachel said. "I'm worried what he might do."

It started to dawn on Susan what Rachel was talking about, and though she didn't understand all of it, she could see that Rachel was genuinely concerned.

"They're not here. I mean Michael and Jamie. My son. They went to release his falcon." She was thinking while she spoke. There were bruises on Rachel's cheek and eye, her lip looked swollen, and there was desperation in the way her gaze didn't stay still.

"Pete carries a rifle in his truck," Rachel said.

Susan grabbed Rachel's arm, infected by her urgency now, fighting down the dread in the pit of her stomach. "You go into town and find Coop. Tell him they've gone up toward Falls Pass. I'll go on ahead."

Rachel hesitated a second, then turned and started running for her car.

———

RACHEL DROVE TO Coop's house, but no one was there, so she turned around and headed back toward the station house, where she saw his car parked outside. She jumped out of her Honda and hammered on the door.

"Coop!" she yelled. "Are you in there?"

She couldn't hear anything from inside, and she hammered again and then thought he might have gone somewhere on foot. She looked down the street, but it was mostly empty this early on a Sunday. She didn't know if the diner was open yet, but she thought she'd go down that way and have a look. If she couldn't find him there, she'd just head up to Falls Pass herself. She kept trying to tell herself that she was panicking, but she still felt this tight knot in her stomach that refused to go away.

As she turned to go, the door opened and Coop stood there with his hand on the jamb, rubbing his face and blinking in the light. He looked like shit, which gave her a moment's pause, but she didn't have time to wonder about it.

"What is it?" he said.

"It's Pete," she said. "I think he might want to kill somebody."

He blinked at her, absorbing what she'd said.

THE DAY WAS perfect for this, Michael thought. Overnight there had been a light snowfall, and the ground was virgin. The sun was behind them, bouncing off the white slope, striking and reflecting off the cliff face a mile distant. The unbroken line of the ridge marked a horizon beyond which the sky beckoned wide and blue like a still ocean.

He wanted to let Cully go from the top of the ridge, where they could watch her soar out over the valley until she chose to leave them. He paused, stroking her breast, beginning to feel the sadness he knew would wash over him as she left. The air was crisp, as if he could take it in his hand and make it crackle between his fingers. He'd come to love the air here. It was dry and rarefied, scented with pine.

Cully detected a breath of wind, and her wings flicked open. Her dark bright eyes fixed on Michael's, as if prompting him to keep their bargain. They began the walk across the snowfield toward the cliff, and halfway there they stopped.

What happened next was stupid and unexplainable. He'd taken off Cully's leash and jesses countless times, and today he meant to cut the leather anklets that attached them to her legs. He took a knife from the bag and then, hesitating, put it in his pocket. He offered Cully a piece of meat that at first she ignored, then, apparently changing her mind, reached for and swallowed.

He thought he'd allow her to eat her fill of the rabbit carcass he'd brought with him. Possibly he was distracted as he unwound the leash from his gloved fingers and reached for the knife again. Unexpectedly she took to the air, startling him, and the leash slipped through his fingers. Before he could stop her, she was rising, flying away from them, trailing her leash underneath her.

Shocked by his own carelessness, it took him seconds to react. In a rush, he saw how serious the situation was. How many times had he read that a bird that escapes with its leash and jesses still attached faces a certain and unpleasant death, caught up somewhere to hang upside down and starve?

Fumbling in his haste, he grabbed the lure and called her name as he swung it at his side. She continued to rise as he called again, desperately willing her to respond, to begin her turn. She flew on, and his terror formed a tight feeling in his throat. He knew that if he lost sight of her now, if she flew on over the valley, he might never find her again, and the knowledge that in the end, after everything, he'd failed her, weighed him down.

Jamie's expression pleaded silently for him to do something, and not knowing what else he could do, he began to run after her.

Normally she would catch a thermal and then rise to wait for the lure, but now she kept on toward the cliff. Lack of hunger made her inattentive. Michael called as he ran. He was thinking that to come so far, to have saved her only to be the cause of her death, was an unbearable prospect. Images of her spinning like a bundle of rags in the wind, caught up in some tree where he'd never find her, tormented him.

He ran, stumbling in the snow, his breath ragged, sometimes sprawling head first and then struggling to his feet again. He tried to reason with himself, to find something that would offer hope. Though she wasn't sharp set, he thought that the effort of flying would quickly burn energy and she would become hungry again soon. All he had to do was keep her in sight until that happened.

He willed her to change direction, to rise and circle high above them—that way, he might eventually be able to call her down. But she was making for the cliff, and it was his real, sickening fear that she would pass beyond it and be lost to him. Her leash would become tangled where she landed, and her efforts to escape would only tire her. She would die slowly and there would be nothing he could do. Finding her would be like searching for a needle in twenty haystacks.

As she drew farther away, he felt that the situation was hopeless. Out of breath, gasping, half choking with remorse, he stopped running. She was almost at the cliff, rising high. Jamie clutched at Michael's arm, his eyes streaming tears. As loud as he could, Michael shouted Cully's name, his voice carrying in the cold still air and echoing faintly. For a second he felt unable to breathe, as if his heart had paused midbeat, and he prayed that she would turn. Then, her image lost briefly in a shadow, he saw the pale flick of a wing as she settled on the cliff face.

The relief he felt was short-lived as he realized she could take off again at any moment. Already he'd lost sight of her, but pinpointing the general area where he thought she'd landed, he started to run on, nurturing a tiny flicker of hope. He stumbled and tripped, Jamie beside him, and soon they arrived at the base of the cliff.

"Can you see her?" Michael said, his voice tense, desperate.

The place he figured she ought to be was a crisscrossed pattern of shadows and rifts in the rock. Incredibly, Jamie nodded, grabbing Michael's arm and pointing.

Michael peered up. At first he couldn't see anything, but then a movement caught his eye. His eye must have passed over her, mistaking her for a pale splash blending with its surroundings, but now he could clearly make her out, perched on a ledge between jagged outcrops about a hundred feet up. She seemed unconcerned.

Michael tried to work out what he should do. If he called her and she left her perch but still refused to come down, there was a good chance she would be lost somewhere in the valley. He reasoned it might be better to wait and hope that the longer she remained up there, the hungrier she would become, that if she would just stay put long enough, the lure might bring her back. He was still weighing his options when Cully made her own decision, and with a flick of her wings she took to the air.

He saw immediately that something was wrong. She remained flapping at the rock face, her wings beating uselessly, propelling her a foot forward before she fell back again. Repeatedly she tried to escape, but her leash had caught on something and she was helpless. As they watched, her efforts tired her, and after a minute she hung suspended by her feet, flapping weakly, spiraling slowly in the breeze.

Michael gave Jamie the lure and searched for a route up the cliff, which was run through with fissures and cracks that would at least give him handholds. He saw that the main problem would be the ledge where her leash was caught, which formed part of an overhang he'd have to get around. It was in permanent shadow, and he could see the cold sheen of ice against the black rock.

He crouched down in front of Jamie and explained what he was going to do. "I have to try and reach her, but when I go up there, there's a chance she might get free." He paused and gripped Jamie's shoulders. "If she does, you have to stop her before we lose sight of her. You have to bring her down." He put the lure in Jamie's hands, clasping his fingers around the rope. "If we lose her with that leash still on her, she'll die, Jamie."

He wished there was another way, but he had no choice, and searching Jamie's expression for reassurance, he was met with a blank look. He didn't know if Jamie understood what he was asking him. "If she gets free, you have to call her. You have to get her attention before she's lost. Okay? You have to call her down, Jamie."

He knew how impossible it seemed. He searched for some sign that Jamie could do what he was asking, but Jamie just looked up at Cully with frightened eyes. He was just a small boy, pale and on the verge of tears.

Michael turned back to the cliff and began to climb.

The rock was smooth in places, worn by the wind and rain over millions of years to defy the frozen hands of a man; it was so cold it felt impregnated with ice. It scraped the flesh from his fingertips as he sought to find each grip, his chafed and reddened hands numbed by a freezing wind. On the ground he couldn't feel it, but thirty feet up the air moved around him, jabbing cold needles wherever flesh was exposed. His ears rang, and his face felt swollen but deadened, as if his cheeks were full of Novocain. In places where the rock was cracked and split into fissures, there were sharp edges that peeled his skin and lacerated his palms.

He paused for breath, his eyes streaming from the cold, and looked for Cully. She was twenty feet away, hanging by her leash, flapping listlessly to try and free herself but caught fast, her efforts only tiring her. She gave up, her wings hanging down as she panted and twisted. He could see her accusing eye, but if she recognized that he was coming to help her, she gave no sign.

As Michael looked down, the ground seemed distant. The pain in his hands and the numbness seeping into his bones allowed him to imagine that falling was a real possibility. He saw himself bouncing against rocks on the way down, breaking bones painfully. He found the next handhold and hauled himself up, and when his toe slipped, his fingers scraped frantically for purchase until he found another hold, leaving faint smears of blood.

As he got closer, he began speaking softly to Cully, trying to calm her, and when she heard his voice, she flapped her wings and pitifully bounced off the rock. She was only ten feet away, but the overhang was above him and there didn't seem a way around it. He thought that if he could climb up beneath it and hook an elbow over the edge to support himself, he might be able to reach her, though having her in his grasp and saving her might not be quite the same thing.

Jamie looked small down below, an elfin dark figure against white snow, pale upturned face watching intently. He held the cord of the lure in both hands, at the ready.

Reaching with outstretched fingers, Michael grasped the edge of the overhang and blindly scrabbled one foot after the other to find a place that would support his weight. The rock was smooth, and the places where his fingers found a hold were too small for his boots. He had climbed into shadow, and the temperature had dropped as the sun was lost from his back so that it felt like being plunged into a deep abyss where daylight never penetrated. If he fell, he knew he'd never be able to climb this far again.

She was so close that if he reached out a hand, he could touch her. He could hear her panting. He spoke soothingly and wondered what he would do next. He was supporting his weight on one forearm, and if he reached for her, he was uncertain he could hang on. Even if he could, and took hold of her, he could do nothing with her. To try and climb down with her would be impossible. He hung motionless, the cold sapping his energy and will with equal measure.

Unable to think of an alternative, he reached into his pocket for his knife, and in that simple action he was convinced that he could hold on for no more than a few seconds. Risking a look below, he glimpsed Jamie and wished he could call down to warn him of what he was going to do, but he was afraid if he did, he might frighten Cully more than she already was. Nevertheless, he turned as best he could before he acted, twisting his head and seeking Jamie's eye.

He wanted Jamie to understand how important it was for Cully to live. She mustn't die fettered by chains, the trust she had placed in him betrayed at the end, her freedom denied her. He looked down to that small pale oval whose expression he couldn't read, then he turned and, reaching up, did the only thing possible. He cut free half of Cully's leash, so that for an instant she fell past him. Then her wings opened and she flew clear, brushing his face as she went.

She rose, riding the breeze that flowed around the edge of the cliff, then sloped and banked toward the valley beyond, out of his sight, trailing the remainder of her leash behind her.

"*Call her, Jamie!*" Michael shouted.

Jamie began to swing the lure, running around the base of the cliff.

"*Call her!*"

He watched helplessly as Jamie and Cully vanished out of his sight. All he could hear was the soft whistle of the cold wind, mournful and steeped in melancholy sadness. After several moments, he thought he heard a thin cry. He listened for it again, but if he'd heard it at all, it was gone now; perhaps it was only the wind and his hope after all.

He hung there, immersed in cold, the feeling in his limbs draining away, and looking back across the snowfield, he saw a figure approaching.

ELLIS HAD FOLLOWED the tracks from the road, and half a mile from the cliff he raised his glasses when he heard a faint voice calling.

He was in time to see the falcon rise and vanish from sight, leaving Somers stuck high up on the rock. He wondered what the hell he was doing there.

Ellis spat into the snow. Sometime during the night it had come to him as clear as if somebody just turned on the lights; all his recent troubles began and ended with Somers. He didn't blame Rachel anymore for doing what she had. He could see now how it had happened, and he thought that Somers was one smart son of a bitch. He must have planned the whole thing right from the start, and Ellis guessed that was why he'd been locked up in the first place, because Somers would do just about anything to get what he wanted. Shit, he'd shot some people, hadn't he?

Ellis had it all worked out. Somers had planned to take Rachel away from him right from the beginning; that was why he'd come back to Little River in the first place. It made sense, and he wondered why he hadn't seen it before. Why the hell else would he have come back? He must have somehow known about the falcon, and so he'd stolen it just because he knew how much Ellis needed the money. He must have figured out all along that before he could steal Rachel, he'd have to prepare the ground.

Ellis was certain it was Somers who had driven him to drink. He'd convinced himself that before all this had started, things with Rachel hadn't been so bad. The yard had just been going through a bad patch that he would have sorted out with the money Tusker had promised him. Things had only gone belly up when Somers had arrived, which he could see now was all to make Rachel feel like she was married to a bum. That was how Somers had got to her, when she didn't know what she was doing.

It occurred to Ellis that in fact this was a test. He'd come to believe in devils and spirits lately; in fact, he'd seen them for himself, hiding in trees and behind chairs in bars, laughing and grinning. He guessed maybe Somers was in with them, and when he took care of him, it'd show whatever was plaguing his life that he deserved a break. Then everything would be okay. He'd stop drinking and get the business going again, and things would get sorted out at home.

He guessed he'd been a little rough on Rachel, but then she had to understand how he'd been feeling at the time. Maybe they both had some apologizing to do. He'd even break the ice. He'd tell her he understood it wasn't her fault that she fucked another guy, that he knew Somers had planned the whole thing, and he'd tell her that was something he'd already taken care of.

Ellis stopped walking. He was about a quarter of a mile from the cliff when he took the rifle from his back. He found Somers easily, and held him steady in the scope.

Son of a bitch, he thought, this is where you get what's coming your way.

AFTER RACHEL LEFT, Susan got in her Ford and fumbled with the key. The engine started. For a moment she paused, gathering her thoughts, reining herself in. It was like being on a roller coaster. Over the past eight hours her whole life had been flipped upside down, and she'd gone with her emotions without having a moment to think. She took a breath to calm herself, her hands gripping the wheel. She had this feeling of dread inside her that just when something good had happened, it was all getting turned around.

She put the Ford in gear and went forward, then stopped and reversed around. The wheels slid and churned up the snow when she stepped too hard on the gas, but her heart was beating too fast, telling her to hurry, and she stamped on the brake and changed gear again, desperate to get moving. The car lurched and the wheels spun, tires whining.

"Damn it!"

She took her foot off the gas and stamped down again, and this time they bit and the car lurched forward, taking her by surprise so that the wheel spun from her grasp. The Ford slewed around and bumped over something so that the front reared up, then it crashed down and she hit her head on the roof. She felt something hit the floor beneath her feet while she grabbed the wheel again. She stopped and tried again, telling herself to take it slowly. She kept thinking about the way Rachel had looked. Now the car wouldn't move. A grinding sound came from down by the wheels, and the engine screamed. Cursing, she threw the door open and got out to see what the problem was. A log on the side of the track was wedged underneath, raising the wheels so they couldn't get a proper grip, and the car was stuck fast.

She kicked a panel, and stopped the panic that was coming over her. She had to think what to do, to be rational, and she started looking around for something to wedge under the wheels. The wood-shed was just on the other side of the house, and she ran over there and burst through the door. Grabbing a couple of hefty logs, she struggled back with them and got down on her knees to shove them into place. She could see she was going to need more and went to fetch them. Minutes were falling away, and she knew this was going to take her some time. There was nothing she could do about that.

In fifteen minutes she'd built a ramp of logs under each of the back wheels, and she got back inside and turned the key. When the Ford was in gear, she let the clutch out slowly, pressing down on the gas, trying to ease free. The wheels bit, and the Ford rocked but didn't come off the logs. She put the clutch in, took a breath, and tried again, giving it more gas this time. The car started to move forward, but underneath, the logs sounded as if they were ripping out the floor. The hood rose, and she thought she was there and gave it just a little more gas. Then everything collapsed. She heard logs fired like cannons from under the wheels as her ramps collapsed under the strain, and she eased off and got out to look at the damage. It was a wreck, the ground all gouged out and the Ford still held fast. She'd have to rebuild the ramps.

She knew she didn't have time, and in frustration she kicked the door panel and put a dent in it the size of a dinner plate. Just then she heard a vehicle turn off the road above, and a second later Coop drove around the bend and stopped. He leaned over and opened his passenger door.

"Get in," he said.

She hesitated, trying to read his thoughts. "Where's Rachel?"

"I told her to fetch Miller."

For a moment she didn't move. He stayed where he was, holding the door open. Then she got in, and Coop started reversing back up the track. The way he looked didn't strike her properly until they were on the road. She could smell liquor coming out of his pores, and his eyes were heavily bloodshot. He didn't look at her but kept his eyes on the road and his face set in a grim way. It was only then that she saw how it all looked, with her being at Michael's house, and she wondered why Coop didn't ask her about it. She didn't know how he knew, but she guessed that he did, and over everything else she felt a deep wash of emotion flood over her. Christ, it was all such a mess.

It took them twenty minutes to find Michael's Nissan. Behind it, abandoned at the side of the road, was an old Chevy truck. All the way she'd thought or hoped that when they got here it would just be nothing. Her panic changed to something like real fear then.

"Oh God," she said aloud. "Please don't let anything happen to him."

Coop looked over at her, and she saw he was wondering whom she meant. She'd been thinking about Jamie, but she meant them both.

The driver's door on Ellis's truck hung open, and a bottle of whiskey, mostly empty, was on the seat. Coop went around and felt the hood.

"Still warm," he said.

He looked across the snowfield, then ran back to his own car and returned carrying binoculars and a rifle. Susan was thinking about Pete Ellis sitting here in his truck drinking, thinking all kinds of fractured thoughts. A long way off, someone was walking across the snow. There were three sets of tracks from the road. Coop was looking through his glasses.

"It's Ellis," he said.

He turned, and she couldn't tell where he was looking. There was no sign of Jamie or Michael, but the tracks went toward the cliffs by the ridge.

"What is it?" she said. She knew something was going on.

Coop gave her the glasses and started to trot across the snow. She couldn't see anything at first. There was just Ellis, and in front of him were two sets of tracks. She followed them to the cliff and still couldn't see anything, then a movement high up on the rock caught her eye and she saw it was Michael. Right then she heard a shot.

MICHAEL WATCHED THE figure getting closer, following the tracks he and Jamie had made across the snow, and he wondered who it was. The figure was too far off to be distinguishable at first, but then Michael could make out a red checked jacket and a rifle and thought it must be a hunter. Some instinct warned him then, and he peered harder as whoever it was got closer. The man stopped and something in the way he stood struck a chord. Michael remembered the hunter he'd first seen stalking Cully in the mountains, and he suddenly knew it was Ellis. For a moment he was surprised, and then it made a kind of peculiar sense. They looked at each other across the snow, and then Ellis raised his rifle to his shoulder.

Michael looked down. It seemed a long way to the bottom, and below there were rocks just beneath the surface of the snow. He already knew he couldn't descend the way he'd come up: He'd lost some of the feeling in his limbs, and he wasn't going to be able to keep his grip. He felt like a target pasted to a board, and it was no longer just the cold that was making him shake.

A shot rang out, and rock chips flew several feet away. Michael twisted himself around. He didn't see that he had much of a choice about trying to get down. A second shot blasted the rock, closer this time. He had the feeling that if Ellis wanted to, he could pick him off anytime. He started to move, and a third shot came—much closer. He froze. Every time he moved, another shot would ring out, and he saw that Ellis wasn't trying to hit him—he just wanted to keep him there, to let him freeze until he couldn't hold on any longer. Michael looked down and wondered which he preferred, slowly freezing or being shot.

He began to make his way down.

Another shot was fired, but now it didn't matter; the nerves in his fingers were frozen, the joints clumsy. Before he'd descended ten feet, he fell, bouncing off the rock face. He heard his own grunts and involuntary exhalations all the way down, and among them the reverberating echoes of gunshots. Flares of bright pain lit the way, until he hit the snow-packed ground at the bottom and all the air was exploded out of him in a soft whoosh.

COOP HEARD SUSAN shouting at him to do something. He'd stopped to see what the hell was going on, and through his glasses he saw Ellis firing at Somers, though he couldn't have meant to hit him, because Somers made a clear target stuck up there on the rocks. Coop moved the glasses to the cliff, where Somers was high up in the shadows. He guessed it would be freezing up there, and he knew what Ellis was doing.

"Do something, Coop," Susan yelled from his side.

He didn't look at her. Another shot rang out, shattering the silence. He raised the rifle and looked through the sight. Somers was still clinging to the rock face. For a moment the sight was squarely on a point dead center in his back, and it wavered there. All kinds of notions went through his mind. He felt Susan's presence at his side, and his finger tightened, then abruptly he dropped the sight and found Pete Ellis on the snow and shouted out his name. There was no reaction, but Coop knew he must have heard. Ellis had his rifle raised. He could have shot Somers off the rock anytime he liked, but that didn't mean he wasn't going to now.

Coop swung his sight back to Somers and held it there. His finger tightened again. Susan spoke his name again, questioningly, as if she didn't know him.

Ellis was still firing. Then Coop saw Somers begin to fall.

"Coop!" Susan screamed.

He wavered, closing his eyes, everything happening in slow motion, Somers peeling away from the rock. He squeezed the trigger.

MICHAEL OPENED HIS eyes, surprised that he could. He was on his back, spread-eagled and numb. He couldn't move, couldn't even think about it. Above, he could see blue sky and the shadow of the rock, then he heard the sound of crunching snow. He thought Ellis would come and finish him off, but it was Jamie who leaned over into his vision. There were tears in the boy's eyes, and Cully was on his fist. The tattered end of her leash showed through his fingers. He was crying as he took off the thongs around her legs.

"I called her and she came down. I called, just like you said. You can hear me, can't you?"

Michael couldn't answer, but he blinked. His eyes were wet, and he felt a tear escape the corner of his eye and fall to join the snow on which he lay. He imagined it forming a crystal of ice. Cully looked around her, proud, bright-eyed. Dusky cream and gray. He could see the pulsing of a strong heart in her breast.

Jamie raised his fist, and she rose into the air.

Small, cold hands turned his head so that he could see her in the cool clear blue of the sky. She climbed, wings outstretched, and Jamie lifted Michael's head so that he could see her as she drifted across the ridge and over the valley.

"She'll be all right now, won't she?"

Yes she will, he thought. He rose with her, and felt the wind in the air. They soared and turned, and far, far below, small converging figures made a tableau on the white ground. The rushing air made a faint whistling sound. Banking, turning, subtly altering the angle and plane of feathers, responding to minute vibrations in muscle and bone.

ON THE GROUND Susan reaches them, and Jamie runs to her. He is sobbing as she holds him. He speaks to her, a fact she absorbs as she looks into Michael's eyes. They seem distant now, and a frost has formed on his eyebrows.

Above them, the snow falcon calls.

32

THE SNOW WAS ALL GONE EXCEPT IN those places high up in the mountains where it remained all year. The soft warm sun of late May fell over the house that Michael had grown up in. Susan looked toward the river and up at the deepening blue sky, thinking it would be a hot summer.

She could hear the sound of men's voices filtering through the woods from her own house, calling to one another with good-natured curses while they loaded furniture into the truck. They'd worked all of the previous day packing, and would be finished, they thought, by midafternoon. Then she and Jamie would get into her Ford with Bob in the back and they would leave. They'd drive up the track and turn away from town, twenty minutes later they'd hit the highway and turn south, and that would be it. Little River Bend would be behind them.

She turned back to the house, hearing a sound, and Jamie came around the corner. "Hi. I thought you'd be over here," she said.

He smiled at her and flicked hair back from his eyes. "I was just looking in the woodshed," he said.

"For Cully?"

"No. I know she's not here anymore." Jamie looked toward the mountains and shrugged. "Maybe I was."

Susan went over and sat on the porch step, patting the space beside her. "Come, sit."

He did, planting his sneakers in the grass. She resisted the urge to touch his hair, because she knew he hated it, and suppressed a smile.

She sometimes thought about how easily she'd become used to hearing his voice after that first time. All the uncertainty she'd held deep within, that somehow she wouldn't recognize him, that he would speak with an alien sound, she now realized was her fear of having lost something of him that she would never recapture. But it hadn't been that way at all. It was as if in the moment she'd heard him speak, the intervening time had vanished and she had him back again, exactly as he was.

It had taken him a while to begin talking about David. Maybe three or four weeks after that day in the mountains when he'd let Cully go, she'd stopped on the way out of town beside the church.

"You can stay here if you like," she'd said.

He'd looked at her with those serious wide brown eyes for a moment, then shook his head.

"No, I'll come with you."

He hadn't said anything else then, and she hadn't pressed him. They'd just stood together for a while quietly, but later that night, after they'd had supper, he'd said to her, "After we leave, we won't be able to go to the church anymore to see Dad, will we?"

"Not as often," she'd said. "But we can get back sometimes."

He'd thought about that. "But we can still remember him, right? I mean, we've got pictures and stuff?"

She'd nodded. "Of course we'll remember him. He'll always be your dad, Jamie."

She'd asked if he wanted to see the albums, and when she'd fetched them, they had sat at the table together going over them. Jamie had listened while she told him about each photograph, where it had been taken and when. He seemed to stare at those of his dad for a long time, as if he were trying to absorb the image deep inside himself.

Before he'd gone upstairs that night, he'd said to her, "I thought I'd forgotten him, but I haven't." Then he'd smiled a little and she'd hugged him, her eyes filling with tears.

He'd agreed to go back to Dr. Carey after that. She'd arranged weekly sessions until they were due to leave, and it was during the second of these that he'd finally talked about what had happened the day David was shot.

They'd been stalking a deer; Jamie had been beside his dad, crouched in the undergrowth, trying to see into a clearing through the trees. The deer had been skittish, sensing their presence, nervously looking all around, then lowering its head to nibble at grass.

David had signaled that they should try to get closer, find somewhere where they had a more open view. He'd lowered his aim and risen, starting to move forward, but Jamie's coat had snagged on a sapling, and as he followed, the sapling had bent with him, then tugged itself free and shot back with a sudden noise. As David turned, startled by the sound, he'd tripped over a root and the gun had fired. It had been as simple as that. An accident caused by a moment's carelessness.

David had remained conscious as he lay on the forest floor, rapidly losing blood. The way Jamie told it, he'd wanted to run for help, but David had stopped him, probably knowing that he was dying. All the same, Jamie had been terrified, shocked by the blood and the pallor of his dad's face, and he'd torn himself from David's weak grasp, running away, stumbling though the undergrowth. In blind panic he'd run back the way they'd come, but he'd become disoriented, and in the state he was in, everything had looked the same. Sobbing, he'd gone back again, and by then David had lost consciousness. Jamie had held him, lying beside him on the wet ground, until they'd been found hours later.

"I think that's what he really feels guilty about," Dr. Carey had said. "He feels he left his dad to die alone, that when he ran off, David was talking and still lucid, but by the time he got back again, his father was unconscious."

The night after that session, Susan had asked Jamie if that's how he felt. He'd thought about it for a long time, and then tears had filled his eyes and rolled down his cheeks. She'd held him while he'd wept and tried to articulate everything that was going on inside himself, speaking spasmodically between gulps for air, and she'd told him it was okay, repeating it over and over, rocking him in her arms.

"I left him, I left him," he'd kept saying.

He was getting better now, Susan thought as they sat together on the porch. They could talk about it without him getting upset, but she saw in his eyes that he hadn't entirely forgiven himself, and she knew that it would take time.

Across the clearing, Bob was sniffing around an old rotting log, his tail wagging, his coat glistening silky red in the sunlight. It looked so different now, without the snow. Now there was grass, and the woods were full and green, the air humming with insects. She imagined Michael standing back there in the cold, calling Cully to his fist from the porch railing, the way she'd seen in the pictures Jamie still drew and now painted.

"We ought to be going," she said eventually, rising to her feet.

Jamie stood with her and took a last look around. The house had been sold; the new owners were due to move in the following month.

"I wonder where she is now," Jamie said. "Cully, I mean. Do you think she's okay?"

"I'm sure she is," Susan said.

She called to Bob, and they started back through the woods.

COOP ARRIVED A short time before they left. He pulled up outside the house and got out of his car, watching the movers carry the last of the big items out to the truck. His expression was closed, and Susan didn't know what he was thinking.

"Hi," she said.

"Hi. Thought I'd drop in, say good-bye." He saw Jamie come out the door, carrying a box to the Ford, and raised his hand. "Jamie, how's it going?"

"Hi, Coop," the boy replied. "Is it okay if I take my plane with us, Mom?"

"We don't have room, Jamie," she said, and he shrugged his acceptance.

There was no trace of the way he used to act around Coop. He was just like a normal kid now, and Susan still couldn't get used to it. She watched him go back into the house, turning away only when he was out of sight. She flicked a strand of hair back from her eye.

"So, everything's all set," Coop commented.

"Just about."

There was an awkward few moments between them. She wasn't sorry that she wouldn't have to see him anymore, because every time she did she was reminded of that day. It was etched in her mind, the way he'd aimed his rifle, the long delay before he'd fired. It might have been just a second or two, but it had seemed like much longer. Much longer.

"Ellis got out of hospital last week," Coop said.

"I heard. What will happen to him?"

"Can't say."

Coop looked away, unable to meet her eye. "Susan . . ." he started to say.

She laid a hand on his arm. "Don't, Coop."

He stopped, then nodded. She'd already asked him once why he'd taken so long to stop Ellis that day, and the answer had been in his eyes. She hadn't talked about it since, and she wasn't about to now.

"Well, I guess I better get going," he said. "I hope everything works out for you."

She nodded. "Thanks."

She watched him walk back to his car, and he paused just for a second as he got in, briefly raised his hand, and drove back up to the road.

THEY STOPPED AT a motel the first night, and after Jamie was asleep, she sat up watching TV until late. Eventually she picked up the phone and dialed a number, then waited while it rang. Somebody answered, and she asked to be transferred, then waited again, listening to the ringing tone.

"Hello?"

"Michael?"

"Hi," he said. "I've been waiting for you to call."

She smiled. "I miss you."

"I miss you, too."

"How's Boston?"

SUSAN AND JAMIE were waiting for him at the airport when he landed in Vancouver. They drove to the hotel Susan had booked, and after they'd had dinner and Jamie had gone to bed, Susan and Michael sat up late, talking.

"How're you feeling?" Susan asked.

He massaged the back of his neck, which still became stiff if he sat in one position for more than a few minutes at a time but which the physiotherapist said would improve if he kept up with his exercises.

"I'm okay," he told her. "How did it go yesterday?"

"Well, we left. Coop came by."

"What did he have to say?"

"Nothing much. Ellis got out of hospital."

"I decided I'm not pressing charges," Michael said.

"I didn't think you would." There was a slight pause, and then Susan asked him the question that was on her mind. "So, what happened?"

He supposed it was something he would have got around to himself sooner or later, but Susan had persuaded him he should go to Boston before they moved to Washington, where they planned to live. While he was in the hospital, they'd spent a lot of time talking when she came each day to visit. There hadn't been much else he could do, immobilized in traction while the multiple fractures he'd sustained in his fall from the cliff had healed. He had told her everything, all that he could remember about his childhood, the way he'd felt after he'd moved away and met Louise. He hadn't left out a thing, uncovering every emotion, every detail of his descent into paranoia.

He'd even admitted that he still didn't know, and probably never would, what he'd meant to do the day he'd returned to his apartment having just shot the man his wife had been seeing.

"I might have meant to shoot her, too. Maybe even Holly," he'd admitted. He'd felt Susan ought to know exactly what had happened, everything that he was capable of.

"But you didn't," she'd said. "You didn't."

It was Susan who'd insisted that he go to Boston, that it was the last thing he needed to do before they could start a new life together, and he'd known she was right.

He got up from the bed while he talked, wincing a little at the stiffness in his back. In the end, Ellis hadn't shot him, though maybe he'd tried to. It had been worked out later that he'd fired off half a dozen shots, the marks where they'd hit the rock descending in a line with Michael's fall to the ground. It was the impact that had caused the injuries to his spine and legs. Ellis himself had taken a bullet in the back, and it had come close to killing him, though at the time Michael hadn't known that.

He went to the window and looked out over the lights of the city.

"You said on the phone that you saw Louise?" Susan prompted. She'd stopped him then, telling him to wait until he got back before he told her, until she could see his face while he talked.

"That's right. She wasn't surprised to hear from me," he said. "I suppose I should have figured she'd know I'd been released. She asked me if I'd called her before."

"Had you?"

"Once," he said. "From Clancys. But I didn't say anything, and she hung up. She said she'd felt it was me, but I'd taken her by surprise."

"So what happened when you met her?" Susan asked.

He detected the very faintest hint of uncertainty in her tone, and guessed it was natural, considering this was his ex-wife they were talking about, a woman he'd once loved enough to try and kill the man he'd thought was taking her away. Even if he had been crazy at the time.

"It was like meeting an old friend, somebody I once knew but hadn't seen for a long time. I think she was a little nervous at first, but she relaxed after a while. We both did. I thought she would hate me, but she didn't. She said she never had. She said she'd been frightened of me."

He went on, telling Susan about their meeting in a coffee shop in the hotel. He didn't say that he still felt a certain pull within him when Louise sat across the table. There was nothing sinister in it; it was just a recognition that he'd loved her once, mixed up with regrets and recollections of good times they'd had.

She'd brought photographs of Holly, and in some of them there was a man, the doctor Louise had married. The snapshots were like any other family pictures. What surprised him was that there were two other children, both boys.

"Matt and Campbell," Louise had told him.

He'd nodded, studying a group shot in which they all smiled at the camera. Her husband looked like a regular guy.

"Alan," Louise had said. "He treats Holly just like his own."

Holly. She was just the way he'd imagined. Long dark blond hair and deep blue eyes, a pretty, happy-looking child. He could see Louise in her, but mostly he could see himself.

"She looks like you," Louise had said, as if reading his thoughts. "She has some of your mannerisms, too."

He couldn't speak for a while, couldn't trust himself to. Louise had reached across the table and tentatively put her hand on his.

"She's happy, Michael," she'd said.

Later, they'd gone for a walk in the park, and he'd heard that

Holly was taking acting lessons, that she seemed to have a talent for it and had already decided she wanted to be a movie star. She was a good student, too, and had a pet dog, and she'd ridden horses for a time but had decided it wasn't something she was crazy about. He learned a myriad of small details about her life, what she liked and disliked, and he listened to it all; soaking it up.

He'd wanted to ask Louise the question that was uppermost in his mind, and she'd stopped at one point and they'd looked at each other.

"She knows about you, Michael. She knows you're her father, she knows everything. She doesn't remember any of it, of course, and she doesn't understand, but she does know about you. She knows you're here, too. I didn't keep anything from her."

He'd had to turn away from her then. He felt an overwhelming gratitude toward her, never having dared to hope for that much, and he was unable to respond. When he related that part to Susan, they were both quiet for a moment, then Susan spoke again.

"Go on."

He couldn't answer for a few seconds, and she said it again. He told her that Louise had taken him to pick up Holly from school, that he'd waited on the sidewalk outside the gates while Louise sat in her car. When she came out, walking with her friends, parting at the gate as they were met, waving to one another, he'd recognized her from her photographs straightaway. Holly had searched for her mother, her smiling eyes ranging over him and going beyond, to the car. Then her brow creased, and she'd looked at him again. Her smile had faltered and faded; then, as he went toward her and crouched down to talk to her, to tell her who he was, she'd done the most unexpected thing and thrown her arms around his neck.

"Daddy," she'd said.

Michael stopped speaking, and Susan brushed hair from his forehead as she leaned down to kiss him. His eyes were shining, moist. God, I love him, she thought, and as if reading her mind, he held her hand and kissed it.

"I love you."

She stood up, keeping hold of his hand. "You look tired. Let's go to bed."

————

IN THE MORNING, they loaded up the Ford and ate breakfast at the hotel. They were driving into Washington State, headed for a town an hour and a half from Seattle that they had picked off the map because it seemed like a decent size, but not so big that it would be choking on its own pollution the way Seattle was these days. When they got there, they would decide what happened next.

While Susan signed her credit-card slip in the lobby, she looked out to the lot and saw Jamie and Michael standing together, leaning against the truck. They didn't look like father and son—they were too physically different for that—but Michael had his arm about Jamie's shoulder and they were both grinning about something. Bob was sniffing around the wheel, his tail wagging, his coat glistening in the sun.

The desk clerk gave her a receipt, and followed her look. "Are you on vacation?"

Susan smiled. "No. We're moving."

"A new life."

"I guess you could say that," Susan said.

"Well, best of luck to you."

"Thanks," Susan said.

A new life, Susan thought. An appropriate phrase. She went over to the truck, reached up and kissed Michael, and as he gave her a quizzical look, she said, "I'll tell you later."

IN THE FAR north, ice and snow gleam across the earth. A falcon takes to the air, rising fast, soaring on thermals, the crisp dry air streaming across her feathers. She banks and turns and comes around above the rocky ledge where a moment ago she rested. There is a faint memory of stiffness in her wing, but it is very distant now and it does not affect the way she flies. The air rushes past. She turns her head and surveys the ground below.

Her mate watches her, his head cocked to one side, then he takes to the air and flies to join her. They wheel in circles, calling out to each other.

Far above the snow.